Crack Up or Play It Cool

Moss Croft

Copyright © Moss Croft 2023

The moral right of Moss Croft to be identified as the author of this work has been asserted by him in accordance with the Copyright, Designs and Patents Act of 1988.

All rights reserved. No part of this publication may be reproduced, transmitted or stored in a retrieval system, in any form or by any means, without permission in writing from Moss Croft, nor be otherwise circulated in any form of binding or cover other than that in which it is published and without a similar condition being imposed on the subsequent purchaser.

ISBN: 9798389249882

The Novels of Moss Croft

Crack Up or Play It Cool

Ghost in the Stables

Rucksack Jumper

The Flophouse Years

Raspberry Jam

God Help the Connipians

Stickerhand

Boscombe

About the Author

Moss Croft is a nom de plume. Pretentious git.

Contents

Prelude: A Memory   Page   7

Chapter One:
That Interview   Page   11

Chapter Two:
First Sightings   Page   69

Chapter Three:
Retford   Page   101

Chapter Four:
Crack Up or Play It Cool   Page   131

Chapter Five:
Mary Jail   Page   183

Chapter Six:
Water Shall Burst Forth in the Wilderness   Page   237

Chapter Seven:
Once a Family   Page   303

Chapter Eight:
The Reckoning   Page   341

Disclaimer

This is a work of fiction and any resemblance to real persons or events is the result of unforeseen coincidence.

Dedication

For Melanie.

Prelude: A Memory

I don't know if Daddy will be able to have affairs in Lancaster. That's the word for it: a married man doing the naughty with someone who is not his wife. I think my Daddy might be the cleverest, he keeps a few on the go at the same time. I am certain of it even though I never see them. His supply might dry up altogether unless Lancashire girls are nicer than I imagine. Or my daddy has poorer taste.

Almost never.

All week while we have been packing up the house, Daddy has been storing things under a tarpaulin in the garden. He says he shall take it all to the tip. I've never been to one but it sounds the most dreadful place. All the rubbish no one wants, dumped in one big heap. 'What on Earth do they do with it, Daddy?' I asked.

'Landfill,' he said.

Fancy putting discarded toys and broken crockery, a black and white television that we left in the attic—everybody has colour in this day and age—all under the ground. Archaeologists of the future will struggle to explain it. The size of a mansion house, junk from one corner to the other. They'll think the maddest hoarder of all time must have lived there.

'Will you take me to see it? Just to see.'

He agrees. Daddy will do almost anything for me. Anything except carry on living here in Epsom, where I belong.

I wonder what it will be like for him in Lancaster. He might only have his wife up there, and I'm sure she's no fun for him. I don't just know about his affairs, I actually like them. I don't expect many daughters would say that but I'm one on my own. That's a phrase my real mummy used to say. 'You're one on your own, Sophie.' I remember it very distinctly, a nice thing to be told. You see, my stepmummy doesn't like his affairs—she hasn't said that to me, I just know that any woman married to a cad looks a complete fool—and if she doesn't like them, then I do. It's like a law of nature. Thinking the opposite of what Stepmummy thinks. A law of *my* nature.

Stepmummy and her crummy baby are in the house. If the nappy-filler is sleeping, she will be putting things into boxes, labelling. Moving out of the family home is quite the undertaking. I have lived here for twice as long as she has and, therefore, I will miss it much, much more.

* * *

Daddy has hitched up a small trailer to the car—to Stepmummy's car actually, I think his is too good for tipping rubbish—it has a replica of the car number plate attached. The problem is, we do not have such a number plate, not a real one. For this reason, Daddy has cut out a large piece of cardboard and written the number upon it. He did it with a thick felt-tipped marker pen. It looks a bit ham-fisted and I tell him as much.

'I'm just obeying the law, Sophie. We're not allowed on the road without it because the trailer attached would prevent the police from seeing the regular number plate if they needed to.'

'Can't you buy a proper one,' I ask.

'For a single trip? I'm leaving this rickety old trailer at the tip too. We can do without rubbish in the new house. No more of that for the Stephensons.'

I wonder if that will prove true. Will we be able to resist holding on to junk when we are living in our new house? Keep only that which has a clear purpose. I can't see it. For one thing, in the pictures I've been shown, the new house looks very old, it might have clung on to some old bric-a-brac of its own accord. And secondly, even now I can't bring myself to throw out half the things that Stepmummy says I should. They remind me too much of my real mother. She discarded everything she owned, except her passport and the clothes she was wearing. Embarked on a new life abroad last September. Seems to be foregoing absolutely everything from her life before. Not a word to me.

* * *

After we have driven only a short distance from our house, Daddy slows the car down. A girl wearing jeans, with long black hair which falls very, very straight, all the way to her waist, is waiting at the roadside. He asks me to move into the backseat. 'A guest should sit in the front,' he says.

I don't know the guest, and Daddy introduces me to her: Alison. I think she must be his latest affair, one that is about to come to an abrupt end unless she is transferring to Lancaster like her tutor-stud.

'Hiya, Sophie, good to meet cha!' she says, like I'm a tiny little child.

'How do you do.' She looks surprised by my formality but she and I can never have a normal relationship. If she's clever—which university students are supposed to be—then the reasons why will soon come to her.

'Sophie,' says Daddy. 'Alison wants to take a photograph of something before we take it on to the tip. I need to carry it into her flat where the lighting is right. Then we'll go on to the tip which was what you wanted to see.' I say nothing at all and he rambles on and on. 'It's a little device we rigged up together in the department. Nowhere to keep it but it will be there for the record. A photo or two.' He really does talk a lot of twaddle. He's going to take her panties down while I sit in the car. If he takes a few photographs of that, I hope Stepmummy sees them. That pair can't row enough for me.

We only drive a short distance. It could be that we are still in Epsom when Daddy parks the car. Then he goes around to the trailer and tries to pick up a hessian bag that is among all the junk. It looks to be mighty heavy judging by the way he struggles. I laugh to myself at the silly things he will do just to keep the pretence that he's on a worthy mission. Hopes I won't guess that he's really just stuffing it to her. Going inside for that thing men inexplicably want to do to girls. He stumbles with the bulging bag towards the front door. It looks like an ordinary house where this Alison girl lives but I can see from the doorbells that it has been divided up into flats. Once a good house, only cash-strapped students living here now.

'Do you have to carry that upstairs,' I shout.

'Ground-floor flat,' says Alison. 'I live on the ground floor.' She has turned her head to me. I didn't see it properly before. Her hair is long but it isn't shiny like mine. She might be very good at science for all I know; she is not a pretty girl. I don't know what that says about my father. It suggests to me that Stepmummy is hopeless at making love—at doing it—that is why Daddy chases these less winsome girls.

Alison opens the front door. I lean across from the back to the front seat and turn the dial for the radio to come on. It does not. Won't. My father has taken the ignition key.

It's as boring as Bognor just waiting in the car while Daddy does what he has to. I've been in similar situations once or twice before, not that he ever tells me what he's really up to. I imagine telling Stepmummy; it might make her cry, only she never does. I have an ice-cold stepmother. I might say, very innocently, I waited in the car, and from there I saw Daddy draw the curtains together very tightly. I expect he and the girl—Alison with the unwashed hair—were doing flash photography.

Chapter One:

That Interview

1.

My name is Sophie Stevens and I am an investigative journalist. It has not always been so. Briefly, I flirted with the name Sophie Hartnell. My mother's maiden name and the one which she reverted to after divorcing my father. It is the name I chose to accompany my very first article to appear in a national magazine. I was sixteen years of age. I had written that week's feature for Girls in the News, a teenagers' weekly that sold well in those days. My piece was an interview with an up-and-coming soap star, her face adorning the front cover, inviting the reader to consume my words. You see, I could claim to be neither an investigative journalist nor Sophie Stevens back then. But I was still me. I think we all undergo many changes in our lives. Happy children, miserable children; successful adults, abject failures. Or is it only me? A peculiarity of the way I look at my own life and the lives of those around me. In this account of, and investigation into, the murder of my mother, it is how I shall present it. Every version you read, of every story under the sun, contains substantial bias. They are all written by humans, there can be no other way. I am laying mine out before you, the baggage that I bring to the telling. I have missed my mother every day since I was eleven years old. I am thirty now and it is only two days ago that I learnt of her murder. A skeleton was unearthed during the landscaping of a garden two miles from our old family home. For the past nineteen years, I have believed her disappearance to be a vanishing act of her own volition. Not that Cynthia Hartnell had obvious reason to flee. To disappear. There were rumours concerning the involvement of a man. I understood that she had run away for love, romance; something in the manner of her leaving made it all feel concurrently sinister. A devilish enchantment. I was a child, the speculation far above my head. Her passport went missing at the same time as she did, not that such a coincidence proves very much at all if you think about it for even a short time. And still the given explanation was that she had taken up a new life abroad. I questioned it at the start, accepted it as I grew older. To the best of my knowledge, neither police nor family believed anything truly untoward had taken place. Or if they did, they never told me, Cynthia Hartnell's daughter, the person who had lost the most. Police enquiries at the time ruled out exactly what we now know to have taken place. There is a detective something-or-other who wishes to speak to me. To my mind, it is he who has all the explaining to do.

In this open declaration of my potential bias, I must make you aware that for a longer period than that in which I have missed my mother, I have also hated my stepmother. I always associated her with my mother's vanishing, without ever imagining her to be directly responsible. Never quite pictured how it now looks. She is under arrest for the murder: a total surprise. I blamed her for taking my mother's place with my father. That she—the second Mrs Stephenson—had usurped Cynthia Hartnell's place in our family house I considered a factor, a reason my mother no longer enjoyed living in Surrey. I confess it made less and less sense as I grew, matured. Grasped the true lay of the relevant facts. My parents separated before my stepmother ever came into the picture. She did not elbow my mother aside. I may have imagined she did when I was a child although even my own memories give me contrary evidence. A headstrong

That Interview

child such as I, had no need of proof in order to blame the one I already hated.

At the time of her disappearance, I—eleven-year-old Sophie—was doubtful that Cynthia Hartnell, my vanished mother, might have fallen in love, given up the life of which I was a part, simply to live with a man. My father thought it, stepmother too, or so they led me to believe. Love is a concept I find both pleasant and troubling, it grants us more joy in principle than in practice. Good for two weeks, sometimes four. Not something to cross an ocean for. The phrase 'I love you' is nice to hear; it has been said to me more than once, and I've repeated it back occasionally. We never use polygraphs, it isn't reliable.

And then there is this awful stepmother of mine. I confess that I hated her the day I first laid eyes on her, and that was six years before my mother's disappearance. The loss of my proper mother was never going to improve the relationship, was it? I think acquiring an unwanted stepmummy was the first blot on an otherwise agreeable childhood. Not always happy but materially comfortable. I lie about comfortable, stinking rich is the truth of it. My father and all the Stephensons up his family tree are more than moneyed. Covered in glue and rolled in the readies, the lot of them. No one turns their nose up at vast wealth. Not Daddy, not I.

My true mummy's vanishing was the tragedy—the ruination, perhaps—that bled innocence from my childhood. Soured me like an old yoghurt. I know it has done that; I force myself to be the vivacious character my friends and colleagues know and love, do so for a short time before they move on. There is bitterness at my core. I can only speculate if learning then that Mummy never left me, not by choice— that she didn't run away for a better life, *sans sa fille*—would have felt any better. Knowing that she suffered instead the indignity of a burial beneath a shed in a garden one village away from where she then lived feels desperately sad.

Doesn't seem like an improvement on the story, even though it means I was not abandoned. The murder of close family must be excruciatingly difficult for a child to come to terms with. I am struggling now, a grown woman whose profession has long shown me how vile we humans can be, one to another. Instead of experiencing that trauma back then, I believed otherwise. That she had left. That I was not good enough for her. She was in Africa or Brazil, one of those faraway places, not really missing me as evidenced by her failure to send for me. To send me a postcard. That is what I imagined. For years and years. All through my teens. Teens and twenties, frankly. You see, I never thought she had left to put distance between herself and my father, long divorced from him as she was. That she resented Mary, his second wife, seemed plausible, but I considered my actual mother to have the upper hand on the stand-in. That was how I saw it before she disappeared, anyhow. My mother was elegant and my Stepmummy a hapless dolt. I have long understood that my father was an ambivalent catch: Mr Moneybags who would poke other girls behind his wife's back. A young daughter shouldn't know such things about her father but I did. Not when he and Cynthia—wife number one—were together. I was too young to tie a shoelace, never mind sniff out an adulterous father. I cracked the code quickly in his second marriage, and I suspect it was the same behaviour that put paid to the first. Men like that can't help it, I suppose. I've not discussed it with him, he doesn't know how much I know, or how young I was when I rumbled him. I've never written a piece of investigative journalism about it. And it really would be the easiest day's work.

For nineteen long years I believed I was the one Mummy had walked out on, even if there was a handsome stranger with whom she had nominally taken up. An excuse. A normal mother doesn't desert a daughter because a normal daughter is too lovable to desert. I didn't seem to fit the bill:

she had gone, and that was proof enough.

I should probably have blamed my father for the family turmoil but didn't. To my childish mind, his marrying a girl only fourteen years older than I am, said everything that needed knowing about him. About the way he was. His chosen replacement for my wonderful mummy showed his immaturity. He had turned forty and still he behaved like a kid in a sweet shop. Mary Stephenson, née Bredbury, might have been an attractive girl—a stunner, I expect; my contrary opinion fuelled by hatred—she was never a substitute for my real mother. A stepmother is actually not a mother at all. You may come across people who tell you otherwise but they are mistaken. Nor was she a better wife than Cynthia Hartnell. Not to my father, I am sure of it.

My father is also under arrest for my mother's murder. For doing away with the first Mrs Stephenson. I'm quite astonished by that. It was my conviction, during those primary school years after my father divorced and married the undergraduate who thus became my stepmother, that secretly he still loved Mummy. I had the makings of an investigative journalist back then; I could back up my assertion with hard facts. My mummy and daddy—although divorced and in his case remarried—still enjoyed sexual relations on something close to a weekly basis. I was too young to know all the ins and outs of it, and yet, even at that tender age, I was able to figure out the bare bones. That it went on. Mine was a strange and wealthy family, not everything was rosy even though the crystal sparkled and oftentimes wine flowed freely. We were all a bit off-kilter. My father's murder charge I did not foresee; I cannot come to terms with it. My stepmother's incarceration is a different story. Detained at Her Majesty's pleasure. I cannot say it without smiling.

Back to my first nationally circulated piece of journalism: I was never employed by Girls in the News; it wasn't a regular job. The piece which appeared under the name I briefly called myself by—this was in nineteen-eighty-six, when I still attended a small private school at Silverdale, in the northernmost reaches of Lancashire—was a one off. I won a competition, earned the right to be a journalist for the day. The assignment was an interview with Mica Barry, the up-and-coming soap actress. It was the planned cover story for a forthcoming issue. I had heard the name, knew nothing at all about her when I got the letter saying I had won, telling me this sought-after interview was to be my prize. However, once I got my teeth into it, I realised there could be no better task for me. Truly.

Nowadays I am a serious journalist. I believe I am, must concede that the scandal-rag I work for has its detractors. My employer adopts a see-you-in-court approach to the publication of story and snapshot alike. It isn't everybody's cup of tea. When I learnt about the discovery of my mother's body, I demanded that I was assigned to the story. Sophie Stevens seemed the ideal reporter for the role, no one could try harder to uncover the truth. Darius—our editor—said no. He said I would not be able to write about it objectively; the daughter of the deceased would bring too much unplumbed emotion to the telling. I had no inclination to explain to him the illusion of objectivity. That to strive for it is to pretend oneself indifferent and we never are. Time enough for that when we are dead. Whether one agrees or disagrees with my viewpoint—my lifestyle even—it always draws a reaction. Everything affects us, one way or another. Far from explaining, I think I just shrieked at him that I had to cover it. The story was mine. He was shaking his head; I was yelling at him. Darius stood his ground and I called him by the C-word. We never print it but people say it all the time in the office. And frankly, no one runs a national newspaper without being one for at least some of the time. To be fair to Darius, he did not sack me, and he has sent others packing for outbursts in a lower register. Compassionate leave he is calling my temporary absence from the office. It has softened my resentment towards him, without easing the feelings that have been roiling within me since learning the shocking news about Mummy. I am still on the payroll without being required to rush here or there. Doorstep an interview or meet a deadline. And of course, I am covering the case. I have the investigatory skills, so what else am I going to do? It is my story, my mother's too, and in the nineteen years since she last lived, I am certain no one on Earth has thought about her more than me. I feel the cruelty of the hidden grave into which the murderers consigned her corpse. My father and stepmother look the likely culprits. If she is coming from the shadows, it is to me she comes. My cold heart feeling stirred by the possibility of learning what happened back then. And I shall find a way to publish what I write. The Sunday Noise has no monopoly on typeface. I think my story—bereaved of a mother for nineteen years without knowing the fact; believing her to have fled abroad, possibly with a disreputable man by her side, when in truth a shed, in a garden she may never even have visited while alive, served as her tombstone—is the one which everybody will want to read.

Oh dear, side-tracked by my pressing thoughts, and I was going to explain about the article. Egged on by my English teacher at Hazelbrook, I won a competition. One which received submissions from schoolgirls nationwide. All entrants wrote essays entitled Why We Are Watching This. Each of us wrote about the appeal of our favourite television programme, five hundred words on the matter. The prize—the interview and penning of the magazine's lead story—appealed to me entirely for the prestige. No one else at my tiny school was going to interview a television star, were they? It quickly got much stranger. Young Mica Barry was to be the interviewee, not as young as me, obviously; however, she was only in her mid-twenties and already a household name. Not in our house, of course. Academics do not watch soap operas. I knew the name, not the actress, quickly learnt that her central role in Shoes and Slippers—which remains a popular programme to this day—was the platform of her burgeoning fame. Mica Barry has long left the cast of the soap, back then many girls in school knew her. Two even confessed to having crushes. Not an admission I would ever have made back then, aloof schoolgirl that I was. When I won, and learnt she was to be the subject of my piece, I had never watched a single episode. Didn't even know what the up-and-coming starlet looked like. Or more accurately, I didn't know what Mica Barry looked like, never before had I put face to name.

The programme I had lauded in my winning essay was the major wildlife documentary of its day; I chose it knowing something worthy must win, plus the advantageous fact that I had actually watched it. I was more book than box. Was then and I haven't changed. I had ten days to prepare for the interview and determined that I must watch the said Shoes and Slippers three times a week for that short period. I could not believe my eyes. Mica Barry is a stage name, I recognised her immediately. I was to interview Monica Bredbury, my stepmother's sister. She had been, four years earlier, a visitor to our home in Lancashire. She visited our home in Epsom once or twice before that. I could clearly recall her at my father's second wedding. The event which turned Mary Bredbury into a Stephenson. Foisted an unwelcome stepmother upon me. I was only six-years old when it took place. I liked Auntie Monica way back at the time of the wedding, always thought her a marvel even while I was hating her sister. To my certain knowledge, my father never slept with her. It more than gave her the edge.

A normal family would celebrate a relative who became a television star. In Carnforth, the small town in which we were by then residing, ours was way off beam. The failure to do so barely registered with me. I already understood that the sisters had fallen out; my aunt succeeding in her chosen career was the news. I had always thought her a talent. Monica made me laugh as no other in the Bredbury clan could come close to doing. Winning this competition was going to enable me to reconnect with her—with my Auntie Monica—that I could achieve that welcome result without making any demand of Stepmummy amused me no end. And it was our side of the family which was at fault for the rift—I never doubted that—Auntie Monica had always treated me well. When I saw her in the soap opera, I realised that my stepmother must have known of her sister's fame, the change of name can't have fooled her. She was in touch with her mother down in Devon—Devon or Dorset, I've never really taken an interest—telephoned her once a month, or so. She no longer spoke of Auntie Monica, not with me, nor at the dinner table. For this reason, the nondisclosure of her sister's soap star status occurred seamlessly. When I watched the programme, alone in the snug, and realised who Mica Barry was, my only inclination was to keep the secret. Whatever caused the falling out between the two sisters—they were once very close—I had no desire to learn it from my stepmother. Auntie Monica was a name from the past, I chose to let the house keep it that way. When Stepmummy and I talked, it was exclusively functional. She might demand that I wash dishes or clear my homework off the dining table before a meal; I would require her to give me a ride into Lancaster if my father was not available. That was the extent of our communication in those days. If she asked me who I was interviewing as a result of winning the competition—and I do not recall such a question—I would have told her to mind her own business. I was not loved and nor did I wish to be.

The interview was to take place in Chorlton-cum-Hardy,

that is where the set of Shoes and Slippers is situated. A television programme with a permanent site for filming indoors and out. At school there were many girls who talked of the twists and turns in the multiple plots which arose on the show: runaway teens, and love affairs between neighbours. That didn't appeal to me; in a family like mine, why import fresh problems to worry over? The new television station which broadcast the show was determined to make its mark, its flagship programme was considered provocative in its early days. I came to understand it comprehensively within the short span of my catch-up episodes—I have always been culturally attuned—it portrayed an accelerated version of reality. More melodrama than any real dramatic tension. Every social problem in the news would be shoehorned into its never-ending storyline. I knew my auntie had been to acting school, I had watched her on stage when she was still a drama student. She had the tiniest role in a period drama on television some years before. Watching the soap in those few preparatory days, I recognised straight away that she is brilliant. An actor among amateurs, and I am certain that mine was a clear-headed appraisal, not simply the view of an almost-relative. And Mica is a star to this day, proof positive that I was right. I should stress at this point that, although I thought myself worldly on account of my school grades and looked-up-to status as a prefect, it was an illusion. I was a clever but protected child, the prospect of travelling to Manchester was a little frightening. An admission which sounds laughable looking back. I had been there once or twice with my father; he had taken me to London too, done that once since moving up to Carnforth. In primary school years—and for the duration of the life I shared with my mother—we lived in Epsom; however, my years in a Lancashire backwater had knocked the cosmopolitan out of me. And for the purpose of the interview, I was to travel alone.

That Interview

Paul Stephenson—who is currently languishing in a Nottinghamshire jail—was, in certain ways, a kind father, always more generous with his money than with his time. He would occasionally go out of his way for me; he also had a wife twenty-one years his junior and, as I have already alluded to, a small coterie of other young ladies he kept on the boil. I like to think I am the one he truly loved—his womanising being an action based upon superficial feelings, not ones of depth or meaning—sadly, the evidence was only ever sporadic. Our relationship was certainly the least complicated: father-daughter, filial love, none of the romantic nonsense which a man like him cannot believe in. I don't think he can, it would be an affront to the logic of the life he has led. And—thankfully—none of the sex either. And that is what he craved with every other woman he clapped eyes on. Plain as daylight, it really was. I say it only for the record, that he has never once been remotely inappropriate with me: if he killed my mother, I hate him. I do not accuse him of doing more than he has done.

When I was on my way down to Manchester, travelling by train, it crossed my mind that I should try to find out if he had, after all, slept with my Auntie Monica. I momentarily thought it a plausible cause of her rift with Mary, my stepmother. Momentary because, on reflection, I could see there was simply no chance. Monica is very pretty but even when performing the role of bridesmaid at his second wedding, the one at which he married her sister, I formed the impression that she hated my father. He went for the girls who fawned over him, the type who think a physics professor sexy. Delusional girls with a scientific bent. I liked Auntie Monica precisely because she hated him. If Mary had done the same, she would never have come into, and blighted, my life. I have felt something akin to love towards my father lifelong—I am revising it in the light of his arrest—never had a problem with others hating him. The young ladies who don't, those charmed with shocking ease, who offer themselves to him tamely, they are the pathetic ones. There was a time when I focussed only on how those affairs might upset Mary, my stepmother. By the age of sixteen, I could see that without them—if those scientific girls had kept their lab-coats on—he and my mother might have lived happily together. No divorce at all. Not necessarily, just possibly. I loved my father and not the Casanova forever lurking below the surface shared with me.

When the train arrived at Manchester Victoria station and I alighted, I looked down the busy platform.

The journalist Pamela Green will be there to meet you.

That was the wording in my letter from the offices of Girls in the News. And at the time I was awe-struck to be meeting her, still too young to fully grasp how crass all teenage journalism actually is. And there she was on the station concourse, holding aloft a small cardboard sign bearing the name, Sophie Hartnell. Technically, I was called Stephenson, decided upon the change at the last minute when I was all but ready to post my entry. How kind of her to trumpet me. I imagined myself to be terribly important on the strength of that cardboard signage. Off to interview *the* Mica Barry. Heady days in the life of a teenage girl living in deepest Lancashire.

'Sophie?' she enquired as I approached the lady with the sign. Pamela Green was young, no more than my current age. I was most impressed with her dress sense: a black and white tartan skirt, just above the knee. Exquisite style and her legs were bronzed as mine were not. Her top was a textured blouse. If it was cheesecloth, then it was made of the finest there is, also coloured black and white but with asymmetrical crimson peppering it. She had blond hair that might have been straight but looked quite uncombed: a positive riot. I did not look so bad, my hair is my mother's black, jet black, and I wore it short. I still do, in a boyish style although my face cannot hide my gender. I agreed with my inquisitor that Sophie was my name, as it still is although the Hartnell has now gone the way of my mother. You must understand that, aged sixteen, I believed my mother had disappeared five years earlier, that she would return to me, whether returning from a round-the-world adventure or after being discovered living in a mental hospital in Naples, Athens, Dar es Salaam, no longer cognisant of her real name. The lunatic idea was all my own, never discussed with my father. It seemed preferable to abandonment. Death was the only possibility I refused to entertain.

Pamela Green took me to a small café just outside the railway station. She said we would taxi to the television set where I was to meet Mica Barry. 'Your hero,' she called my aunt, a phrase which amused me hopelessly. I realised from her manner that Pamela believed she was giving a schoolchild an opportunity of a lifetime, an experience of stepping into her journalistic shoes. At this point, I feared bursting her bubble. When Mica Barry was plain Monica Bredbury, she visited my home in Carnforth. A four-year hiatus could not make us strangers.

In the café, Pamela asked if she could see my prepared questions. This is amusing to recall. Girls in the News sent me some sample questions along with the train tickets and arrival instructions. ***What is your favourite food?*** and ***If you were not an actor, what job do you think you might be doing?*** were on the list which the magazine proposed. I had in mind, why do you no longer speak to my stepmother? I hadn't written it down but it was the one I was most keen to ask. Pamela called herself my mentor; even at that young age I could sense that she thought herself ironic. Never allowed herself the thought that I might rise far above her in the world of journalism. I showed her the side of A4 I had prepared. All in my best handwriting:

> *Have you considered acting in Shakespeare in the future?*
>
> *Do you share any characteristics with your on-screen character, Sarah Best?*
>
> *Might you have children one day?*

Monica and I have always got on well, these questions were only to kickstart a conversation. That is how an interview works, I was cognisant with the process instinctively. Knew the favourite-food question was a dud. We all conduct interviews several times a day, always have. We simply neglect to write them down, and the fact that we all do it makes it two-way rather than one-way, sparkier and more interesting. I wanted that with my aunt. I was quite prepared to answer any question she asked of me. I recognised also that avoiding the fawning claptrap would result in an article superior to the usual fare. It was bound to: Girls in News was rubbish, week in and week out.

Pamela was concerned when she read my prompts. She feared Mica would take offence at the first, might believe it poo-pooed her work in soap opera. The second question was interesting and potentially explosive: Sarah Best enjoyed the attention of several young men in the programme while always seeming more comfortable in the company of Kath Wyatt, a woman ten years her senior. It was for viewers to imagine why—this was early evening fare—if they guessed Sarah to have romantic feelings for Kath, it was because the notion was *in the air*. Girls did not kiss girls on television in those long-gone days. Lavatory stalls and nowhere else, that is as I understood sapphism at the age of sixteen. My third question, Pamela told me directly not to ask. 'It is not the policy of Girls in the News to either promote or denigrate motherhood. It may be part of women's lives, may or may not. What makes our gender newsworthy lies elsewhere.'

That Interview

Then she looked at me with searching eyes. Pitying, I inferred. 'Is that what they prepare you for at Hazelbrook?'

As she said it, I sensed from her body language that she was hoping to rescue me, show me a world beyond the small-minded private girls' school that held me back. Ridiculous. Child-rearing was no part of our education; I never gave it a thought. Half the staff were lesbians; everybody said so and I said it too. Said it disdainfully, they were the lesser half. I was wrong, should never have held such a prejudice. Surely just a dollop of that teenage denial, considering how I have turned out.

Maybe I should have anticipated her criticism before writing the question on my list. I was interested in acquiring a cousin or two, I think, and Pamela Green was not yet aware of this dimension in our relationship. I shouldn't have put it on my pad because I knew that the magazine looked for a girl-empowerment angle in every article. And I would be required to squeeze a gender-specific quote or two from my aunt. The magazine was full of that nonsense: it was never political but noted that we had a woman Prime Minister with tedious regularity. Female newsreaders were praised for breaking the mould. Laughable: reading off a cue-card isn't empowerment, and Maggie Thatcher only ever behaved like the men she surrounded herself with.

No. My interest in this lay far beyond the formulaic rubbish of mid-eighties journalism for teenagers: I wanted to ascertain how Monica viewed her sister. Mary had, by this time, borne two children of her own. She had long ago learnt that I was distinctly not hers, not even on the basis of salvage. My two half-brothers were very young, five and two. She cared for them more resolutely than she did for me but I never thought her a natural. Monica was in Mary's life before the children and not since it seemed. I couldn't imagine a connection between those issues. I assumed that the dislike of her little boys would be all mine. Grown-ups seemed to like babies far more than I ever did, although her first was a very strange one. Not much of a baby at all, as far as my younger self could tell. My best guess was that my aunt had simply got sick of my stepmother, as I had done at a much earlier stage in our relationship. First sight was too much for me.

'The interview might feel like a dream to you; the important thing is that you pull it all together during the write-up afterwards,' advised Pamela. 'And these young stars can sometimes be relaxed, very forthcoming, or they can be prima donnas. May only give you the briefest time. Nevertheless, you can write up how they look, what they were doing before they met you, and why they had limited time. It can give the reader a good insight into the life of a working actress.'

'If you don't like the person you interview, do you say so in the article?'

Pamela looked shocked, even a little cross. I think she feared I was going to declare war on the star whose time she had secured for me. That was never my intent; as I have said, I liked my almost-Aunt from the day I met her. 'We are promoting the names women are chiselling out for themselves in this male-dominated world. It wouldn't do for us to be fighting amongst ourselves.'

I shook my head. 'I won't criticise her, if that's what worries you, Pamela. I know Mica Barry a little. She is the sister of my stepmother.'

There. I said it, and Pamela, once more, looked at me with a frown on her face.

'How has this happened?'

Well, I had won her silly competition fair and square. That's how. It amused me to think about the conversation we were having. Pamela will have been the one worrying over the character of the star we were to meet. I was simply thinking aloud. Seeking a few journalistic tips, and wondering what I might ask the family member who disappeared from view four years earlier. Not a vanishing act as resolute as my mother's, I hadn't for a second imagined she was other than plying her trade in London or even her and Mary's childhood home of Charmouth. I favoured London; being any kind of actor sounded improbable in the one-horse town she and Mary grew up in. My missing knowledge had been her meteoric rise. And I saw Monica only infrequently in the five or six years before the rift between the sisters occurred. If I sound incurious, not asking Stepmummy about her for so long, I should also say that my Auntie Sarah and Uncle Phillip visited Carnforth only in our first year. Perhaps they'd be back but it was yet to occur. Uncle Stephen was unseen for three years. My insipid step-uncle.

I had known her when she was named Monica Bredbury—attended a drama school—a step-aunt with aspirations. The nicer of the three Bredbury children by a longer distance than a flight to the moon. I knew she had undertaken one or two minor roles in television. A name change, and four years further down the line, I was to meet a star.

2.

'Hey, it is Sophie, isn't it?'

She wears jeans, tight fitting, and my aunt is in terrific shape. Looking her Sarah Best, one might say, she approaches us across the front garden of a house I recognise from the opening credits of Shoes and Slippers. Monica is alone, only I have a chaperone. Too young to meet a television star solo although I can recall being alone in a room with her once or twice in the past. Her pre-Mica Barry days, I suppose.

'It's me. Yes.'

'Ha. That's a turn-up. I expected a schoolkid, not family.'

'Miss Barry,' states Pamela Green, 'the connection between Miss Hartnell and yourself was news to me. We would have advised you, had we...'

'No. It's great. This is the girls' magazine interview, isn't it?'

'Girls in the News,' says Pamela. 'Your agreeing to our request is the most fantastic honour...'

'Ha! Nice touch Soph. The Hartnell name threw me. Never figured. And I thought being interviewed by a kiddie was going to be proper easy. Ha! Not now, you're streets cleverer than most.'

I like my aunt enormously; she looks casually glamorous—T-shirt of cardinal red—and yet it is her disposition which makes the strongest impression. Never a moment when she isn't resolutely present, being herself. Monica's hair is fairer than Pamela's, fairer than my stepmother's too. She may have dyed it. I wonder if the television studio requires this of her, she is mid-filming, after all. She has it arranged in a tight ponytail, combed and pulled so that her forehead is prominent. Monica Bredbury looks more film-star than soap-star. To me she does. Only three years younger than my stepmother, Monica is the more radiant by far. I realise as we meet why some in school feel a girl crush towards her. Stupid to say it but in her presence, I am one of them. I don't react to her talk of me being cleverer than most. It might sound conceited, and I've always thought myself cleverer than her sister. Mary has a PhD.

'If I'd known you were coming, I'd have cleared more time. A proper catch up.'

Now, this I do like. Monica Bredbury is my friend, whatever has gone on between her and Stepmummy.

* * *

Pamela has finally left us alone. My wonderful relative—I forgive her all the step-nonsense, she is not to blame for her sister—has shown us all over the Shoes and Slippers set. There were many people present, some technical, some thespian. Pamela knew many of their names and I knew none. Oops, must research better. I think it amused Monica—Mica, as Pamela continued to call her, although I do not—to conduct the interview in the lounge of the Best family home. Initially, Pamela and I stood like visitors to a stately home while Monica flopped onto a sofa, scuffing off her training shoes and lifting her legs beneath her in the manner which I do only in our Carnforth lounge.

'Sit, girls,' she beamed. 'Make yourselves comfortable. Half the country thinks this is my real home, you know?'

Pamela laughed, fawned in my view. 'Of course, Mica, the realism of your acting gives them no room to think other.'

Monica nodded but I am sure it was hiding laughter. Shoes and Slippers is a succession of emotionally overcharged scenes. Sarah Best's father is an alcoholic and, in preparation for this interview, I watched touching scenes of love between father and daughter—her acting is very fine, my aunt has presence—not a word of it could I believe. The writing is sentimental tosh. They add in a little swearing, also known as social realism for the masses. I will be taking A-level literature next year. I understand exactly how they put these stories together.

I took an easy chair, and my Auntie—my friend, as I am coming to think her—said, 'You could have sat here, you know?' She patted the sofa cushion exactly beside her. 'In better circumstances, you might have been like the kid sister I once was to your stepmum.' I felt many complicated things hearing her off-the-cuff remark. And I regret not taking myself to sit beside her. I should have liked to share space—a hug—with Monica Bredbury, even put my arm around her slim waist. She is magnetic. That could be the psychological effect of my having seen her on television, and she is currently made-up—hair tied back, discreet eye-liner—

exactly as the nation sees her. It is also true to recall, years ago, before her fame which I am still acclimatising myself to, that she never lorded it over me with the Aunt Monica nonsense. My stepmother would ask me to call her by that name, and she would say, 'Monica's fine.' I have always thought it a phrase laden with meaning. Always thought Monica to be very fine indeed.

I asked her the prepared questions and one or two more in a similar vein. I have brought along a notepad and a small hand-held dictating machine. Monica consented to the use of it, Pamela making quite a song and dance about the matter. 'We shall erase the tape once Miss Hartnell has written the article. The magazine will print only what Mica Barry wishes the world to hear.' On and on she wittered. 'Anything indiscreetly said, may be unsaid.' That phrase of Pamela's jumped the needle in my brain. Jarred. It sounded like a cunning journalistic trick. Lure the interviewee into feelings of easy conviviality. It is not true for a second. Time moves forward; all that we have done remains done. We undo shoelaces and precisely nothing else. I am not a philosopher—those mental rabbit holes hold no interest for me whatsoever—but nor am I a thicky. What's said is said. I understand the permanence of what has gone on. Including all those things I would rather set back to the way they were.

'Would you like to appear in Shakespeare one day?' I ventured.

'For sure, Sophie.' She was leaning back on the sofa, scratching herself just beneath the buckle of the belt of her jeans. The flesh upon her tummy is a pasty white although her arms are the lightest brown. I wonder if it is make-up. The tan might be more Sarah Best than it is Monica Bredbury. 'I have done a little. Drama school, everyone does it there. I think I was a terrible Desdemona, just not so bad that I failed the course. The snag is, Shakespeare is all male roles. Desdemona was just a muse. The prettier an actress they can put on the stage the more it explains why Othello goes a bit gaga. Looks get the nod over acting prowess, there's too much of it in this game. I was middling, I suppose. Shakespeare is a maybe for me.' Then she flashed me a smile. 'For Mica Barry.' I sensed some disassociation in the form of words she chose. And I have not read Othello, couldn't make a coherent reply about the role she spoke of; only Julius Caesar and Macbeth are in my compass. If she was saying that she is middling in the realm of attractiveness she is oblivious to an obvious truth. I can imagine boys, girls even, going quite off their rockers with unrequited love for my step-aunt. It is the easiest thing in the world to picture. 'Ibsen or Pinter appeal more to me. They wrote better roles for us girls, Sophie.'

'And Sarah Best, do you think you share any characteristics with her?'

My young aunt, to whom I hope to be like a kid sister, laughed uproariously at that hurried question. 'You and I need to talk about all that privately, Sophie,' she said, glancing at my primly clad minder. 'My character is in thrall to her dad, isn't she? Stupidly drawn to a wastrel. I scarcely know your dad, Sophie—my bro-in-law, Paul—but that is still a lot more than I know my own.' Monica tapped the side of her head. 'Not a memory in here. My father had gone from the house before I was two.' Her honesty captivated me; she doesn't just act well, she lives out in the open, unabashed by the presence of the obsequious journalist. Of Pamela who we are finally rid of. Watching the movement of her lips, the intensity in Monica's green eyes was a joy. 'Oh God, Sophie. I don't mean to sound self-pitying or any of that. I know all about your mum. That's awful...' Monica arose from her sofa; barefoot she crossed the floor and took a hold of my hand. 'We must arouse funny memories in each other, Sophie. It's all good. Great to see you, and I'm sorry if my tongue is going faster than my brain.' She had released my hand and put her own upon the side of my head, fingers touching my ear. For a second, I believed she might kiss me—both a shocking and a pleasing thought—then she stepped away, slid back upon her sofa.

At this point Pamela behaved like an idiot. 'Mica,' she said, 'if you wish to speak privately with your niece, I understand. Nothing will leave this room. I have a responsibility to remain because Sophie is a minor and Girls in the News has a duty to accompany her at all times.'

'Sophie and I will have a little one-on-one time when the interview's done,' said Monica quietly. I saw Pamela turn red in the face. My aunt putting Miss Busybody in her place without recourse to any disagreement.

'Are there any other characteristics which you and Sarah Best might...'

Monica was laughing again, quite openly, and I may have been going back to the question for all the wrong reasons. 'Sarah pushes the men away, doesn't she? I've let too many into my life, got that wrong once or twice, not that we'll write about it in the teeny magazine, please. And the show flirts with Sarah's feelings for other girls, very tastefully, but it does. I don't have those feelings. No need to print it, I'm not some weird anti-lesbian crusader. I don't share Sarah's feelings towards other girls, that's all there is to that one.'

I nodded with enthusiastic righteousness. Shoes and Slippers only hints at Sarah's feelings towards other girls, it is a subtle contrast from the boy-girl relationships that all the other characters hop between. Girls loving girls isn't quite right. The silly hand-holding in my school is probably because there are no boys there and I, for one, have nothing to do with it.

And now we are enjoying the alone time of which Monica foretold. Pamela ran out of reasons to stay once I'd switched off the dictating machine, concluded the interview, if that is what it was. A good talk with my aunt already and now I shall enjoy a better one, unobserved. Monica has promised to put me in a cab to the station. When my minder asked me if I was satisfied with the arrangement, Monica and I laughed.

'When did the two of you meet?' said Monica.

'At the railway station this lunchtime,' confessed Pamela. Then she too started to laugh. Understood. She must represent a graver danger to the vulnerable youth whom she portrays me to be. Auntie Monica is family. 'It has been a delight to meet you, Mica. We shall get the first draft of the article couriered to you on the set here next Monday. It might make next Wednesday's edition, or a later date if you feel it needs more work.'

'And I'm on the cover?'

'Yes, Mica. On the cover, our brightest star to appear there in weeks. In months.'

'Your photographer was here this morning; my agent will look over the pictures. Agree on the one.' Monica looked at me very directly as she spoke. 'The article will be great but the picture is the one that gets imprinted on the most brains. Do you see? Very few people use their brain quite as much as you do yours, Sophie.' I smiled; understood that the compliment was to alleviate the put down of the words I was to write. And I have read Girls in the News, know a shallow diatribe when I read one. My ambition is to write about crime—robberies and murders—it crossed my mind that Auntie Monica was guiding me down such a route. To a place of analysis and deduction, where words will mean more than a photograph.

* * *

'I hope you don't imagine I am taking you into my bedroom,' says Monica. Her voice has changed to that of an upper-class girl, it is as though she is pretending this a period drama. And I believe utterly: her acting is remarkable.

As we were climbing the stairs, I said, 'Is that where you

sleep?' Silly of me, as if I was confusing Monica with Sarah Best who spoke to her father from just outside this door in the very last episode I watched.

'We never film inside,' she says as she opens the door. 'Sarah's bed is much too private for the viewing public. This is actually a break-out room. Can I fix you a coffee?'

This would be the second bedroom of a modest suburban house—the principal bedroom makes it into the show, Sarah's parents arguing in the sexless marital bed—this one is off camera, a kitchenette with a sofa and three hard-backed chairs against the far wall. No bed in here; actors may rest but it is not where they sleep.

'A coffee would be lovely. If it's no trouble.'

She gestures for me to take a seat. 'We've only instant here unless we send out for one.'

'I like instant,' I tell her. And I actually do. Strong coffee can turn my stomach. 'Only half a teaspoon, please.'

She turns to me and smiles. 'A lot of water under the bridge.'

That is an expression I consider to be a catchall. I am not certain which stream of consciousness she refers to, so many might we choose from. 'Monica,' I say tentatively, 'I should probably tell you that Mary sends her best wishes, the truth is I never told her that it was you I was coming to interview.'

She looks at me but no understanding shows on her face. I calculate that the estrangement from her sister has been of at least four years duration. She has never, to the very best of my knowledge, seen her nephew Craig, who is now two. She met Simon only when he was a small baby, and now he walks. He should talk, by rights, but he doesn't. God knows what will happen when he starts school in September. He should have gone last January but there would not have been much point to it. None at all, quite frankly. The elder of my two half-brothers is a dead weight.

'She and I were close as peas in a pod when we were both

in school. You know that don't you?'

'But you are so unalike. Mary is uptight, anxious. You take life as it comes.'

'Ha,' laughs Monica. 'Are you studying psychology in school or simply taking the teeny magazines too seriously?'

I tell her that I am a good student.

'Of course, you are,' she replies. I am almost a child of physicists. My father a professor, my stepmother has a PhD. Not that my interests begin or end with the sciences. 'Back there we touched on fathers. Your question about Sarah Best. Am I anything like her in real life? I guess I can drag out the sentimentality of the script. Even an alcoholic father might be better than none at all. That's all Mary and I knew. Me particularly, although I guess it was worse for Stephen. And for Mary. They were older and might have taken the abandonment personally. I couldn't possibly.'

I watch her very carefully as she speaks. My stepmother has spoken to me about this only fleetingly. I know it is true, that her parents were divorced when she was an infant, her older brother no more than seven- or eight-years old. I have no insight into the exact circumstances; my stepmother doesn't interest me. Monica has a forthrightness unlike all other family members—Stephenson or Bredbury—I admire it. My true mother was the same. Honest to the core. I am still young enough to learn from my Auntie Monica should she give me the opportunity. I can be tetchy at school, and I hope it will not become a life-long characteristic. I like my aunt more than I do myself.

'It was easier for us than for you, Sophie. Our father ran away with the babysitter, he has a child with her who is older than I am. I know her name but we've never met. When my mother learnt that he was paying someone to babysit her baby while she came around to look after us, it was the end. How she never learnt of the pregnancy at the time beats me. Deception. It's the strangest game. That was a quarter of a century ago. The family moved from Warminster down to Charmouth—mum and the three of us—to get away from the shame of it all. Do you know this? It split my mother from her father. Your late grandfather. He was a Reverend back in the day. A Church of England man of the cloth. He blamed mum for not being enough for my father, so poor a wife that he had to seek solace elsewhere. Girls in the News nineteen-fifties style was a disgusting pile of crap. We've come a long way. Like I said, Sophie, I know you've had it worse. With your mother.'

I bow my head, determined not to cry although Monica is more sympathetic with every gesture and inflexion than her sister has ever been. It is five years since my mother left. Abandoned me without a word of where she has gone, or why she has taken herself there. If that is what she has done. For a few weeks, the police were all over the issue, asked questions, searched her house top to bottom. Later, my father received a letter from them—the Surrey Constabulary—they concluded that there was no foul play after all. At least, that is what he told me when I asked a year or two back. I never saw the letter. He thinks she is in another country, the only explanation for her missing passport. It is odd though. Money remained in her account. It is frozen. Daddy says it will be mine after seven years but I don't want it. I want Mummy, not her money. Cash is no replacement whatsoever.

'I never really know what to think,' I say. The mother I recall would not have left me like she did. But the mother I have most certainly did. Have or had? Perhaps if I give up hope, I will gain the perspective my aunt has upon her own fraught past. I must think this over more fully when all that churns within me has settled down.

* * *

It has happened. I did not wish it but tears have overtaken

That Interview

me as they have not done since I was twelve years old. Monica has an arm around my shoulders, a warm and caring embrace. I think her compassion was writ clear upon her face. It undid me and I no longer mind that it has occurred. I feel consoled by her. Warmed by her action and I am only an object of her sympathy.

'I can scarcely talk about it. As you described your family's reckoning with a runaway father—"shame buried where it does not belong," I think that was your phrase—it resonated inside me. Glorious and nauseous all at once. Knowing that someone as successful as you can feel like I do...'

'Sophie, Sophie...' As she speaks, she cradles the whole of my upper body in her arms, pulling me tightly against her thin T-shirt. My upper arm is trapped between our respective chests. '...you live with Mary. She feels what I feel. I'm sure she does.'

'You know how it is between she and I.' If anyone can take my plain speaking it is Auntie Monica. Something has riven her and Mary apart; the fact that I was there before her— never liked Mary one iota—should not offend. I turn my tear-laden face towards hers.

'You know who I blame for that, don't you Sophie?' she says, holding my gaze.

'Blame for my dislike of your sister?'

'Yep. That little stone in the stomach.'

'Do you blame me, Monica?'

'I certainly do not. I blame Mary. I've been telling her so— back when we actually met, of course—since before she even married Paul. Your father. You were a tiny little one, already had a mother back then so probably didn't want another. Mary wanted you to treat her like you did your real mum. I told her she was being ludicrous. Not just to want the impossible but to imagine she might deserve it. But hey...' Monica touches the side of my face, puts her own quite close to mine. It feels intimate. '...the big problem you probably don't need reminding of is this: Mary was twenty when she married Paul. Not really stepmum ready, was she? A kid herself. Kid from a small town in Dorset. I was the same and I'm still not married. I may not be as attractive as Mary but I think I have more sense.'

Monica laughs at her line. A half-laugh, I don't know which part she finds funny. 'You are far better looking than my stepmother?' I feel myself blush as I say it. They are the truest words I shall ever speak.

'I get my mug on the tele. It helps, I think. Mary looks spectacular. Always did. Or do you think motherhood is wearing her down?'

I wonder now whether to burden her with the darkness that pervades our household in Carnforth. Mary is worried sick about Simon, her simpleton child. I care little for either and do not know if I can even raise the matter. The second baby seems fine to me. Not that I am any more interested in little Craig but he says a few words. Uses a potty more reliably than his older sibling has yet to manage.

'She has never told me why you and she fell out.' I think the mask of tears has helped me bring this delicate matter to the fore.

I feel the grip of the arm around me loosen but she does not remove it entirely. There is a warmth in Monica that is absent in her sister. 'We were disagreeing for quite a long time. Pretended we weren't, I suppose. Like I've already said, I told her to give you a break. More than a break really. I suppose that was coming to a head after your mother...' Monica seems to be stuck for a word, not something I have so far noticed during two hours in her company. '...was no longer in your life. I didn't think...' Again, she pauses for the longest time. Inside I want to say it's okay, she doesn't have to tell me if she doesn't want to. However, the journalist who gave a talk at our school last term, said one should never fill in the silences for an interviewee. They will come out with

That Interview

the most amazing things if you just let them keep filling in the blanks. '...there ever was very much love in your father.'

'He loves me, Auntie Monica.' Even as I say it, I feel the chill of doubt. I had not expected this stinging rebuke of my father. He has not been faithful to her sister—a state which I celebrate in my more spiteful moments—and that is surely because Mary is such a cold fish. How to tell her sister that this is the reason he appears as she sees him, is quite beyond me. Once more, I am crying and bawling. A shocking state of affairs.

* * *

'I learnt young that many people go through life oblivious to the emotional havoc they cause along the way. I didn't mean to upset you about your dad, Sophie. He can't seem to help himself. I can be the same, you know. It's why I try not to let anyone get too attached.'

I look at her as best I can from within this prolonged embrace. She really is a comfort although there may be some bad news here that I ought to know already. What Monica is telling me about herself—in a roundabout way that has obscured it so far—might upset me more. If she is a slapper, I really don't want to know. And it doesn't make sense either. She is so pretty. No need for any of that, she could keep any man she wanted hanging on a thread. Mica Barry has no need throw herself at them. 'Daddy works with undergraduates who are a long way from home. They are tempted by each other.'

I see from her eye movement that Monica is laughing silently at my thoughtful pronouncement. 'I don't think Prof Paul is a long way from home. He doesn't value home enough is the problem. And he's not the only one, like I say. Just can't get enough of a good thing, that's the scale of it. And I think my sister should be enough. I always did think that. You probably thought it—think it unconsciously—

39

about your mum. Wife number one. What your father does hurts Mary, you know? I never thought she should put herself through it. I kind-of warned her before the marriage, although my obsession at the time was the age gap, not the expectations of their respective marital behaviour. I was a kid, remember. Same age you are now.'

My father and Mary will celebrate their tenth wedding anniversary later this summer. I know he is unfaithful but have thought Mary to be the sort to put her head in the sand. Not exactly grin and bear it, simply let it look that way. What she has said to Monica, I have never been privy to.

'You can't be the same, Auntie Monica. You're an actress, you don't have undergraduates.'

'Hey Sophie, less of the auntie. I'm just Monica, right. You're a grown-up now. Sixteen is when you have to take everything seriously. Look. I can't talk to you about my love-life, I hardly told Mary anything, she was so cross about my first. But one time, a man that really seemed like he might be right for me, I just pushed away after about four dates when he admitted to having two children already. I can enter any consenting life that I like—he was no longer with the mother or anything—but causing collateral damage to some random kids in the background? No. I'm never going to do that.' She puts her hand behind her head. Briefly holds the ponytail, lips tightened together as if she has found something unexpected back there. 'I think Mary was impressed by your dad. The big-shot physicist. Weird really, I never got that. Impressed by the house, probably. You remember your old one, in Epsom; about five times the size of the house which Stephen, Mary and I grew up in. She didn't think wider, look deeper. Too immature to go there...hey, your little tape machine is off, right?'

She looks at me quite warily, leans away from the hug she has been giving me since first I cried. I nod vigorously, truthfully. I want to be a proper journalist, not a spiller of family secrets.

'I think Mary loved Paul; I couldn't see it entirely, him being so old, still, I guess he was good-looking. She respected all he'd done, his career. Written a book on something or other. On physics...' She gives a little laugh at this sad fact. '...as I say, that stuff is beyond me. The sheer wealth of the man was probably a bonus. We were poor as church mice. Down there in Charmouth. You know that, right?'

I nod again although I struggle with what I know about Mary, and her wider family. I think I have resented them. All except Monica. Resented Stepmummy like she was the chickenpox. It is actually very good to hear that our poor relationship is basically her fault. I was probably a brat, and I am pleased Monica hasn't raised that. Implies it was justified.

'At the start, she thought you would mostly be with your real mum. None of us could guess how it would turn out, and I told her before all that she was being selfish. Not giving you enough thought. Mary doesn't like that kind of feedback. Everyone loves her because she's always been a diligent student. Always seemed concerned for others, tries to do the right thing. I guess they're the ones who can't see the blind spot. Paul won't tell her because she could probably throw a hundred worse things back at him. And you see, you aren't affected by his—the undergraduate rubbish—only by hers. By Mary not coming up to scratch at mothering in those early years when no self-respecting girl should be raising tots. Kiddies.'

'Monica?' I say tentatively, 'was my father the first man that Mary ever...slept...did...had...'

'Whoa, whoa. Sophie, I cannot answer that question. I want Mary to work out a better relationship with you, I'm not giving you ammunition to throw at her. Dialogue, not psychoanalysis. That bullshit solves nothing. You know that?'

I don't know anything about psychoanalysis but I think Monica Bredbury very wise. My wrong turn in the conversation starts me crying again. It is not from thinking about my mother this time, it is being impertinent with Monica. I am cleverer than that, I know I am. I don't want to explain this to her. She holds me close, once more. If it is she who has made me cry, the volatility seems to be all mine. She is most level-headed, more so than my father or stepmother. They are far, far easier to steel myself from.

* * *

Monica has been exceptionally kind. She has telephoned Windermere Court, our Carnforth home, spoken to her sister for the first time in forever, taken this step all because of me. Because I cried, and I hope she has not shared that sorry detail with my stepmother. She has told me only that she explained the happenstance of our meeting, my surprising interviewee. She has about ninety minutes filming to do. That is to be her third and final shoot of the day. This evening she will take me out in Manchester and let me stay in her hotel room. I shall not return to Carnforth until tomorrow lunchtime. I try not to visualise the hotel room. She said it is very large, so I don't imagine we shall share a bed. In principle I would not share with a girl. Ever. For a hand should stray where it mustn't and that would be mortifying. Mine or the girl's I shared with. My friend, Caroline, told me that another schoolfriend of ours, Helen Green, spent the night in her bed platonically. Helen's parents had gone to a wedding in Scotland. Platonic means there was no funny business. I know that Caroline is not remotely interested in that sort of silliness. In fact, I too might safely spend a platonic night with her. With Caroline who I like enormously. I would never climb into a bed with Helen Green. Not in a month of monthlies. She has freckly legs, looks like the plague has swallowed her up and spat her out.

Whilst Monica films another scene for Shoes and Slippers,

That Interview

a man from the production company has driven me the short journey to what he and my aunt call 'basecamp.' It is a large portacabin; a lady gives me a cup of tea, offers me a pastry which I turn down. The prospect of the evening ahead has stirred me, my stomach is jittery. I think many of the people in the large waiting room are actors—they talk television incessantly—however, I do not recognise a single face. They certainly haven't starred in any wildlife programmes.

Monica has promised she will be back with me as quickly as she is able.

In this large anteroom, I fail my journalistic assignment although I am confident that I can later rescue it. Now is the time for going over my notes, planning the core of the story, and even thinking if there are any points to clarify. Monopolising my auntie, as I am to do this evening, is a terrific opportunity for me to get a story of more depth than Girls in the News has ever done before. Sift out the too personal, keep Mica Barry's wise outlook to the fore. Instead, it is my rekindled adoration of her that has the better of me; I dwell upon our meeting before this: I was far younger, and Monica visiting Carnforth quite soon after we moved up north. Simon, my unwanted half-brother, was a babe in arms. I must attest that I am the only one who clearly doesn't want him. His mother attends the boy diligently, and our father takes a sporadic interest. Simon's developmental delay is not the result of neglect. He is seriously not all there. Born that way and it is a sad state of affairs. No physics and no winning of journalistic assignments for Simon, I am certain of it. Couldn't have known it when he was a baby, not in the early weeks. He is five years old now, stares and doesn't speak.

I recall that Granny Bredbury, my third and utterly superfluous granny, mother of Stepmummy, came to visit when Simon was born, and Auntie Monica did so too, accompanied her, for a few days. That was in Epsom, and then over a year later, after we had moved up north, Monica came alone, stayed about a week. It was the last time I saw her before today. Not that I had any sense then that there was to be such a hiatus. She was already an actress but to the best of my knowledge had still to adopt the stage name she now goes by. I connected the name to Shoes and Slippers from the talk of square-eyed girls at school. Funny that I had to win Pamela's mundane competition to discover it was my aunt. Just before that visit, Stepmummy and I watched Auntie Monica make a brief appearance as a maid in a television drama set a hundred years ago. My father may have sat with us as we did, or he may have been out getting closer to someone Monica's age than could happen through the medium of television. I could not adjudge my auntie's skill, so few words had she to speak. I liked her appearance in our house, the set of her face, the way she carried herself, far more than I did her portrayal of a maid. The character was subservient, demanded pity. Helpless in life and equally so at her menial job. I suppose she was always a good actress. Convincing. There is nothing analogous in my auntie's real life to that pathetic screen self.

Although Monica spent the bulk of that visit with Mary and even cradled the small baby, Simon, whose subsequent delayed development was still to be fully disclosed, she also spent a little time with me. An exclusive half-hour; quite a contrast to how my stepmother and I interact. Never in a room together unless we have food to eat, and even that can be a strain.

Our house in Carnforth is a grand, if ugly, old Victorian place set in an acre of gardens. The visit occurred in February; I am sure that was the month because Daddy made pancakes. They were good to eat, nicely browned but never burnt. Not that he is any kind of chef, he has acquired the ability to cook precisely nothing else. The day was not Shrove Tuesday but the day before, or the day after. Most years he

That Interview

makes them every day that week. Before the food, Monica joined me in the garden. I was making sure that there were openings for the hedgehogs to come in and out of the kitchen garden, and also supplying a little cat food for them. I was going through a very pro-wildlife phase, young girl that I was. I remember a book I kept by my bedside, it told how best to protect the wild animals found in English gardens, I followed its instructions diligently. Monica joined me and asked many questions, complimented me on my awareness and care. It might have been that I only took an interest because another girl at school did the same. It is important to remember that I had lived in Carnforth no more than three months at this point. It was far short of a year since my mother had disappeared. When the niceties of her initial conversation were over, Monica asked if I was missing my proper granny—Granny Hartnell, mother of my true mother—this was a most astute question, one that neither her sister nor my father ever raised. When Mummy disappeared, I began to spend significant time at Granny's house. A sort of replacement for my mother, and I could not stand spending all my time with Stepmummy although our move to Lancashire was soon to require it. I think, in those first weeks after the disappearance, those overnight stays offered me continuity of the life I'd had before. Granny Hartnell and I were always close; she loved me dearly. She missed her daughter, of course—went a little out of her mind, once or twice, worrying where her beloved Cynthia had taken herself—I hope that I was consolation. Behaved better in her company than ever I did with Stepmummy, most certainly. My grandfather, Mummy's daddy, lived too, he simply wasn't a man for speaking with. Not as silent as Simon; yes and no and a grunted thank-you would come forth from his tongue. Granny often complained about having to look after him, he was newly retired at that time. Her worry resulted in a hospitalisation or two—psychiatric:

depression, I now think, the term was not bandied around at the time—which meant I could spend time there only very occasionally. I remember Mary stating that, as an old and unwell lady with a near-silent husband, Granny wasn't able to look after me any longer. I argued, said that I required no looking after, could even help them. I was eleven, and a child that young cannot defeat an adult in argument, even if their reasoning was as sound as mine. Within weeks my father secured the post of Chair of Department at the University of Lancaster and my life became stranger still. Surrounded by northerners, attending Hazelbrook. Frankly, I think the fees at my school are ridiculously low, and the girls it caters for can be of surprisingly humble origin. Some of the accents one hears are a joke.

'I miss her terribly,' I told Monica. 'I feel she has been cut adrift from her family. We talk on the phone; I've no idea when I will see her next.'

Monica was most sympathetic; she asked me a string of questions about my granny and listened attentively to each answer. I realise now, in this waiting room while she performs for the camera, that she is a most wise and sensitive person. I think it is the coldness of physics that has ravaged my father of feeling. Contemplating space, stars and planets. Worlds other than ours with geology but no life. Not a shred of it out there, I'm sure of it although I am not a scientist. That is his burden. Of Mary, I choose not to dwell upon cause or effect of her cold, cold heart. She means nothing to me.

* * *

When Monica arrives at the door, I notice how all eyes alight upon her. Mine are but one of many admiring pairs. As I stand, a girl with several strands of pink in her otherwise black hair says, 'Is that you for the day, Mica?'

Several heads turn to her, to peer at the one who deigned

to speak to the leading actress. My auntie says, 'In the can.' Nonchalant, funny. She isn't American, nor even trying the accent. She is being ironic; I am certain of it. 'Come then, Sophie,' she adds, and I rise and go toward her. Chosen.

When we leave the room, heading for a waiting car, I whisper to her that it was weird in the portacabin. Only the one girl spoke to her but all watched my auntie like hawks.

'Jesse was signing me out,' says Monica. 'The extras can't speak, it's in their contract. I feel kind of sorry for them. Not a role I could tolerate. I open my mouth when anyone in their right mind would keep schtum. Always have.' Monica is not a blood relative and yet she and I appear to be cut from the same cloth.

In the car, I press her again on the awkwardness of my unplanned overnight stop. I have no change of clothes and I left Carnforth over nine hours ago. We are sitting beside each other on the back seat, she has spoken to the driver. Calls him Roger and I think it touching that she remembers the name of one who occupies so lowly a role. She gently touches my knee. A tap, not a touch that lingers. 'I've a couple of inches on you and you might need to pull the belt in, what's mine is yours, sis.'

I love the way she says this. I am sitting so close to a star: knees touching; family.

* * *

The Bedford Hotel is terribly old-fashioned. It has very wide and carpeted corridors, a lift with lights which illuminate the designated number of each floor it passes or stops on. My auntie's hotel room is on the fourth floor. Exceedingly large, a double and a single bed, a large en-suite shower room. She lives in it for weeks on end, a flat in London and she films here in Manchester. The wardrobe is a cache of beautiful clothing. All hers apparently.

Monica picks out a summer dress and a cardigan which

she thinks will suit me well. 'Are you sure?' I ask, only because it is not one which I would have chosen. If she wishes to see me in red, then red it shall be.

'I'm showering before we go out,' says Monica. 'You too?'

I agree to do so; we are civilised girls embarking on an evening in the city. I hope we go somewhere glamorous, the habitat of television stars. She hasn't said where yet, only that we shall eat together. I know I shouldn't be excited about showering just before or after my aunt but I am. I touch the fabric of the dress, it is silky, I accept some rather flimsy white knickers—lace edging—that she hands to me. 'You had best keep your own...' She makes a hand gesture, pointing at me quite vaguely, at a particular part of my body. '...bra. They never fit across, I'm afraid.'

'No.' I agree. I am rather flat-chested and contemplate foregoing a bra altogether for I have worn this one for too long. It may not work in the dress she has chosen for me. I do not plan to make an exhibition of myself.

'Do you mind?' she asks, as she goes to shower first. I try not to stare as she disrobes in our bedroom. I have no erotic interest in the female form. Nor have I any wish to see a naked male of the species and I know this might mean I am funny. It is her expressive face that I wish to gaze constantly upon. The appearance of a star, an icon of early-evening television is of interest to me for aesthetic reasons. I see how thin her waist is while noticing her legs are not skinny. They are muscular, in the manner of girls sportier than I. Monica is not nearly as tall as the models one sees in fashion magazines, and nor is she so angular. I am sure hers is the finer look.

While she is in the shower, I glance at her many clothes which cram the two rails. They are of every colour. Almost all are casual. Jeans and T-shirts—I put my nose to them—laundered beautifully. I quickly come to understand my auntie's style. The dress she chose for me is elegant but

That Interview

hardly formal. Summer wear, above the knee; for her if not for me. When I hear the water stop, I step away from her things and go to sit on the single bed. Monica emerges from the shower room with a white towel wrapped around her. Again, I see how pale most of her skin is. I think even her arms look less tanned than they did earlier. It must have been television makeup that enriched her pallor. I do not mind; I understand that a tan can age the skin.

'Plenty of hot water,' she states, sitting on the double bed. She leans forward and removes the towel. I instinctively look away, stand, turn my back, remove my own clothing. She has allotted me a towel and I take it with me into the bathroom, accidently knocking my knee on the half-open door. I stifle an urge to yelp, must not lose any poise that I might have chanced upon. At Hazelbrook, I am a bit of a star-turn. Not to everybody's taste but a cool customer. With Mica Barry in the room, all others must fade like month-old flowers.

* * *

When I am dressing—the white knickers fit me well, Monica is very slim—I dislike the idea of wearing an unwashed bra but cannot picture going without in this dress. The material is too thin.

'What size are you?' I ask.

Monica is browsing through a small Filofax. She reaches into a drawer beside her bed and throws a white bra straight at me. I reach a hand out to catch it, around which her garment wraps itself, so forceful is her throw. 'Might be too big,' she says, a smile on her face. 'You'll be my size in ten years, Sophie. Sooner if you go in for babies, like our Mary has.'

'I think it might be nicer than wearing the used one,' I say, stretching it out and beginning to place it around my chest.

'Let's do the old trick then,' she says, picking herself from the bed and walking straight into the en-suite. She returns with a toilet roll in her hand. I have clasped her bra to myself, found that it does not really fit at all.

'Stay still,' she instructs.

I feel her hands on my back, not upon my chest at all. As she has said, she is not of that sort. Then, very carefully, she pads each cup with a copious amount of the tissue paper, all at the bottom of the hollow.

'If the acting goes belly up, I could move into costume,' says Monica as she stands behind me. Adeptly, she clasps shut the bra, all the paper staying within. I think a little may be showing but only on the underside, the dress will cover it. She picks the dress off the bed—it is a lovely shade of red—and with her eyes she indicates that I should raise my hands. Within seconds it is upon me. 'The mirror's over there,' she says.

I walk to it, feeling most self-conscious. See immediately that she has chosen well. The padding makes my figure curve as it never has before. I believe my legs are more tanned than hers, although it is only from a day on Morecambe beach, and a little sitting out in the garden at Carnforth. I like to read in the clearing beyond the orchard, away from the crying of my younger half-brother and the depressing silence of the older.

Monica wears a black and white wrap-around skirt, very long, and a near-white blouse with a faint pattern of pink and blue stencilled across it; she comes and stands beside me. An arm across my shoulder. 'We could go to a club,' she giggles. 'You look as eighteen as I do with your bog-role boobies.'

Finally, I laugh with her. It is relief. I have felt nervous to be going out in Manchester, a far cry from staid Lancaster, and doing so with the famous Mica Barry. I agree that we look as companions, not really a generation apart. 'A meal will be all right. I don't really dance very much.'

She pulls me into a small hug. 'A meal is the plan, little sis. I'm filming a lot more tomorrow. Strictly no alcohol down my gullet tonight. No dancing, little buddy, but you actually do look like starlight.'

'Thank you,' I say. I want to ask her to be my stepmother, although I have already learnt that she dislikes my father. I would be delighted if he and her sister gave me up. Let this better relative adopt me until Mummy returns.

* * *

When we step out into the streets of Manchester, I imagine myself to be a man, going on a date with the magnificent woman beside me. I am a fraction shorter and my clothing more girlish than Monica's, not that I have any illusions about who is the lady. Monica has released her hair from the tight ponytail that belongs to Sarah Best. She did not spend long upon it but the look is rare: lively hair. It does not lie flat, not neat hair and nor is it untidy. Many shades from ochre to sunshine glisten, perhaps a skilled hairdresser has put in the streaks, or it may be only the summer light bringing out the contrast in her natural hair. What a star! Her clothing appears the more stylish for the effortlessness of her movement; she has adorned herself with a blue-grey scarf of fabric so thin it is barely out with us. A slither of wispy cloud. She takes me to a restaurant called The Copperhouse: it is rather wonderful. The thick wooden blades of large fans rotate close to its high ceiling, enormous palm trees in large silver buckets punctuate the walls. I say, 'Do you come here often,' and feel like a common fool for doing so.

Monica tells me I may order anything I like, then laughs when I pick up the wine list. It was not meant as an impertinence, I am simply curious about the venue. I am sure my father is richer than my aunt, and yet he takes us only to country pubs with pies and chicken dishes on offer. I apologise and view the food menu; it contains exotically named dishes without explanation of their content. I tell her I shall order cassoulet, and she says, 'Good choice.' I took my serviette from the silver ring, fiddled with it, and now I am frantically trying to put it back. We shall not be eating until they cook it. 'Would you like to share some of the courgette fritters first?' she asks. I agree enthusiastically. When Monica lifts a hand, a waitress in a dark green skirt is instantly by her side.

'Oh God, it's you. Sarah...no, Miss Barry, isn't it?'

'Call me Mica,' she says.

The waitress smiles as if Monica has tipped her a thousand pounds. Then I notice her glance quickly towards the rear of the restaurant, nod her head briefly at the man behind the bar. He acknowledges her. I understand they have recognised my aunt from afar and this has been its verification.

'I watch the omnibus each weekend. I work when it's on through the week. I love Sarah.'

'I'm delighted to hear it,' says Monica in a low voice. 'I was hoping for a quiet meal with my friend here.' She glances at me. I am her friend, a status I feel heartened by. Not her niece. Well, I am that also but it is only a coincidence. 'What's your name?'

'I understand,' says the waitress. 'It's Anna.'

'May we order the following, please, Anna...?' The girl holds her small pad and pencil to her bosom. Writes down the dishes which Monica names. 'And mineral water, for me.' My aunt looks purposefully into my eyes. 'You'd like a gin and tonic?'

I think my eyes enlarge. I nod at her suggestion, try not to let my enthusiasm show me up as uncouth. Tomorrow I will be filming nothing.

* * *

As we wait for our food, Monica asks me about my school, my friends. The gentleman from behind the bar arrives at our table bearing a tray. 'Mineral water for the most glamorous actress in the whole of England,' he says. He has an accent

That Interview

that could be French or possibly Italian. I am untravelled although visitors from the world over come to our house. 'And the gin-tonic, for her pretty friend,' he adds.

I blush at the compliment. Monica says the simplest, 'Thank you.' She is not rude at all whilst cutting off further discussion with her admirer. She hardly needs the attention of bar staff or waitresses. When he has gone, she says to me, 'A hundred girls? Jesus, that sounds like hell.' She refers to Hazelbrook. It is the smallest of schools. 'Oh Sophie, that must be way weirder than growing up in Charmouth. My upbringing was small town but secondary school was decent. Pretty stimulating actually. Is Prof Paul trying to hide you away from the gazes of all the dirty men like himself?'

I ignore her commentary about Daddy. I can understand why she says it but he isn't really like that. 'I went to the state school in Epsom. The primary. My father isn't at all scared of ordinary people. He simply wants the best education for me.'

'And you? Is it okay in a girls' school? Do you ever get to meet boys?'

I don't tell her this but I have often pictured myself having a boyfriend. I imagine spending time with this make-believe young man in the outdoors of a summer evening, fending off his physical advances. Not fending them off if he were to offer the particular intimacies I might enjoy. I fear I am a bit strange—cooped up in a girls' school is as good an explanation as any—I have pictured these acts with boys and girls. Touching each other's flesh while leaving alone the more outrageous parts of bodies. The privates. Tummies and bottoms interest me, the fleshy parts. The bum-hole itself not at all, I should ask him—my imaginary suitor—to put gauze or a strip of masking tape across it. I've spoken of these longings to no one on Earth. If I were to tell Monica she would surely drop me instantly. I have already learnt that she is quite the lover; I expect her taste in men is top of the range. She is a star, and they can have whom they please. 'I

53

will be entering Lancaster Grammar in September. For my A-levels?'

'You'll finally be meeting a few boys then.'

Her smile is encouraging but I have conceived of no plan that might achieve my imagined future. 'It's actually a girls' grammar school. I think there is some crossover with the other one. The boys' school across town. There might be dances; it all sounds old-fashioned to me.'

'To me and all, Sophie. He really is keeping you away from them, isn't he?'

'It's all right. I'm much too young for boys.'

Monica nods very politely, although my comment sounds stupid even to my own ears. I think she mutters, 'More sense than Mary and I,' but it is to herself. I don't ask her to explain. I have often wondered if her sister threw herself at my father, although such an action would not explain all the other girls in his life.

'He's very clever, you know?'

Monica looks at me with interest. Paul Stephenson is her brother-in-law; I seldom saw them speak together when she visited us in Surrey or the one time in Carnforth. Her time staying with us was centred upon Mary. And she would always spend a little of it with me. 'He's a professor. A serious scientist. I get that. Do you think he's been good for Mary?'

I'm surprised by the question—cannot answer—I have always posed it the opposite way around.

'Ten years they've been together,' adds my aunt.

By this time next year, the dreadful Mary will have been a part of my life longer than my true mother was. Unless she comes back. I still believe she might. She could give her Brazilian lover the sharp elbow and return to England. Reunite with her top-of-the-class daughter. French lover. I sometimes think she might be living with a large American woman. A black woman who wears loud and colourful clothing, hair as short as my own. An odd fantasy, I know, but I have no reality to cling to. The more unlikely a fiction, the more probable it can seem that it might be true. And if she returns, I will forgive her anything. She can bring a big lesbian; I'm not a fan but I want my mother back. And the latent longings of my own night-time imagination can be a little disgusting. On a much, much smaller scale. 'He can't help how he is. None of us can.'

'I don't really go along with that,' Sophie. 'We all have it in ourselves to be murderers, or bank robbers. At the very least, to seriously trash other people's feelings. We make choices, choose better. It's difficult, Sophie. Love is difficult. I think everyone confuses it with lust—fancying the pants off somebody is a good feeling—declare love for more selfish reasons than they ever dare to admit to themselves. If you intend to treat someone shabbily you should let them know at the start. I've done that. Told a guy not to think long-term. More than a single guy. Don't print this in your teenagers' magazine, right. Nothing wrong with it if everything is clear from the off.'

I feel her eyes upon me, sense that she is weighing me up. I listen in silence, slightly unclear what she is advising me to do, and what she is warding me away from.

'I don't mean to embarrass you, Sophie. None of it excuses how Mary has treated you; I don't think she gets the mum bit. She might do now she's got her own. A bit late for you, I know. I also picked up that you never went out of your way to accommodate her. You could be prickly with her but, then again, why wouldn't you be? It makes sense; she was always coming a distant second until...well, you know I'm so sorry for all that. But it's not been easy for her. For my sister. She isn't a happy wife, you know? Repeatedly hurt by your father.'

I don't know if it will cement my relationship, or make Monica put a distance between us, I decide to answer her honesty with my own. 'I don't really think about their marriage at all. I have tried to remember how Mummy and Daddy were together. Paul and Cynthia. I think they rubbed along more smoothly, I was so young it is difficult to trust the memory. I know something that Mary never learnt, and it doesn't really make sense.'

'What's that, Sophie?'

Before I have a chance to answer, a face I recognise is walking across the restaurant, and I see that Monica, like me, has seen the man approaching. She grimaces, teeth clenched. Then, as he arrives at our table, he fixes her with a trademark smile.

'Mica, Mica. They told me you were here. Carrie and I are dining with a couple of others in the Bamboo. Johnny Hall is with us. Would you care to come across when you've finished eating?'

'Word gets around, Bobby. It's a quiet night for us, I'm afraid. Just going to keep it to Sophie and I in here. A family reunion.'

Robert McIlroy is an admired detective. An actor, who can convince us all he is the former. It is astonishing to see him standing beside my aunt. He bends and she turns her cheek, allows him to kiss her upon it.

'You are both welcome to join us. We have a private room.'

'A kind offer, Bobby, but like I say, I'm taking a little precious time with my very sweetest cousin.'

'Very good,' he says, then Robert McIlroy turns to me and says, 'Sophie, enchanted to meet you,' turns away and leaves the restaurant. I think he was being funny, I never enchanted him at all. Didn't wish to when I saw my aunt's initial pained expression. I love becoming her cousin. A step-niece sounds an ugly thing.

'His partner, Carrie, is a lovely girl,' she says softly to me. 'Bobby McIlroy is a dick. Tell everyone you know; tell them you heard it from me. Print it in your magazine, if you wish.'

I am shocked, deliciously so. I have never entertained a

fantasy involving DI Spoon; I know girls in my school who do exactly that. He is a heartthrob against which mine is now doubly sealed. To consider him attractive would be to betray my cousin Monica. 'What is it you do not like about him?'

'Vanity, Sophie. Trust me, that can be enough.'

'Is it not...' I struggle to frame my question. I do not wish to imply that Monica is vain, I have not found her so. However, she exudes a confidence I cannot find in myself nor see in others. '...fame must instil arrogance in many people. Wouldn't you say?'

'Ha! Right again. I want to act. To experience being someone other than myself. Bobby just now, he wants something that proves he's a cut above. Which it really doesn't. None of us are famous on Mars.'

'And would you like to be?'

'This is Mars. The world is teeming with people who live without reference to my soap opera. That's okay with me. Watching it makes me money, I like that, not that I would watch it, mine or the other soaps, if I wasn't professionally interested. Looking to learn from them. See how the best of them act.'

I am that Martian, hadn't realised she was even in Shoes and Slippers until this assignment fell into my lap. 'I don't,' I say, then pick up my gin and tonic. Put it to my lips with my eyes down, not sure whether I have confessed to a crime or good taste.

'Pleased to hear it, Sophie. You do your homework at that time of day, I hope.'

'Do you know that Mary never told me you were in it? That you had a major role on television. She never speaks your name within the walls of our house.'

Monica exhales long and hard, I fear I have said something upsetting. 'I get that,' she says. 'I haven't spoken to her since a good while before I was cast in the role. Not until that little phone call earlier. She doesn't watch it either, I'm sure.

Slippery Shoes isn't highbrow enough for her. Not by any stretch.'

I had not thought of this, that my stepmother's sister is a household name, but the one she goes by may be unknown in our home. I doubt it but who knows what she and Granny Bredbury speak about on the phone. I don't eavesdrop.

'You were saying that you knew something she doesn't. Before Bobby Loves-Himself came in. I think it was important.'

I have put my gin down and my face has coloured instantly. I pick it back up, do so too late to hide my blush.

'Is it concerning your father and another woman?'

I nod my head, try to speak but I have a little blockage of air. Not the breathing sort, just the speaking. 'My mother,' I eventually say. 'He used to take me from his house to hers, and on arrival, not every time, but many, he would tell me to go into a different room while he spoke with Mummy. I could hear them through the walls. I was very young but I've always known what grown-ups get up to. I don't think I understood the whole thing. Too young to know about intercourse...' I find I am coughing and take another sip of gin to quell it. I keep my eyes on the tablecloth, I don't know why. '...I knew that they liked to undress in each other's company. Making a lot of noise as they went about it. I no longer know what is memory and what is imagination, I guess it was the same before and after the divorce. I think he probably liked doing it better with Mummy than he does with your sister.'

'Oh God, I'm sorry, Sophie. I didn't know that you knew. It's really fucked-up, I know. Mary told me about it, not until after your mother disappeared, after you'd moved up to darkest Lancashire. We quarrelled about it. I said she should leave him, that the marriage was never worth a whore's kiss. She begged to differ.'

She is on her feet, has come around the table and put an

That Interview

arm around me. Hugging. She puts her cheek next to mine. Why I am crying—my secret is not so secret but it makes little difference to me—I cannot explain, nor do I wish to. I love my mother and my father; the fact that they continued to make love to each other long after they had separated has always given me solace. I did not expect Monica to believe me. I thought she would put it down to the fantasy of a young mind, battered by a fractured home. Learning that Mary knows, Monica knows, Uncle Tom Cobleigh too, I did not expect. For all I know my father and stepmother may have rowed about the matter, it might have contributed to the frosting that has settled upon our Carnforth home. A shared roof but everything inside is individually wrapped; life experienced in the respective solitude of Paul, Mary and I. It might be a disease that Simon has caught, uncommunicative little sod that he is. And none of it is a secret: Monica sees right into my soul.

* * *

We are back in the hotel room. I did eat a little courgette and a some of the strange concoction that is cassoulet. Not very much. I refused pudding, and Monica advised that she never eats it. I accepted a second gin and tonic. She said, 'Last one,' before I'd even put it to my lips. True stepmother material, my aunt. The waitress, Anna, attended with serviettes and handkerchiefs and never once asked what was wrong with me. The Copperhouse is a high-class restaurant. Mica Barry's cousin-cum-step-niece blubbing for about fifteen minutes over not much at all—or everything that matters; I cannot tell which—was handled with discretion.

Monica is in the en-suite, brushing her teeth, I presume. Before she went in there, she handed me a nightie. Very pleasing on the eye. It is blue and the material rather thin. Many of the girls in school would say it is sexy, and so shall I. Only inside my head, of course, mustn't bother Auntie

Monica with a schoolgirl's silly blather.

Back in the restaurant, while eating our food, Monica talked and talked about growing up with my stepmother. A little about boring Uncle Stephen although she never designated him as I do, and even about the mysterious Dennis Harris. This man writes to Mary occasionally, I have seen the letters. I've not a clue as to why he is so important. A former beau, most likely. Monica encouraged me to speak my mind, never pushily, did it by sharing her own intimacies. Her qualities might be the opposite of her sister's; Monica is the loveliest woman on Earth. I told her more about my mother, and about Granny Hartnell as well. I said that my mother must have found a better lover than my father. 'I hope so,' she replied, and I felt a small chill in it. I know that the police considered other possibilities at the time she took her leave. Dismissed them too but one never knows what has really gone on until an explanation more insightful than conjecture is abroad. A letter, better still a sighting.

When Monica returns from the shower, she holds a towel over her most private area. Wears nothing at all on her person, then picks a nightie from beneath her pillow. 'Shy?' she enquires, for I am still in the dress she lent me, still padded to the bust which could be hilarious while also making me look exceptionally feminine. I know I shall try the trick she has shown me again and again. She turns out the wall light, there is a glow from the bathroom. I see her drop the towel to the floor and pull the crimson nightdress upon herself. I take my clothes off, say 'Thank you' for the bra which I return to her, walking to her bed with my own small orbs exposed. I may have shocked her, or perhaps actresses see this all the time. At school we change for sports together, I am more than familiar with the sight of girls undressed. I quite like it but do not know how to behave in its presence. Always feign disinterest.

'You need the bathroom?' she asks. Monica has slipped

That Interview

between the sheets; she did not look embarrassed by my brazen display.

I assent. I shall use it. I slip off my knickers, Monica's in fact, and pull the blue nightie over myself. I step into the bathroom and shut the door. Toilet and teeth.

When I step back into the room, it is in darkness. 'Goodnight, Sophie,' she says.

I should like to talk more. Even to hear more tales of my stepmother's youth. I climb into my own bed. I understand that Monica has been kind to me, does not share the worst of the feelings I harbour toward Mary. 'I have never been to Charmouth,' I say from my bed. Into the darkness.

'You've never been to my mother's? The bungalow?'

'When I was young, and Mary went down there, I stayed with my mother or with Granny Hartnell. I know your mother—Granny Bredbury—only from her visits to us.'

'No holidays in Dorset or Devon?'

'I've been to Torquay, never to Dorset.'

'Beach, sea, this country's finest fossil hunting ground. A lot going for it. The trouble is its size. We were a pretty finite number of girls and boys growing up in Charmouth. Like your girls' school but at least I had boys to ogle.'

It is my impression that Monica enjoys the sight and feel of them more than I have yet had opportunity or inclination. 'Do you think I should be doing that?' She doesn't answer and so I expound the point. 'Throw myself at boys.'

Monica laughs. She is a difficult girl to offend. 'I only did that once or twice.' Then in a more serious tone, she offers advice I've already worked out for myself. 'Don't do anything you don't want to do. Never ever do that.'

We talk more. She tells me how very poor her family was when she was growing up. Doesn't make a sob story of it. I think she draws some pride from the hard work of her mother: she raised three children up into higher education with precious little help from the world around her. Even I must admit it is a worthy achievement, no matter what a dull person Granny Bredbury has become as result of her self-sacrifice. And nowadays Monica rests her head in the finest hotel rooms by dint of her own talent, her hard work on stage and before the camera. I do not sense any dig at me—my fortunate circumstances—in her telling. There is a different silver spoon in our house for every hot dinner served. I suppose I should be grateful; I have known no other life. Monica—even Mary, who I do not really wish to bring into mind in this hotel room—endured true hardship before arriving somewhere worth staying.

3.

I returned to Carnforth by train the following morning. It is not a long journey, and although I started to write up the interview—bland and fawning to suit the magazine's style—my mind was elsewhere. When I first recognised that I was to meet Monica behind her sister's back, it excited me. When my aunt telephoned my stepmother to arrange the overnight stay, I think I was primarily thrilled that I might spend still more time—intimate, personal time—with one so deservedly famous. I did not realise that the call would trigger a rapprochement between Mary and Monica. Odd, and although I was the catalyst, I suspect I could never compete with Mary for her sister's affection. They go back too far. I believe Monica was seventeen when first I met her; Mary was her comforter before she set foot in a schoolroom. Big stuff, sharing a childhood in that impoverished Charmouth home. I even think their bond is as strong as mine was with my mother. It explains why I have missed her so. She was there at my beginning.

It was my stepmother who met me at Carnforth railway station. Both her own children with her. She was, for reasons I cannot explain, unusually warm with me. 'You're a little tinker,' she said, and it is a phrase my father also used to deploy if praising me for something less than straightforward. 'I'm so glad you have been able to spend time with Auntie Monica. I love that girl, whatever you may think.'

It was during that short car ride that I first resolved to seek truth over security, to let discomfort be my friend in its careless wake. 'You never told me she had become a star. I had to discover it for myself.'

'You quite correct, child,' she said. 'I understood she had a role for which she is being handsomely recompensed. I've never watched an episode of Shoes and Slippers, long ago resolved that I should watch Monica on the stage or not at all.'

'You have a dismissive attitude?' I tried not to sound overly accusative. Spoke it as though we were fun-sparring. She'd never talked about Monica. Not in four years.

'Perhaps, but not of my sister's talent. I would hope to watch something finite: a work of contained art. Soap operas go on and on. We will all die wondering how the story might end.'

I was to study literature in Sixth Form the following school year, might already have known more about it than my stepmother, although hers was an interesting observation. 'Art is not a scientific problem to be laid out and evaluated. I think it hits you in the gut. If you connect with the lives of the characters—Shoes and Slippers or the miserable Henrik Ibsen—then it affects you. You don't have to say precisely how, or know why. It just does.'

'Wow, Sophie. I remember you looking down your nose at Shoes and Slippers before you won the competition. Got the interview with the big star.'

She wasn't wrong about that. Nor when she called me child. I think it was part of the normal development of a sixteen-year-old girl. Changing my mind; growing into my future opinions.

At home that evening, my father, who had been working late at the university—working or screwing, always a thin line—came into my room. I had already prepared for bed; my light was still on. I read copiously and eclectically in those days.

'How was Manchester?' he asked. 'The big assignment?'

'You know who I met, don't you? Mary has told you.'

'Uh...yes.' He sounded vague, like he didn't know or he had forgotten.

'Monica. She calls herself Mica and she stars in the biggest soap opera of them all.'

'Mary's little sister?'

'Did she not tell you?'

'She might have mentioned it.'

When I told him about her role, the central young generation character in Shoes and Slippers, he admitted he had never heard of the programme. It is tabloid fare and they never entered Windermere Court. Our home was the habitat of science, not of art. Shoes and Slippers a fairly crude stab at the latter.

'Did you like her, Dad? Do you like her?'

'Monica? She's done very well for herself. Hats off, but no, I never cared for her. Noisy and full of herself. I've known her since she was your age and she really was very brassy.' I don't think his comment concerned me at all. My mother aside, my father has no taste in girls. I valued his opinion on other subjects, not on the relative merits of females younger than himself. I thought his opinion about Auntie Monica quite worthless. Then and now. His evaluation of the opposite sex—myself aside—is driven only by the scent of availability. He will have been bitter about one as alluring as Monica giving him so evident a cold shoulder.

* * *

That Interview

The following day was to be one of home study. My exams in the offing, school virtually over, and Hazelbrook soon to be consigned to history. Within the context of my life anyhow, my life and my Daddy's chequing account. The boys went to nursery and my parents to the university, where both were working at that time in their lives. The telephone rang.

'I will need it today, if we are to have Miss Barry read and confirm for Wednesday,' said Pamela Green. It was very stupid of me—not yet a pro—I had done no more work on the interview for Girls in the News than I had managed on the train during the early part of the previous day.

'My step-auntie told me countless more tales which I can include; ordering them is causing me some delay,' I lied, and there was a grain of truth in the reference to additional material gleaned from our private conversation. I knew most of it would need to remain strictly off the record. Even the scathing reference to Bobby McIlroy was a joke, Monica wouldn't mind but I could never smuggle that one past Pamela.

'Can a courier pick it up at the end of the day?' she asked.

'End. Ten in the evening?'

'Six.'

'Can we say eight?'

'Miss Hartnell, I do appreciate that your relationship with our cover star may have enabled you to draw more from Mica Barry than a less connected interviewer might have managed, that doesn't alter a print deadline, I'm afraid. Can we say seven, please?'

'Eight,' I repeated.

'Very good. I have your address. A motorcycle will be there at eight. Will it be typed?'

'I'm sorry...' This was not an expectation I was prepared for.

'I'll have someone stay back to do that. It is terribly inconvenient.' Then Pamela Green laughed. 'You told me that you aspire to be a journalist when you grow up, Miss Hartnell. We are all awkward sods, deep down. Make the story yours, make it good. And don't write a word that might offend Mica. Anyone else is fair game.'

I had no inclination to offend Monica Bredbury. I did wonder if Pamela's comment made McIlroy our sitting duck, chose not to chance it. That day I met my first deadline. First of thousands, I do believe.

* * *

The article which I wrote—forgoing revision, and done without ill-effect upon my smooth passage to Lancaster Grammar School for Girls—did draw on our evening together. Although very young, I correctly discerned which elements of our conversation I should not reveal to the wider world and which were on the money. I gambled and won. Monica spoke to me of Charmouth, growing up poor of money but not of love. I put it centre stage. I dismissed titles like POOR LITTLE RICH GIRL and FROM GENTEEL POVERTY before hitting upon a line which I knew she would relish.

PLENTY TO BE THANKFUL FOR

It made the front page of Girls in the News the following week. A picture of my aunt—hair tied back in the style of Sarah Best—adorned the cover. A small insert in my two-page article—pages four and five—had her smiling warmly and hair untethered. I looked at that one time and again over the following years. Monica posed for those photographs in advance of my arrival in Chorlton-cum-Hardy and still I felt that it was me at whom she smiled.

I had written, succinctly but central to the tale, that Mica Barry was the youngest of three children brought up by a single mother on the windswept Dorset coast. She credited the endeavour of that loving mother with her own success, and that of her two high achieving siblings. I did not write anything further about Mary, and that throwaway line sounded more complimentary than anything I ever said out loud. But it was also true: Mary Stephenson had earned her PhD and worked in some capacity or other at the University. I said it because I was sure Monica would have wanted me to. My praise of the Bredbury family was entirely selfish in its motivation. The glamorous auntie was the only one in the bunch who I actually cared for. Stephen had a degree but as far as I could fathom, the hospital-lab job which occupied him at that time consisted mostly of rinsing out test tubes. The praise I gave him in the slipstream of his sisters was entirely insincere. For Mary, I believe it was technically true, if said grudgingly on my part. I have always been a stickler for journalistic accuracy.

Two or three weeks later, my stepmother gave me a handwritten letter from Monica; she had enclosed it within another sent from sister to sister. Monica had written to tell me the article was great; she made zero changes, and that had never happened in any previous interview. She said that she loved spending time getting to know me again. Some lines in that letter have stayed with me over the years; I believe I replicate them accurately although the original is long lost.

You were great company.

She assured me that I would achieve well in life, it was obvious; then she wrote a few lines which I read time and again. Treasured in my sometimes-unhappy adolescence.

Hey, Sophie, I really didn't mean to make you cry, talking over family troubles like we did. It sometimes happens simply from being who we are, and facing up to all that goes on in our lives. That you confront the most painful memories with unflinching honesty is a strength of your character, and the only real strategy for getting through. It can mean being brutal in our opinions of our own selves sometimes, and that really mustn't get you down. You've so much to be proud of Sophie. I've always loved having you as family.

Chapter Two:

First Sightings

1.

I began the conduct of my investigation with a simple exercise in retrieval. I have an excellent memory. I am certain that I saw Mary Bredbury—that being her name before her imprudent marriage to my father—some weeks or months before she ever laid eyes on me. My parents had separated when I was four years old. I can recall with great clarity the day when Mummy moved her belongings out of the family home. I remember she returned later the same day to take me to her new house. It was a strange time, neither parent explained a damned thing. Too disturbing for them to try, most probably. Mummy and I had already spent some weeks together living in a hotel, alternating it with weeks at Epsom, with Daddy. That one is the family home: I always thought of it that way. Did so when I preferred spending time in my mother's new house, continued to when it was sold on. When we upped sticks for Lancashire. Another family has lived in it for almost two decades, return it to us only in my night-time dreams. I understand with clarity—not a scintilla of doubt—that another family lives there now. It is utterly absurd; I was born to it.

On the day of her move, a large removal van came and loaded up a few items. Not many items, quite frankly. Other than a chaise longue with elephant's feet and a dark-wood wardrobe from her and Daddy's bedroom, I can remember missing nothing in the old house—family home—where my father continued to reside after the separation. I lived in both, me being one of a couple of things they continued to share even after the divorcing was done. The chaise longue fascinated me and, of course, I became reacquainted with it on my every stay with Mummy. I also remember the ridiculous size of the removal van; everything we owned might have fitted inside, and yet she took so little. Left a married life with a holdall and a couple of middle-range antiques. And a small daughter cut in two.

Six months or so after the moving-out day which had upset me and neither parent, my father threw a party in our house. Mummy was there also, came as a guest to her former home. For this and other reasons, I always thought my parents were going to move back together. They spoke cordially with each other when Mummy came to collect me, or if Daddy dropped me off at her house. It seemed normal to me that she would come to his party. She was his wife who lived in another house, never really an ex-wife as far as I was concerned even though I had cried and cried the day the removal lorry confirmed the permanence of their arrangement. And she was never an ex-mummy. Always had time and thought and love for me, far above anything my father offered. Never ever was she an ex-mummy. Not for one day of her life, I now know. And for nineteen years I have been thinking to the contrary.

On the night of the party, with me in bed early, or possibly the usual time—four-year-olds don't get to see much of the evening—the house was teeming with people. I certainly wasn't going to sleep, not with music playing, the chattering of a monkey house accompanying those more melodic sounds. Strangers wandered throughout the downstairs rooms, all with a plate of finger food in one hand and a glass of wine in the other. My father employed a neighbour's girl to babysit although he and Mummy were both in the house.

First Sightings

Looking back, I suspect she was meant to be my jailer, ensure I witnessed nothing of the grown-up party. Not that their social engagements needed censoring, it was simply that young children were deemed out of place. The wicked stuff happened in Daddy's private time, not at wider social engagements. I cannot recollect the babysitter's name, or if father was doing the business with her. I don't expect I understood that side of his relationships when I was four. Four or five, my memory of the wider background to this party is imprecise. She sat in my room and talked to me; I was meant to be in bed; a wilful child, I was more frequently out of it than under the covers. I think the babysitter was the one who let me pull her hair—jet black, sometimes worn in two side plaits but I enjoyed pulling it most when she let it hang loosely—I hope I have not confused her with the next one. I had many; if my antics drove them away, Daddy never said. Whichever it was, she made a bargain with me, agreed that I could look through the balustrade but on no account make my way down the staircase. I agreed to her demand because I was crafty, saw that it was the most I should wisely extract. If I ran away from her and into the party—where only the patronising bonhomie of strangers awaited me—it would result in the dismissal of this easy-to-manipulate babysitter. I liked pulling her hair and getting my own way; stick not twist, whatever a less-calculating four-year-old might have done. Decisions have usually come easily to me, except when fate has been at its most capricious.

The babysitter and I both ventured upon the landing. The old house in Epsom was a marvel, technically smaller than Windermere Court, Carnforth, but more elegant by any measure. A small porch led straight into the large wooden-panelled dining hall and for social gatherings, including my own birthday parties up to the age of eleven, it provided a truly marvellous setting. The ceiling of this room reached up a floor, double the height of any room I came across in my friends' houses. The staircase climbed up one side and then at the top the landing included a ninety-degree turn. From that vantage point, all was laid out before us. I could survey the party from within the gloom of the unlit upper floor. Guests might go into the kitchen or sitting room out of view; however, the great hall was the principal gathering place. For this party, my father had moved the dining table, which usually occupied the centre of the room, placing it against the interior wall. It was draped in white linen and strewn with drinks, snacks, big round cheeses. Alcoholic drinks will have been in abundance; however, I recall no behaviour indicative of it. No falling-down drunk at an Epsom gathering. My father's friends were enquiring scientists, and excessive drinking was not on their playlist. I am sure they all had a glass or two of red or white but they didn't 'go for it' as my generation is apt to do. Myself occasionally. And some in my father's time doubtless did, some of the lads and lasses in our house might have got inebriated when home alone, or in a public house; it was not acceptable behaviour at a house party on our road. Daddy acted far more lordly than louche; first rule of journalism: never imagine one can deduce a person's character from their public face.

'Who's that?' I asked the babysitter, pointing at one person and then another. We were in near darkness where the staircase turned to landing. The bannisters of ornate wood might not have hidden us entirely; however, everyone at the party was talking to those on their own level. A teenage girl with plaited or messy hair—I forget how she wore it that night—and a child in reception class, away up in the gods, held no interest for them.

I asked my who's-that question once more when I saw Daddy doing a tiny bit more than talking with a young girl. Quite pretty, I expect, I had no eye for all that at so young an age. Mummy was the true beauty in my eye, and I understood that her move away to a smaller house, a short drive beyond my primary school, where I had another bedroom of my own—not a nicer room, smaller, and laden with more dollies, with hundreds of them, another added between my every stay—was in part because she struggled to compete on that front. Struggled against whoever it was my daddy was then pawing, most probably. Since Mummy left, Daddy had entertained other ladies in his house. It had happened a few times. Breakfast with Bethany, dinner with Diana. A long and lazy lunch with Linda. I hated him having other ladies in his bedroom. Girls really, always very young. The girl he was homing in on that evening seemed a bit unresponsive to his tactile communication. Stiff as a board, I would say. I hope it is a true memory, I shall always believe it. A central characteristic of my stepmother is that she hasn't an ounce of spontaneity within her. She must have enjoyed my father's attention—she hopped into his bed sooner or later, that very night perhaps although if that was their first conjoining, she steered clear of breakfast—my infant observation told me nothing on that front. She could have been advising him to reunite with my mother for all the body language she emoted. And that is central to my gripe with Mary Stephenson: she has been as cold with the man she allegedly loved as she has with me. Interesting that I now write loved, put it in the past tense. I understand from my initial enquiries that the police have arrested both Paul and Mary Stephenson, my father and my stepmother, for the murder of Celia Hartnell, my true mother. She—Mary who I never liked—denies it completely. He says that he didn't murder his ex, that Mary did that part of the terrible deed on her own, he admits only to having a role in the disposal of her body. The burial beneath a garden shed. I have not heard that Mary has stopped loving Paul, only surmised it. After all, he has fingered her for the murder, confessed on Mary's behalf while partially absolving himself. That would put a strain on any relationship. And the feelings she held for him before this turn of events cannot have been simple. She knew that he frequently took advantage of the undergraduate, and even the post-graduate system, designed by and for randy professors. I learned long ago, from my Auntie Monica, that she even knew he cheated on her with his ex-wife and forgave it after some fashion or other. I strongly suspect that finding herself dobbed in it for the murder of my mother has finally exhausted her love for him. I should ruddy hope so. And it finally proves he felt the same about her as I always have. I fear he hid it to save his own sorry skin. I really wonder if they stayed together only because each feared the other going to the police about whatever the hell it is that went on in September, nineteen-eighty-one. The events that put my mother under a shed. Family can turn out to be such beasts; I've covered other news stories in which that was the central message. This one is the very, very worst.

The police have asked to interview me tomorrow. They were very clear that it is 'only for background.' The detective who spoke to me on the telephone had a very kindly manner. 'I've read your work in The Noise,'—not such a surprise, I'm a crime reporter and he is police—'it will be a pleasure to meet you. And, Miss Stevens, if you wish to bring a supporter, they shall be most welcome. I appreciate that what happened in your childhood can be upsetting. We simply need to hear as much as we can about it in order to form our most productive lines of enquiry.'

'Detective Yorke,' I said, 'by supporter, do you mean a lawyer or a solicitor?'

'Miss Stevens...' He softened his voice at this point, spoke to me as he might if he were delivering news of a death although that terrible disclosure had been given me two days earlier. Nineteen years too late, also. '...you may bring who you wish but we have no suspicion of your involvement in the unexplained death of your mother. Nothing of that sort, truly. Our concern is the state of both of your father's marriages, the relationships between the adult parties. We know you were a child, uninvolved beyond the tragedy of bereavement.'

I agreed to attend—they are running the operation from a station in Banstead, I can't think why—I did not say whether I would be alone or accompanied. I am minded to ask Grace to go there with me; I feel closer to her than to anyone else right now. The catch is, we have been a couple for only the shortest time. I should not like to destroy whatever it is that we have by asking too much of her. By allowing her to see me get upset, and the contemplation of this is having that effect almost every hour of my day. I am distraught, cannot believe what either of them may have done while finding a renewal of the hatred for my stepmother which I had not previously dwelt upon for years. Or if not years then months. Weeks. I think weeks covers it quite aptly.

* * *

In the summer of nineteen-seventy-five, some weeks or months after the party at which I first saw my father circling young Mary Bredbury as she was then called, I gained an inkling that she was to play a bigger role in my life than I would have chosen for her were this world a fair and rational place. There were many meetings before the marriage, before Mary made herself a permanent fixture in my family home. Three stand out. She came to tea, entering the house with my father, at the end of the university day, when she was still—I have worked this out—a first year student, possibly eighteen, no more than nineteen, years of age. A trip to London Zoo: I adored animals at that age; during this trip, I think Mary competed with me for my father's attention, stupid girl that she was. Then, some weeks before their wedding, not many although I cannot place the precise date—summer of seventy-six, certainly, and over a year after seeing her through the balustrade that looked onto our dining hall—I accompanied the pair to an outdoor eatery. A beer garden is my best guess. There, my father told me—you will learn much about his innate sensitivity from this—that Mary was to be my 'new mother', no less.

I have, until very recently, loved my father, while always known him to be an oaf. Not at science, and he is apparently *au fait* with the art of seduction, an activity I have never directly witnessed. Thank you, God. Back then my mother remained my mother, the only one. Mary replaced nothing. Later, when my mother sadly disappeared—deposited beneath a shed, robbed of life, the burial surely performed without ceremony, although this event has only very recently become known to me—Mary still replaced nothing. She is a vapid, purposeless soul, devoid of presence. She might know physics, begrudgingly I admit she has a pretty face, a slim figure, not that either attracted me even when I finally admitted to myself that I am not immune to such charms. Even to her own boys, I think her no more than a modestly able mother. Simon, whom I am ashamed to say, I used to ridicule, was a hard-to-reach child. To this day he chooses not to speak, never has, but he writes notes, texts, has quite a vocabulary. He displays a directness of thought that is not to everybody's taste. In my teenage years, perhaps even when I was first a university student, I believed him to be the cursed child which my stepmother deserved. More recently I have thought that an unkind sentiment to wish upon poor Simon. I have even wondered if it was me, if I am the cursed child. There were signs. The divorce, the disappearance, even being so much smarter than all my friends was a bit of a curse. It made my childhood more difficult to navigate. I upset others because they could not see their own stupidity, that is how I understood it. Looking back, I can see that for all my talents, I made one or two poor choices: unkind comments don't win anybody's affection. For one or two, read thousands. I was a catty child, and my behaviour towards Mary will have given her pause for thought along the same lines although I scarcely regret it, not my ill-will towards her. Perhaps she tried her best with all of us, still it has been a pretty poor show. Craig is normal. Always has been. One out of three is not much of a return; Mary is a pretty crummy mother-cum-stepmother. That's as close to an objective summary as I can manage.

2.

A girl called Thea collects me from school. I'm a first-year but I might be the cleverest in the place. I've not talked to all the other boys and girls yet; they are mostly of the screamy and shouty type, and I don't like to. Not intelligent at all, I can tell. I've known Thea for about a month and I don't like her. When I am at the other house, Mummy comes by car to collect me from school. Daddy spoils me with words and presents but shares his time only sparingly. Hires stand-ins to look after me when it is his turn. The last one was useless, so I made myself sick all over the new trouser-suit that she was wearing because it was a Saturday. That got rid of her very nicely. I've not riled this one as spectacularly, currently I'm thinking about it. Plotting. Thea takes my hand and advises that I must walk. She says I am too big to be carried.

'Doesn't that depend on how strong you are?' I query.

It is hot today, scorching hot, and I try to give this girl—whose job is to assist me and make my life comfortable—my cardigan to carry.

'I have this schoolbag of my own,' she replies. Meaning no. It's a pathetic line of argument. Hers is a satchel which she might easily strap across her back; she carries it in her hand exclusively to look modern. Many girls carry shoulder bags but this dolt has a satchel. It is no excuse at all. I shove my cardigan into her hands and she fails to take a hold. It falls onto the dirty pavement. I begin to cry and tell her she has made my school clothes dirty. Thea picks it up from the ground, threads it through the straps of her satchel and finally puts it all upon her shoulders. This babysitter needs a real shove if I'm to get her to do her job properly.

The walk is long and I think about crying again; however, I cannot work out exactly what it would achieve. Thea is a pale and skinny girl. I think she looks very stupid, albeit with interesting knees. The knobbly kind. She tells me about the girls in her school, says that many of them are in love with Danny Clare. Several, it seems, and when I subsequently learn that the said Mr Clare is known to them only through the mediums of television and gramophone records, it becomes evident that she attends Idiot School. One which heaves with morons who think themselves on a date while watching a singer on a silly pop-chart show. I shudder just thinking of them.

Finally, we arrive at my father's house, the one I have lived in since birth although I now alternate my weeks between here and the other house which belongs only to my mother. Mummy would never hire a goon to look after me in her stead. She does some work, buying and selling old things. Dressing tables and chairs of pleasing design. I don't know where she does this, she has no shop of her own. She has taken me into some old houses where we looked upon elegant furniture. Mummy talked about the carvings along the sides of each piece, the grain of the wood. Since she has lived separately from Daddy, she has told me that physics can drive a person round the bend. Apparently, even looking into space with a telescope tells you very little. The scientists work out what space is like through doing sums that go on for pages and pages. I should rather they did drawings, then I might understand what is out there. Stars are very interesting: they twinkle and apparently the sun is one but bigger. A thousand times bigger by the look of it. I am not averse to doing a page of sums but I can see no connection between my times-tables and space.

* * *

Inside the house, dumbbell puts the television on. I never watch it. A bald man reads a story to children who can't read it for themselves. This nonsense isn't for me. As soon as Thea goes to the kitchen to make herself a drink, I turn off the set. Daddy says it ruins young minds, and so I shan't let it take the edge off mine.

'What are you doing?' says Thea, on returning to the room.

I have a book from the shelf that belongs to my father. I don't understand it but some of the words are simple enough. A few. I think it is about his work, about universities and science. 'Read it to me,' I say. 'I was not interested in the little-children's story.'

This girl takes the book from me and holds it away from her face like it might give her the measles. 'I don't think you'll understand this, Sophie,' she says.

If she doesn't read it to me, then I cannot possibly.

While we are sparring—Thea wants me to watch television so that she can do her homework, a raw deal from my side of the fence—my father comes home with a young woman on his arm. I swear she is no older than the babysitter. I know the face but not why I know it. Perhaps she was at his last party.

'Is everything all right, Thea?' he asks.

'Sophie is so funny,' she says. 'She wanted me to read Principles of Electro-Magnetism to her. I think she adores you and your work.'

'Really?' asks the new girl whose name I have yet to learn. 'Do you think she knows what it is about?' Why is she asking Thea? I have a perfectly good tongue in my head.

My father goes down on one knee next to the sofa on which I sit. 'Sophie, dearest, this is Mary. My special friend, Mary. I have a feeling the pair of you are going to get along like a house on fire.'

'Can she read that book?' I ask, pointing at The Principles of Electro-Magnetism, at the shelf to which Thea has returned it.

'Mary could explain it very well indeed. A top, top student...'

I interrupt his glowing praise because it is not about me. 'Does that mean you are giving dumb-dumb Thea the boot?'

The Mary-girl gasps as if what I have said puts her down, when I think it elevates her. She looks prettier than stupid Thea, who looks away at my comment. Won't face facts. Daddy shakes his head. 'Thea is your babysitter and I'd like you to be more grateful for all she does for us. Mary isn't replacing her at all. She is my friend...' He clasps the university student's hand as if they are about to cross a busy street. '...and I'd like her to be yours.'

She might be a bit brighter than the kids I endure in first year infants but it doesn't make this my-friends-are-your-friends balderdash genuine. She's come around to see him, not me. I can see that in the way she holds his gaze, allows my father to put an arm around her waist. Her interest in me began and ended with the gasp about the physics book. And if she understands it—the magnetism and everything that Daddy teaches—then she is streets ahead of Thea; it still doesn't mean she is on my level.

* * *

My father fusses in the kitchen. I don't know what he is playing at, he usually eats a slice of gala pie with pickles in mustard. I can't abide the sour taste and will only eat cucumber with a small piece of the pie. Sometimes he lets me have tinned ravioli which is much nicer. My mother is an excellent cook—a lady chef, indeed—prepares me hot meals in winter and proper salads with sliced meats in summer. It isn't that Daddy doesn't care about me, simply that he is not very interested in food. Eats whatever is in front of him; that is what my mother says and she knows him well. And has subsequently tired of him, I have surmised.

I am being entertained in the lounge by the two young ladies. I presume only one is earning money for being here. Funny to think that she is the more stupid. What on Earth is the clever, pretty one even doing in our house? Thea is in her school uniform, a navy-blue skirt which exposes her creepy knees. They are like the biggest burls one sees on a weather-worn tree. Her top is light blue, a school blouse. She is as skinny as me. I can see the outline of her brassiere beneath the thin shirt but why she wears one is unknowable. She could be a boy looking at the shape of her. Her hair is black and straight, and I believe she ties it back at school, often has it loose by the time she is in my company. Mine is black also, and with a far greater shine. I have told her many times that she should wash hers more frequently. Perhaps she hopes to repel boys rather than attract them. I am grateful if she repels my father.

The new girl's face is rather sweet. I only steal glances at it because I do not want her to think she has won me over. It is an odd thing to report, her eyebrows are darker than her fair hair. They are not deep brown but definitely not yellow. Her hair looks better cared for than the dolt's. There is a wave or a curl about it that might be natural or might be the result of an hour's preening. She wears jeans, which I think to be workman's clothing; Mary's are clean, perfectly so. Beryl, who gardens for us, always looks shapeless and rather dirty—like a man—in her blue jeans. I sometimes watch her in the back garden, when she bends over and shows the world the top of two moons peeping out because she wears no belt. It's hilarious: getting to see half of a big old lady's bottom. I enjoy laughing at those who make a pig's ear out of life, although Mummy says I shouldn't. It shows bad taste apparently; however, I cannot see any connection between enjoying both my food and other people's stupidity. This Mary-person wears a yellow-patterned blouse above the jeans. She has undone the bottom few buttons and tied the ends together above her tummy button. This trick reveals three or four inches of midriff. She has the top two buttons undone also; her breasts are not large but the very tops of them are visible when she bends over. I think the whole point of clothing is that it covers you up. She might be as stupid as Beryl, just does it without looking like a fella.

When father calls us into the dining hall, I see he has laid the table with napkins. Why he has done such a thing is beyond me: entertaining schoolchildren and then he believes himself in high society. Upon the table are slices of smoked salmon, and a potato salad that comes from I don't know where. Perhaps you can buy these things ready prepared, my father has never before shown an aptitude for food preparation and there are no caterers in the house. There is green salad: lettuce with a small amount of chicory, and sliced tomato in there too, vinegar and olive oil upon it. I can do that—dress a salad properly—Mummy has shown me how. I didn't think Daddy had a clue about that sort of thing.

Mary makes a point of serving potato salad onto every plate. She touches the back of my father's hand, serving spoon still in hers, and says, 'Would you like more, Paul.' It is an intimate gesture, a physical familiarity. When the puffed-up girl comes to serve me, before so much as raising a potato she touches the back of my hand also. 'Do you like potato salad, Sophie?' Her voice is a notch higher than the one she addressed my father with. If it is because I am a child, it is patronising; if the earlier voice was her being sultry, bring me a sick bowl.

3.

Leaves are upon the ground, puddles here and there, and yet the day is pleasingly warm. It is a boon at this time of the year. I am walking between my father and the girl he treats too nicely, Mary Bredbury. Each holds a hand of mine. They swing me over puddles if they are large and situated in the centre of the path. I have no choice in the matter, they have determined that I am their prop. In return for my obedience, I shall see the sea lions. They are funny creatures; big fat tummies. They can't really walk, and when they slither around, it is comical, not scary like the ugly snakes with their scaly faces. I don't like to see them at all. I am certain that Mummy has taken me to London Zoo before; this isn't my first time, whatever Daddy keeps saying. I think she brought me here during the first weeks after she had moved out of our Epsom home, when she and I were sharing a hotel bedroom on the alternate weeks I spent with her. Before the big moving van came. The facts of zoos are known clearly to me. Animals in cages, and many even have gardens too. However, I recognise nothing: whatever I saw when last here has slipped from my mind. Like an eraser has been used upon it, and vigorously too. All gone. The zoos in books and the zoo in my memory have merged into one. I might even know of them mostly from the moronic television. I like watching animals whenever there is a programme which is exclusively about them; it is having stupid people enter one's house through that medium which makes me press the off button.

I see a sign that says, 'Snake House.' I want to walk past it without mentioning the horrible creatures; Mary has turned towards me and stooped down onto one knee like she is going to propose marriage. I am a girl, a very young one, asking that of me would be sillier than stupid. She wears a thick brown coat of a stiff and hairy material that I would like to touch but not when she can notice: I fear she might misinterpret the gesture. I like the coat, cannot stand the girl inside it. 'We can see some snakes, little Sophie, unless you think them too scary for you? They will all be behind glass. Slithery, but they can't bite or wrap themselves around you from there.' If Mary Green-Eyes were behind glass, my world would be a lot less nauseating. My father has a stuffed owl in his study that spends its entire day—day and night, its flying days terminated by the stuffing—within a glass dome. I should like Mary Bredbury far more if that were her. She is a good-looking specimen but every utterance, each tilt of her head or gesture with her hand, I find very annoying. I think it the inverse effect to that which she has upon my unworldly father. He is in thrall to her which is duck-brain daft. My daddy is a university teacher, and they are supposed to be the cleverest kind of teacher there is. Why he drools over a student who has still to learn the first quarter of what he knows is beyond me. I think it is to do with her looking very nice which she sort-of does. But she isn't nice like Mummy, it's completely false. Tries too hard, and that means she isn't really it. A pretend person. I even wonder if her brown eyebrows are dyed. So much darker than her fair hair, it is the most likely explanation. And my Daddy keeps touching her. Just now it was the nape of her neck, a hand in the collar of her lovely coat. Her skin must feel slimy like the snakes which I agree to go and see. I don't want Mary to think I'm scared of anything. Just so long as I am not made to touch them, I'll be all right. Pretend that I like them. It is only Mary's coat which I really wish to feel with my hands. It is the same colour as her eyebrows, and I like the coat better.

* * *

It is dark and unpleasant in the snake house. I think the zookeepers keep it this way so that one can ignore the horrible creatures more easily. The trouble is, my imagination might be scarier than the hosepipe-like reptiles. My fear is difficult to pin down, they have no arms, cannot punch us, but I understand that they spit. I am very pleased that there is glass between the snakes and I, so however much they try, their sputum cannot reach me. And they have poisonous spit which makes them even worse than the boys at school. Mary—whose coat I think her only worthwhile feature—tries to tell me about them. She is only reading off signs by each glass enclosure. They are a bit high for me to read. You see, she is taller than me, not smarter.

'Can you see that one?' she says as she points. 'There! Curled up in the corner.'

'Why is it so dark in here?'

'You're quite right, Sophie, they are a bit hard to see. But if the lights were brighter the snakes would be frightened and just cower under their logs where they couldn't be seen.'

That would suit me very well. Better that the snakes are frightened than that I am. I don't discuss this with Mary. Whether truth or lie, I want her to think me brave.

'Look at that,' she points as we pass another of the glass tanks. I hadn't seen it because this snake is the same colour as the large branch of tree which runs through the enclosure. A swathe across the snake pens. Branch and snake are as still as each other. 'It is a boring snake,' I say. 'We could leave it, go back into the sunshine.'

'Don't you like the snake? Is it a bit scary. I was terrified of snakes at your age. You're doing great, Sophie.'

'No, it isn't because I am scared at all. The snake simply isn't doing anything.' I look into her face when I say this, looking at the horrible snake might make sick come into my mouth. I don't like them at all but I shan't be letting this girl know any weaknesses of mine. She says that she was terrified of snakes at my age, and I wouldn't have known about it if she hadn't said. I am acting like I'm not scared at all—want to leave only because it's boring in here—I like the subterfuge of fooling her. Making her think one thing when another is true. I wonder if this girl knows she is one of many. It is months since she first came around the house, and she is an infrequent visitor. Last week—and this was after I had gone to bed—a different student called at the house. Although I did not see her, I heard my father bring her into his bedroom. He called her by the name Louise. There is a girl in my class with the same name. Momentarily, I thought to go onto the landing to greet her, mistakenly thought that the late evening visitor had come to play with me. 'Oh Paul, you are the devil they say you are,' said this other Louise. Just the sound of her voice was enough for me to realise she was not from my school. My Louise has a squeaky voice and this one's was definitely deeper. She must attend Daddy's school, his fancy university, the same as Mary here. It's a bit silly that my father brings his students back home. I would not go to my teacher's house of an evening. I've had quite enough of Mrs Appleton by the time the bell goes.

My father imagines I sleep from a quarter past seven each evening and it was after nine o'clock that I heard him with the girl upstairs. With his Louise. I will sleep from seven-fifteen if my day has been busy, fun, tiring. That is something Mummy seems better at arranging than Daddy. I listened to Daddy and Louise in his bedroom. I understand that grownups like to look upon each other without clothing concealing their skin. This pair made noises. Oohs and aahs. To me it sounded like they were eating ice cream but we have none in the house. If there is another explanation, I have yet to learn it.

I don't know what happens when I am at Mummy's house but, to the best of my knowledge, Mary hasn't had a proper sleepover with Daddy yet.

First Sightings

* * *

Father wished to stay longer in the snake house while his little admirer insisted that I had spent enough time in there. 'She's being very brave, Paul, and they are sinister-looking creatures. I think she'd rather go.' I am unsure what the word she used means but it sounds desirable only in the most sinful way. Snakes just look thin, the wrong shape to be real animals even though they actually are. I think Mary Bredbury might be the sinister-looking one, do not say it. It is best not to use a word until one is more certain of its purpose than I currently feel.

The monkey house beats the snake-place hands down. It is rather wonderful. I see the biggest chimpanzee beating its chest; Father nods his head in the beast's direction, recognition in his eyes. Mary laughs and laughs, occasionally flexes herself down, almost sitting on her heels, so that our faces are aligned. She points things out to me, the monkeys' many antics. They amuse—that is beyond doubt—broad jaws of teeth display smiles which stretch impudence to its limit. The monkeys have superior accommodation to that of the snakes. The slithering freaks were all kept in small dark tanks, while the monkeys enjoy an indoor-outdoor playground. Trees and tyres. There are a few small monkeys—they look more like spindly toys—which live only inside the house. Caged off from the rougher, breast-beating apes. The girl picks me up so that my head is level with a tiny monkey. Its saucer eyes gaze into my own. The little monkey has no one to hold it to her chest as Mary Bredbury does with me. I like looking at the animal, and more so I like the fuzzy feel of Mary's coat within my hands and even upon my cheek as she pulls me closer to her. Still, I would gladly change places with the monkey. Mary should be handling a jungle beast, it is more akin to any child she might bear than I, the daughter of Cynthia Stephenson, or Cynthia Hartnell. I know her names—the one she shares with Daddy and the one which is only hers—not which one she is now known by. Mummy, that is as I call her, and always will. She stopped being called Hartnell when she married Daddy, and now she has got a house of her own she might have gone back to it. Stephenson is his name more than it is hers. Mine to but Sophie Stephenson sounds like a snake talking. I might call myself Hartnell—I could try it when I'm in her house, that seems the way of names—it sounds rather nice to me. A name with a heart in it. And it is in Mummy's arms that I would rather be. This girl is just using me to ensnare Daddy. Prevent Mummy from ever coming to live back where she really belongs.

I will be going to Mummy's house tomorrow evening, spending the week there from which to attend school. I know that Mummy knows all about Mary, I can even remember that she was at the party where first I saw this girl. The horrible thing is that I understand everything that's going on. Daddy is nice to me but generally he's stupid; thinks that Mary can replace Mummy when she cannot possibly. Those months ago, when I looked through the banister rail and first saw Mary Bredbury attending a party in my home, I thought her very pretty indeed. That is what she has, eyes and nose and mouth that are well placed. It doesn't make anyone a nice person. She seems to have fooled Daddy but that could even be a trick he is playing on her. It is the only way I can explain Louise. The girl I heard on the landing. I think he just likes playdates; tells everyone they are his best friend, when you can only truthfully have one. And I don't think Mary is clever enough to figure out what he is really like. If he says he loves her, she is sure to believe it; he's her teacher, after all. It's her job to remember everything he says. She only pretends to care for me. I don't eat pretend fruit. There is no love in her hollow heart; not for me and I'm not sure what she feels for Daddy. Playing Mister and Missus at their age is a silly game. She should have grown out of it long ago. Mary

First Sightings

is not Mummy and so I yell at the top of my lungs for her to put me down. Away in the main enclosure, a monkey mimics my cry.

* * *

As we move around the zoo the never-ending smell of poo, which is caused by the animals' inability to defecate within, nor manually operate the handle of, a proper toilet, makes me lose interest. Many of them look nice but none have manners. I find myself thinking about one particular tea-time before I had started school. Before Mummy ever moved to her own house. I remember little from that time, and this one has stuck in my mind. We had a guest at tea, a man from Daddy's work. He was talking about the new student intake. My daddy works as a teacher at Imperial College. I know all about the word imperial. It means that it is the best school in the world, and my daddy the cleverest teacher. He works there, and so he must be. Daddy's friend said something about the girls who are joining the course. I think he teaches them about space rockets and I understand boys to be more drawn to this subject, although I should rather study rockets than dolls. Dolls are vacant, dead. Even Mary is a couple of notches better than a doll.

'They can be as clever as the lads but they never have the dedication.' My daddy's friend said this. I don't know what it means but my parents greeted his words with a stony silence, then he added, 'It's wanting babies. Happens to all of them once they're in their twenties. It makes them lose interest.'

My father argued with him, quite forcibly. 'Rubbish, Rinus. We don't have enough girls on the course. There is no difference between the sexes. For every girl with a baby there is a man who has one too, you know. And that isn't some whacky feminist's opinion, it's scientific fact. We need more girls at Imperial, more girls studying physics and chemistry and maths. We have to lead the way on this. I am not chaining our university to the past on the back of some outdated notion that was wrong a hundred years ago. Wrong when everything was so stacked against women, that men never got a glimpse of their own prejudices, never gave a thought to how clever many girls really were.'

I liked hearing Daddy's point of view. What he said about men having babies surprised me, they must keep them in their garages or something, I never see them pushing prams like the ladies do. His job sounds more important than Mummy's, and it seemed to mean I would be able to do anything I chose. Antiques are not for every girl.

To my surprise, Mummy sided with the other man. She rose from the table, throwing down her napkin. 'Two-faced nonsense, Paul,' she shouted. There were tears in her eyes that made no sense to me. 'You want all the girls you can get coming on to your course for all the wrong reasons, you animal. You make a clever argument but you don't fool a soul. Not even on the corridors of Imperial. They let you get away with it because you know your Newton and your Einstein but you've ruined your career...' She started walking out of the room and I could hear her voice breaking as she finished what she had to say. '...and your marriage.'

Now, in this zoo, I think Mary Bredbury is one of the girls Daddy wanted on the course for all the wrong reasons. She is his student but he hasn't said a word about rockets all day. She comes around the zoo with us like a replacement mummy, and that is the last thing I need. If Daddy needs a replacement wife, it is his own fault for upsetting the first one.

My memories of that time are very blurred but soon after the argument I was living with Mummy in a hotel. It was in London. I didn't like it very much because London is for visiting and not for living in. Epsom is a proper place with houses, not hotels. While at the hotel, I went to school in a taxi which was rather nice. I believe it is the same way that the Queen travels.

* * *

When we leave the zoo—and this is after eating fish and chips at the cafeteria, something Mary enjoyed and Daddy laughed at; I despised it—we go down the escalator to the tube. Zipping out of London on the underground. My mouth feels sticky and horrible from the greasy awful chips. At the cafeteria there were a lot of dirty-looking children who seemed to enjoy the fare. I expect that Mary was once that sort of child. And not so very long ago. Fourteen years older than me, that is as much as she is. I asked her what her age is and then worked it out. I like doing sums. They insist upon me sitting in between them on the train, wedged between Daddy and Mary. I would rather have Mummy right now, in fact, if I could sit with Mummy, and she were wearing Mary's furry brown coat, then these would be the most wonderful of times. We came here the same way we return. I have grown used to going on the tube-train; I'm not frightened by the screeching noises, nor the darkness of the endless tunnels. No snakes down here. The doors are funny, nobody can stop them from closing and I imagine that stupid people allow themselves to get decapitated by them once in a while. Because I am clever—always noticing how things work—I am able to avoid a beheading.

A little time later we are in a proper train, one that travels above ground. These London trains are very sneaky; this one must have come up its very own escalator to get here. Now that there is daylight all around us, I imagine loss of limbs or noggin would not go unnoticed. The dead must all be along the trackside in the tunnels; it is a more civilised lifestyle above ground. I still sit at Mary's side but the fluffy-coat wearer has moved centre stage. Daddy is by her side not mine, he has his arm around her shoulder, once or twice the pair put their foreheads together. I think he kisses her, not certain because I look away. It is disgusting: I don't really want to see him kissing his real wife, and I don't think she would let him do that any longer. Not my mummy, and not in a railway carriage of all places. You would think they could wait until they are out of sight. Back underground or when I am supposed to be in bed. Louise was better mannered than Mary, waited until it had gone dark.

* * *

When we arrive home, Daddy talks to me about tiredness. I know all about his snake-charmer tricks and I am impervious to them. Still, I would rather play in my room alone than be in the company of Mary, although I rather think she tried hard today. Behaved in a similar way towards me as Mummy would have done had she accompanied us. Similar but unconvincing, she's the wrong one. In my room, I change into pyjamas. I often like to wear a simple nightdress, the ones I have are thin. At Mummy's house I always do, and she lets me climb into her bed and snuggle up next to her, my skin against hers. Tonight, I choose flannel pyjamas, a blue and black tartan. I shall not be under my covers. In fact, I might be anywhere in the house that the adults are not. Hide and seek is easy when those who might find me are otherwise occupied.

Downstairs, my daddy and his student drink a bottle of something which he fetched up from the cellar. Daddy is a bit of a wine-guzzler; I don't think Mary knows about vineyards and how the country girls stomp upon grapes in large barrels, because she is common. Not unless she grew up doing the stomping which is actually done by common girls of the country sort. I think burp-inducing beer is the drink which is meant to accompany fish and chips. Big pots of stinking beer drunk by the rough men of London and all points north.

I am very good at sneaking down the stairs undetected. I

shall eat some dry cereal from the pantry. I wish to replace the slimy texture of chip fat from my lips.

Mary and my father are in the lounge and the door is ever so slightly ajar. A record is playing. Vulgar pop music which I understand appeals to students. I think it is the drumming that captivates them. Boom-boom-boom, like a chimpanzee beating upon its chest. I glance into the room from the dining hall; Mary slouches upon the sofa. I realise that she is no longer wearing her coat, the clothing she has on looks all wrong, not a lot of it, and I notice her blouse is upon the rug. What she does or does not wear is of little interest to me, the house is warming up so she won't freeze. I take myself to the porch. The nice furry coat will be hanging there, I expect.

I find it, she has hung it on quite a high peg and I am small. There are two lower pegs on which I am able to hang my own coats. I can reach hold of Mary's and shake it but the hanging loop won't slide off for me because the peg is angled upwards. I remember the monkeys in the zoo and the way they swung on ropes and trees. I understand from my father that, although our grandparents are not monkeys, nor even their grandparents, our grandparents' grandparents' grandparents actually were. They were apes and baboons and silly little macaques and that might mean that I have the inherited ability to climb as well as those funny creatures do. I give it a go, grip hard on Mary's coat, start to clamber up. At the top I shall pull the hanging loop over the point of the peg, it should come down then.

Bang! Ouch! Disaster!

I think the thread on the little bit of fabric which the coat was hanging from has snapped. I've hurt my ankle. I can hear my father, even Mary too, shushing each other. They might think I'm a burglar, and hit me over the head. It is what I will do each time I find one. Burglars are such brutes: they've got it coming, they really have. I wait as quietly as I can. I hear the girl giggle. That is not the noise you make when approaching a burglar, not unless you have a gun with which to finish them off. I hear Daddy say, 'Squirrels.' It is to my relief that they do not believe me an intruder; I should not like to be shot by Mary. I suppose Daddy would finally see how stupid she is, were she to do that. And God help us should burglars ever enter our house. This pair don't have a clue how to protect a homestead. I fell from halfway up the wall like a falling chimney, and my ankle aches and aches; it could be coming apart. The coat feels lovely; I made a right racket getting hold of it. Squirrels, my eye.

I roll the coat into a ball so that it won't drag on the carpet, and therefore won't make a noise. I walk gingerly across the dining hall. I can scarcely bear weight on my right ankle, it's very painful. Throbbing. I hope the foot doesn't have to come off. Giggly Mary is still making her childish noises, thankfully the pair of them are back in the lounge. The silly music plays. As I pass the open door and glance quickly in, I see Daddy standing on one leg removing his trousers. At school, two of the girls undressed in a toilet cubicle to look upon each other naked. I should have liked to have joined in but they never asked me.

* * *

I sleep long into the next morning. I was playing in the glamorous coat in front of my mirror for hours last night: a lady about town. As I awake the smell of coffee, and of bacon—which is cheap meat, basically just pigskin, but very nice to the detecting nose—are wafting up the stairs. I hope there are croissants, I like to eat neither of the items I can smell, it is only their aromas I enjoy. Better than the monkey house by a distance. I am awake but my eyes keep closing. To my surprise the door flies open, Daddy and his girl are standing in front of me.

'I've cut it up very small for you, Sophie,' says Mary. She is holding a small plate with a sandwich on it. Fatty bacon, I presume. A sandwich in bed: they must think three's a crowd, don't want to have me downstairs with them. Then Mary exclaims, 'My coat!' I am beneath the covers but it must stick out and I have worn it all night.

Now I am very embarrassed. She will want it back, and I wear nothing beneath it. Some of the rough hair touches my skin. It is a marvellous feeling. 'I like it. I want to keep it.'

'Oh Mary,' says Daddy. 'She's really taken to you. Wanted something of yours in bed with her.'

I say nothing, he's way off beam but I've no wish to argue with him at this time. I hold my hand out for the sandwich. 'You can have it back later,' I say in my very firmest voice. 'Please?'

Mary laughs. 'All girls like dressing up,' she declares. I hope they haven't noticed the crumpled-up pyjamas at the side of my bed.

4.

I have been six years old for six months now, which means I am six and a half. Six being half of twelve and that is the number of months in a year. I am explaining this to Mary and she seems to alternate between knowing it already and not knowing it at all. She tells me I am very clever but this is not long multiplication and I can do that too. With a pen and paper. I use a funny word that Daddy uses when things are simple. 'This is rudimentary. I worked it out inside my head.' Funny because it sounds rude. In fact, rudimentary sounds like it is meant to be rude; a lot of words mean something very different to what they sound like. Words were all invented by idiots and now we must put up with them.

'Gosh, Paul,' says Mary, 'she is so good with language. A marvel.'

Mary sleeps in our house quite often. In the same bed as my father. She also has a student room somewhere near

Imperial College, and she goes and sleeps there sometimes too. I think she doesn't really know what she wants. Students should keep to their student halls, to the buildings which are named for that purpose. I think she is greedy and wants to live in two houses. I do that because my mummy and daddy each maintain a house, Mary Bredbury has no such excuse. She has told me that she has a mummy of her own who lives in a bungalow by the sea. I shouldn't like to live in a bungalow because anyone who cared to disturb you could rap on your windows and wake you from your sleep. Living by the sea must be very fine, I must grant her that. I asked Mary if she could swim and she said yes, said that she will take me. I am nervous about that. Daddy likes seeing her without her clothes on but I am not interested in any of that. Worse still, I might drown in the water. It can do that if you are better at drinking than swimming, and that is definitely my current state. I am to have lessons next year—first year juniors get taken across Epsom to the swimming baths, walking in a crocodile, and that is another silly word—I would rather wait until I have received instruction before letting Mary see me splashing about. I prefer it if she sees me doing things at which I am better than her. My twelve times table. And if she actually stopped me from drowning, it might oblige me to like her. Not a sequence of events I wish to be beholden to.

Today we are sitting around an outdoor table in the garden of a big restaurant. It is a good place to be in the warm weather. Daddy calls it a beer garden which is silly because he drinks wine, and Mary has coca cola. I think she drinks the smelly cola with rummy mixed up in it. It tickles the nose like fresh paint. I have regular cola. I think it is a funny drink, when you swallow it, the taste, and even a bit of liquid, can come back down your nose. I am just trying to understand it. I shall stop drinking the stuff once I have done that. Move on to wine like Daddy has.

First Sightings

We have ordered food, and it is the right day for eating outdoors. Sunshine and not a cloud. The waitress who served us wears a black dress which has frilly white hems. I told the grownups that I should like to wear something similar, that I enjoyed looking upon it. Mary said, 'Would you like to work as a waitress, Sophie?' I think she is very unimaginative, thinks the clothing fit only for one purpose, and yet I expect a lady-detective could wear a black and white dress, even the funny white Alice band that the girl has through her hair. I tried to explain this, and Mary simply pulled out a ribbon she wears, which is yellow not white, and tried to tie it across my hair. Daddy told me this accessory suits me well, so now I await food with a yellow ribbon across my forehead, although my hair is so short, it serves no purpose. If I become a detective, and wear a white Alice band, I shall first grow my hair longer. I think it is easier to predict what one will do in the future if one is also very, very determined. I can make events fall in my favour much of the time. I will pull the ribbon off when no one is looking and say it was the wind.

Daddy has pie and chips, and Mary just a salad. I have chicken which is also accompanied by chips, and I am pleased to say they are dry on the outside and quite crisp. Mary offers to cut my chicken up, so I must explain to her that I have mastered cutlery. It is easier than skipping, and I can do that better than any of the other girls in my class.

'Sophie,' says Daddy, and the tone he deploys indicates I have done something wrong when I have not—the stupid ribbon still pretends to shape my hair—'we have something important to tell you.' I look up from my food. It seems to be about them and not me. Perhaps Mary has done something naughty, and I should like to hear about that. Particularly if she is to be given the boot. 'I think you understand that your mother and I recently finalised our divorce. That we are no longer married. I have asked Mary, here, to be my wife, and she has accepted.'

I look back at my food but before I do I see that his wife-to-be is nodding like the little dogs that sit on the sills at the rear of many a car on the road. Nod, nod, nod. I'm going to marry your Daddy. Her face looks like that of a nodding dog; like a plastic toy. A sweet smile upon it that might fool someone into an unnecessary purchase, a stupid face nonetheless. Daddy has known her for more than a year, I'm surprised he isn't sick to death of her by now.

'What do you think about that?'

I put some chicken in my mouth because it is rude to eat and talk at the same time and I have no wish to answer. The trouble is, I start to swallow before I've chewed it properly and this makes me cough and cough. I can hardly breathe, it's awful: I think I am doing what they call choking. And choking is actually a prelude to dying. First a bit of gasping and heaving, then the main event. Before I know what's what, Mary thumps me quite hard on the back. It brings the chicken back into my mouth and I spit it out onto the grass. There are tears in my eyes from the coughing and I try to thump Mary. I'm allowed because she started it. 'Hey,' she says, taking a hold of the hand that was meant for her chest. 'I hope I didn't hurt you, it's just what you do when something is stuck in a passageway.'

I hadn't thought of this, that she was thumping me to be nice. It seems quite unlikely. I suspect she was waiting for me to choke because it is, apparently, an opportunity to start bashing people. I can think of a couple of girls at school whom I would like to find choking on the corridor.

'Passageway?' I query. 'Daddy said it was a beer garden.'

'Your throat is a passageway, Sophie. A passage down which food travels, all the way to your tummy. Food that you haven't chewed thoroughly can go down like a fat lady trying to climb through a tyre. Their fat tummy can get stuck.' This makes me laugh although I wish it didn't. Fat people are ridiculous, and Mary has chanced upon a funny joke, but this is not the time for laughter. She hasn't let go of me since stopping me from thumping her, and now she tries to hug me. 'I'm going to be your new mummy,' she says. 'Your mummy number two.'

I struggle out of her grip and shout, 'Never!' This time I manage to strike her properly. I hit one of her squishy bosoms very, very hard.

'Ow,' says Mary.

I am crying quite a lot now but also emitting richer laughter than her silly joke prompted in me. She confused me really, making me laugh when I hate her. Hurting her was just plain funny. I wanted to, so I did. I have wanted it for a long time.

'Sophie!' Daddy addresses me, and once more he is using his cross voice. Cross with me and I know why. 'Mary virtually saved your life when you were choking just now. She is a very quick-thinking girl, and...' He looks into her eyes, no longer seeming to address me at all. '...I love her very much. She shall be living in our house after the wedding, and that is only six weeks away.' He has taken hold of her hand, and while doing so, turns again to me. 'You must say sorry to her, Sophie.'

This is like a terrible dream. I get what I want most of the time, and that is the way it should be. Mary Bredbury stays in our house more often than I would like but she is not at meals or in the lounge terribly often. I have thought of her like a television set. Jane Gosling, at school, has told me that her parents are divorced and her daddy now has his own television set up in the bedroom. He watches it from there every evening until the picture turns into a small white dot. My daddy isn't so keen on television so he keeps a girl there. Not every day but a lot. I think he has one or two spares for when Mary stays in her student halls. Standbys in case she is on the blink. I am able to quell my tears, even a little of my anger and say what I need to say. 'I'm very sorry that I punched you...' Mary nods again—woof, woof, woof—nods like a doe-eyed puppy. She places a hand upon mine, carefully, gently. '...but you will never ever be my mummy. I have one already and she suits me perfectly. I shall never have need of another.'

Chapter Three:

Retford

1.

Grace has dropped everything to make her way to my flat in Bayswater; it is quite a journey and I appreciate the effort she is making. I telephoned her after arriving back from Banstead. I went to the police station alone because I could not bear for my new friend to hear the entire story of my sorry childhood. Poor little rich girl, and all the brouhaha that goes with that. Now, I fear I shall spill it all, I am so grateful not to be by myself. She will stay the night which I appreciate more than I know how to tell her.

When my buzzer sounds, I feel truly loved. She must have flown from Herne Hill; I have barely recovered from the tears I shed on the telephone call which summonsed her. 'Coming up,' she calls through the intercom, before I say a thing, confirm I am letting her in. She might be the love of my life.

Grace is only a little older than I—four years—many of my partners have been far older than that. The girls and not the boys, the latter have often been quite young, although I have long been disenchanted with them. The comfort of a man is only fleeting, and I have come to understand my own mentality better with time. Grace works in theatre, and her profession has no bearing on my journalistic life. I enjoy the separation—the otherness—of our working lives. And I have met her only five times before tonight, stayed at her small flat only once. She has not been to mine before, although I gave her my address on our first encounter. The spontaneous date that it was.

* * *

She is fully five inches taller than me, a young face but her black hair has just a tiny number of grey ones nosing their way into the light. Grace is the type to embrace it: will not fight nature, has no reason to do such a thing. A beautiful girl. She takes both my hands in hers and draws me towards her, pecks me on the cheek. An old-fashioned greeting in the light of one or two intimacies we have shared. Recently shared. I put a hand behind her head and plant a firm kiss on her lips. 'Thank you so much for coming. You are a godsend.'

'Tell me, Sophie. I haven't followed this case. It was so long ago. And you knew the victim. You were so young, I can't...'

I interrupt my lover. In my babble on the telephone, I made nothing clear except the extent of my upset. That someone close to me is in prison; that there is a murder in the mix. 'The lady beneath the shed was my mother. I've never told you about her because it is difficult to talk about it. Was difficult before, and now it has become irrecoverably worse.'

'My God. That's so awful. But it was years...'

'Nineteen years ago. My mother has lain there, unknown to me. I thought her whereabouts were outside the knowledge of my father and stepmother, both are currently under arrest for her murder. It seems I have been duped by them for much of my life. Not that the police have charged either, not yet. Perhaps it will not happen. I don't know quite what to think, thoughts running everywhere at the present time. I must be prepared for it though. They could be murderers, and of the person most dear to me life-long. Absent from my life since I first started secondary school. The police were cagey. They talked to me only to help them build a picture. For me, it is already fully formed. The truth behind the nineteen loveless years.' I realise tears are tracking down my cheeks, contrasting with my controlled words.

We have walked to the sofa and seated ourselves side by side. Grace has a kindly arm around my back. 'Poor dear,' she says. 'You must have been so very young. The police shouldn't have been questioning you.'

'It's routine. And I am no longer young. Good luck to anyone trying to understand the Stephenson household circa nineteen-eighty-one. Strange goings on, start to finish.'

'Your name is Stevens?'

'Stephenson. My newspaper name is derived from it but I decided long ago never to publish under any name that might be associated with my stepmother.' Grace looks at me with alarm. I realise I have no idea if she has living parents, divorced parents, a stepmother whom she has come to love. She is thirty-four years of age and has made a living from acting for half of her life. She would not tell me her television credits, except to repeat that they are unexceptional, no starring roles. In the theatre, she has spent hours in the spotlight. Some repertory, up and down the country, some in the West End. As much as possible there. It sounds like a hard life, money a stranger for significant periods of it. The night we met she had appeared in Closed Heart at the Roundhouse Theatre. I was in a neighbouring bar, jilted of a man. The following night I was able to get one of the banquet seats, observe Grace at her craft. She played a woman determined to only wound in the future, to allow no one to hurt her again. It was more than relatable. After that show, I took her to dinner. Paid. Promised I could do more for her but she was initially reticent. We have since forded that river, and I can confirm that I am Grace Topping's first girlfriend. Another one for the team. 'And nor am I anyone's son,' I say. Hope a little levity will relax my Grace. 'I always thought my mother had been driven away. It is complicated,

Grace. Mummy divorced Daddy but continued to sleep with him. Does that shock you? I expect it must. And my stepmother was a child. Not literally but more than twenty years his junior which is far too much. I never understood any of his relationships. Inexplicable, the carryings on of promiscuous academics from a bygone age. Mummy started seeing a man. Finally started seeing a man, and I've no idea whether it put paid to sex with Daddy or not...' Grace is open-mouthed. '...I am not explaining this properly at all. I go long periods not thinking about it, cannot achieve that blissful state for five minutes since this turn up. The dreadful certainty of my mother's death. The...'

'I am so sorry that all this is happening to you, Sophie.'

'Not happening. It has happened. The shocking thing is not knowing for so long. Mummy was seeing a Maltese man. I never met him but Daddy told me all about it. I don't believe she ever saw him when I was at home. At her home. I understood there were other men too, gathered no picture of any in my mind. As an eleven-year-old, my father, stepmother too, good as told me she had absconded with one of them. There was no alternative explanation offered. Forging a new life in a faraway land. Not a jot of proof, no goodbyes or letters promising imminent reunion. Granny Hartnell—the one down my maternal line—always said it was an error that Mummy left me. I think she meant that I was collateral damage. She hoped Mummy found happiness, understood that she had known little of it with my errant father.'

The more I explain myself and my family background to Grace, the more I realise what a complicated story it is, how very bewildering my childhood must seem to an outsider. Up until now, Grace has understood me to be a well-to-do northerner. Hazelbrook School; the University of York. I am as southern as she, better spoken but I don't say it. Grace can speak like anyone in the world when she chooses to put it on, such is her acting range. Born in Sittingbourne, while I am Surrey; her innate vowel sounds are the coarser.

'When did you stop hating your stepmother?' she asks.

'I never said I've stopped.'

'Your father's affairs must have been hard to stomach?'

'My parents divorced when I was six; I liked it if Mary was hurt. The hated stepmother. His many liaisons with students never affected me. Daddy bought me this flat.' I feel odd after I have said it. Praise for the patronage of a relative now banged up in prison. It is not how life should turn out but it is mine. I find the tears come rapidly now. I even make those wailing noises that so distress me when I have had to endure hearing others make them.

'Oh, you poor dear,' says Grace, an arm around me once more. I fear she doesn't know what she has got herself into. And we neither have a clue where it will end.

* * *

It is not yet four weeks since, stood up by Aaron Morley, Grace and I fell into a relationship of warmth. I am talking about *the* Aaron Morley, the writer of occasional leaders in The Messenger, a man who supposedly filed eye-witness accounts of the Chernobyl disaster—he was actually in Kiev—the arrogant sod is also the sort to arrange a second date and then fail to show. And for that reason, I have never seen his legendary dick. If I never see another it will be no loss; moving quickly on to Grace has been my salvation. Back to what I know best.

On the evening in question, I left the restaurant, at which Aaron had a table booked, thirty minutes after the time we arranged to meet. If I'd had any wit about me, I would have gone sooner; what on earth was I thinking? The maître d' tried to press me for some kind of cover charge but I just kept walking. I went a couple of roads away.

The Kilderkin is only a small bar and it can get very busy. I drank four gins in there on my own. On me tod, as a friend from Leeds always used to say. Of course, I was not entirely alone, done up to the nines for the overrated Aaron. Many men approached me; however, I had already concluded that they were of the wrong gender. There may be two sides to every street, it doesn't make the window displays of equal artistry. Women have always been my first love; if my first sexual experiences—first year Uni—were of boys humping, it was only the immature version of myself bowing to convention. Which is why, at this more circumspect stage in my life, it was vain and idiotic of me to agree to go on a date with that ridiculous man, Aaron. Girls, girls, girls: that's what I know and love—Aaron Morley, briefly married to the popstar, Carrie Collins—I suppose I'd puzzled over what all the fuss was about. The second date was an utter humiliation, the no-show in the restaurant. In the pub, The Kilderkin, I was getting lightheaded—being dumped has that effect on me—late in the evening three truly gorgeous-looking girls entered the bar. I swear they were each a decade apart in age. I could have chosen any, or all three, so pleasingly did they fall into my eye. Grace—whom I confidently estimated to be the middle in their widely disparate age order—happened to be the one who came to the bar, stood beside the stool on which I sat, as she sought to order drinks, gain the attention of the barman. She had a hold of mine already. Since first standing in the doorway.

'You've been somewhere?' I said to her. Three girls arriving in a bar at ten forty-five? It was a drunken observation rather than a clever one. She smiled at me despite my poor opening gambit. Her hair sculpted her face most wonderfully. I could see a small amount of makeup on her, darkening of eyelashes and brows, which gave an intensity to her stare.

'Do I know you?' she asked. I told her my name, mentioned the Sunday Noise, it impresses a few. 'Were you watching?' She is a girl of many questions. It has the potential to be bothersome but not so on that night. The prolonging of our conversation was oxygen. Of course, this misunderstanding took a little unpicking. I had not been in the Roundhouse, nor even recognised her. I suspect I have seen a television programme or even a play with her in it in the last half a dozen years. Could not bring them to mind on that barstool. Told her that I am not a culture critic, crime and intrigue my stock in trade. Crime: I reported upon it but was still to learn that a family of criminals raised me. The night I met Grace Topping predated this sorry turn of events. Mary Stephenson was a nuisance in my life. I never guessed her a murderess, yet now it looks the case. And my own father's role I still cannot bear to dwell upon. Digression over.

On that barstool I simply made enquiries about the play she performed in, told her then that I must see it. She invited me to join her friends. When the barman finally came to her, I added another gin and tonic to the order and insisted I pay. 'Struggling actors,' I explained.

'I never said we were struggling,' she replied and I apologised. Papered over it. I sat with her two lovely friends who spoke mostly with each other—quite wrapped up—performances past, actor talk. Not revelling in each other in the way I had already started to with Grace. And she with me, although I believe she had yet to fully understand that aspect of herself. I remember the younger actress commenting upon the looks of one or two men in the bar. That can be quite a vulgar trait in a girl. I do not know if it was chance or if the two were well attuned, when I said that I knew a bar we could move to which would keep serving after hours, the other two dipped out while Grace agreed.

The tale of our drink in Filchers was neither romantic nor steamy. I did share with Grace how attractive I found her; she nodded at that. I realised it was a small overstep. She did not slap me down, walk away, brag about her most recent male lover. When I suggested we swap telephone numbers, she agreed to the request. I sensed the will to lean towards me, even as she leant away.

* * *

I have to flush the notion that I am northern from my girlfriend's overheating brain. 'I was eleven years old when we left Surrey,' I say. 'Only did so because my father was made Chair of Physics at Lancaster Uni. I think...'

She interrupts. 'I thought he was the lord of the manor, or something. Buying you this fantastic flat. I've known academics but not...'

'It's true,' I confirm. 'Daddy is a physicist and also the lord of the manor. A coincidence. Not actually titled, just born into money. Pots of the stuff. When we moved up north it was to a house with gardens running up a Lancashire hillside. I think we employed a rhododendron pruner on a full-time basis. Or perhaps he doubled and dug out dandelions half the week. I didn't watch.' I am a little worried, from her facial expressions and one or two conversations past, that Grace likes to draw upon the poverty of her youth, the faux misery which I recall my stepmother also used to relish. Grace spent her childhood in a semi-detached house, I believe, on an estate of identical three-bedroomed houses. Like Mary, it was hardly a pit village. Sittingbourne. I am only glad that she has learned some refinement. 'I think it was wrenching me out of Surrey that turned me into a bit of a loner,' I tell her. This is not strictly true and happy loners are less inclined to view themselves as alone, so much as self-contained. And in my school in Surrey, I had a set, a group of girls who considered me their friend, as I mostly did them. 'Up north, the girls were different. Quite physical. I was clever in every classroom subject but an abject hockey player. My popularity plummeted.'

'Poor you,' says Grace, but I do not detect the sincerity in it that marked her sympathy over my father being in prison, my mother beneath a shed. I do not wish to talk about it, although we are more in step on that ground. The stuff of real drama. Childhoods might be for forgetting, and it is an aberration that I recall mine so clearly.

* * *

Two Saturdays past was the final performance of Closed Heart. I was again upon a banquet seat. I chose to sit there for the proximity it gave me to the actors. To one actor in particular. Cherie, the younger girl who I also met in The Kilderkin on the night Grace found me, looked stunning throughout their performance. She played the sister of Grace's character. She is a beautiful specimen. In those seats alongside the stage, one can also smell the actors. Cherie gave not a whiff of the desire I could sense when Grace was just a few feet from me. Or was I smelling myself? A heat arising from my own person in the wake of seeing the girl I had determined should be mine. If it was so, it was a surprisingly pleasing experience. The following day I called at the flat of the out-of-work actor—by agreement; relationships only work by consent—and whisked her away to a rather trendy club in Clapham. By cab. On me. She drank and drank as she had not when each day was to contain a performance in which she had a central, indeed a starring, role. We danced together and she allowed me to place my hands upon her neck and midriff. An occasional kiss. Men tried to cut in. For her and for me. Once or twice, we allowed it, something to laugh about after. I correctly sensed that her interest in me was strong, included a physical element. I think I had plain tonics half of the time, did so to ensure that I was in control of myself—I have a tendency to lose it when shit-faced—I let my hair down but without the unpredictability of the bacchanalian. At the end of the evening, we took a cab back to hers. She did not argue when

I suggested I stay the night in her flat. It is a rather drab affair. Posters on the walls in the way that a teenager might adorn her bedroom. Odd in a woman of thirty-four; a couple of them reminded her of performances she had given. I can imagine that is nice to bring to mind. She allowed me into her bed, confessed how tired she was, seemed not averse to my performance anyhow. I gave a good one. The morning after had the potential for embarrassment, not that any arose. Seeing me again remained on her to do list.

* * *

'I used to move backwards and forwards between my mother's and my father's houses. It started when I was barely four, before I even had a stepmother to hate. When Mary became part of my father's household, the arrangement became most unbalanced, and my life a see-saw of ups and downs. The oddity was, much as I loved my mother, I hated the ordinariness of her new house. It was no better than many of those my friends lived in. Perhaps like yours in Sittingbourne, although it had four bedrooms, not three. Of course, Daddy screwed her in the divorce, Spenser Avenue is alright, I suppose, but it's a box compared to the house she gave up. He screwed her before, during and after the divorce. I think I've told you that already.'

Grace has fixed us drinks from the fridge. Not alcoholic drinks, I think we are neither in the mood for them. I advised that there was a lemon to slice in the pantry. She has made them very well. Only a smidgen of sugar. 'When Mummy disappeared—and I was eleven years old, my memory most reliable—the conversations around the house were fierce and mad. Mary may have been quite the actress, on a murder charge as she is now. I remember her weeping for the woman she knew to be her predecessor, and one she has never truly replaced. "Do you think Joe has done something to her?" she demanded of Daddy. Joe Azzopardi was the name of her

Maltese lover. Daddy seemed to know something of the man. Said anything was possible but he did not imagine Cynthia involving herself with a low-life. He knew nothing tangible about him. Respectable or disreputable. He was simply Maltese Joe. The police were looking into it, he told me. Days later I sat on the landing and listened to Daddy explaining all that the police had told him, telling it to Mary in the dining hall. Joe Azzopardi had broken off whatever affair he was having with my mother, claimed that she was cheating on him. Up on the landing, I contemplated that my father might be the third party in this. I'd no idea how the Maltese man might have known about him. Mary asked what was known about this other, potentially new, lover that my mother had taken. "Fled with him," said my father. "Passport. Quite a lot of clothing. Fled with him." Isn't that the oddest thing?'

Grace is sympathetic, looks a little frazzled by the shocking story I tell. 'It is only contemplating the matter now that I see it, both parties to that conversation imprisoned. If they knew what really happened, then they must have been staging their conversation on the off chance I was eavesdropping. Or could one have been kidding the other? It was an astonishing performance.'

* * *

Grace repeatedly says how awful it is for me. At one point she says, 'I'm glad you've got it off your chest,' referencing the interview with the police. I do not want any policeman near my chest, thank you. I feel surprised that my current girlfriend is not a more attuned listener. I thought actresses had to be, to appear spontaneous when on the stage, reacting precisely to every cue. All an act, I presume, a devious craft. And my tale is one that any normal person would find riveting, if I can only tell it without breaking down. Is it not?

When I have exhausted myself of talk, I just sit, let her again wrap an arm around me. 'It is scary,' says Grace

Topping. 'My first relationship with another girl and it's turning into a murder mystery.' I think she must see my eyes go down. 'I'm sorry,' she says. 'It's your mum, I know that.' She turns her face into mine, kisses my lips with a passion I have needed since first she entered the flat. 'Will you stay,' I ask. With her eyes she consents. I love looking into her eyes, drinking in her beautifully drawn body, feel a little apprehensive that she might make further crass comments.

2.

Relationships confuse me more than they satisfy. When Grace takes her leave the following morning, I feel frustrated by the words she uses. The departure itself is unremarkable. Girls may stay the night; I am joined to no one at the hip. Boys have stayed here once or twice but I believe I have grown out of it.

'Thanks, I'll be in touch,' were her words. I might have received such an accolade after performing poorly at a job interview, and that does not describe the night we had. More than once, Grace said I was taking things too fast for her, and I wasn't really taking them anywhere. Taking pleasures that I believe better shared. Is there more to it? Grace looks superb, yet I am finding her a most confused person. A pity really. For me and for her. I hope first-date Grace re-emerges or it might have to be adios.

Alone in my flat at nine o'clock in the morning, and I've nothing to pursue but the terrible matter of my mother's murder. It is the only thing on my mind. Grace was a pleasing distraction and too quickly did she depart. I shower and put on light clothes, a pair of green trousers, three-quarter length, a blouse that I used to wear to the office precisely because it is casual, unexpected. Red decoration on its sleeves, otherwise rich white. I might be a country and western singer taking to the stage. It lifts my mood for only the time it takes to dress. I go down to the shop on the corner. Buy croissants. Three. I do not know why I choose this number. I determined on entry that I would not give the smug young assistant the satisfaction of seeing me purchase but a single one. She need not learn I live alone. I think that a plain, an almond, and a chocolate are the right choices. I expect to eat a third of each. The pigeons which alight on my balcony are the luckiest in London.

Back in the flat, I percolate coffee, place the three croissants on a large plate. I am a slim girl; I have bought this number before. Never scoffed the lot, never will. 'You're missing out on almond croissant, Grace Topping!' I shout at the radio. It was telling me the news and I have grown tired of hearing it. My mother gets no mention today, and it is neither a good nor a bad thing. I want to hear that it has all been a mistake, that their reporter has discovered Cynthia Hartnell living as a nun in Cape Town. The bones beneath the shed an old fox. Want delivers little that it conjectures. Nothing at all for nineteen years, and now this.

I know what I must do. Grace did not talk me into it, although she raised the subject of my wider family. How we are all seeing things since the arrest and incarceration of Paul and Mary Stephenson. If it comes to trial, I think we may hope for disparate outcomes. It is not the way in all families, mine is unable to put up a united front. I hated my stepmother from day one; Simon and Craig, her children with my father actually like her—love her, I dare say—and might believe her claim of innocence. Neither met my mother, their perspective quite disparate from mine.

I am still to feel in my bones what I know in my conscious brain: that my mother is not in Monte Carlo, Buenos Aires or any of the myriad of other places I have dreamed her to be since nineteen-eighty-one. She is no longer beneath a shed, and that might be a blessing. The knowledge that she lay there so long haunts my soul. I told Grace about Mary, and her hapless brother, Stephen, describing both in some detail. I did not mention Mica Barry to her, never hinted at the existence of a younger sister for my stepmother. The issue was one of tact. Grace acts well upon the stage; however, her name does not exactly appear in lights. I am happy to namedrop every news reporter and feature writer that I know. I have earned my friendship with each and every one. My enmity in a few instances. Aaron Morley certainly, and I fear my big mouth has put Darius Pleydwell on that side of the page too. My connection to Mica, a celebrated star of stage and screen, is a fluke. It is via a route that I regret. The familial link with my stepmother. I admire Monica greatly. Step-aunty, I might call her. A ridiculous term and so I do not, she is family to me however tenuous the link. And Monica Bredbury, who is a decade older than I, is more beautiful than Grace by some distance. It might be wrong of me to think it but I cannot delude myself. If I am anything it is searingly honest. I was right to keep mum, although it may have made no difference, judging by the latter's perfunctory departure. Name-dropping might have won me Grace's pleasures a little longer. And there were some in there, truly. She has her charms. Properly woman shaped which I like a lot.

I have to scrabble about the flat for my old phone book. Find it at the back of a drawer stuffed with bank statements and credit card bills. My phone contains all the numbers I regularly dial, Aunt Sarah and Uncle Phil are not even occasional. It has been years. They still live in Surrey, in Redhill, nearer to the old family seat than we ever were in Epsom. I have not lived down in that corner of England since January, nineteen-eighty-two. Sarah is my father's older sister. The only reason she hasn't phoned me is our mutual dislike. Mutual, profound, bitter. Never spoken of. We can, as must happen in all families, pretend to hold each other in good regard provided our meetings are infrequent, and occur only when plenty of other people are present.

'Oh, hi Auntie Sarah. Sophie here. How are you? How are you bearing up?'

'Sophie, I've been so worried about you.'

'Yeah, yeah. I'm a tough cookie, it's been a shock. Have you been to see him?'

'Paul. Yes, I'm planning to. I can't imagine what it's like for him.'

'Remand, Auntie Sarah. He's only on remand. I can't believe he had anything...' I stop myself. I am about to declare the innocence of a man I know to have admitted a role in the disposal of my mother's body. It is just how I see him; I have always forgiven him because I am a daughter and not a wife. Because all the wrongs I previously attributed to him hurt Mary and not I. I think my view is going to change in the coming weeks and months as his actions in nineteen-eighty-one become clearer to me. Sink in. It may be seismic. '...can you believe what they are saying?'

'He's your father, Sophie. It isn't in my nature to speculate. I am shocked. I believe what the police have told me. They wouldn't lie to us, not the police. They say he has confessed a role but pleads innocent of the murder. He blames Mary, I have gathered. That shocks me too. A sweet girl, however inappropriate the marriage. I can't understand that one either. Can't see what Mary ever had against poor Cynthia.'

Mary must have had a lot against my mother, must have realised that she was not even a match in the bedroom, whatever decoration her looks provided before the lights went out. I don't think Sarah needs to know about all that. To think about her brother's circular philandering. God knows, it will probably come out in court. That tends to be the way of these cases. It's a year off by my reckoning, so I shan't broach the subject this morning. 'Have I understood correctly that the boys are with you?'

'Craig and Simon? Yes, they are.'

'With you right now?'

'Yes, they are both in the house.'

'You don't think Craig would come to the phone, do you? I know I'm seldom in touch but I do care about them, you know?'

'I can ask, Sophie. I'm sure he will. Not Simon, I'm afraid. You understand how he is?'

'Yes, yes. I shared a household with him. The idiosyncrasies. How has Simon...'

'Craig says he is the same as usual. Seems very withdrawn to me. All texts and emails. It's nothing new, apparently. I think he misses Mary. He used to smile for her—I remember that from years ago—and there is none of it now. He's no trouble, I just feel very sad about him.'

She is woffling, not saying anything of note. I'm pleased—astonished actually—that Simon is no trouble. Having a big strapping lad in the house who takes up air and food and electricity—truly, he is as good as plugged in, such is his internet use—occupying a room with the curtains drawn. It troubled me back when they were still calling it a phase. The oddest thing is that he is not stupid; terribly clever and still he lives like a mole. That is the self-imposed lot of my extraordinary half-brother.

'Hello...Sophie?'

Craig has come to the phone. Lightening quick. I love this boy. Shouldn't get sentimental, I suppose; we never saw eye to eye about his mother, and I'm going to struggle not to rub it in now that my perspective is looking the truer. Love him as much as I have anyone; I get a bit conditional around love much of the time.

'Craig. I'm sorry I've not been in touch earlier. How are you bearing up?'

'Sis, sis, I'm good. I mean, everything is a bit shit but it's not me, is it? Done nothing, me. It's the other buggers.'

'Have you been to see Dad?' I must admit, I pause a while before adding, 'or your mummy?'

'Sophs, our father has as good as admitted it. I never knew wife number one—your mum, wasn't she?—but it's bloody terrible. Terrible what he's done. I don't believe a word about Mummy. Not a word. Why would she?'

'Yes...' His mother's integrity is the very subject he and I don't see eye to eye upon. '...the police must have something though. She has been arrested.'

'Sophie, they have the word of a man who's trying to keep his own neck out of the noose.'

'Craigy, sweetie, that is a bit over-dramatic. I always thought Daddy had a soft spot for young Mary whatever else was going on. Surprised he doesn't take the wrap for the whole thing just to protect her...'

The little bugger cuts me off. 'You weren't living up there the last five years. Barely in the last ten. Everything between them stank, Sophs. I think she would have gone; my mum would have walked out but for me and Simon. Simon mostly. She worried herself sick about him. I think she was just coming to terms with everything. That he's a happy oddball. And now this.'

'Is Simon all right?'

'He's in his own world, and it might be a better one than this. You can email him, Sophs, he always replies. A meeting in person is rarer. If you're a doctor and he's developed an inflamed rash, then you've got a sporting chance.'

'How did he get from Carnforth down to Auntie Sarah's?'

'That. Well, good old Uncle Phillip agreed to his request— texted not spoken, of course—to drive through the night.'

'Is he a saint or what?' I think I say it to keep the peace. Uncle Phillip is a privileged idiot.

'The other. A grumpy bugger who reluctantly does whatever his wife asks of him.'

'Ha-ha. I've missed you, Craigy. What do you say to me

taking you up to see Mummy before long?'

'I don't know, sis. Won't she be out soon? I want to see her out of prison, not in it. She's not a criminal, my mum.'

'That's not how it's looking, sweetie. Who knows where it will end? She's on remand. The detectives build a case all the way to prosecution. Unless it all collapses. Daddy's testimony looks to be keeping her there, from what I can...'

'Come and see me, sis. Maybe I'll go to see Mummy. Tricky and horrid; I need to steel myself for that. And sis...?'

'Yes, Craig.'

'I'm not sure she will be especially pleased to see you across a prison visiting room. It'd be just like you to gloat about it all.'

* * *

My little stepbrother is more astute than I'd thought; however, gloating is not on the agenda at all. I want him there so that Mary will talk, say something. I don't expect her to be overly indiscreet, to confess all to her teenage son. I am an investigative journalist—a few big stories under my belt—I have learnt to read between the lines. The meaning of each intake of breath.

I have agreed to go down to Redhill. Poor Craig can't attend school, his being the boy's grammar up in Lancaster. Residing in Surrey prevents it. Auntie Sarah says there is a private school nearby which he could attend but for some misalignment of syllabuses. It isn't the biggest deal in the world, and I am grateful that he studies the arts, not physics. He might be talented with a brush, young Craig, although it really is too early to tell. Nice choices of colour and way above average drawing skills. It's the Art History A-level which sold Lancaster Grammar for him—very niche—and which is proving hard to find in the vicinity of his new home. His stop-gap home. The charges against both parents might make it an inordinately long gap. The Carnforth home may never reopen; the two whose names are on the title deeds, shut away for the longest time.

I have promised to email Simon in fairyland. Promised Craig, and so I shall. It might be revealing, his make-believe world is a shade or ten darker than the one the rest of us live in. It can be quite edifying to converse with him. Tricky but stimulating.

Things to do, people to see.

3.

What it says about the prison system, I do not know. That it is in chaos, most probably. Police in Surrey—specifically those working out of Banstead—will wish to visit and speak with my father quite often during this information-gathering stage. Unless he has buttoned up his lip, having made his written statement. Owned up to a little, not a lot. For his sins—and to the inconvenience of all—Retford Jail is Daddy's temporary home. I think it has a fancier name; Retford was the place I had to look up on the map. Nottinghamshire, knocking on Yorkshire's door. The northern tip of a county which holds no interest for me. I have a hire car. Living where I do, I don't keep one or drive regularly. The newspaper provides me with wheels when needed, if I'm sent to cover stories outside London, and that is not a task I volunteer for. For this one, I must foot the bill. Must go straight up the M1 to my father's scary new domicile. Straight up and a hell of a way up. I dislike motorway driving. It has been my excuse for steering clear of Carnforth, give or take, for a considerable time. And I have no family there now. Windermere Court closed up like a clam.

I can't really believe what has happened; the task I face is the worst. I shall not kill my father on my visit to the prison in which he stays. I don't imagine I could smuggle in a stiletto, nor am I the type of daughter to slit her father's throat across the visiting room table. It is a thought. He has played some role or other—direct or indirect—in the murder of my mother. He has certainly—and this alone makes me feel as if the world has gone mad—kept his knowledge of her death from me for nineteen years. A knife in my gut, it truly is. My years of confusion and bewilderment while the smug face across the dinner table knew the exact location. How the story ended.

They were not frequent—just now and then—growing up in Carnforth, there were conversations.

'Why doesn't she write?'

'I think it is her parents she is hiding from most of all. They hit the roof when they learnt she and I were doing more than attending dances. That she was entering my rooms of an evening. And I always intended to marry her. Whatever would they make of whoever she has shacked up with, wherever she has made her home. Mortified is my guess.'

I never doubted him at the time; it sounds silly looking back. A made-up excuse.

'But me! I'm her daughter,' I would shriek at him. I loved Mummy while wanting to yell similarly at her. How could she leave me, a child of eleven? And now I know she did not. Never left me. Resided one village away. Partaking in a long and silent death.

'I think, Sophie, that parents have the fortitude to face their children with anything. Illness, disciplining, sacrificing hard-won gains: we see it through. It is as children, children to our parents of whatever age, that we fear how they will view our actions.'

I recall that conversation terribly well. I did not disbelieve my father's apparent wisdom, not at the time. From the wise old age of thirty I see what errant nonsense he spoke. Children judge their parents with a fiercer dose of realism than the doe-eyed Hartnell's ever applied to their daughter. They were distraught, would have forgiven her shacking up with the Springboks rugby team if only she'd sent a letter or made a telephone call. And they knew no more than me. Had heard of the Maltese, never met him. And come to that, he was never the one suspected of whisking her off. The police long ago cleared him. We have all been duped.

My maternal grandmother was the one who telephoned me just five days ago, advised me that my mother is dead. Has been so for too long. She didn't do grisly details, just the broad outline. The police had her address from the old missing persons enquiry, notified her before they could get hold of me. Before making anything public. They'd told her within a matter of hours of making the discovery. Granny Hartnell telephoned me as soon as she was off that call. The poor lady has turned eighty, her husband in a care home. And then this. I have seen her more often in the last five years than I have since leaving Surrey shortly before my twelfth birthday. I have not seen her since this awful news. It is simply too upsetting. For her and for me.

The drive is dull. The sloping verges of the motorway cut through countryside that must look nicer from a raised position. From a helicopter. I am a cautious driver, not much of a driver at all, quite frankly. I do not fear death. If it comes to pass that a man, whose wife I have seduced—lured from his bed to my own—should stab me to death, the story alone will render me a most interesting footnote. A fun ending. To expire in a car wreck would be wasteful. Too meaningless to think about. I drive slowly no matter what fumes through my veins.

I don't expect my imagining the rousing of jealousy in others has anything to do with my father. He is a half-baked Don Juan who, for the most part, simply preyed on the unattached and the inexperienced. I even think his day has departed, gone with his waning virility. Girls enter physics nowadays because their minds are the equal or better of any man's. Mary Bredbury and all her contemporaries felt they had to prove it. Earn their place at the shoulders of men. Drop their knickers for the privilege in about fifty percent of cases, by my simple estimation. I wish my father had belonged to this time, not that. Even when he was cheating on the hated Mary, I would often contemplate that this same behaviour must have driven my mother to despair. To divorce. Whenever I try to think it over, I become stuck on his two oddest decisions. Why did he marry the hated one? I know it was only me that hated her but I saw very little love on his part. A daft fling that went on and fucking on. And why did he continue to sleep with Mummy, and she with him, when everything else was half-cocked. Even in this mad old world that we inhabit with the swagger of our dinosaur forebears, you'd think there would be reasons.

I approach the new services, still under construction last time I drove a car on this motorway. I decide it is time for a toilet break, a cup of tea. I never top sixty on these roads, rain or shine, so a break from the boredom is essential. The vehicle is easy to park up. Small. I leave it with a little bleep of the key, very nice. Had one like it before but it's quite the gimmick. I walk through the automatic entrance doors, see that the toilet signs are nice and clear. Shiny new services, best thing so far today.

As I sit, I see that the graffiti artists include girls in these parts. A phone number I shan't be noting down and an inexpertly drawn cock and balls. Odd stuff but I think I entered the right ones. There was always something different about my stepmother. I recall thinking how ordinary she was when I was very, very small. The time of those first meetings. The thing is, she clearly never got the memo. We can see how plain she is, and then she thinks she is something special. I don't know how that translated itself for my dad, he expected undergraduates to come to his bed—or the back seat of his car, most probably—and they did. When this one didn't, he had to do what it took. I have always understood that Mummy and Daddy separated long before Mary came on the scene. I suppose it could be as mundane as wanting someone to cook his meals for him. Cynthia had decided it was no longer her, and I expect someone who makes you feel horny beats an ageing housekeeper. She was at least young and pretty when they started out. I'd like Grace to decorate my place—with her presence, a comfort in my bed which is a little large for one—although I'm a little worried that our connection may have run its course. She has gone off the boil and never learnt how to bring me to it. More's the pity. Which might—by association—get to the heart of the matter. My mother's relationship with my father was successful only on that rather basic physical level. I can relish the stimulation only a man can give, although I find many of them inattentive, and their looks never match up to the more stunning of the ladies. Not close. My father's track record suggests he supplied some level of satisfaction. Yuk! I don't like to think about it but I am trying to piece things together. Be the investigative journalist I profess.

Did Mummy break it off? Did my mother put an end to her easy-to-arrange not even terribly furtive trysts with my father? Mostly configured in the lee of dropping off or picking me up. Five-minute fucks, not that I was ever the clock-watcher. I may do them a disservice. Any time is too long in my book. Kids don't want their parents doing that stuff, and I expect I even had Mary on my side in this instance. My mummy kiboshed his weekly leg-over in order to devote herself to Maltese Joe. It's plausible, and I expect the police found out some of this back in nineteen-eighty-one. Not the stuff with my dad, just the strength of her other relationships. There was no sign of foul play, no sign of my mother.

And what's Mary got to do with any of it. Jealous of her bedhopping with Dad and unaware it was over? My father says it was her, and I am—all my biases put to one side—

inclined to agree with him. Not figured out the methods and reasons yet. Daddy is a slippery bastard but I will take him on trust just this once. Mary's the man.

* * *

If you don't understand modern Britain yet, just think over this little bit of heartlessness. A pay and display car park at Retford Prison. Talk about a captive audience. No one comes here without a pitiful reason and still they take your pound. I've visited four others and this is the first to charge for parking up. And the money doesn't bother me, Daddy can pay. It's the mugger's wives I feel sorry for. Girlfriends, daughters and little lost waifs, all scrabbling about for a bit of change in order to see their banged-up loved ones. Or hated ones if their situation is as messed up as mine.

Entering the place is a scary business. Always the case. A man behind a desk and grill talks to me, needs to know who I am and who I plan to visit before allowing me into the foyer, the enclosed capsule in which a lady comes and pats me down. It used to be men taking these over-intrusive liberties but now they leave it to the lesbians. She takes my mobile phone and the handbag I carry. She permits me to retain the packet of biscuits I intend to give to Daddy. They are upmarket, wrapped in cellophane around a navy-blue cardboard design. Oats and dates and what have you. Everyone must fear finding themselves constipated if they have become cooped up in prison. Or is that just me?

The lady doing the patting is most severe, and I should have thought she enjoyed her job more. It's a role I could fulfil were my dignity completely spent. Feeling the curves and pockets on the lady visitors. I hand over everything I carry; she insists upon it. Oat biscuits, lip balm and a packet of tissues; no tunnelling tools or crack-cocaine. At this point in time, I am in favour of Daddy staying in prison, having a hard time of it whilst he's here. What he did to Mummy is unforgivable.

In a small side room, the same lady takes my photograph and, within a minute and a half, I am handed a lanyard stating I am a visitor, and from which my facsimile stares out. The point of my wearing this is that I cannot subsequently change places with a prisoner, enable an escape and then claim wrongful imprisonment to ensure my own release soon after. That I am an attractive girl in a prison of scarred, tattooed and downtrodden men does not exempt me, although I don't see how I could pull it off.

My father, of course, looks better than most in here and his hair and eye colour match my own. We have no other similarities. My hairline recedes not a jot, and even our characters turn out poles apart. This last point is only a recent appraisal. A reimagining of he and I. My father is nothing like me. If I have enjoyed more bedroom partners than many, it was without obvious deceit or hurt to anyone on Earth. Excluding a couple of husbands whose wives chose to try a little playfulness my way, of course, I didn't tell. As I said, I am not much like my father, and might even work on erasing any latent similarities. My days of loving him are in the past. He knew where my mother was and lied and lied and lied. Lied to me, his daughter, firstborn. Bastard!

* * *

In fact, he looks terrible. Daddy has some horrible bruising on the side of his head, a visible scar and I can see that it has bled recently. I point and ask how it has arisen; he waves it away. Does not wish to explain, and I know what these places are like. Every crime reporter does. Scores settled that were not known to require redress until the beating was complete.

The table we sit across is wooden, varnished ash to my eye, or it may be a hybrid, a cheap imitation. I could unmask it but scrutinising furniture is not the order of the day. The room we are in is smaller than I anticipated. Only four such tables and each spaced about a metre from the next. A single guard stands watch, his presence in so confined a space may ensure that the conversations taking place are not private at all. It might be unwise for Daddy to tell me anything in here but I am eager to hear it. If he is guilty of her murder, I should order another beating. Not that I have the connections to make it happen. Au contraire, at heart I am but a squeamish girlie.

There is one other woman in the room—quite young—she wears a short skirt and I imagine it is a boyfriend she visits, dresses this way to please him. I notice even Daddy's eyes stray to the fake tan of her legs. The knees beneath the table. The fella she is here to see has the worst view of all. The table will obscure the shapely pins which she displays to others. One of the guards looks nowhere else. And I must grant that they are worth a peek. Nicest legs in Retford Jail.

'What have you told them?' I ask my father.

'I've told them, Sophie. It's not pleasant, I felt I must tell them all I know. I've never been a dishonest man.'

The snag with this assertion is that everybody who knows him must be aware of his never-ending untruths. My father has—I understand this better than any well-adjusted daughter possibly could—been consistently dishonest in relation to his sex life, if nothing else. Denied what was obviously true; schemed to hide what he did not wish brought into the light. He played down the significance of meetings with students in pubs. Played dumb to enquiries of late-night arrivals back in the house by Mrs Stephenson number two—I heard many—and number one also, I could bet every pound to my name without my heart changing its steady beat. The subject which led him to lie was always that singular little motivator: sex. Murder is a new addition. Or maybe not. For nineteen years he has hidden from me his knowledge that my mother did not live. He has recently admitted involvement in the disposal of a body while telling me for years and years that he guessed his ex-wife to be in South Africa. For all I know, half the sheds in Epsom and Carnforth might be impromptu gravestones for a slew of victims. He used to be hard to trust, and now I do not. Not a slither of trust for him, not any longer. Daddy is a baddy. Throughout my life I have depended on him for financial security; his wise counsel was always fly. I don't say that I hate him, the feelings are still forming within me. What once was love now curdles in my acidic stomach. He will have figured that out if he knows me at all.

'Why did she do it?'

He glances quickly at the guards. Their eyes are not upon us; I have dressed conservatively. 'The usual, I expect. We never talked about it.'

'Daddy?' I can believe they have not talked about it for years. But before agreeing to bury the body, he must have learned the general drift of things. Nobody would aid and abet without. Not to murder, the big one. He shrugs. I do not like to see that—his dismissal of the worth of my question—it is worse than lying. It diminishes the questioner. 'Why did you protect her then? For years and years and years.' It is my stepmother I refer to. He has accused her in the same story in which he has implicated himself. Putting her where she lay.

'Sophie, you've no idea what it's like. Loving two ladies.'

Twenty-two more like, and I know exactly what it is like. That is the number of partners I have found the space for in my heart. Grace Topping is number twenty-two; Aaron Morley never made the cut. I seldom allow an overlap and have quickly made my mind up when there has been such a misalignment.

'You call that love…' I try not to let my voice rise up. It is an outrageous declaration he makes.

'Sophie, not here,' he hisses.

'Sorry. Let us go for a walk in the woods.'

'Sophie!' He looks at a guard. We are not supposed to talk about the case but the official has a nice pair of legs to occupy him.

'How? How did it even happen? I thought they seldom met?'

'Seldom. But Mary figured...Sophie, do you already know what it is she figured? Learnt?'

'Tell me, Daddy. From the horse's mouth. I don't want to guess, no margin for error, please.'

'It will all come out in court, Sophie.'

'Tell me!' I hiss.

'Cynthia and I still enjoyed carnal relations,' he mutters under his breath. 'Unusual, it was simply... It doesn't matter why. Your mother and I just chanced across it. Then Mary chanced across us.'

'I don't buy all that. What about Maltese Joe? Your little bit of extra was going on for years.' Then, mouthing more than speaking, I say, 'Mary didn't bump off the other twenty, thirty. Fifty? Your never-ending supply of undergraduates.'

'Sophie, I'm so sorry, it's just the way I'm made.'

A guard is suddenly crossing the floor towards us, and I burst into tears. I don't see why Daddy didn't just bump off Mary, let Mummy live back in the old Epsom house. I would have had a much nicer life, and if he had gone to prison, at least Mummy and I would still have been there. Where we belonged. My father is such a selfish bastard.

* * *

'Who did the face?' I ask. 'Roughed you over. Who and why? If you get off scot-free, you will be due compensation, you know?' I am dabbing my cheeks with a handkerchief. If I hadn't cried, I think the guard would have terminated the visit. He had overheard enough. They put the bat-eared ones in this room; saucer-eyes for the girl's legs don't stop their ears from functioning altogether. Nor me, actually. I keep looking at those lovely long pins, while it is Daddy's misdemeanours I'm trying to understand. Marys too. The cow who killed my mother.

'They think I'm a wife murderer. Which I'm not. It doesn't get you good treatment in here. I might be better off in Broadmoor. Everyone there has done much worse than they could accuse me of doing. I...' Daddy looks at the guard, then speaks very levelly, as if he is answering a question about where the fuse box is to be found. '...buried her as we might have anywhere. Consecrated ground meant nothing to Cynthia. It seemed like the way to keep the family together. You never liked Mary, Sophie. But we have the boys. There are many considerations when your partner goes berserk and butchers your lover. I think those feelings are inside us all. Self-control is all that separates us from hyenas. I implore you to keep your life simpler than I have managed to do mine.' Then the guard turns his head and Daddy lets the volume in his voice rise. 'They took me to the medical room right away.' He touches the swelling to the side of his right eye. 'First rate they were. Very prompt, very thorough. Kept me under obs for about twenty-four hours but it's pretty superficial.'

Chapter Four:

Crack Up or Play It Cool

1.

I send a text to Simon:

> *All right bro. I am hoping to call in at Auntie Sarah's tomorrow. Can we talk? Besties - Sophie*

I receive a reply after about one second.

> *Text*

I wonder what to say next when another comes in.

> *Text, text, text. I don't talk and you know it*

He speaks the truth, although it seems rude to assume he never will. Nothing wrong with mouth or ability to co-ordinate lips and tongue. He just won't.

> *How are you bearing up, Simon?*

I use this line a lot. It covers all the bases. I am back in my flat, it was straight in and straight out of prison for me. No hanging around; I've done nothing wrong. Must listen out for the car rental chappie. Super Rentals pick up from the door, which I like.

> *Philip says I am getting on his nerves*
>
> *He told you that?*
>
> *Uncle Philip told Craig. Craig told me. I've told you, and you can print it in the Noise*

Hmmm. Funny boy. I haven't told anyone in the family that I'm having a little break from work. Suspended or pushed out on sick leave, whatever humiliating way they choose to dress it up. I think it's being termed compassionate leave, and I assume it means that I am a little off my head. I don't see it that way but the Sunday Noise has standards. Chooses to inflame the base emotions of the nation through the application of a workforce that must keep their own under wraps. As I think this, I realise my answer to the bearing-up question would be pretty mental. Blown a girlfriend—I think that is what has happened—and not in a good or an enjoyable way. Upset Dad in prison; or he was upset that I was upset. I think that counts. Swore at Darius Pleydwell, although I am neither the first nor the most vehement.

> *Don't worry about him. His bark is not as bad as his haircut*
>
> *I never said I was worried, I just told you how it is*
>
> *Are you missing Dad and Mum?*
>
> *I am missing their texts*

I think that is actually very funny. Not sure whether to text back a smiley face. Simon hates sarcasm, so I better hadn't.

> *I'm off work. Put on compash leave on account of it all*
>
> *Compash?*
>
> *Compassionate*
>
> *You are not that, Sophie. Caustic leave? Can they give you that?*

Wow. I've flicked the switch and I wasn't even trying.

> *I asked Darius to assign me to the story. Our*

family's story. He refused to play ball.

?

Then I swore at him

Very compassionate, Sophs

Funny boy. It bothers me, Simon. You too, I think? Having parents in prison is bad form

Emotions. Shut up

They are in all of us, matey. You and I have the bespoke wiring

Just flick over the off switch. It's lazy but effective

Better to have loved and lost...

*B*ll*cks*

I don't think he is right, not that I've tried living his way for even a single day, and he's managed more than twenty years of it. Weird as fuck but a truly interesting kid.

Thumbs are wearing out. Talk to you when I'm in Redhill

My texting facility will remain available to you

* * *

While I shower, I think about my drive back here from that wretched prison. It started to rain—heavy rain—the very driving conditions which frighten me. I slowed down to about fifty, caring not that my driving-style infuriated all the men on the motorway. They were behind the wheels of about nine out of every ten cars as far as I could tell. The cocked ones. Women do their driving in towns, it is men who like to speed, channelling down three lanes, white lines keeping them apart like they are taking part in a swimming race. The one in ten, women like myself, were probably all there

Crack Up or Play It Cool

reluctantly. Not got a fella to drive for us. Better off without the fuckers, motorways notwithstanding.

The awful drive was actually better than the visit. As it rained, I remembered how Daddy coughed as if to get permission from a guard—fair enough, I suppose, they are in charge—before daring to place his hand upon mine. Rub gently, flesh on flesh. And I was soundlessly bawling like a baby. I don't do that in normal life. Did a lot of it when I was eleven. When Mummy disappeared. Staring at the man who buried her beneath a shed, my father who has been a dishonest bastard his whole life—to me in spades for nineteen years—became all too much. I liked feeling his hand upon my own, only because it meant I was not entirely alone. And perhaps I'm not, Grace Topping could still come good. A beautiful girl but I worry she doesn't think the same of me. She may have been no more than consolation, not the soul mate I need and never have come close to finding. The rain was pummelling the windscreen faster than the little wipers could cope with, and once more I was leaking like the sky. Tears streaking down my cheeks. Inside and out that Renault Clio was feeling the inclemency of the world. Crazy. I've pulled myself together for the last eighteen years. After the wobbly start. Or maybe I just froze myself over. Granny Hartnell was such a dear support. Easy to cry in her company. Our move up north seemed to harden my resolve but perhaps I lost something too. Lost all but the most infrequent connection to the Hartnells. Became someone else, someone harder to reach. I put on a lot of airs—quite the show off in my school days—I am not really a fan of me.

I've come out of the shower, still drying myself with a towel—quite nude—when the buzzer goes. The intercom. I answer it. 'Here to collect the Clio,' says a lady's voice.

'Oh, right.' I've forgotten all about this. 'I'm not dressed. Can you come to flat fourteen to collect the keys? I can buzz you through.'

'Righto,' she says. Bright and breezy. It's a relief. Some of these service types can be quite uppity. That class of people want to get their own back on us toffs these days, not that I'm in the least stuck up. I buzz her up the stairs and then look among my clothing for the keys. My hair is really very short, scrunchy short, not shaven, I don't go in for that rough-girl look. I finally find them when there is the faintest rap upon the door. I go and open it, and honestly, the most gorgeous little black girl is at my door. She looks a bit surprised, I have only an orange towel around me, at least it is a large one. I am lucky a girl is picking up the car, wouldn't let a strange man in my flat wearing so little. If this girl wants to take advantage of me, she should step right to it. I hand her the keys, then say, 'Can I give you something for your trouble?'

She looks a bit uncertain, stepped over the threshold as I indicated she should, you see, I don't even frighten the young ones. I push the door to, and say, 'Wait, please.' Back in my bedroom, I find my purse, pull out a twenty.

'You don't have to, you know?' she calls, standing stock-still, her bottom touching my door. I like her voice. It is throatier than one would imagine coming from such a tiny girl. 'No one else does.'

'A-ha,' I tell her, stepping back into the lounge, holding out the twenty-pound note. 'I'm me, not anyone else.' As I take another step, the towel falls. I'm not going to lie, I planned it but in a manner that could have happened by accident. Nothing too burlesque. I just wished to see her reaction, didn't go out of my way to embarrass her. Not far out.

'I've got the keys,' she says. 'No time to lose.' She turns her back on twenty pounds. And on me in the buff, a sight which pleases most with whom I share it. Gone, pulled the door closed behind her.

I open it and put a head around. No more than that, not

letting the neighbours see my specials. She looks around, then breaks into a little run. 'Are you old enough to even drive?' I shout. Laughing a bit manically as I do it. Sweet little girl.

I may have misjudged that one, sent a rather gorgeous looking girl into the arms of some hulk of a man after the fright the pretty older lady gave her. That's me, you'll understand. If she'd have taken the bait, it might have been the coolest stunt I've ever pulled. In fact, I never tried anything remotely similar before. It could also be that I'm sailing closer to the wind. Mother truly gone; Grace sounding worse than conflicted. Chin up, that was definitely worth a shot. Everything going on at the present time has brought me to this crossroads: crack up or play it cool? Sophie Stevens won't be changing her stripes.

* * *

It isn't even eight o'clock yet, so I swear this gin and tonic will be my only one. A night in and a single bevvy. Winding down after a bloody awful day. When I was a young reporter, not at the Noise—when I was twenty-three, I was covering crime for the London freebie—the office had an away day. This was at a Golf Club outside of Horsham. A stupid team-building day. I was new but already understood that reporters aren't a team. If you are lucky, you can find someone who'll cover your back; generally, it's as competitive as hell. At the Noise, a chappie named Johnson covered mine for a time, during my early months. Then I did the stupid thing, slept with him which was what he wanted, and then that was that. I mean, if I'd married him or whatever the hell he was looking for, perhaps he would have watched out for me throughout newspaper eternity. Or chained me to sink, cot, and a bottle of Valium. I observed my stepmother's life—remember—I know how it works. I think I let him do what he did to me because he seemed to have earned it. He didn't know that I was far more the other way, although I'm not averse to feeling a man's hydraulic appendage inside me. It is the wider package I find off-putting. Their tub-thumping personalities.

Anyhow, the golf club. There was the usual rubbish with trust exercises and trying—as a team—to complete a task that no individual would likely have all the skills for. It forces you to listen to each other. Then there was Locate Your Colleague. A big chart was pinned to the wall showing the Jungian personality wheel. Carl Jung, psychoanalyst or Terry Jung, the TV comedian. Could have been either, all psychology is a joke to me. We each had a bagful of our colleague's names written in felt-tip on small cardboard rectangles. The task was to put each name alongside whichever character trait we thought most suited the person. I can't remember where I put my colleague's names. If there was a rubbish bin, it would have been in there. One after another of the blighters put mine next to the word assertive. It's a good word, I think I am a bit, but when twenty or more call you assertive—co-operative, approachable, dependable, were all reasonable alternatives—a picture builds. One wag wrote the word, frigid, on a blank piece of paper and stuck my name by it. It told only of his own frustrations, not a characteristic that is remotely mine. I had done two of the older women at the paper, so he clearly wasn't even in on the gossip.

It might be this trait, my assertiveness bug, that prompts me to telephone Grace. It is early enough, of course, she could be out with friends; she performs in no show at present.

She picks up.

'It's me. About the other night, I am so sorry if I came across as clingy and needy. I am not usually like that. It was just a shit day. The police, my mother, and everything. Grace, you are such a sweetie. I'm frightened that I've pushed you...'

Crack Up or Play It Cool

'Sophie, it isn't that. All a bit fast. Being...' She pauses, and I don't want to interrupt and say the wrong thing. '...a girlfriend isn't something I have really contemplated. You are a marvel, that's how you won me over...'

'Not me, Gracie. You're every woman's dream. Sorry if I was overexcited at finding you. Do you know...' The fridge starts making a much louder noise than it usually does. The kitchen is an alcove off my lounge and this buzzing is a new phenomenon. Annoying that it should start up now. '...I had to go to prison today. Not had to, not for corrective purposes. To visit Daddy. It was such a depressing thing to do.'

'I feel for you, Sophie. It's a terrible time for you, I know. I don't think I'm the one to see you through it, my love. Not in the way...'

'Oh Grace. I could send a cab to collect you. Come around. I promise not to be so...'

'No, Sophie. Not me, I'm afraid. I do feel for you but I can't...'

'I'm not asking for a long term...'

'No, Sophie. I'm sorry.'

The phone has gone dead. Not even a goodbye. I think about texting Simon again. He says all the wrong things but at least I'm prepared. Know that it is all I will get. Agree with him generally, however harsh his commentary.

Another gin and tonic in hand, plenty more measures in the bottle. I'll see if there's a game show to watch. The contestants on them can be so fucking stupid, if I can just find the right one, I'll be able to laugh through these tears.

* * *

When the phone rings I am three sheets to the wind. Out of gin, tears still streaming but surely near to the bottom of the barrel by now. I keep thinking about Gracie. I really, really liked her. And I had thought she would opt for the ladies' team long term—she was getting into it more than many a late starter—all for nothing, that might even be the bigger tragedy. Nobody seems to stick with me for very long; I had the loveliest mummy in the world for just eleven years.

'Sophie, it's me. Monica.'

A phone call from Mica Barry who has the lead role in a Pinter, on at the Marlowe Theatre. Or the run may have finished. I read all the reviews four months ago. She has come a long way since Shoes and Slippers. I didn't go, Pinter is too miserable for me at the best of times; it's always nice to hear how well she's doing. 'Monica. Or should I say Auntie Monica?' I don't know if I've said anything at all, so slurred are my words.

'Monica, please? Sophie, I've disturbed you. Are you in company?'

'No, no, it's fine.' Shit-fuck. I should have said I have friends over. Drunk in company equals fun; all on your tod and it is the most maudlin state. 'I've taken the phone into the bedroom. All alone for now.'

'Sophie. Not sure what you make of everything going on. It's shocking, I know.'

As Monica Bredbury rambles on about the sorry situation which entwines her family and mine, I think about her. My feelings. Odd that I like her as intensely as I do. My stepmother's sister and everything. I think her partner is a handsome actor. James Bond, probably. Not sure that I can prise her away from all that but it is nice to dream. I have missed most of what she is telling me; will try a little of my own scintillating conversation in recompense.

'I saw my dad in prison today.' Oh, God. I start crying like I'm eleven again. It doesn't fit. Monica doesn't need to hear this.

'Oh, Sophie, I'm sure it was simply horrible.'

She is offering me her sympathy. Probably doesn't care tuppence about Daddy's incarceration. 'I think he's in the right place.' I say it loudly, through tears. I really do. He put my mother under a shed in a stranger's garden. Not quite a stranger, if my research is cutting the mustard. 'I hate it because I've lost everything but I don't love him any longer, Monica. I can't. I love Mummy.'

'Oh, Sophs. It must be so, so hard.'

'Would you like to come around. I've a flat in Bayswater where...'

'Now? I can't do now, Sophie. I've rehearsals in the morning. And...well...Gary has a couple of friends over. I think I'm meant to be entertaining but I was thinking of you.'

'That is sweet. I think about you, Monica.'

'And Mary?'

As she says this, I realise I pitched my last comment too amorously. She is thinking about me because of our plight. Not more generally. I've been in love with Monica Bredbury since I was sixteen. An on and off love. Mostly on a break, rekindled those sporadic occasions when I see her lovely face. That is how one-way traffic works. 'I can't believe she did it,' I say.

'Me neither.'

Oh. I think she means she can't believe it in the absolute sense whereas I was speaking figuratively. It seemed unlikely but, for my money, her older sister is a bitch. Monica has never really been on board with my perspective. Not entirely anyhow.

'Sophie, I'm going to see her. A visit like you did to your father. In two days.'

'Been to prison before?' I ask it as casually as my gin-laden bloodstream will allow. 'I've done loads but today was the worst.'

'Never. I pretended, ten years back, but it was all done in a TV studio. I don't know how I'm going to cope.'

That is quite an admission. Monica copes with everything, or perhaps that is just Mica Barry. Monica might be the vulnerable one. Even assertive Sophie seems to have a couple of weak spots: the drink; my lovely auntie; I'm beginning to think I should have kept my towel on earlier, too. A tad tarty, or was it cool? It's a very fine line.

'Things have not been great between Mary and I in many a year, Sophie. I remember when you brought us together. Do you still remember that? The interview.'

'Of course, I do, Auntie Monica. My first story in wide-circulation print.'

I actually remember the crimson nightdress she wore in the hotel room she and I shared, find the wherewithal not to blurt it out.

'I was wondering—and I really understand if you don't want to—but would you come along. Me and you, the prison part will be awful, so I'll buy you a meal out. Or come back afterwards and meet Gary.'

'Yes. I'd love to visit my stepmother in prison. And I'll be helping you. Yes. I should love to do that. What time?'

2.

I won't replenish my gin supplies until I have regained a little composure, understood myself in the light of all that has happened. I have recently learned a disturbing truth which occurred in my family long ago, and still the detail—the exact lay of it—evades me. The how and the why. I'll drink nothing before I have seen Auntie Monica, not until after we've made the trip together to South Kent Women's Prison. I am thankful that she will drive. When we were speaking, I offered. It came to me that she is so famous she might have limousines drive her about but that's actually rubbish. My own fantasy of being so feted, were I the film star. She might have had them on opening nights once or twice, I expect, but Monica makes a point of being a regular person. More so than I'll ever manage. And I think it was a no-brainer for her to overrule my offer, to bring her car down from

Crack Up or Play It Cool

Buckinghamshire, where she lives, and call upon me. I was off-my-tits drunk, hid it as best I could. Which was not very well. I would have sobered up before driving, if she had wished it—I hope she can recognise that—not sure I was very clear on the phone; I offered to drive and added, 'But I don't have a car.' And I am grateful that the pretty girl has collected the rental jobbie. Been and gone. If it were still here, I might have driven across town to Grace's and made a fool of myself there too. Or I could have called a cab, the problem is she was pretty explicit about not seeing me anymore. At one point she said, 'We can be friends,' and that formulation actually means we can't. Every time. For lack of an alternative, I went to bed and thought about how fantastic the girl from Super Rentals looked. If she was doing the same about me, she'll be back. I am utterly pessimistic on that front too.

Two or three coffees and then I'll take the underground and all the rest of it. Out to Redhill. I think I can meet family without crying so long as they haven't been lying to me for nineteen years. And I've not had a skinful of gin.

* * *

The journey is quite as one might expect. The tube from Bayswater to Edgeware Road is busy, not excessively so, and the travellers are clean, well groomed. When I change to travel to Farringdon, the class of my fellow tube-users deteriorates. I do not look up from my seat when a yob throws himself into the vacant space next to me, jolting my thin frame with the violence of his sitting. I glance very quickly into his face, expecting an apology, find that he is not in this world. He looks Pakistani, or similar, and I must stress that I have no antipathy to people from that or any other place. Indeed, he is surely a Londoner, a Pakistani upbringing would have instilled better manners in a boy than has occurred with this one. He wears earplugs which have garnered all the attention he has for this life. In his hands he clutches what I think is a Cornish pastie—hardly halal but it is not my place to judge such matters—and every bite brings crumbs of the flaking pastry onto his clothing, some carry to my own summer dress. I glance down the carriage; this man is younger than me and there are several vacant seats he could have occupied. I think it is my siren beauty which has attracted him. I don't mean to sound as pig-headed as that phrase may appear but, believe me, he has a pockmarked face and a wall-eye. His chances of getting close to girls like me are reliant upon the opportunities public transport offers him.

I have a book in my bag, I do not like to retrieve it with this oaf sitting beside me. Any inadvertent stimulation of our physical closeness, he will misinterpret. I have no doubt about it, extensive pre-knowledge of the type. I stare at the advertisements on the sloping interior of the carriage. One is for a theatre performance but with no sign of Monica's name. Or Grace Topping's and, for all the dismal inevitability of our parting, I wish her well. Ouch. The thug beside me has elbowed me in the ribs.

'Sorry cuz,' he says, 'fetchin' dis from me pocket.'

He holds up an electrical adaptor, something that might attach to the earpiece. I don't wear one, nor care to learn how it operates. My newest cousin balances the half-eaten pasty on his knee while attaching a new device to one end of his audio apparatus. I put my hand to my mouth to hide a smile when I see the foodstuff slip to the floor. His hip nudges deliberately into mine in the movement with which he stoops to pick it up. Now he turns into me, pasty back in hand.

'I've 'ad enough,' he tells me. 'You want it?'

'Thank you, sir, but no.' I put a hand up to the side of my face. He is vicious of public space but otherwise inoffensive. 'I don't eat other people's food. Anybody's.'

'We all eat other people's food, cuz. We do that or you are the farmer. The farmer of the cereal and the meat and the breakfast, dinner, tea. Pizza farmer, the Cornish pasty farmer...'

He goes on, and I find myself laughing. I think he makes a good point although it is not really in opposition to my own. I intended only that I do not eat food which other people have had first go at. I explain my rule.

'Hey, cuz, do I know you from somewhere?'

I tell him he does not, and he pulls a piece of paper from his pocket, a pen. Scribbles.

'What's your name?'

I give him a look. I liked his joke; it does not make us intimate. 'I am Sophie,' I say.

'Me number. Call if you like. Your hair is proper buzzin'. Love it.'

And then the man is on his feet, the doors of our transportation are opening and he gets out at Euston Square. I think my hair is elfin, will accept buzzing as a compliment. I see from the paper thrust into my hand that his name is Mushtaq. Very nice. I don't expect to call it, I'm not that desperate yet. It is good to have options, I suppose. The fellow bruised me twice in a ten-minute tube journey: love-making would be hell, the knock-knock-knocking of heads and pelvises. I surreptitiously slip his note into the open carrier bag of the lady to my other side. If her husband comes across it and rings the number this evening, it could all get rather funny. Sorry to miss it but I can picture him already. The short balding husband with an indignant pink face. The lady in question has white hair; it buzzes not at all.

* * *

It is a twenty-minute walk from the station to my Auntie's house; when I arrive, I feel more out of breath than I can justify. A hint of anxiety within me, perhaps, the rarest thing but these are not normal times. I cannot truly warm to Uncle Phil, and Auntie Sarah is insufferable; what long ago happened to my mother never leaves my mind. My half-siblings are great; I confess that I hated them a dozen years ago. Not so much Craig but the strange one certainly. And, if I think on that time with blistering honesty, I have long thought myself to be equally strange. Perhaps we all are, and back then my attack was also my defence. Maybe all prejudice is a form of self-loathing. It's plausible; however, I am more of an It-girl than a philosopher. Float the ideas, never wait around for the drawing of conclusions.

'Sophie, do come in. I would hope to tell you how fine you look but frankly this has aged you. Shocked describes it best. Uncle Philip is at work, I'm afraid.'

Oh dear, oh dear, my aunt has lost her good manners. And I thought myself beautiful in the mirror this morning. Nor is Uncle Philip at work: golf is a leisure pursuit, not a job. I don't tell her this. In fact, it is possible that I am wrong; he remains a partner in a small accountancy firm but others count the beans. I am not wrong about my looks; on the train this morning, wall-eyed Mushtaq was clearly smitten. It is walking a mile from the station—along the side of the A25 for the most part—which has taken it out of me.

'The boys are in?'

'I am sure Craig will be very pleased to see you, Sophie. You know how it is with Simon.'

She lets me in, indicating I must take off my shoes—how very Japanese—and ushers me through into the lounge. Auntie goes up the stairs, speaking with Craig, I expect, and I text the other one.

> ***Oy, Matey, big sister is in the house. Why not give me a scare and show your ugly face?***

I can hear talking upstairs but it can't possibly be him: the silent one. Little 'un and Auntie Sarah, I'm sure.

145

I'm not speaking to the press

He is very drole, isn't he? I have to think a little before I can reply to that.

Did the coppers try and speak to you? How did you bat them off? They can be as persistent as big sisters in my experience

There is a sound on the stairs. The door opens but only Auntie appears.

'Craig wants to shower. I'm most surprised he is not dressed yet.' She looks very flustered as if she is responsible for his tardiness. I blame the parents, not her at all; being banged up in prison would knock a hole in the smooth running of any family. 'He had breakfast in his dressing gown before Uncle Philip left.'

'No worries, Aunt Sarah. He's been through a lot, poor lad.'

'Still.' She says this single word, leaves it hanging as if Craig is the one letting us down. Mother on a murder charge clearly not something to stay in your pyjamas over, not in Auntie Sarah's estimation. I reckon it actually is, although getting up and doing something about it might be the better trajectory. I feel my phone vibrate. 'Do you mind waiting? I've got an especially busy wash day. You and I can have a little catch-up later.'

I nod a yes to that. 'Which is Simon's room?'

'Will he see you?' She is pointing at my phone.

I guess that she has to text what is coming up the stairs for his tea. Leaves it outside his door most probably. 'Not there yet.' Before I look at my screen, she points to a door up the stairs, first on the left, and then Auntie takes herself into the kitchen. Her laundry is through there, I presume.

Detective Inspector Woodcock and I text. Not sure when that one will end

They do that? Not tape recorded

It's a permanent record, Doofus

He knows that I dislike the name with which he abuses me. There is no reason to stray far from Sophie, the name that has suited me my whole life. Quite short, no nonsense. I used to call him worse but I didn't know he took it in when I was a mean older sister.

When I've done with Craig, I'm coming in

The reply comes in no time at all.

No can do

Hmmm. I shall consult with younger brother.

* * *

'We're freaks and we have been since birth. You called us as much when you really were our big sister.'

'Craigy,' I say, a little surprised by this self-pitying turn, 'if I wasn't the nicest older half-sister which you two boys could have had—and I clearly was the cleverest—I have apologised for it several times over the years. No hard feelings.'

'But I'm not talking about you. It was Mum and Dad who marked us out. I didn't see it back then—God knows how I missed it—small, I suppose. Their marriage was a train wreck. Always a train wreck.'

'Yes, and I understood but was mostly too nice to tell you and Simon. I hated Mary, didn't intend for you to feel like I do towards her.'

'Mary, Mary, Mary. You think Dad is blameless? Just because he's your dad too. We're the same fucked-up DNA. Both marked, me and you, sis. Bad blood.'

'Daddy is not blameless. A bit of a shit, that's ever clearer. I've never understood what made him marry her. The other way around makes a bit of sense. The Bredburys were no one in the world. West Country thickies.' I am seeing Monica tomorrow, a Bredbury I adore, and even as I say it, I recognise the abuse which I've been hurling at Mary for years can't really stick. Stephen is a bit thick; got himself a PhD five years after the younger Mary, which might make him cleverer than me on paper, and that is evidence only of the pin-headedness of a scientific education. Mary and Monica are not thick at all. Mary probably matches my father as an academic physicist. She had a couple of children and all that goes with that. Must have made it harder for her to prove her worth in papers written but she is academically gifted. Far more so than I. Monica is one of the finest actors of her generation. Wins accolades and she is underrated. The objective opinion of an admiring step-niece. Truly, she can move an audience with a soliloquy or put in a comic performance that is deft and bemusing in equal measure. I think Mary married for the Stephenson dosh. Daddy usually slept with undergrads for nothing. Or passing a paper he might otherwise have failed, I suspect. Squeezing a marriage out of him suggests that Mary possesses impressive skills in manipulation. She was a useless mother to me—not a mother at all but, cards on the table, I never gave her a chance—if she is the cause of Simon's difficulties it is disturbing, if not, I must grant that she has put up with him like a saint. Craig here is not as messed-up as he is feeling today. She brought him up with the love I wouldn't allow her to shower on me. Not that she was keen to try in any way likely to succeed. My stepmother was just nice enough to me to instil guilt for how I treated her. And I've never felt more than a smidgen of that.

'Murder. A murderer's child.' Dear me, he is internalising this unhelpfully, poor mite. 'This was not the life I thought I was born to, all the darkness happened before my birth. It was going to come out sooner or later; why could I not see it?'

'Do you get any facetime with big brother? Does he see it like you do, Craigy, or has he a weirder take?'

'Sophie, I talk to him for hours. I don't wait outside, he's okay with me in the room. Never talks, of course. When I've gone, after an hour's rant or however long, he texts me. Thumbs up, thumbs down. Gives me his views. He's an interesting guy, my Simon. I think I'm the only one who gets him. Me and Mum. And he's as confused as I am about her now.'

'What does he reckon? What do you reckon? Is Dad being honest? No more involved than this awful and illegal burial.' I pause, Craig doesn't answer but he is looking at me quite intently. 'If he's telling the truth, then your mother is the woman who murdered my mother. Not a pleasant thought, Craigy, and really, I am very fond of you whatever has gone on. I am not the sort to confuse her actions with those of her offspring.'

'Simon thinks it might all be his fault. He doesn't quite say it—text it—but it's there between the lines.'

'He might be responsible? He was a new-born baby. Short of a year old, anyhow.'

'Sent Mum post-natal crazy. He got that term into one text although he writes very little about himself. Deflects it mostly.'

'I was there, Craig. Remember that. I was eleven years old. I didn't like your mother on account of her not being my mother—that was my principal gripe—and she wasn't really right with me. None of that is the point here. Post-natal depression? I don't remember any of that. And nor can Simon. Six-month-olds remember nothing. Not even clever sods like him.'

Craig is in a funny mood. He usually looks up to me—admires his big sister—my name appearing in a Sunday newspaper now and again, it's a big deal for kids his age. Today he is on his own tracks. I ask whether he has been to see Mary. 'She hates it in there,' is all he says; it is clear he has yet to make the dismal pilgrimage. I tell him that Monica and I are visiting tomorrow. 'Aunt Mon sent me a card,' he says.

I feel a little surprised by this, then realise I should not. He is her blood relative, not mine. I try asking what it says.

'Polite, polite. I don't think Auntie Monica knows what to think anymore.'

I was drunk when I spoke with her, so perhaps I missed a bit of nuance. 'I thought she believes her sister is innocent.' It was as much as I heard, not that we discussed a single detail.

'I think that but I know I think it mostly because she's my mum. Would never hurt me. I don't know...' Craig buries his face in his hands, won't let me see his expression as he talks on. '...what she might have done to your mother, Sophie. I wish we could make it all right, make it not have happened. You never liked her but she was all right with you from everything I saw. Wasn't mean.'

'She didn't kill me, Craig. No poison or bash on the head. I was mean to her and she matched it much of the time. Some of the time. She was more adult about it; I was the sulky teen. That is how I remember it anyway. Now Daddy says she did it. The murder. What am I supposed to think?'

* * *

After a bit of coercion, I am standing in the doorway of Simon's smelly bedroom. He has tightly drawn blackout blinds; no sunlight enters this room. Craig is two steps in front, actually inside the room. Since older brother has occupied it, following their flight from Carnforth, only younger brother has put a step inside. Plus Simon, of course. From my two paces behind, I tell Craigy that I feel like Buzz Aldrin.

'Simon, darling, my thumbs don't type fast enough to say all I want to say to you. Forgive me for entering your domain but it is in the spirit of love and kinship that I come. Whatever has transpired—your mother, my mother—it does not alter my affection for you and for young Craig here.'

I don't get so much as a grunt back. Simon was sitting on a swivel chair by his writing desk—his uncle's, I expect, he's most likely commandeered it—when Craigy knocked and entered in a single manoeuvre. I caught a glimpse of him, the poor boy is enormous. Twenty stone, I would hazard a guess. The last time I saw him, he was big but nothing like this. It might have been three years. The texts are his thing. Before I could catch his eye, he had pulled up the counterpane from his bed, an old-fashioned green one, rather elegant stitching. Candlewick. He threw it over himself. Craig and I are talking to a small unresponsive mountain.

'Might want to see her, Simon,' says little brother. 'Big sis hasn't lost her looks yet.'

'Not any time soon, darlings. A small fortune in skincare products has turned me into the delectable creature set before you.'

Now my little half-brother is staring at me in a way I consider a little creepy. 'No tights on,' he tells the boy beneath the blanket. I suppose this objectifying of the female form is the way of brothers and half-brothers the world over, I am not a fan of listening in. The more he talks the more alluring I find myself but that's an observation for another day. To dwell upon with one's bathroom mirror, or better yet a loving lady-friend. Not a blood relative. 'Don't be crude, Craig. I am here, and our Simon might be gay for all we know.'

That prompts neither confirmation nor denial but the mountain doth move. A little wobble on its swivel chair. The creak of metal hinges too. It means something. Whether it is the unearthing of a hidden truth or the prodding of a homophobe, I have yet to learn.

I tell Simon that Auntie Monica and I shall be visiting his mother in prison.

Craig butts in. 'She hates it. They're only keeping her in there because of Dad. All the crap that he's said.' I see how his face reddens as he says it. My youngest brother is very aerated about this. Very pro-Mary. 'Dad is probably cross about something else she's done. A million things they could have rowed about. I bet Mum knows nothing about the murder of the ex-wife. She thought the woman had gone abroad, the same as everyone else did.' It's a bit of a rant and I don't like hearing him refer to my mother as 'the woman', he is in too fragile a state for me to start putting him straight.

Simon is beneath his blanket. I see it move once or twice, a little tunnel into the shadow beneath. I think he is trying to look at me without allowing me to see him. That's Simon. No word or text yet; I have no idea if he thinks similarly to Craig. If he's on the same page about his mother's likely innocence; or about the pleasure to be had looking over his half-sister's tight-free legs. Big brother keeps mum.

'I think we may never know anything beyond our own wishes and fears until we hear what the jury also has to hear. Is that right, Si?' I ask. 'Although I am not sure if you will sit in court for a second. Not sure if I can bear it either, quite frankly.' I think I saw a pair of eyes in the brief raising of the blanket. Quickly dropped back down again. 'Simon, you are always sensible. Measured. Do you understand what I said at the beginning? That this mustn't come between us. Me and the pair of you.' The blanket doesn't say yes or no. 'Well, I know you understand on account of being such a cleverclogs. I just wanted to remind you. It's all rather upsetting. Upsetting for me. I've never stopped loving Mummy, and I always thought I would see her once again. Now I know it cannot happen, and I am feeling more mixed up than ever about Mary, about your mother. I am unchanged in my feelings towards you. Love and kisses, Si.'

I turn and step away from the open bedroom door. I will be getting nil by mouth from Simon Stephenson. A flood of texts later, I'm sure.

Crack Up or Play It Cool

* * *

Auntie Sarah and I talk in the garden. I asked Craig to join us but he gave a teenage, 'Nuh.' He has been all right with me. Thoroughly. Even Simon, I cannot complain about. I've always known he was as he is.

'I spoke to Philip, I'm afraid he's tied up with work. Can't get back just now.'

'No, Sarah. It is you I wanted to hear from. I went to see Daddy; tried to get the truth out of him, find I've still no idea what he has and hasn't done.'

'I can't believe he has kept this secret.' She reaches a hand out as if to touch me. A comforting gesture but then she stops short of actual contact. Can't quite make it. 'You deserved better than all this, Sophie. He lied to you; we can all see that now.'

We are sitting on her fancy folding garden chairs; they make us tilt back a little. My dress rides up. I swear I have seen a movement, a shimmering, of the blackout blind that stands out amid the array of otherwise open windows. I feel an impulse to tug my dress down, I think one or more brother is watching me. I do wonder about blanket-boy in there. Like Quasimodo, he inhabits the dark for fear of what a girl might think of the sight of him. And I should like to see Simon again. I talk a little judgementally, I know, but I love him as a sister should a brother. Wobbly start aside. First ten years or so. There is light shining in my eyes from the glass of his window, although the blind still looks fully drawn from here. He might have little spyholes for binoculars, for all I know. Auntie Sarah is by my side, a sunhat and looking forward. I raise the skirt an extra inch. Give the boy a treat. They might both be jacking off in there but this is sisterly love for you. 'He lied because he knew I couldn't keep a secret. Just a little kid at the time.'

3.

'Why hasn't she come?' It is the end of my second week since starting at Long Grove Prep. Friday. For every day of my first week, my mother drove me to and from school, this week—living with Daddy and his slapper—I have walked it. Only seven hundred yards, I don't complain. And I have not moaned about my mother's delay in picking me up—five o'clock was the agreed time—until now, fully one hour and ten minutes after she should have arrived. I show not a sign of weakness in front of Mary Bredbury, as I call her although she and my father performed a sham wedding some years ago. Not a woman with whom I care to share a name.

Daddy is home, just arrived, and that is why I have enquired. I am less resolute in his company.

'No idea,' he says in reply to my question.

Mary Moron is cooking an early supper. She has set places for only the pair of them; I have told her repeatedly that I will eat at Mummy's, not here. Not with them. The ugly little baby—which cannot crawl yet, although I've read in 'Baby's Doing Fine,' an overoptimistically named tome which the Moron also browses, that he should be doing it by now—seldom gets wedged into his high chair at meal times. She feeds him with a spoon, holding the fat sprog to her person as she does when breastfeeding. I bet Mary was just as stupid when she was a little cry-baby.

He has a quick word with his slapper. I hear most or all that they say. Still, he insists on speaking to me as though he is placating me, and I simply want to go to the other house. The one with the best parent in it. 'Sophie-sweetie...' What patronising language he uses; I'm eleven years old, dammit. '...Mummy says you've tried phoning Mummy-Cynthia but she isn't at home. Give it half an hour and try again, and after we've eaten here, I'll run you over. Shepherd's pie, sweetie. There's plenty for you, Sophie. Plenty.'

'I'm eating with Mummy. I always eat with Mummy when she collects me...'

'Yes, sweetie, it's just...'

'I'm not going to ruin my appetite with Mary's muck.'

'Sweetie, I know you are upset. I'm sure Mummy-Cynthia hasn't forgotten you. And there is no need to be rude about Mummy's cooking.'

Mary Moron is—unbelievably—only twenty-five years of age. I cannot call her mummy although my father would like me to. It would make her an even more disgusting and depraved slapper than she already is. If I was hers, she would have had me at fourteen. And children that young can't physically have babies unless they are the naughtiest children of the lot. In exactly five days, my father will celebrate his forty-fifth birthday. I don't mind his age but don't think much of him giving my mother the push to take up with a floozy like this. Not much at all. I am glad that I will be at Mummy's when he and Mary raise a glass to his approaching old age. They might have a night out, go into town for all I know. Unlikely though. There is a girl they've tried as a baby-sitter, did it only once. I think it might be too spooky looking after Simple Simon. Sleeps and stares and shits. That's your lot, folks. Sleeps, stares, shits. Mary took him to the doctor on account of the staring, told Dr Temple that her baby doesn't blink. It was after school on Monday so I had to tag along, although I had no need of a doctor. I'm normal, you see, don't stare into space hour after hour. Totally normal. I had to listen to Mary pleading for medical assistance. 'He will, Mrs Stephenson,' said the doctor. 'I'm sure he will.' Dr Temple is hopeless, can't do his job. Doesn't know the mother's name is Moron, hasn't spotted baby is a freak.

'Sorry,' I say to my father. I don't mean it but he is not the one I'm trying to annoy.

'It's Mummy you need to apologise to, Sophie,' he says, glancing at the young woman now wearing his ring.

'Uh, soz,' I tell her. I heard a boy say that when a bullish father was berating him at the play park. Good and insincere, I've thought that since first hearing it. 'Uh, soz.' I even give her a second dose.

I mope around and then sit and watch my father and stepmother eat shepherd's pie. It doesn't look so special but watching makes me hungry. Daddy says, 'We'll leave some back, just in case.'

I don't say, in case of what? Or even, stick Mary's food up where you do your business with her. I think it, elect not to say it. It's very strange that my mother has failed to collect me. She has done exactly that on every day she has needed to since I was four years old. Ever since she lived in a house apart from my father. He is making out she is unreliable but his floozy is the rubbish one. Mary Moron cannot be depended upon. Can't even make a decent shepherd's pie.

Before they have finished eating, the sprog starts to whinge. Not really a cry at all, just the kind of unhappy moan I would probably make if Mary Moron was my mother. 'Eur, eur, eur.' It could be the faintest ambulance siren. 'Eur, eur.' I think it means, put me out of my misery. I should tell her, instruct her, but I don't. They need to work everything out for themselves. Drown him when squeamish Sophie isn't looking. Really, I wouldn't want to watch, and I hate him. He's of no use to this world but I won't be the one to dispatch him. I believe they are going to make me cut up a mouse in biology class at this new school, and I go woozy just thinking about it.

'Mary, I'll run Sophie up to Spenser Avenue. See what's going on. Or Sophie, would you like to phone Mummy-Cynthia one more time?'

'Take me,' I say. I know when Daddy sees Mummy, they

sometimes spend a little time together. Hop into bed, I'm sure of it. I think she must be better at it than Mary. At the business. The more he sees her, the more chance there is that he will divorce this cretin and let Mummy live back in her proper house. Everything was better when I had my proper mummy every day. Not just half the time.

'Is that all right, dear?'

'I suppose so,' says Mary.

As we are heading out the door, he says, 'Leave the pots for me, Mary. You just look after Simon.'

I think he is quite smart even though he's married to a moron. I would rather wash pots than change the nappy, endure stench or stare of the fatty lump with its brain on the blink.

* * *

When we arrive at Mummy's house my hopes rise straight up to the stratosphere. Up into Daddy's world of astrophysics. Her car is on the drive, parked where she always leaves it. There are no lights on in the house, it's only early evening.

'Do you think she's asleep?' I ask.

'We'll see,' is all I get out of Dad. He rings the bell on the doorstep.

I wait a few seconds but Mummy doesn't answer, and I say, 'Shall I go round the back?'

'Wait a minute. I'll come with you if she doesn't answer soon.'

It is a bit odd, her car on the drive, so why didn't she come and collect me. The upstairs windows are open. I go round the back all the time during my weeks living here. Throughout the day, Mummy leaves the back door unlocked. Epsom is not London.

He rings the bell twice more. Waits with an impatience I dislike. It is as though he is blaming my mother, and I am worried something has happened to her. That she is on the floor in a faint, or sick in bed unable to move or even call out. I think she must have laryngitis, the illness which causes that. Eventually we go around the side of the house. There is no obstacle, and when we come to the kitchen door, it is wide open.

'I'm home, Mummy,' I shout, stepping inside.

My father has a hold of me before I am properly through the doorway. 'Sophie,' he hisses, 'there might be burglars here.'

This notion scares the wits out of me. I should not like to meet a burglar or any sort of ruffian. They can kill you, might do it just to stop you from identifying them in a police line-up. We talked about it at my old school. All the girls were very frightened. Didn't even want to go to the line-ups. 'Wouldn't he have heard our car?' I ask. I really hope there is no intruder in Mummy's house. He might have killed her, unless she has feigned blindness. That is what I said I would do in the school lesson about it. Mrs Spalding didn't even praise me; I think she was jealous on account of not thinking of it herself. It would be the best ruse; the ruffian mistakenly thinking I would be no bother at the line-up. And that's exactly when I would stop pretending, and finger him for his misdemeanours.

'Cynthia,' my father calls. No reply comes. 'Cynthia,' he tries again.

'Mummy, Mummy, Mummy.'

I think any burglar would have fled by now, out the front door because we are at the back. Two voices, so he would know he is outnumbered. We walk through the kitchen to the hallway. Daddy opens the lounge door, there is an open magazine in the middle of the sofa. The television is on, pictures but no sound.

'Is it always like this?' Daddy asks me.

'What?'

'This messy?'

'It isn't messy. Mummy's much tidier than Stepmummy. And she never leaves the television on if she isn't watching. She gets cross about electric.'

'I'm going into her bedroom. Stay down here please, Sophie.'

I know this trick. Daddy and Mummy are going to do sex again, and I'm not meant to know about it. I would rather Mummy had come and picked me up like she was supposed to, although I like them doing this. I think proper parents are always up to it. Divorce is actually very inconvenient: they aren't really supposed to do sex until their children are in bed. I think this pair get fewer opportunities on account of Mary Moron back at our proper house.

In no time at all Daddy is back downstairs. 'The bed isn't made,' he says. 'She isn't here, and yet it doesn't feel like she's far away.'

I start to cry. This is very, very strange. Mummy lives for me. She likes her antiques but I come first. I know I do. She says that she loves me every single day I spend in this house. Every day except this one, and this is only because she isn't here. 'Has she been kidnapped?' I ask through tears.

My daddy goes to the phone. I can't think why initially, and then feel very cross when I hear him talking to Mary. It's got nothing to do with her.

'I can't come back until I've sorted things here. The house was open round the back but no sign of Cynthia.' For a minute or so I think they are arguing. Perhaps Mary thinks he should leave me here, and take himself back to her and Sprog but I don't want that. I think it would be very scary to be left alone here. I'd not thought about it before; Mummy has always been with me in this house. Every second. 'I'll be back with Sophie as soon as I'm able. I hope you've kept on to that shepherd's pie.'

I suddenly chuck up—I didn't feel it coming on—smelly sick right down my blouse front. All over it. I don't give a fig about the shepherd's pie. Mary's cooking is that dreadful, I think it might be the thought of it which has made me spew so horribly.

'Oh dear, oh dear,' says Daddy. He takes me upstairs to the bathroom and tries to sponge away the vomit on my clothing.

I hear a door creak down the passageway and shout, 'Mummy,' once more, shout it so loudly that Daddy flinches.

He stops cleaning me for a moment and steps onto the landing, opens and closes a couple of doors.

When he comes back, he says only the word, 'Wind.' I start to cry once more, and he says, 'Sophie, the wind is in because she's left windows open in every room.'

Back downstairs he uses the telephone again and this time he starts talking to the police. I know it's them because it's who asked the operator for. I heard it even though he said it quietly: 'Police, please.' Then he explains that his first wife seems to be missing and he is very worried. Her car is here and the backdoor was left open. When he has finished talking, he looks down at me and says, 'Sophie, we mustn't touch anything, and we've to wait.' I nod at this, and he adds, 'You are being very brave.'

I'm not. I didn't volunteer for this. I came here because Mummy is loads better than Mary. Huggy and lovely, I like being here. I didn't know I was going to be waiting for the police with no Mummy in the house at all. It isn't brave finding yourself in a horrible situation. Maybe it is if you deal with it very calmly, I've already emptied my stomach. This is what it has done to me, not knowing where Mummy has gone. Made me physically sick. The shepherd's pie is insignificant. It's having my mummy missing which makes me feel ill. Nothing is as it should be. Needing the police to help work out where your mummy is would not happen in a normal child's life. I have a sick feeling that won't go away until she holds me close to her person once more.

Crack Up or Play It Cool

* * *

By the time the police come, it's pitch-black outside. I'm sitting on a kitchen chair, half asleep. The other half is terrified. Two uniformed men come into the house. Daddy talks to them, points to me, and steps out of the kitchen into the hallway. I hear him say something about burglars, then he says, 'The lock wasn't forced.' I think he is trying to say it probably wasn't burglars but this is Epsom. Nobody locks their backdoor early because everybody in the area has a job. There is no time for robbing until after dark. I suppose—and I am working this out as I sit and listen to them—a London burglar could have come on the train and then just walked in. A clever one.

I shout out what I think. 'They will want a ransom. You should put a trace on all the telephone calls.' I know about this. Kidnapping is very lucrative if the ones doing the snatching know what they are about. My father laughs, not nastily, just saying something about too much television. I hardly watch any. My suggestion is very clever. Probably on the right lines. I am frightened but not stupid.

One of the policemen seems to agree with me. 'Is this a family with a lot of money?' he asks. The answer to that is yes. Yes, a thousand times over, with a big fat riddle on the end. It is Stephenson money, not much at all on the Hartnell's end of the see-saw. They are not poor—not as penniless as the stupid Bredburys—they couldn't raise a million pounds. Granny Hartnell has never driven a car and Granddaddy spends more time under his than he does driving it. Mummy married into money and divorced right back out of it, that's why her house is a semi-detached.

'You've got to pay it, Daddy,' I shout from the lounge. 'I want my Mummy back.'

* * *

Daddy stays in the house with the policemen, all searching

Crack Up or Play It Cool

for clues. A police lady drives me across Epsom, to my other house. Mary, who is not my mummy, acts very nicely with me. Pats my hair and hugs me quite tightly. I tell her she is hurting me but she isn't. I am simply in the arms of the wrong mother. Then she asks me what I saw at the house. I tell her everything. Ringing the doorbell lots of times; the open kitchen door and windows. 'Nothing has been stolen as far as I could see.'

'It's very strange,' she says.

I think exactly the same, I scream at her anyway. 'Mummy has been kidnapped, or done away with. And you're not even crying.' Then I cry more than I have ever done in this false mummy's presence. My chest heaves and Mary hugs me tightly. I don't even complain. I want it and I don't want it. I want everything to be different but that is what you can never have.

* * *

I am in my bedroom, still very much awake, when Daddy finally comes home. It is two o'clock. I don't think Mary has even been to bed. The sprog is awake now, in her arms as she talks to Daddy. I can hear them, see them too. They are in the dining hall and I have stepped out onto the landing.

'For over ninety minutes they kept me at the police station. Wrote down every word I said. They had a policewoman sitting in; probably one who knew shorthand. It felt like they suspected me of doing away with her. And I'm worried about her—about Cynthia—can't think what has happened. Of course, she might be in town, turn up in the morning. Can't see why not. Odd that she left the house the way she did. All the windows, the back door.'

Mary talks in a low voice; I can't hear what point she is trying to make.

Daddy interrupts her. 'They will wish to speak to you tomorrow. I'll look after Simon while you are there.'

'Me?'

'Routine. To tell them when you last saw her, that kind of thing. I said she might be with Azzopardi. Not like her to forget about Sophie, it's the only explanation I can come up with.'

Mary says something back. Quietly, I don't hear it. And I've not heard the name Azzopardi before. I guess he's the one Daddy calls Maltese Joe. Daddy and Mary are always laughing about him, my mother's new boyfriend. I've never met him. I think Maltese Joe is their name for him; either that or he's a professional wrestler. And in the summer holidays, Daddy told me she had stopped seeing him. Mummy never said a word about anyone called Joe, Azzopardi or otherwise. Wouldn't need a boyfriend if only Mary-Moron would push off. I never liked them talking about him—Daddy laughing, implying the Maltese man was not very suitable—Mary lapping it up. I should have asked Mummy about him but didn't like to. He can't have been any worse than the slapper Daddy has got himself tied to. Got himself another baby with, and Burping Sprog is a hopeless case. Proper Mummy had me. And I'm better than normal: top of the class. And if Mummy and Maltese Joe have run away together then he can't be that bad. She only likes pleasing things, that's how she describes the antiques she buys. If that's what's happened—gone to Malta—then they are sure to send for me. I might have to live on a tiny island but I won't mind that. It's a long way from Mary and the freaky baby. On-The-Blink who can't blink. Daddy can fly over when he wants to see me, he has pots of money. He flew to a conference in Rome in the summer and that was only for silly physics.

4.

I feel like a stuffed toy, so little have I slept. Like the tatty little grey bear that sits unattended at the foot of Simple Simon's cot. There was a morning a few months ago, after a party for a lot of people from the university, when I heard my daddy say, 'I feel like shit.' Crude words, I know, but that is precisely how I feel today. I have woken in the wrong bed and the whereabouts of my mother is a mystery. Not a nice juicy one, the upsetting sort. The worst.

I can hear people moving about downstairs. Daddy and the moron, I suppose. I get myself dressed but only in jeans, not the kind of clothes I usually wear when I can choose anything that I like. My father is alone in the kitchen; I presume Mary is with Sprog, and then I hear a bit of a cry from the baby, and Daddy says, 'Oh hell.' As he is heading for the sound, he says over his shoulder, 'I'll make you some breakfast in a moment, Sophie.' This is unnecessary. Even pancakes I can make myself, and today a piece of toast with marmalade will suffice. I'm not in the mood for proper eating. I feel close to tears and that is not how I am when things are as they should be.

While Daddy is tending his inferior child, the doorbell rings. I go to the window to find out who it is. Mrs Hooper is on the doorstep. Her daughter is my best friend but I do not see Emily with her. Then I remember, she was to come around and play with me, and it was supposed to have been at Mummy's house. I expect Emily is sitting in the car.

'Daddy,' I shout. 'I don't want to. I don't want to. Can't.'

He comes into the dining hall holding the baby across his shoulder. Silent, which is preferable to his whinge. Daddy is rubbing the sprog's back, trying to make him burp. Quite unnecessary: he's as windy as a winter's day in West Wittering. 'Emily has come to play but I don't want to.' I have to make sure Daddy gets the point.

'I'll explain,' says my father. He goes to the door, which is directly off the dining hall. I stand back, not wishing Emily or Mrs Hooper to see that I have been crying. Or that I am wearing inelegant jeans.

'Professor Stephenson, I'm so sorry to trouble you. I was to drop Em off at Cynthia's house. To play with Sophie. There was a police car on the drive. An officer told me no one was home, and I couldn't get any more than that out of him. I do hope they are both all right.

'Mrs...?'

'Hooper. Please call me Deborah.'

'Deborah, I'm so sorry I didn't phone. Sophie's here but it has been an upsetting time. My ex-wife has disappeared. We can't explain it at all at this moment. Hence the police. Sophie's been here the whole time. Tell young Emily that her friend will be in school on Monday, it's just that she's not up to playing today.'

'Disappeared. Good gracious. The poor girl must be worried sick?'

'I think that's the size of it. Very puzzling. I can't make head nor tail. Deborah, were you and Cynthia close?'

'We talked. About our girls mostly. What...'

'Do you know if she has been seeing anybody?'

'Good grief, Professor Stephenson, we never spoke about anything of that sort. Her personal life is none of my business and I have never been one to probe.'

'No, no. Sorry to have raised it,' says my daddy. I am standing next to the display cabinet along the wall—cannot see Mrs Hooper's face—but I know she is lying. She said it far too quickly, and I know that her and Mummy would talk for hours when Emily and I played. Not every time but some of them. I never listened in to what they said because I behave much better around Mummy than I ever do with Mary Barely-Left-School. I treat anybody well who deserves it. I remember that they sometimes talked in hushed voices, like people who tell secrets do. If she told anyone about Joe Azzopardi and why she is no longer seeing him—or if they planned to run away together—it will be Deborah Hooper. I hope Mummy never told her about the dirty things she and Daddy used to do together even after they got a divorce. I don't imagine she ever said about that, it always seemed like it was top secret. I wasn't in on it except I worked it out. Like a Private Eye. I suppose, if she had blabbed about all that, Mrs Hooper might have told Mummy that she and Daddy should get back together. Do the right thing if they like doing it so much. It would have been good advice, although to my knowledge they haven't sneaked off into a bedroom in months. Maltese Joe could be the cause of that; if he has disappeared too, that would prove they have eloped. It's very, very upsetting having a mother who has run away. Going away without telling me when she is coming back. I stop listening to the conversation and run up the stairs, tears streaming down my face once more.

* * *

By lunchtime, Mary is home and she says, in front of me, 'I couldn't help them much but I told them everything I could.' I realise she has been at the police station all morning. I understand that the police sometimes rough people over to make them talk more but there are no bruises or cuts on her face. I think they have gone easy with her, and I would have advised the exact opposite.

She has popped into the study where Simon has a second cot, looks upon him with concern but there is nothing to be done. The little lump sleeps day and night, give or take the odd whinge. Daddy tells her he has had a good morning, and by that I think he means he never had to change a nappy. Stupid Simon certainly didn't crawl, laugh or speak his first words.

'We should talk this through with Sophie,' Daddy says to Mary.

'I'll fix us all some lunch first,' she replies.

I get a sinking feeling. It might be that they know exactly

where she is, or that Daddy has been asked for a ransom and he's trying to decide whether to pay or not. I would rather they just tell me, without food in their mouths. And I also don't want to hear it. I might start crying again, and I hate doing that in front of Mary the Fair-Haired Moron.

We have cold quiche, bread and cheese, and celery sticks. I didn't finish my toast earlier, so I eat the bread and cheese. I think Mary made the quiche, and Mummy's is far tastier. None of that muck for me.

My stepmother puts her hand upon mine. Touch can be very comforting; my father probably wouldn't think to do it. He seldom touches me at all. I realise tears are running down my cheeks, I know they are going to tell me something horrible.

'Sophie,' says my father, 'last night I tried to help the police. I went through some papers at your mother's house. I told them that, from what I could see, Mummy's passport has gone missing. They've told Mary this morning that they have yet to find it. It could be with her. Do you know what that means?'

'She's been kidnapped and taken far away.'

'No sign of a struggle, Sophie. We never saw...'

'Taken at gunpoint.' I am crying a lot more now. I know that I am talking tripe. I can't say that she has chosen to leave me, gone to Paris for the weekend even though I should be with her. It is too sickening by far.

Mary speaks. 'It seems more probable that your mother has left of her own accord. Possibly with a gentleman in tow. We don't...'

'You don't know that! You just want her gone! You don't know if somebody has hit her on the head. Mummy might have lost her memory, gone to Scotland because she thinks she lives there. Hitting on the head can do that. Don't just say what you want. You're horrible to me!'

As I am storming away, food scarcely touched, my father

says, 'Sophie, I understand how upsetting this is.' I don't think he does. He cares about me, and still he spends most of the time in his own little world of physics. Giving the girl undergraduates extra lessons on the backseat of his car. I have told my friend, Emily, that he is a very randy man. That he had a girl from the university over to babysit for me and Ugly Sprog, and later that night Mary and Daddy had a blazing row about her. I think he kissed her, and some worse things too. The student pretending to breastfeed Daddy, all that sexy rubbish. Probably not on the night they argued but that was definitely what made Mary cross. I also told Emily that when Daddy drops me off at Mummy's, he likes to go upstairs, where he and Mummy 'take their clothes off for old time's sake.'

It's true but Emily wouldn't believe me. 'Why would he do that, when your stepmother is so much prettier,' she said. For a moment I hated Emily for saying it. Mary is only younger, and that isn't anything to do with pretty at all. The accident of birth, they call it. But then I worried that she might tell everyone in school how depraved my family are, so I said that she was probably right and for that reason, she should probably forget I said it. I think having a randy father could give a girl a stinker of a reputation.

When I am lying on my front on the outside of my bed, the rough blankets on my face and forearms offering some solace on a miserable day, Daddy enters my room. 'There was no need to speak to Mummy like that.'

'Stepmummy.'

'Stepmummy. You know she is only trying to help. Where your other mummy has taken herself is a mystery to us. Had you heard about...' My father doesn't finish his question, always wants to treat me like a child.

'About her boyfriend? About Joe Azzopardi?' I can sense Daddy jump a little when I say that name. He doesn't expect me to know it. Thinks I'm a child; it would shock him if he knew that I rumbled what he gets up to with Mummy, figured it out years and years ago. 'She wouldn't choose him over me.'

'Well, she might have, Sophie. We don't know one way or another. I don't have an address for Mr Azzopardi; I told the police what I knew and they are trying to trace him, speak to him. If they are together, I'll be so cross with her.'

'You're not married to her, Daddy. Not any longer. Nothing she does is any of your business.' I hate the way he is talking; this isn't Mummy's fault. I still think there might be a ransom note. The kidnappers could have left it on her dressing table, and then the wind blew it off—behind the furniture or suchlike—so the police never found it. Written in capital letters; demanding hundreds of thousands of pounds or else they will keep Mummy in a cave and pull her teeth out with pliers. Kidnappers are the nastiest people there are. And that is more likely than running away. She loves me, I know she does. I don't even remember what her passport looks like. It will be black, like mine, but I can't think which photograph appears in it. Mine looks awful; I want a new passport so that I can see a nicer picture of myself in it. I might have seen hers when we went to France. That was a long time ago; I was very, very little. Before they divorced, so I can't actually remember it. Daddy and Mary took me to West Germany two years ago, and France last summer; Mummy has only taken me to Southwold, and to a little cottage in Wales. She didn't need her passport and nor did I need mine.

* * *

I don't go to school on Monday because I'm too upset by all that has happened. Can't sit in a classroom; can't even sit still at home. My school is new to me—first year of secondary— and I hardly know any of the girls; I couldn't bear for them to see me crying.

Crack Up or Play It Cool

In the afternoon, the police lady—the very one who took me home from my mother's house on Friday evening—comes around with another policeman. He doesn't even wear a uniform and Mary says he's so important that he doesn't have to. They want to interview me. They do it in our lounge; I'm not a suspect, so they don't have to take me to the station for roughing up. Because I'm a child, Mary Moron has to sit in on the talk. I think it should be my Daddy, my blood relative who does that. He went to work this morning as if nothing has happened. Doesn't care that he has lost his wife just because he has another one. I have only one mummy. That's all anyone has. Stepmummies are rubbish.

The policeman does all the talking, and the woman police officer just smiles like she is sucking on a boiled sweet. It's chronic, my mum has disappeared and she acts like she's trying to coax a smile out of me. When she drove me home three days ago, I was crying and crying, and the police lady said it was all right, said that she'd have done the same if she had no idea where her mummy was. I can't see why she has changed her tune. Trying to act manly with the important policeman in the room, I expect. It is daft, really. Men get it wrong trying not to cry when they are upset, acting like death and war and car crashes are the most normal things on Earth. I think Daddy has gone to work to prove the very same point. He's probably getting all the physics wrong, muddled and befuddled. He must feel something. He was married to her for seven years. Didn't want to divorce Mummy at all, judging by how they carried on afterwards. She might have chosen to move out because of all the undergraduates. They never said. Parents always tell their children as little as they can get away with.

'When you last saw your mother, how would you describe her behaviour?' asks the plainclothes policeman.

'She behaved like she always does. Just looked after me.'

'Do you know if she was still seeing Joe Azzopardi?'

'She never told me about him. I only know what Daddy and Stepmummy have said to me.' Mary listens like I might hold the key to the mystery but I don't: I know nothing at all. Mary wears a green skirt, quite a long one but you can see her sun-tanned calves, they have been that dark since May and it is September now. Above the skirt, she has a white blouse with some red stitching over the breast and on the cuff. It is nice but she dresses like Daddy's undergraduate students. She was doing something called post-graduate research before she had the stupid baby, and then she stopped doing anything but nappy-changing and having the sprog suck on her titty-pa-pas. Rocking the unblinking blob close to her chest all day long. She sits on the edge of the sofa, beside me. I think it might not even be me she is listening to but straining in case Simon starts crying in the next room. He sleeps, twenty hours a day. I know he's only very, very young but I could tell her now, he won't make it to the post-graduate research. Can't sit up properly yet.

The policeman seems to write a lot down even though I can tell them nothing that will lead them to where Mummy is hiding. He confers with the police lady. Eventually, he asks, 'Do you think she was ashamed of her relationship with Mr Azzopardi.'

'No, I don't think so. I'm a child and no one talks to me about anything. Have you closed the ports in case they are trying to leave the country? She might be in the boot of a car.'

'You have some very good ideas, young lady, but there is only so much we are able to do. At this point in time, it looks like your mother left home by choice. The way she did it is unusual, so we are keeping an open mind. We are asking people who know her if they know of anyone else—a friend of hers, male or female—who might also have gone away around the same time. Do you have any thoughts?'

I think it would be less disgusting if she has run away with a girlfriend but it still wouldn't make any sense. Girls behave themselves in each other's company—keep their clothes on—even grown-up ones. 'She has a lot of friends but I don't know if any are missing.'

'Any special friends? A man. Or even a woman.'

'Daddy is her special friend,' I say very quietly. The police people both look at Mary. She says nothing. I think she looks a bit worried. Like she knows I could tell them some juicy gossip. I don't because none of it explains where Mummy has gone.

'Anyone else?' asks the policeman.

'Maltese Joe, only I never saw him. It's what Daddy said. And her.' I point my thumb at my stepmother.

The policeman nods. I don't get the impression that I am much help to them, and I want to find my mummy so much, I'd do anything. The trouble is, the police are not much good either. I know they haven't found a ransom note but I still think kidnapping is the most likely explanation. The kidnapper might have taken her passport too, and then hypnotised her so she doesn't say anything when they walk through customs. France or Holland probably, where the boats go. I don't say it, because I don't know what's happened and detectives don't take much notice of schoolgirls like me. I don't know why they've even bothered to come round. They should be searching her house more thoroughly. Azzopardi's house too. Looking everywhere.

* * *

The following weekend—and I went to school on Thursday and Friday, couldn't concentrate, but I went—Daddy sits me down for another of these terrible and serious talks. Thankfully, Mary and Simon are out of the house, visiting a friend; Mary's friend, Simon doesn't have any.

He tells me that the police have located Joe Azzopardi. He lives in Fulham and he told them that he hasn't seen my mother in weeks.

Daddy says that the police were thorough. 'They searched his flat but no one thinks he's lying.'

There is another man that someone has said Mummy has been seeing. I know that seeing, in this context, means looking into each other's eyes and then getting under the bedcovers. I don't pick up who said it exactly because I don't like the talk at all. It makes Mummy sound like a slapper, and she isn't one in the slightest. I thought she only did naughty things with her husband, ex-husband too, but it is the same person. And she is better than him. He's the one with the undergraduates. 'She might be in touch, and I'm putting a notice in newspapers here and abroad to ask her to do just that. It is all we can do for now, Sophie.'

I ask all the questions I can think of. No one has phoned asking for a ransom. The police have not found any evidence of a struggle in her house. Her bank account had a cash withdrawal three days before she went missing. Two hundred and fifty pounds: it doesn't really explain it. Quite a lot but she has far more left behind.

'Your mother is still quite attractive,' says my father. 'She might have found herself a rich man.' I glare at him. Quite attractive? He's been doing Jolly Roger with her for the last dozen years, a divorce didn't stop him. 'It's the most likely explanation but we won't know for sure until she's back in touch.'

Daddy sounds like he doesn't care a jot. I start crying again. Loud awful crying. If she's found someone better to kiss than a few stolen moments with my father, it is no surprise. It is me she should have run away with; I would even have put up with another man. Any man. It couldn't be worse than doe-eyed Mary and her stupid bug-baby.

5.

I have been home for over three hours before the texts start to come in. I'm unsure why it has taken him so long. Simon is a bright boy. Bright, weird and an awful lot larger than I had understood before today. And I set eyes upon him for only half a second. The blink of an eye. Not a moment more.

> ***Craig is a dirty-minded little git. My sincere apologies if he embarrassed you earlier***

So, there it is. Simon is the gentleman of the household, and their previous abode in Carnforth too. My father would doubtless have tried it on if I'd been an undergrad and not his daughter. Probably wouldn't give me a second look now I'm thirty, although my figure is exactly as it was at university. My weight too. Craig was embarrassing. What he said did not need the airing; however, I must admit, I actually had put the short dress on with Simon in mind. I was trying to nudge him out of his never-see-a-soul groove. And his room stank: perhaps it was sweat not wank if he is truly a gentleman. I've never lived with teenage boys, left before those guys got there. Or gigantic twenty-one-year-olds.

> ***I have heard not so much as a hint of wedding bells in connection with your name, Sophie. I think that means you lead a racier life than young Craig dare imagine***

Fuck. Was I wrong? He is a twisted little fucker—great big fucker, in fact—how long has Simon been imagining my racy life. An hour ago, I telephoned Topping, tried my luck once more with Grace. I tried to explain how I needed a little physical comfort, somebody to hold me in her arms. Nothing more. I don't think she quite believed me, recalled only how I ravaged her during our first private meeting. Away from the gazes of men, she and I both attracting plenty of those when we were in Filchers or The Kilderkin. I fear Grace Topping has tried and rejected sapphism, although she seemed to lap it up for those few hours we spent in each other's company. I told her, simply because she is an actor and might have been interested in a fellow thespian, that I was seeing Mica Barry the following day. That she would be driving me to see my stepmother in the women's prison in Kent. Grace was curious about this, asked me what my connection with Mica is. This was a stumbling block. I realised that the newspapers have never connected the murder of Cynthia Hartnell, or the subsequent arrest of Mary Stephenson, with the celebrated actress. I would hate to fall out with Monica, knew better than to be the source of such a leak. I tried to imply it was my journalistic connections, Mica Barry phoning me out of the blue.

'Tell me about it afterwards,' she replied. The obscure theatre performer, Grace Topping, believed my assertion a fantasy, I'm sure she did. A sexual fantasy probably, going inside a women's prison with Mica. My wicked stepmother locked up in there too. If it were not true, I expect she would have a point.

I could text Simon back, ask if he was looking through the blackout window or not. I am unsure how he copes with those questions. His own proclivities. He might be more honest than even I would wish to hear him tell.

> *I meant what I said; nothing has changed between us*
>
> *But everything has changed*
>
> *An awful lot, Simon, not anything between you and I*

The reply to this one is not immediate. It is difficult to guess what this means. I don't think any of us really knows what he is doing in his room all day. He might have put his phone down and picked up a book. It may mean nothing at all. I didn't tell him directly that I will be seeing his mother tomorrow but Craig did. He knows now. Perhaps I would have got around to it but it is hard to get the measure of a man beneath a blanket. I actually envy Craig's easy rapport—he says what he feels—bugger the oddity of getting no reciprocity until the texts start to arrive.

Monica has an uneasy relationship with both her nephews, Mary's boys. I think she gets along with me to make up for it. Or to get one over on her sister. Theirs is a complicated kinship. She has said—a time or two over the years—that Mary should have treated me better, not approached me differently than her own simply because I am step. She also excuses her, saying she was 'too immature, too full of herself, too much the science nerd, to see the world from a small child's perspective,' when she first came into my life. That stuff does nothing for me. I doubt if she believes Mary's tales of how bloody awkward a kid I was. Sophie the shocker, that was young me. Kid-bitch. Before my mother disappeared, I could spend an entire day in Mary's company holding my tongue out as a rude display. She was actually quite patient but I knew how to make her crack. Be the stronger! And this all comes down to my true gripe: Mary doesn't belong. Monica has told me that her sister had no idea of all my father's affairs until long after she was married. She married for love and a life of mutual scientific endeavour. It is hard for me to remember anything precise from that long ago, and still I think I could have put her straight before the ceremony. If she'd only asked. My mother certainly could have and should have. None of this would have happened then, surely. Monica said that Mary knew only my father's highly sanitised version of the first marital breakdown. You'd think she'd have gone in for scientific enquiry. When I was young, I thought she married for the money. There is an awful lot of it. Always thought that was her motivation. Both for marrying and for staying.

Can you pass a message from me to Monica?

And I expected he might have one for the sainted Mary. Craig tried to send her his love, and then couldn't quite say the L-word.

Of course, I can. Or could you text her?

You say it. She is to weigh up the body language and report back to me what she thinks: innocent or guilty?

No beating around the bush with Simon.

I'll ask; can't guess how much she will like the question. A sister is not a judge

I can tell if Craig is lying or telling the truth. It's sibling knowledge not a mystical power. I expect the same of Monica

Auntie Monica, to you

Monica

I really don't give a damn what he calls her. And I believe his faith misplaced. Craig is his little brother and he knows his experience, may catch him out lying on the coattails of that. Whether he will have the same skill in twenty-years-time is quite another matter. I have only half-siblings, a father who has hidden my mother's death from me these nineteen years. He is my closest blood relative. Ignorance is not just an easy state, it may be our natural state. Knowledge hurts like buggery, it really does.

* * *

I have tried to go to sleep, achieved it to the most modest degree although my phone buzzes and the visit I am to undertake with Auntie Monica weighs heavily on my mind. It is ten to one, I look at the eleven texts which Simon Stephenson has sent me. He is a hard-hearted boy, I like that.

Our father is a liar of the very worst kind. Presents himself in the nicest possible light knowing full well that it is not regular phooey but utter deceit. He could be a murderer; he plays a similar game with the police

I am sorry one or more of my parents' actions have denied you the opportunity to grieve properly for your mother. I do not think I am culpable but my birth may be a significant factor in the events which unfolded. NB. I mean it, but 'grieve properly' is as alien a thought to me as 'praising the Lord.' Neither action registers squat outside the carousels of our own minds. Apologies if I am missing something on this point

Craig says our mother is innocent. She certainly hasn't confessed to anything, contrary to our father. I have read about fugue states in which the mentally ill act out behaviours which they afterwards cannot recall. I think she had some post-natal meltdown when I was refusing to play baby ball, being my static self. Might she have gone crazy and not known about it? I think I gave her a hatful of reasons

I don't enjoy reading this particular text. I recall no such illness in Mary, although it might have been my inability to comprehend adult behaviour when I was young. That she did it has become my overarching belief, the how and the why elude me completely. This explains and excuses in equal measure; however, whatever the chain of events, I shall not be forgiving. I'm not made that way. I also dislike hearing Simon talk so analytically of fugue states. He has had one or two of his own in the past. I don't know what he remembers. Eleven windows he broke in the house in Carnforth. In about fifteen minutes. I called him psycho for several months on the back of that. I regret it enormously; happened in my kid-bitch phase. From the age of eleven to about seventeen.

> *No one else was involved. Dad would be indicating who with an introductory drumroll if there was such a person. They have the culprit(s), we just don't understand the detail yet*

Yes, Simon. If only it made sense.

> *Craig bursts into my room, as my mother used to at Windermere Court, because they are trying to make our abnormal family normal. Dad too. Seldom, but he tried it once or twice. My relationship with you has long been on a sounder footing. No pretence. I was disappointed that you showed your face at the door today. Profoundly. Obviously, I forgive you, Sophie, but for clarity, please read this text again*

I do as he asks—Simon is unflinchingly honest with me—I owe him that.

> *Like Craig and I, you have been granted respite from normal life mid the melee that is our family's sorry state. The Sunday Noise is not worth reading without an article in your name*

I text back a reply to this one.

> *Sweet of you to say it; sadly, many of my own articles are just the dross that the owners of the said Noise insist upon. I can but try*

After pressing send, I spot the flaw in his question. Craig and I are taking a breather from the world. Simon the Pieman never joined.

> ***Do you remember the stray cat which Craig adopted about eight years ago? It disappeared two years ago, only our mother feeding it by then. It was one day in September that it went, possibly the same date, plus seventeen years, as poor Cynthia Hartnell. Coincidence?***

God, this is Simon at his insensitive best. I cannot recall the cat. I left Carnforth for York long before then, still went back now and then—I was a student—found my way to London at twenty-one. Before this cat entered Windermere Court, I fancy. The dates suggest it was my replacement. Apt, I suppose. Perhaps it was there when I visited but I am not really an animal lover. It wouldn't have registered with me; I consider animals to be pointless except for bees. I take honey in my tea, and have a soft spot for them for that reason alone. I think his text is a speculative admission that Mary is responsible. Possibly for the disappearance of one of God's creatures for each of the last eighteen years.

> ***What was the cat's name?***

He will fathom that I don't recall it, and may reveal more of his theory when replying.

> ***I enjoy knowing Father is in prison. He has never been able to empathise with me. This will be edifying for him***
>
> ***You wanted me to see you sunning yourself on the lawn this afternoon, Sophie. You looked cheap. I wish you hadn't***

Is that ouch, or is Simon struggling with the recollection. Loving what he professes to hate. God knows what I will do next time. Bikini or burqa, I could flip a coin.

Channel 5 is showing early episodes of Shoes and Slippers, midnight Tuesdays and Thursdays. Monica is hilarious. An intense young woman, one might say

Tell Mother that I am missing her. I appreciate all she has put up with on my account. She doesn't deserve this

I cannot reply to this. She deserves hell on Earth if I am right about what she has done. I thought her misfortune in having spawned Simple Simon to be exactly that for the longest time. I was wrong; he is not simple but weirdly delightful. I am fallible. Wow, has that thought just crossed my mind?

It has passed one o'clock in the morning and a single-word text arrive in my phone.

Marmalade

That is an old-fashioned drivel of a name for any cat.

Mary named him—this is speculation on my part but it isn't a lad's name; if Daddy were to name anything, it would be a comet or a distant galaxy, never something as mundane as a cat—*so why would she kill him?*

One neither remembers nor forgets fugue states. They come back to you each time you slip back there

My thumbs could not have written it as quickly as it came in. And Simon should know. The more I think about this, the truer it gets, and the more frightened I feel. Psycho-stepmother had nothing against Cynthia Hartnell, her devilish alter ego hit upon the surest way to shatter my world, my peace, my heart. I was a rum stepdaughter. Might have deserved it but Mummy really didn't.

Chapter Five:

Mary Jail

1.

I am awake at five-thirty. It is absurd. I like Monica, have nothing to fear from her. To share time will be a pleasure. The visit might be the oddest of my life—South Kent Women's Prison—I will not be telling my aunt of the pleasure which seeing my stepmother banged-up might bring me. I have climbed out of bed, the flat is still warm, such is this balmy September. I feel I should dress up but it might be a poor choice. I am long over my teenage crush on this beloved relative who is only eleven years my senior. I think grown-up crushes may be worse. I am worried that I will blurt out inappropriate phrases to her. Advise her of my life-long lesbianism, which the occasional boy has thus far hidden from my family. Advise her that I've converted a couple of one-time heterosexual ladies to the cause. Tipped Grace Topping that way if only temporarily.

I must do none of this. Today I research the most important case I have ever worked on. Mary will speak to Monica as she never would to me. I climb back under the covers. Monica does not look the same as she did seven or eight years ago. Has not been on a magazine cover in that time, although I found a small picture of her inside my television guide last week. They are showing repeats of Oakengates. For fully three years she played Lady Hornchurch. The Noise christened her Lady Hornychurch.

Half the men in the country watched, collectively they put the rating of a period drama up miles above where it belonged. And it was pretty chaste stuff. To the best of my knowledge, Monica has never appeared in a sex scene. An on-screen snog her raciest, although the camera has caught many a cheeky smile. I didn't make up the name, the Horny thing, didn't work on the paper at the time. I think she looks even better now—comfortable in her pleasing skin—and if my eye for the older woman is a minority taste, so be it. I dare not sleep for fear of oversleeping. I cannot imagine that we will hear a confession; Mary is of too rigid a construction for any little cracks to tug her apart. I must look for signs, subtle signs. I will not advise Monica of my quest, she loves Mary. Does it with a big fatty lump of dislike in the mix. They have fallen out many times, I have concluded. Mary has told me nothing of that; Monica is the more honest, and sadly, only a sporadic companion. My once-in-a-blue-moon friend.

It is funny to relate. Many people—inside the family and out, those who know of my almost-kinship to the famous Mica—have told me that my stepmother is the more beautiful sister. The finer features. Mary went physics, Monica acting. It is a daunting profession; nothing can upstage talent. Looks help but not without a true aptitude to begin with. Monica is a serious performer. She can convince an audience that she is any kind of woman imaginable. Mary is just herself. A young siren who got my father's pecker up, never realised that her desirability on his arm at faculty functions cannot make up for whatever lacklustre bedroom antics are her limit. I even think Daddy used her as a lightning rod. Other young girls saw the professor parading his slight consort. Wished themselves in her shoes, and with the thought of mimicking her he drew them in. It's a blood sport for Daddy: he admires the odd catch but it is the tally—knife-carved notches on the bedpost—which motivates him. A competitive snooker player will always keep his cue chalked. I think he has gone off the boil since this semi-retirement. And prison must have cramped his style completely. Back to Mary, her looks did nothing for me. I see why people say it but her connection to others is insipid; there is no joy in her smile. It is as meaningful as the silk scarves she may drape across her shoulders. An adornment.

Monica has connected to us all, one role or another has touched every theatregoer and television watcher in the country. Me more than most. I might ask her to be my surrogate mother. If her sister killed my actual one—and I think she did—it would be the best redress the Bredbury family could offer. By a thousand miles. I mustn't say it; she would have me admitted to the lunatic asylum. And that might be the only place on Earth as grim as South Kent Women's Prison.

* * *

When she arrives and buzzes the intercom. I say, 'Hi. Would you like to come up?'

'I'm not properly parked, sorry. I'll wait in the car. I'm just in front of your building.'

This pours cold water on my plan, flusters me a little. I hoped to have a coffee with Monica before leaving Bayswater. A catch up. 'Just a mo and I'll be down.' I don't think I can contradict my famous aunt, so we must start with a drive and not a coffee. I look for the right shoes. It's a little cooler today but I look best in summer dresses. I carry a cardigan too, won't wear it unless the heating in her car is defunct.

I make it out in one minute. Cannot keep Mica Barry waiting. Actually, I suspect I can but shouldn't push it, this is our first meet-up in about four years.

'Hiya.' I open the rear door a little tentatively. 'I'll just pop this down here,' I say, placing my cardigan on the backseat.

'God, Sophie, you look a million dollars.' Her compliment

is a melody in my ears. Then she adds, 'Bait for the lezzers in the women's prison, I fear.'

Yuk. My step-auntie hates my type, and she won't have even guessed that her comment offends me. I see that she wears a shell suit. It might be still more offensive than her throwaway remark. Clothing I do not—and would not—own. I have standards. Expected them of Auntie Monica, likewise. As I slide into the front seat, beside her, tugging my shortish dress down as far as the seated posture will allow, a different perspective enters my mind. In the past, Mica Barry's face has been on the front of the TV Times: the first time was when she was leaving the soap opera, Shoes and Slippers; and she was there again when she first played the young aristocrat in Oakengates, the oft-repeated period drama. I'm sure that—visiting a women's prison—she has no wish to be recognised. Sensible clothing for the task. Even her gorgeous fair hair looks mousier today, a simple grip keeping it left. Not a way I have seen her wear it before. I can also see that the two sisters were the fairest sights in titchy little Charmouth, Dorset, in their younger days. Attracted boys a-plenty, I'm sure. 'I've been in these places before and got out in one piece,' I tell her.

'Soph's,' she says, and I think I like her familiarity although I am prevaricating, 'I've got every sympathy with you. It's going to be a most difficult visit. The best of us can muck our lives up. God knows, Mary's done a bit of that. And as well as looking great, you have dressed perfectly for my purposes. The attention will be on you, and I'm keen not to make it into the Sunday Noise. Not for visiting a suspected murderer. So far, so good on that front. I must thank you for that, surely. Putting family before a scoop, and not a family you can be too enamoured with.' Interesting. I think her lezzers comment may have been no more than casual talk. Thespians are usually liberal-minded, or that is how they purport to be, managing it in practice might challenge a few.

The traffic is snarled up, the car quite stationary. She looks across at me again. The nicest smile on her handsome features. 'Sophie, it must be so tough. How are you?'

'Fine.' Before the word is out properly, I find tears welling behind my eyes. This step-relative of mine has a hold over me that I cannot define. 'You ask more nicely than anyone else,' I tell her, shaking a hand, meaning she must ignore my tears. Trying to explain what I cannot.

As we make our way out of London, edging towards the M25, I tell her a little about how it has been. I speak of Simon and Craig. Tell her that I called around to support them but cannot really tell how any family member received it. Except for Uncle Phil who simply didn't.

'You are so good. I sent Craig a card but I've no idea what to say to them. I haven't been. I'm not close like you, Sophie.' When there is a short silence, she asks, 'How's Simon coping.'

'He is a most objective young man.'

Monica laughs. At my serious tone, I think. 'Objective, not objectionable. That's a blessing. I feel for him, Sophie, I really do. And he is brighter than anyone thought likely before he got his fingers on texting facilities. Wilful in the extreme, don't you think? I'm not sure how it makes him objective; suppose I should bow to your superior knowledge. To your closer relationship.'

'Monica, you ask how he is bearing up: Simon doesn't really let the ebb and flow of life affect him. If emotions pass him by, he believes it makes his opinions less cluttered.'

She thinks about this for a moment. Quite a ponderous look, no smile on her face. 'What does he make of all this?'

'I think he has it in for my father. Our father. Your brother-in-law.'

The certainty my brother expressed surprised me yesterday, and now Monica is laughing about it. 'I'm objective too then, Sophie.'

I don't think that is objectivity. I know Monica never thought Mary wise to marry Paul Stephenson, hated all that he did behind her back. She is protective of her sister, although it was all Mary's stupid fault. She should have had her fling and then walked away from him, then my mother would still live. I am sure of it, although I have no certainty over the precise order of events. No insight at all into how Cynthia Hartnell came to rest in that awful grave.

* * *

Even finding the motorway does not allow us any greater speed in our journey towards South Kent Prison. The traffic is crawling. I have told Monica all I know of Craig's and Simon's respective views on the events that have befallen our family. Monica spoke quite coolly of her sister's predicament. My stepmother's. She does not believe her capable of murder. 'She is flawed, Sophie,' she said at one point, 'but she has a pervading honesty. If she had done it, she would have admitted it. Wouldn't be able to lie in the faces of police officers. You know what I think? I think there is no proof. Your father's admission is part of the picture, his accusations about Mary are a mystery.'

Once again, as I did all those years ago when the famous Mica Barry took her schoolgirl interviewer for dinner, I raised the issue of my mother hooking up with my father to cheat on Mary. A pretty odd way around, the first wife usurping the second, and all on the sly. 'And you know the order of events, Sophie,' she reminded me. 'Mary had reason all her married life, and it sounds like your mother finally gave your miscreant father the shove when she began to see other people.'

'Who knows how any of them thought in that messed up love triangle,' I said. I can't fathom it at all. I'm not a jealous sort, or maybe it would come upon me if I ever sustained a relationship beyond a dozen dates. Guy or girl; the latter suit me better.

Now having talked out the Stephensons—civilly, Monica is always that—she asks what she has never asked before. 'Do you have someone, Sophie? A fella. Somebody you can lean on through this.'

I am not sure what it is that makes me so taciturn about all that is at the heart of this question, with this lovely woman, and with my wider family too. I am proud of what I am, what I do. Opt to keep it under wraps a little longer, say only a bit of daft bravado. 'I'm a singleton on a mission, Monica. There was someone for a week or two but it's over. A guy called Mushtaq gave me his number yesterday. I might call it. I can be game for that.' As I say it, I recall that I never kept the piece of paper. And the lad had a wall-eye.

'Fast and loose,' she says. 'Whatever suits. For myself, I've found that a regular, reliable confidante can be more...' Monica concentrates on the road for a moment; I wonder if she is off-piste giving relationship advice. She confessed it was not her strong suit back in the day. '...emotionally stabilising.'

'Yeah. But me and Simon don't bother with emotions, remember. Simon's alternatives I don't fathom. I'm good if the sex is good.' I know that my face has reddened a little. Ridiculous, I am more than old enough to do anything I please. It would be tragic if I hadn't. This auntie is important to me or was before this strange journey began. I don't know if I am exploding our once-good rapport, or taking it to a new level of honesty. I am not being quite as honest as I could be, perhaps these are the approaches. Travelling in this car I think with a little longing about Monica, about the content of her absurd shell suit, and I have never given a moment's consideration to Mushtaq. I believe his Cornish pastie was his greatest attraction and I wouldn't eat one of those if you paid me.

'As you please, Sophie. I was enquiring, not lecturing. That kind of life has never been mine.'

'Never? No quick and meaningless hook-ups.'

'Not since Charmouth. Acting school maybe. And I didn't think them meaningless at the time. After the event, I reappraised. You know how it is?'

'Did you and Mary share all these thoughts when you were young? Talk about who you'd kissed.'

'Ha. You were like an only child, weren't you, Sophie? The boys along a hell of a lot later. Mary's boys.'

'Yes, That's right.'

'I had a brother six years older—Stephen, you've met him—he'd left the little hometown before I was ready to kiss. And Mary, three years. She tried to warn me off doing everything she'd done; really cross that I took no notice. And we were neither truly wild. Just a little teenage curiosity. Nothing to make a song and dance over.'

I think about this for a moment. I led a chaste life, almost a nun's life, until I found freedom at university. Went a bit mad in that first term. Dates with two or three different boys each week for a short number of weeks. Before I found the courage for girls. 'You and me, both,' I tell Monica. It doesn't cover it but it's all I dare tell her. Must suffice.

* * *

Our entry into South Kent Women's Prison is every bit as intrusive and degrading as my earlier visit to Retford. Monica glances enlarged eyes my way with every pat down she receives. The prison staff appears to be a workforce of women, strong of arm and scary of scowl. Monica may have had a point: wall to wall lezzers and not one of them a proper girl's girl. They are more likely to bed skunks than actual human ladies. I see one or two looking me over. I am not entirely stupid, wear thin tights, they can only imagine the flesh of my legs although I allow them to see the shape. All the other visitors dress like Monica. I expect that for most, if

Mary Jail

not all, it is the extent of their wardrobe. Shell suits or leopard-print leggings. My step-aunt is acting, plying her trade. For her alone it is a cunning disguise.

The names on our passes are obscure. Mica Barry does not make the form, Monica Bredbury still the most honest—and inconspicuous—name she can give. I write Sophie Stephenson; it is Mary Stephenson I have come to visit. Still the portly, butch, short-haired prison guard says, 'Don't I know you.' She is looking me up and down, every which way. Sophie Stevens is the name that makes the newspaper, and my columns do not carry a photograph. I did once speak for about ten seconds on the main ITV news, eighteen months ago now. The story was about a thieving councillor, one who took his own life before the laborious arm of the law could finally corner him for the corruption which I had been honing in on for months. I cannot imagine a know-nothing prison warder recognising me from that fugacious clip. I expect she recognises my type, fantasises about slim girls with short black hair in her free time; knowledge of me, she will have none. Monica looks around as I deal with this unlikely query, tries not to smile, I think, for fear of making herself known. She was in a crime drama last year—mother of a murdered child—and this sort probably stay in and watch them. The guard couldn't really go clubbing with a face like hers. Not unless they have special clubs in Ashford or Dover, or wherever it is we have driven to. Ugly Heaven or Gay and Gormless, clubs of that ilk. Dread to think what the fat sods get up to in there.

* * *

The corridor down which we walk is low-ceilinged, bare in every respect, and it smells of urine. Not sharp but I've an enquiring nose. Not that ladies' urine is a bouquet I hanker for. Again, I wear a lanyard with my likeness printed within: the visitors pass. I look good in the photo. Monica, on the other hand, managed a momentary scowl at the flash of the camera. She looks awkward and even a little unpleasant in that passport-sized photograph. What a professional! The lesbian-in-charge opens a door and we see prisoners already sitting at eight or nine tables. They have tea, served in pastel-coloured plastic beakers, held in hand or resting upon the tables before them. It brings a children's party to mind.

It is unusual for me to think anything good about my stepmother; however, I have to grant that she is the most attractive prisoner in the room by about a zillion miles, prisoner or guard. A model among monkeys. And only one of the women I refer to as a monkey is black in skin colour. My comment is not racist. They are all ungroomed, the entire roost. Might have knits, they are clearly miserable, lacking in poise. The whites in particular. The downtrodden of this Earth. Imprisoned and they can't blame it on a police force that targets them. I find myself feeling sorry that Mary Stephenson—who never really lifted a finger for me but we shared formative time, her early marital years, my school days—has come to rest among such human detritus. She has lived a life far above this; seeing her brought so low might be more difficult than I anticipated. As we cross the room, she erupts in tears. I feel most uncomfortable. Monica steps around the table and hugs her. Before we know it, a light is flashing and two of the big lesbian guards have stepped into the fray, pulled the sisters apart. Four more come to the door, the room is suddenly anarchic, and it is at my stepmother's table alone that the pandemonium bug has struck. I have no inclination to hug the distraught woman, but allow my face to show a measure of sympathy. I see that incoming guards make eye contact with each prisoner. Assure themselves it is not a riot. The other prisoners look too slovenly for that. The fat prison officer who brought us here has a hold of Monica.

'Get off,' shouts my wonderful aunt.

Mary Jail

Another one has pulled Mary up from her chair.

'Pat them down,' instructs the one who doesn't know she is holding a TV star.

These two fatties rummage their hungry paws all over Monica and her sister. I see how she puts her hands on my aunt's breasts. 'Got to check you've put nothing in there,' she tells her, as if a bra might be a shopping basket. Monica is allowing the patting down. She turns when the fat guard swivels her. It could be a dance, then the woman pats her behind, dips a hand inside her shell suit bottom, right around the front as I would never dare without a signal of consent. And Monica looks positively against it.

'Nothing down there. You're in the clear.'

'I gave her a hug because she was upset,' says Monica.

'We explained the rules,' says fatty.

I wasn't watching the other tussle but I think the more acned guard was just as physical with my stepmother. Intrusive. Mary looks shocked, and the tears which flooded out of her upon seeing us have slowed but not ceased. She is snivelling. I think I will be pleased about it this evening, for the time being my false sympathy feels genuine, even to me. It is a horrible place to be, and then she is denied the comfort of a caring sister.

Prison visits do send one's feelings skidding hither and thither; I wonder what my nemesis has to say for herself.

* * *

She has been speaking for an age. The guards might be deaf; they have let her speak about the most important of issues. Watching faces and not listening to any words is my best explanation. Mary tells all—truth or lie—it is preparation for the forthcoming police interviews, the distant trial. It is why she is here, and I am rapt. Out of the blue, she takes my hand across the table. 'So good of you to come, Sophie. I know I haven't always been the mother you needed. And now you've all of this to cope with. It must be so awful for you. And your father's role...' Mary has been stating her innocence, her surprise at the discovery of the body. Her complete mystification as to why her husband should finger her for the murder. She has hinted at a reason while also acknowledging that it is all beyond her. '...he told me she'd fled. South Africa, he was sure of it. Sounded to be sure of it. I go over and over it. Cynthia had connections there, you see. He said that she did, I wouldn't have known. Scarcely knew her.'

I am actually aware of these supposed connections. Not when I was a child, later, in one or two conversations with my father, he told me that my mother had 'long ago developed feelings' for a man called Van der Linde. Marick Van der Linde, of Cape Town. 'Could be anywhere now,' said Daddy. 'Montevideo or bloody Scotland. Anywhere at all.' Even when we talked about this in my mid-twenties, I struggled to believe she would have walked out on me for a smooth-talking man. She loved me as a proper mother should. 'Diamonds. And he was the shadiest dealer in them, I have to say. His skulduggery was common knowledge—not in my circles—found out only when I made enquiries. I'm surprised she ever fell for him. Met him when we were still married too. I don't know if she got up to anything she shouldn't have back then.' I remember laughing at him when he said that. If he could screw every undergraduate who enrolled on his silly physics course without bringing their own willy, why shouldn't Mummy have a fling. It was the thought that the man had taken her from me that rankled, not her taking of a little pleasure. And I never figured out how Maltese Joe came into the picture. When or why.

While she talks, she cries. At first, I liked it. I cannot push from my mind the thought that my father has been telling the truth. He helped bury the woman my stepmother killed. That Mary, who sits before me, may have murdered my own mother. The alternative would be that Daddy acted alone;

even if the arrival of Maltese Joe and this other guy meant his sex on tap dried up, it would not constitute a reason for killing, surely it wouldn't. My mother was only one of many sources of pleasure for Imperial College's own playboy.

Her hand remains on mine, Mary speaks with both a warmth and an insecurity I have never before detected. Or perhaps I have seen her that way with the two boys but never with me. I have always thought of her as the cold scientist, a contrast to my father. The warm and fickle one.

'I can't imagine what you're going through, Sophie. Finding out after all these years. I try to imagine, honestly, I do. Prison makes for a contemplative outlook. I don't think I deserve this. Arrested for what I never did. I think that if I'd known, understood that you were truly motherless, I would have tried harder. Should have. Should have done it regardless, I know that, Sophie.' The tears tracking down her cheeks make Mary Stephenson look ugly. I often thought to myself that she looked stupid, not physics-stupid but life-stupid. Ugly? Never. Yet that is now the case. Monica, the more famous—not necessarily the better boned of the pair—is trying to look inconspicuous, pulling it off nonchalantly, and yet she is a thousand times more glamourous than Mary right now. That must be what prison has done to her. Am I pleased? I think I should be but my feelings have gone haywire. I cannot work her out. 'Can I talk about your father,' says Mary. 'I want to say it for myself, not to upset you.'

I nod assent. I'm at the end of the road with him, anyhow. For nineteen years the only person who has consistently spoken of loving me—and of whom I believed it true for the longest time—has kept my mother's true fate a secret. Denied me simple grief.

'He courted me in nineteen-seventy-five. You will have seen me a handful of times that year but you were too young to remember. He was divorcing Cynthia at the time. In fact, I thought he was divorced when I met him. If he didn't say it, he implied it. It was terribly strange looking back. Paul was my tutor; I was just eighteen.' She looks at me levelly, tears abated, now. 'Am I embarrassing you with this, Sophie?'

'Go on,' I say.

Monica sits unstirred. Not without interest; she is waiting, anticipating. I understand from our infrequent, and occasionally intense, conversations that she has always pressed Mary to be more open and honest with me than she has previously achieved. Incarceration seems to have improved her.

'I grew up in West Dorset, so being in London, having a tutor with a published book on applied physics, might have gone to my head. Our courtship was old-fashioned, I practiced a restraint I'd not known I had. That seemed to be as Paul wanted. Your father. That is the strangest thing, looking back. He is an animal in his pursuit of girls. Rather early in my marriage, I realised this. And it sickened me. But before I married him, that was not the man I perceived. Courteous, winning. Oftentimes he seemed too aware of the vast age difference. Wished me to continue seeing people my own age, trusted me to do so. Completely trusting, I thought. The awful thing...' Mary glances at a guard, before turning her eyes again to my own, holding my gaze. '...I blamed myself. Thought I was failing in the bedroom. In the back of the car too; he was that sort of a lover. If he wanted more than I could offer, then I feared it was I who was not up to being the wife so famous a physicist needed. I was rather stupid about it all, I know. What once was so blurred, so difficult to understand becomes clear as a crystal looking back.'

I don't know anything about this at all. Never has she said anything like it to me, nor did I think about his infidelities beyond enjoying the notion that they might hurt her. And as an angry and precocious child, I figured his antics to be proof that Mary was deficient in the department she says she doubted herself. I knew nothing practical about sex when I made that link. Young and naïve, knew nothing whatsoever. Cruel of me, wasn't it? If a relationship is open, so be it. Clearly, there was no such arrangement between them. My father once told me—and I quote—that he 'loved women too much.' It was only the feeling of having his dick inside them that he loved. I think I knew that by the time he told me. Never feel sorry for Don Juan, if he looks forlorn it is simply his facial muscles at rest between conquests. Something has to give.

'Cynthia said to me...' Mary glances up from her own hands which she has been studying, again takes my eyes with her sad gaze. '...perhaps as a word of warning, that he had cheated on her more than she could bear. Before we were married, she said that. I didn't dare ask Paul. Looking back at it from here, I was still a child. I rationalised it. He implied their marriage was over, I thought Cynthia was trying to sow discord...' She reaches across the table, strokes the back of my hand once more. '...she said he'd started quite quickly after your birth. I think it may not be so unusual. The brief hiatus in relations presaging a bigger one.'

Oh dear, oh dear. My stepmother, a woman in her mid-forties, is blushing with some memory that she scarcely dares to disclose. If she is recalling making love to my father, I'd rather she says nothing. Some sounds are easily distinguished, however large one's house. I never watched—never ever—but Mary used to gasp a lot when they were humping. Five minutes tops. I should have long ago conceded how beautiful Mary looks but I wouldn't have stood for five minutes and on your bike. Why would he? And why else did he keep on screwing Mummy? Cynthia won that demeaning contest, even a pudding-brain could work it out, and I was far from that.

'You know all about the twenty-year age gap. At my wedding, our wedding, one of his colleagues...no, not just a colleague...the best man's speech...he said that Paul's bewitchment by me—that was the very phrase, "bewitchment by young Mary,"—said it had brought the "lecherous lecturer" back on track. Everyone laughed, and truly, I thought it was only the wordplay. Not that he had ever been so obvious. So blatant. You see, Sophie, it was not like that between us. When he touched my hand—back when we were nothing, no relationship above tutor student—touched my hand for no greater reason than handing back a paper, I felt something I wished to reciprocate. Didn't dare, being so young. Nor did he make any kind of advance. I thought he was the perfect gentleman. Thought it as a flood in my brain when he invited me to his house, a dinner party or something. I met his relatives—met Cynthia—and we weren't quite a couple. I was just a favoured student, one he took a proprietorial interest in. When it became apparent to both of us that our feelings for each other were romantic ones, he asked after my family. Considered how he might appear in my mother's eyes. She was a church-goer, you will recall. Strong views on the order of play in a courtship.' Then she turns her head. 'Monica, you remember that first summer?'

Monica raises a hand to her mouth as if to suppress an unintended smile. Or a scowl, I am not a mind-reader. 'Yeah, yeah. Tell Sophie, Mary. It's all good.'

'He was a gentleman. I feel ridiculous saying it after all that has gone on but it is how I saw it. How I still see it when I remember those days. Brief days, looking back. It was the nineteen-seventies, Sophie, I was not a virgin bride. Your father wooed me discreetly although...' Her eyes go back to her hands. '...we enjoyed relations before the wedding ceremony, did so many times. Paul had more concern for proprietary than any boy in Charmouth ever showed me. Or any boy but one. And Paul completely charmed my mother. Not slimily; got himself on her wavelength, at least after a fashion. Our mother was protective of us...' She smiles an aside to her sister. '...wasn't she Monica? But ambitious with it, on our behalf. Marrying a man with a detached house in Epsom and a family burial plot. Ha! She rather liked all that. And we honeymooned in the Loire. I'd never known a life like it. Blissful. I think you know that I returned from that first trip abroad—the honeymoon—to complete my degree. I was no longer living among other students. Back when I had been—my first two years of study, before I married your father—I had never heard a word of his advances towards other female students. Not a word. I didn't really know the older students. I think Cynthia's warning implied they had occurred. I felt myself to be in love with him; thought it reciprocated. Had need to know nothing more. He was all I knew of Imperial College, London, him and a bit of physics. Being a student, my hours were odd. And some days I stayed in Epsom, others were in the university, staying until evening. Paul encouraged me to keep up with my old friends, fellow students. There was an incident, towards the end of the autumn term. Three months after I'd married, around about then. We were meeting up in a little pub near Ravenscourt Park. A dive, we called it. As my little gaggle of friends and I arrived, three girls at a corner table stood up. Fits of laughter, and not sharing the joke at all. As they passed me, I heard one say, "It is her. It's his wife." That brought about another flume of unenjoyable laughter. The flailing, despairing kind. I could not interpret the deeper meaning of the words, something about them made me feel wretched. My friends were all for beers and wines. I ordered a glass of mineral water and left without drinking it.'

'Mary,' says Monica, across her, 'I think Soph knows how her father treated you. Are you going to tell her why you stayed?'

'But Monica, it was complicated. I was living in a house four times the size of any other I'd ever lived in; my husband was a leading authority in his field. I thought he deserved to be Chair of Faculty; he was the brightest at Imperial. Much later I learnt that there were reputational concerns...' Mary shakes her head as she completes the sentence. '...about his behaviour with the undergraduates. The girls.'

'Is that why?' I ask. Interrupt, and I feel I should have figured this long before now. 'Did we move up to darkest Lancashire all because he was persona non grata at Imperial? Or any decent university, come to that?'

Mary is nodding. And judging by Monica's face, I'm the last to know. Some investigative journalist I've turned out to be. 'Lancaster was a terrific opportunity. It was even a chance for Paul and I to start again. We had some rows, Sophie, but I think they all happened when you were out of the house...'

'Not all.'

'...I'm sorry about that. You see, Sophie, what Monica was referring to, why I stayed with your father despite everything. I had many reasons maybe. Young and in love, whatever that amounts to. I think the love of my life came before your father and we were...' She glances at her sister. '...never mind.' Mary drops her head into her hands. Her still-fair hair covers it in its entirety, hands and face, I can see her no longer. Just that hair, the best washed in this room, at least among the inmates, hanging above the odd red T-shirt that she wears. I don't think it is prison-issue clothing, it is certainly bland. Ensures she is not too different from her fellow inmates. 'We were going to split...he didn't know. Let me start again. I had just about had enough, soon after Simon was born. Even the pregnancy was dire. Paul smelling of other women.' I hear a shiver of hatred in her voice as Mary says this. It surprises me, I had always thought her a doormat. 'Then Cynthia disappeared. I had told Monica of my plan to leave, take Simon to my own mother's little bungalow, and work it out from there. I was nothing. A physics graduate with barely any research behind me, not

Mary Jail

that I cared about that. Not with a child whom I would always put first. Then the awful thing with Cynthia. Well, at the time the awful thing was you, Sophie. Not personally, awful that we—you, it was you I was thinking of, Sophie—had lost all contact with your mother. Been abandoned by her...' Mary puts her hand on top of mine once more. '...which we now know did not happen. Not of Cynthia's volition. At the time I thought, believed your father thought also—although I have recently reappraised this—that she was the only one having a decent time. Halfway around the world with a man who might make her happy. God knows, Cynthia deserved that. Never deserved what really transpired. No one does.'

My stepmother looks ashen faced as she contemplates this. It confuses me: is she dwelling on how unfathomable it all is, or recalling a murder for which she is culpable? If she is an open book, it is written in an illegible hand.

'I couldn't leave you, Sophie. I wanted to leave him, then couldn't leave you as I thought your actual mother had. Do you understand?'

I have hardly spoken during this visit. Thoughts and words run amok inside me; it is from my stepmother that they flow. 'Cards on the table,' I say. Mary nods. She will listen. 'I was old enough to know quite a bit. My mother and father still carried on...you know.' She nods as if she does but I haven't made myself clear. 'They were still having sex until a few months before she disappeared.'

'I know that, Sophie. I knew at the time.'

This is a complicated issue. I didn't know she knew, not when I was eleven but—some five years later—Monica let me know that she did. I never knew she ever planned to leave him. I only knew of the relocation. Lancaster, Carnforth. I thought they were taking advantage of my mother's flight. I saw it as their chance to start again. Never imagined they had engineered it. 'I never thought she was dead until a week ago;

however, I always thought you wanted her out of the picture. I can see why you would.'

I've set her off again. Mary is crying like a teenager stood up by the rattiest heartthrob in Christendom. Monica is on her feet, glancing across at the guards. Wanting to comfort her sister without giving them another chance to feel her boobs and crotch. Which I expect the bored prison guards are all itching to do.

'I'm all right,' says Mary, gesturing with her hand for Monica to sit back down. 'It wasn't like that, Sophie, but I cannot blame you for anything you think or feel. I stayed for you; sadly, I never managed to make it right between us. I think you tied me to your father who I no longer loved.' There is a silence around these last words. The three of us contemplate them; the biggest of the lesbian prison guards walks across. Despite our current silence, ours might be the noisiest table in the room. 'Respect,' says Mary. 'I could never respect him again. I think I loved him a little, wanted what I once had while fearing it could never be rekindled.'

'It's still no touching,' says the guard. I scrutinise her; honestly, she has the tiniest little patch of chin stubble.

'Nobody is touching anyone,' I tell her. 'I'm sorry if it has been an emotional visit. We are not a close family, and I feel much closer for having our talk. If you could leave us to it, please.'

The fat lump nods and turns heel. Result. I am not certain in my own mind if I am being sincere or kidding. I want Mary to carry on talking. I cannot trust a word she says, and I wish to remember them all. Analyse them in my own time. Knowing what has gone before and understanding what it all means exist on two different planes.

* * *

A bell rings telling us that it is time to leave. I feel quite astonished by all that my stepmother has told me, although I know I should not be. An intelligent woman who has battled for twenty years in a shockingly bad marriage. What did I expect? Monica rises, so I do to. The fat lesbian has come across to our table, and Mary—more composed now than at any time this afternoon—says, 'May I hug my daughter, please?'

'Your daughter?' The guard is more astute than she appears.

'Stepdaughter.'

After a long pause, she replies. 'I'll monitor it.'

This is the strangest hug of my life. With a feeling that mixes the intense sympathy I have today extended, plus several remaining gallons of residual hatred, Mary, the blight of my youth, is holding me in a closer clasp than ever occurred when I was a child. 'I'm so sorry, I'm so sorry,' she repeats. Our cheeks are touching, and I wonder again if she is sorry for doing away with my mother. It would contradict everything she has said. She won't let me go, and then I feel a hand upon my breast, it must be upon Mary's too, so entwined are we. 'Just checking you're passing nothing between you,' says the guard with the chin stubble. Honestly, this old dyke is feeling better boobs than she could ever get her hands on through an honest night's schmoozing. In the wrong job, as surely as she must think it the right one. Mary won't let me go, and I worry that the hand between will start checking our lower parts too, although those particular lady-bits are not so close as to raise suspicions. It's what her sort does.

When we have finally desisted, Mary mouthing the words, 'I love you,' at me, words I cannot return, she takes Monica's hand. 'Thank you so much for coming. I love you, Mon.' Then a different guard turns her shoulder, points her at the door back into the heart of the prison, as her sister and I drift out where we came from, shepherded by the big ugly guard who just now had her sweaty palm on my breasts.

When we have traversed the corridor, arrived at the foyer in which we entered, taken off the lanyards, the butch one says, 'I've to pat you down again. Can't say fairer than that.'

* * *

Monica pulls the car off the motorway. 'Can I get you something to eat?' she says. We have driven through spells of silence and others of intense talk. So wrapped up in the past that I keep forgetting how much I love this woman beside me. And how little I probably mean to her; thankfully, she is always more than civil. Warm and caring. Monica is everything Mary isn't. Or wasn't. Prison might have changed her big sister. For the better but it means nothing if she really did do away with my mother.

'Or we could just stretch our legs.'

'Not hungry, Sophie?'

'Mmm.' I don't know what I am. Delaying our arrival in London is good. And Monica's help in analysing the day is most welcome. 'Eat if you want. I can always snack, Auntie Monica.'

She slaps my thigh, incredibly lightly but my dress is thin. I feel the palm of her hand. 'Get away with auntie.' She laughs as she says it. An affectionate slap, nothing more. And I have to say, I liked it.

It is in a little town called Farningham that she parks up and we leave the car. A needed walk. I am wearing my cardigan; the late afternoon is cloudy. This place looks more inconsequential than Carnforth; without thinking, I say as much.

'Hey Sophie, Mary and I were raised by the sea out where Dorset meets Devon. We'd have called this the big city back then. I...' She pauses, puts a hand into the crook of my elbow; I let her link arms. '...know you had the more sophisticated upbringing; maybe try not to rub it in quite so much.'

'Oh God, sorry. Was I being awful? When I was a girl, I

was such a snob; for me it was just something to hold on to. Living in Carnforth, I could have been swallowed up, become...' I think Monica is listening as she has in our most intense conversations, and I am simply trying to excuse myself. I am still a snob. '...a pregnancy statistic.'

'You? Nope. Never pictured you pulling that one.' She is amused, and something about the way she says it is too knowing. I feel slightly outed but I am not ready to test it. My aunt may be more broad-minded about my predisposition than I momentarily feared this morning, although I have as good as ascertained that she will not join in. She has Gary.

We walk down High Street, and it really might as well be a back lane, so narrow and remote does it feel. At one end there are a couple of pubs. The Star Inn must take her eye. 'You need gin,' says my aunt.

This is quite perceptive although I have not drunk anything since the night my Grace concluded she was not mine after all. Now this visit is behind me, I think I can return. Keep it together. 'You're driving,' I say. Drinking alone is good, just not as good as going down together.

'It's food, I'm after,' says Monica. I follow her inside.

She is most intent on her stomach-filling objective. Her first question for the barman is whether they are serving everything on the menu. I tell her that the more discerning customers choose only a dish or two. 'Not the whole fucking lot.' I am pleased with how she laughs. We have been through so much.

When we are at a table, some chicken dish being prepared for her and a plain salad for me, we talk alone, quietly. Not wishing to share our emotional day with the clientele of the Star Inn. There are a few, drinking more than eating, one or two of the latter.

'Who is this Dennis she was going starry-eyed about?' I ask. During our visit, Monica and Mary had a little exchange that went over my head. All about some guy whom they both expressed a certain warmth towards. Mary even said he may be of help in her current predicament, although I did not understand how he could be.

'I believe he's in Boston, America—or thereabouts—just for a short while. He grew up in Charmouth with us.'

I had gathered the fellow was known to them in childhood; it seemed to be a frustration that they had no contact address. 'Was he Mary's first love?' She never said it, just alluded to having had one before she went to university. It joins the dots.

'I don't really know what they were,' says Monica. She is looking around the pub as she answers. Something about this subject is touching a nerve.

'And would she have had a better life with him than with my father. This Dorset Don Juan.'

At this Monica finally looks me in the face, laughs, but I am not sure at what in particular. 'I never really worked out if Dennis Harris was the coolest kid in Charmouth or the least cool guy on this Earth. A little bit of each. Mary and I disagreed about him, it's all water under the bridge. You know, good-looking lad in a small town. And...' Now she smiles at me with a certain resignation. '...he was a better man than your father. I don't intend to be mean to you, I know it might hurt, he's your dad and everything. Prof Paul deserves to be in prison. For what he's there for and some other stuff that he'll never be charged with. Serial cheating on both wives, you'd think.'

'And Mary doesn't? You believe she is innocent.'

I am holding my gin and tonic as Monica puts her hand upon mine. 'What did you reckon, Sophie? I knew it would be difficult, visiting with all this up in the air. What did you reckon?'

'These last few days have been very strange,' I mumble, before finding my stride. Articulating my thoughts. 'My father said very little—nothing—not a murmur of whatever he has confessed to the police; my stepmother confessed nothing. Her denial seemed heartfelt but is she preparing, practising for a jury?'

'Wow,' says Monica. 'I love you, Sophie, you know that. But you can be more cynical than I know how to be.'

That might be the nicest thing anyone has ever said to me. On both counts. We each tuck in to our modest fare. Monica is embracing the anonymity of her shell suit, dining in a commonplace pub. I imagine she is preparing for the role of scouser or benefit claimant. Will not say it. I fear she thinks me condescending when I only find such people amusing. Live and let live, however pitiable the life one must. It's been my motto lifelong. I raise the topic that we neither really picked up with Mary. Heard but didn't question. We let her have the floor for most of the visit. Gobbled up what she said, and I suspect neither of us has digested it. Not properly. While I have been making a name for myself as a great reporter in the nation's capital, and my father reduced his teaching hours to next to nothing up at Lancaster University, my stepmother—who has also been lecturing in physics in recent years—told us she bedded a post-graduate. Not quite her words. She was determined to share her theory with Monica. My presence probably made it harder, not easier, but share it she did.

In a low voice, Monica asks me, 'Would Prof Paul really go nuts at that?'

This is at the heart of Mary's reasoning. She has conducted a relationship with a man—and one much younger than herself for which I offer her a small dollop of sincere respect—been at it for a few years. Quite a few if she is to be believed. Only one fella. She would not name the boy concerned, although she confirmed when Monica asked, that she has shared it, and the attached story, with her solicitor. I am none the wiser who it might be. Keep wracking my little brain; however, I've spent as little time as I could get away with up there in the culture-free north during recent years. I concede she has the looks to attract such a guy. A younger man. Had the looks; prison does not become her. She always thought she had maintained this illicit relationship without my father knowing or even suspecting its existence. Briefly, she troubled our simple brains with her twisted logic, postulating that, were he to know, he would deem himself absolved of the many infidelities for which she has never forgiven him. She has—only since her arrest—reappraised her notion of exactly what my father knew about her tryst with the said postgraduate student. She says that his fabrication of her involvement in Cynthia's death must be some kind of payback. I must admit, everything in this strange labyrinth confused me. I have always thought Mary too much the goody-two-shoes to ever have an affair. Perhaps she needed better sex than her ageing husband could muster. Clapped out as he must be. Or she has made it all up; this is also in my range of plausible explanations.

'He has other hypocrisies in him but that would be rich. Being bitter about her having a fling.' Then I put on a northern accent as I used to hear every time I ventured onto the streets of Carnforth. 'Nout so queer as folk.' Monica doesn't laugh, I don't have her timing skills. 'Seriously, I struggle to believe your sister would conduct an affair without separating from my father first. She is very ordered.'

'God, Sophie...' I see a tear roll down my aunt's cheek. '...she should have treated you better but don't begrudge her some pleasure away from that sham of a marriage. You heard her, she stayed for you. Couldn't get it together, maybe you never felt it...' Tears positively streak down Monica's face.

I think my own face is flushing as I signal to the watching barman that we are all right. Wish for no intervention from him. 'You may be right.' I can hear the anger in my voice which I did not intend to display. 'I was not even a teenager. Losing my mother, having to live with a cold front as the alternative. It was dire. I felt for her today, Monica. I'm sure I should be forgiving but it is not exactly in my nature. And she is still in the frame...might be the one responsible for my mother's fate.' As I complete the phrase my face is as tear-laden as Monica's. What a crazy decision to even accompany her today.

Monica has risen to her feet, come around the table and hugs me. It is the nicest gesture, and I fear we are not close to agreeing about Mary. 'I know. I know. I remember that age, and I had none of the shit you had to deal with, Soph. I'm wrapped up in Mary's story, and I can't believe she is...' Her voice becomes inaudible but for its proximity, virtually kissing my ear. '...a murderer.'

I return the hug, hold her tightly. Head-to-head.

We can neither finish our food. Mostly, we look into each other's faces with a combination of love and sorrow. I have always been proud of my famous almost-relative, and now, my sporadic animosity towards her sister feels like a dormant beast—an alligator or a sleeping wild cat—that will prevent us from ever having the relationship we would enjoy if life was fair. I manage to drain the gin; the salad has lost its appeal. Monica suggests she drives me back to Bayswater to collect an overnight bag. 'You shouldn't be alone at this time, Sophie. Stay with Gary and I. Stay as long as you like. If it gets too much, I'll pay you a cab home. Please come. I can see how cut up you are over this.'

Tears come to me again as I nod, agree. I am not sure how she will ever get me out of her home. I am already hoping that Gary will be the first to leave.

2.

'No, Sophie, I am really not cross at all. Simply surprised that you neglected to tell us in advance.'

'In advance of what?'

'Publication of your article, of course.'

'And what does it matter to you anyway. I'm not yours.'

'The name you choose to call yourself by doesn't matter to me, perhaps it does to your father...'

Why should I give a fig about him? It is the name of Mary Stephenson which I was determined not to be associated with when I chose to use the surname Hartnell for my article. And the interview with Mica Barry makes no reference to either surname my stepmother has deployed in her life. I detect that she is upset, which is good. Very good. 'Daddy knows I still love Mummy. Says it is normal. That's why I'm using her name.'

'And I do understand how important she is to you, Sophie. Such a shame...'

I simply walk away. Up the stairs of our large house and into my bedroom; once there, I pack a small bag that fits on my bicycle carrier. Then when I come back down, as I pass the kitchen door, I shout, 'Revising with Caz. No supper for me, thanks.' I can hear her saying some reply or other but I keep on moving. Straight to the bike shed, push it to the side gate. What she has to say means nothing to me.

* * *

Mrs Reynolds has read my article—Girls in the News—she tells me how interesting it is. I detect that she wants to ask me more about Mica Barry. Natural enough, I suppose, and I have already told her that the television star bought me dinner, while mentioning to no one—not to my friend Caroline or her mother—that she is a relative. It would put my stepmother in a light too interesting for my liking.

'Now Sophie, I think your name, Sophie Stephenson, is a good one for a writer. Alliteration. But you have chosen Hartnell.'

'For my mother in Africa. I am sending her a copy of the magazine and so I used her name.' It might be foolish of me to invoke my mother more directly than I can justify; however, if I am to be a writer, a little embellishment will always be an applied tool. We none of us like the truth to unduly restrict a good tale.

'Hartnell is your mother's name. I see. And Caroline has asked if you can have supper with us...'

'If it's all right, Mrs Reynolds. We revise well together...'

'Having a famous journalist to supper will be a pleasure, Sophie.' She smiles as she says it. A bit patronising and, in the future, I think I will be exactly what she calls me. My article is good, and I can do better than a teenagers' magazine. Can and will. 'Should I phone your mother?'

'No need,' I interject. 'She isn't expecting me back until quite late.'

* * *

When it is only Caz and I, my friend asks me more about Mica. I go over the hotel story—sharing a twin room—although I told her all this at school last week. She is quite in awe of me, envious. Who wouldn't be in the light of my revelations? I describe Mica in minute detail but never share the Monica Bredbury name. Nor her connection to my stepmother. I do not believe it would be my aunt's wish, nor in her interests. She is a fabulous star, my stepmother a housewife with a physics degree. Still does something or other at the university, and I think that's only because my daddy is in charge of the place. One cannot call it a proper job.

Caz and I manage a certain amount of revision between gossiping. We are the top performers in our year. The very brightest at Hazelbrook. Mrs Ansell, the headmistress, is devastated that we shall both switch to Lancaster Grammar for sixth form. It was my idea, and now Caroline is as keen as I am to have a proper town to explore during our free periods. An education in the sticks is barely an education at all.

At supper, Mrs Reynolds asks many obvious questions. 'Did you see what Mica looked like without makeup?' This is one.

Before I can answer, Caz jumps in. 'Without make-up? Without clothes on more like. She took Sophie into her hotel room all night.'

The look on Mrs Reynolds' face amuses me but then I have a second, more disturbing thought. 'No, Mrs Reynolds, it wasn't like that. Mica is no...' I look down at my plate as I say the needed word. '...sapphist.' Have to put her straight on that. 'And, of course, I would not have shared her room if she were. She simply had a large hotel room with two beds. And we showered before dining out in the evening.'

'I see,' says Mrs Reynolds. I am not certain that she does, she simply reverts to the question about her make-up.

'I think Mica's skin is quite unblemished.' I tell her.

'And does she dress like Sarah Best? Wear her hair the same?'

I answer all her questions and keep glancing at Caz as I do so. Mrs Reynold queries her accent. It is true that she sounds like a Manchester girl in Shoes and Slippers and speaks properly when the cameras are not rolling. The Queen's English but I don't use that phrase. Mrs Reynolds is pleasant enough, her own vowels are a little flat, can't lose that dulled northern buzz. At least Caz speaks properly, has risen above parents who might limit many a child. Her brother is hopeless.

The mother seems star-struck. Mica is so famous and my name—the Sophie Hartnell one—is beneath hers, and in only slightly smaller typeface, on the magazine cover. Mica's face alone accompanies the names, and I fear mine would look wrong were it there; provincial next to her beautiful features. Strange but true, for my aunt hails from tiny Charmouth, and I from dazzling Epsom. Caz and I have long agreed that Shoes and Slippers is actually dross. I thought it before I watched a single episode; Caroline described the programme and I saw the flaws. A mind-numbing regurgitation of the trivial challenges of everyday life made watchable by decent acting. It entertains those who cannot think outside their dire station in life. Around the tea-table, I gather that Mrs Reynolds is one of them. It is as if viewers think they are watching themselves navigate life's mundane dilemmas. In truth, it is my prettier and better scripted aunt doing it for them.

Gordon, the fourteen-year-old brother, asks me if I will be a newspaper reporter when I grow up. I tell him that I am already a grown-up. 'In print, as they say.' Gordon's face turns deep red. It lets me know he fancies me. I like that a lot, although it will go unreciprocated. Caz looks nearly as eye catching as I do; however, her brother has spots and his voice is higher than hers.

Later, she and I are studying history and French, may move on to algebra which is my friend's weakest strand of mathematics. Gordon has the nerve to enter a girl's bedroom uninvited. Does so on three occasions. We could have been trying on clothes or anything. Not that we were.

The first time is to borrow an eraser from Caz, and then the second and this third, are simply to ask questions of me. Daring little beetroot face.

'Will you go to see your mother in Africa?'

'Gordon, I am not allowed to see her, according to my father. Forbidden because she has brought shame to our family. She lives with two men, and makes a nightly choice which one to allow in her bed. It is not common knowledge but most women live like that in rural Zambia. When I am eighteen, I shall go there and do the same, although I have yet to find even a single boy with whom I should really like to go beneath the bed covers.'

I am a cruel girl saying this tosh to him, aren't I? Gordon's face might as well be hooked up to the mains electric. If he lay on the bed, I could grill sausages on it.

'I see,' he says and hurries out.

Caz bursts into laughter, as do I. 'I remember,' she says, 'that in fourth year you told me you didn't know where she'd gone.'

I swallow quite hard. I am not a natural liar but nor do I enjoy other people seeing me get upset. 'She might live with two men. I won't do that though. I'm not immoral, it's simply funny to watch your brother think I might be. I don't care about Mummy anymore. She clearly doesn't care about me.'

'Really? But I thought you used the name because...'

'Can we just study?'

Caz nods. Revision it is.

* * *

At ten minutes to nine, I go outside to my bicycle and both Caz and her mother wave me goodbye. Then, as I have agreed with Caz, I go out onto the lane and circle around a couple of times before heading back towards the Reynolds' house. Quietly, I push my bike into the back garden, lean it against the far side of the shed, hidden from the house. Then I take myself to the backdoor. I slide my hand ever so gently across it, as I simultaneously take off my shoes. My action makes the tiniest sound, detectable only to one standing close and listening. The handle turns and Caz lets me back inside. With my shoes in my hand, we cross the kitchen and quietly climb the stairs. Her parents are watching television. Gordon is dutifully in bed, possibly asleep, more probably cogitating over my future lovers. We enter her bedroom. I whisper to Caz that I hope the nuisance doesn't come a-pestering anymore. She puts a hand behind my head in order to whisper most quietly in my ear. 'He doesn't know you're here, otherwise he definitely would.' Caroline has seen what I have seen, and it makes me feel ever so slightly glamorous.

The point of this furtive sleepover is mostly to upset my stepmother. If my father worries about where I have gone—a little collateral damage—so be it. I am not a Stephenson, that is now a matter of public record. I do not dislike my true mother but if I pretend that I do, tears cannot fall. I attend a girls' school, and this makes it difficult to come to the attention of boys. Gordon has been a useful canary. In the future they will all swoon before me, that's what his behaviour presages. I do not need my parents any longer. I expect I could attract myself a protector when I am at school in Lancaster but it sounds stifling, being a boy's girl. I would not wish to be owned. Two lovers indeed! And this secret night at Caz's is only a game. I plan to go home in the morning; a recce, not the great escape which I will do in years to come. I'll leave her room at first light, spend a little time in Carnforth—watch it waking up—before getting back to Windermere Court at about nine. That should have caused sufficient upset. They will think I've done a Cynthia.

I put my hand around Caz's head as she earlier did mine. 'Should I sleep under the bed, in case someone looks in?' I whisper.

'We can top and tail,' she says. 'More comfortable.' Talking so embraced feels most intimate. I would never kiss a girl but find myself partial to her proximity.

* * *

Caroline sleeps, and I can feel her breath upon my cheek. We started off by topping and tailing but I think we both prefer the face of the other to the feet. Nothing wrong with them, just odd to accidentally feel toes with one's nose. When I turned around, we struggled not to giggle. The bed is a bit narrow but Caz is a good friend. Not of the funny sort—Jane Coates at Hazelbrook boasts about seeing our sports teacher take a shower, and if she had any self-respect she would have looked away—a girl's school can teem with the wrong kind.

While I lie awake, I hear the phone ring, and then, although I cannot make out anything that is said—I hear Mrs Reynolds voice. I am not a psychic but I realise I accidentally told dumb-dumb Mary to which friend's house I was venturing out. I cannot really guess if we have fooled Caz's mum with my staged leaving, or if she will look in the room in the next few minutes. My plan was good but certainly falls short of great. The next few minutes will find out if it succeeds or not.

When I hear her coming up the stair, I turn into Caz and hug her, dip my head right under the sheet. I hope this makes the body in the bed look like a single one. The light from the landing enters the room with the opening of the door. Caz gurgles noisily awake, from either my hug or her mother's entry.

'Sophie?' says Mrs Reynold's, 'you were meant to have left over two hours ago. I think you've tried to trick me.'

'Not you,' I object. 'You've been so good to me.' I dry up. Can't think of anything more to say.

'Mum,' says Caroline—I have let go of my grip upon her—'Sophie really needs a better family to live with. Can't she stay here?'

'She cannot,' says Mrs Reynolds. 'Sophie, dear, talk to me, whenever you like—not at this time of night—I can see that you are a clever and an unhappy child. Both of these things. Tales of sharing a bed with Mica Barry, and whatever nonsense you filled Gordon's head with about your poor mother, indicate all is not right. What are you wearing, dear?'

'A nightie.' I am wearing a long one. It happens to be the same colour as Caroline's. I brought this one with me from my own home. In the little bag.

'I'll leave the room while you change. And I will phone your mother back. Stepmother. She will be here in minutes. She must be simply beside herself. Do try and think of others, however unhappy you are.'

I glare at her but I am in the shadow of the room, not the

light of the landing. She may not even see my scowl although it must penetrate through darkness, enter her skull in some manner. I hate how she talks about me. Happiness and unhappiness are complicated states and we should not assume one good and the other bad, but better consider how best to use our time in each state. I shall not cry about this. When her mother leaves, and Caz places a comforting hand upon my back, I shrug it off. I might spit in Mary's face when she collects me. It's been years.

* * *

My father has gone back to bed, the boys are sleeping too. It is one o'clock in the morning and Mary and I each nurse a second cup of cocoa. I think she is trying to be nice to me but her efforts are hollow.

'I never minded the name,' she repeats. 'I said I was surprised you didn't tell us before the copy came out. It is for you to determine which name you use, Sophie. And adopting your mother's name makes a lot of sense. I do understand that you miss her, you know.' Although we sit in the kitchen, she has left the strip lighting off, and the only illumination is from the hallway and a small light beneath the cooker hood. I recall she and Daddy having heart to hearts late into the evening with this same arrangement. Probably Daddy explaining away his most recent conquest. Denying whatever Mary had uncovered. 'I think it embarrassed Caroline's mum, and I hope that doesn't prove awkward. She was very understanding though. She hasn't banned you from going around the house or anything.' Mary gives a little laugh. 'Thank God. She is very clued in.'

'Why the "thank God" phrase?'

'I think you came across as a little louche. Claiming a disreputable mother, a shared hotel room with a famous soap star, and then worming your way into her daughter's room in the middle of the night. "A phase," she called it. And maybe it is.'

'But Stepmummy, you know that I really did share with Auntie Monica...'

'I know. The most outrageous of the lot is always going to be the true one. And Sophie...' She places a hand upon mine, warm from being around her cocoa mug before this touch. '...Daddy says your mother is in Southern Africa but I don't think he knows anything for certain. It's okay to be upset about this. I don't think making up stories will bring you a good return. Not in the long run.'

I've had enough. I stand up, pushing her hand off me and it knocks my cocoa to the floor. 'You haven't a clue what it feels like!' I shout. If I wake the boys, I really don't care in the slightest. 'You fell out with Monica and she's tonnes nicer than you are. You drag me back from a better house across town but you can't drag Daddy back if he chooses someone better than you for the night. I hate you!'

As I am going up the stairs, Daddy has come out of his room. 'Sophie, Sophie,' he says.

I look up; he stands at the top of the stairs, open arms. 'You wish I was in Africa like Mummy. You wouldn't need to bother about me then, would you? I bet you'd send Simon there by post if you could. I'm going to be a famous reporter and I don't need you telling me what to do. Or hugging me because you think you ought to. Bugger off!' I push past him, storm into my bedroom. Leave the door open. If I am louche, I can undress this way.

My night in Manchester with Auntie Monica was the best I've had in an age. Ever. I don't think I can stand much more of this. Of Carnforth. Mary looks a bit like her; I see that more than I ever used to. Looks like is a reminder of everything she isn't. She's Mica Barry's waxwork dummy.

Simple Simon is out of his room. Standing in my doorway, staring. Staring at me as he does. I wear only my underwear, his face registers nothing. The blankest stare. I give him a V-sign. It's mean, he is not as simple as I used to think. But he never says a fucking dickie bird. Whatever is going on in his brain, it's going to stay there unheard. I'm just going to be myself from here on. This menagerie of freaks is going to have to learn to live with it. With the real me.

3.

I have not been to Monica's house before. It is delightful. A cottage outside Aylesbury. People often say, a little cottage, the phrase making one assume all cottages are smaller than regular houses. Not so. Auntie Monica's is enormous. Long as a great ship and it backs onto fields. As we are getting out of the car, I say, 'Is it yours?'

'Sure, it's mine, Soph,' she says. But this has not answered my intended question. I wasn't sure how to ask if she and Gary share ownership, or if he remains on sale or return. I am interested in the types of relationships the people I care about enjoy. Not angling for a route in. Not seriously. I have long surmised that Monica is hetero to the core. I will stay the night, possibly a couple more. My life is in Bayswater.

Then he is standing on the drive. Dr Alsop, as he is known to most of us. That is the character he inhabits in the long-running television adaptations of Millicent Wise's Victorian-set novels. His other name is Gary Fielding, of course. It is the contemporary-era version who is Monica's boyfriend. I don't watch his programme, nor do I read low-brow historical melodramas. I am sure it pays well. And he is terribly handsome, that will have helped getting the TV role and the gorgeous girlfriend too. Played its part.

'Family, family. Welcome to Westlington,' he says. I think it is the name of the little hamlet. He is not my family: Monica wears no ring.

'Sophie, Gary. Gary, Sophie.'

A television heartthrob kisses me generously. On the

cheek but proximate to the right corner of my lips. I feel absolutely nothing. Return it with a little peck. Lubricate the façade.

'I hope I am not imposing?'

'Mon has told me so much about you, Sophie. And it must be such a traumatic time.'

'Port in a storm,' I manage, looking at my aunt. If he starts talking garden sheds, I shall cry, and surely none of us are angling for that.

* * *

Monica shows me a spare room, I think there are several. The bed looks like it has come from the set of Gary's TV series. The curtains too. They display a pattern of leafless trees, identical to the bedcover. Chintz, it is called. Or imitation chintz, I am a little uncertain about this. My mother knew furniture, furnishings; I've not followed those particular footsteps. It's certainly an elegant room which Monica has put me in.

'I might have a bath, Soph,' she says. 'Gary will entertain you. Maybe eat a little cheese, later?'

'That would be lovely.' I showered at Bayswater when we called in for my things. It is only early evening. I think a bottle of red makes a good accompaniment for cheese, fear drinking too much of the stuff. I have been known to make a fool of myself once or twice.

I take a seat in the lounge—it's a tasteful mix of the old and the modern, a corner sofa and an antique-looking display cabinet with a few awards muddled in with photographs—and her man Gary begins a monologue. 'Known her years and years. We were together in the West End. I think I met Mary eight years ago, and that was after a performance. Hard to take in. Met her twice earlier this year. Mon and I have only been sharing a house since last Christmas. Mary stayed here for a couple of nights at Easter.

Brought her youngest. I've never met him. The husband. The philanderer. Nor the other boy...'

'Gary, the man you call "the philanderer" is my father.'

'Oh God,' he splutters.

I see laughter lines crease his handsome face but he also colours more than I expected. The coolest man on Sunday-night television is embarrassed speaking to me. Quite a coup. I no longer give tuppence for my father. Philanderer, liar, mother-burier. My mother. And where he chose to put her, I will never forgive.

'I really should work out the family tree before I start spouting my mouth...'

I let my laughter be more overt than his but I am faking it. 'He's a lot worse than just a philanderer, Gary. I hope I am a very different person from him. For years I have felt more kinship with Monica than I have with my father or stepmother.' I gulp slightly, cover it, just. I hope I haven't said that in a clingy or creepy way. 'For years I thought my mother would come back, then for years I hated her because she didn't. It is only in the last few days that I have learnt she had no choice. Never left me. Taken in the cruellest possible way.' He is listening closely; I sense genuine interest. It makes me think his interest in Monica goes beyond being close to someone famous. I am pleased for her; she deserves contentment. 'I disliked my half-brothers when we were growing up, and now—not that I see them often enough—we are really very close.'

'Yeah. Mon has been talking about them. I liked Craig.' I look at him, want him to elaborate. How others see my family is a revelation. 'Everything I hear about Simon tells me he's autistic, and then Mon says he's not. She thinks it's something else.'

'I think the doctors have been diagnosing for twenty years. Whatever they come up with, he reads up on and then behaves his way out of that pigeonhole. He is the one and only Simon.'

'Mon says she can't see him. That he won't be seen.'

'Hmmm. I barged in a couple of days back. Talking is what he will not do. An elective mute. You can hear his message before leaving a voicemail. He doesn't mind recording his voice. Won't give it to you face to face. Mr Text.'

'And he's clever, right?'

'I think so. But I'm losing track of what clever really is. I thought I was clever. I spent my whole life thinking myself cleverer than Mary. Now I wonder if I've only been more fortunate. Didn't accidentally marry Casanova. Which must be hell. A marriage where only the other one has a good time.'

'Sophie, Monica says it is terribly hard for you. She wasn't sure you'd go today. We were so pleased you gave it a go. And with Mary charged for your mother's murder, your head must be spinning...'

'Remanded for it,' I correct.

'Monica doesn't believe it but...' He looks across at the door to the room. It is open, his voice might carry. Monica is still upstairs as far as my reading of the house noises go. Dressing herself directly above us, if I'm not mistaken. '...she admits she can't be sure-sure. She just grew up with Mary. Always thought her a gentle soul. God knows what you do after the hundredth adultery.'

'Cut his cock off. Anything but murder my mother.' I say it as a joke but tears are escaping from my eyes. My watery head.

* * *

'We usually go herbal tea, Sophie. It might be the better shout. It's been one emotional day.'

Monica has a selection of fine cheeses upon a board but her planned accompaniment is not the wine I'd hoped for. She talks sense. After bathing, she came down in just a kimono, something underneath, that I can't see. Her legs are really quite white. I like that, try not to think about it. Gary smiles from her to me and back again. He has no banged-up relatives, no murdered mother. Life is a doddle for Victorian-era doctors.

'Yes, chai is good for me. Sorry for suggesting it.'

'Don't be silly. I just...drinking alone is no fun, and I'm very occasional, Soph.'

I only had the one gin and tonic earlier, because it would not do to get blotto all on my own. I agree with everything Monica says. And I did sneak down a small sherry when we were in Bayswater collecting my clobber. Bottle in the bedroom, you see. Fortification. I thought actors did the same, apparently not these two. 'How long...this house...I can't remember where you used to live.' I am dissembling, and she is right about the emotional day. I keep picturing Mary in that funny red T-shirt. Dressed as she might for gardening or housework, not how she ever presented herself to the wider world. She looked raggedy. And, God knows, I have seen her upset on many occasions, that discomposure always looked momentary; today she was slipping from reach. I would once have been gleeful; the world has turned into one too complicated for any of that. This affair she had, whatever she has done, I don't begrudge it. A last hurrah. She threw happiness away on my father. He might have made her more miserable than I would have liked her to be, and I was the meanest stepdaughter. I have no illusions on that score.

'I know, Sophie. I think I would have liked to see more of you than I did. Even that interview felt disloyal to Mary. Being out of the blue, like it was. Behind her back. She and I have one strange relationship. She was a great older sister, you know. When I was a kid. It is adult choices that...'

'Was it to do with Dennis Harris?' I feel like an investigative reporter again, seizing on the oddest exchange of the afternoon. There was something weird with him.

Discomfort all round when his name came up.

'No. Well...not really. Dennis was Charmouth. I sometimes think, when I'm having a hard time—which is mostly shit like now, happening to Mary not me, my life being so charmed and all—that whatever we go through, that kid, Dennis, had it worse when he was too young to know what he was seeing through tears. At seventeen-years of age the poor guy became an orphan. The weirdest tragedy. I was way, way younger. Thought he was the coolest kid in a nothing place. He had his own house...Sophie, I can only tell you that Mary and I both remember him fondly. He's in America, we understand. Another tough chapter. A friend of his is battling cancer. Closest thing to family poor Dennis has ever had. She's dying, I believe. She—a girl he knows, not someone Mary or I ever met—is dying and he can only be there to hold a hand. We can't change very much in this world. I feel so sorry...'

'You're right, Monica. It's nothing to do with me. Sorry to pry.' I can hear in the quaver of her voice that I struck a nerve, was onto something. I am not heartless, only pretend for the kudos it gives me at the Noise. I care about Auntie Monica. Always will.

'I may have told you that I never warmed to Paul. Prof Paul, your dad. He was more than twice Mary's age when they married. I was seventeen at the time. In a bridesmaid's dress. I thought it ludicrous that she would shackle herself to someone not of her own generation. I never got the Mr Physics vibe. I think only the science kids ever did.' She looks up at me, half smiling. 'Everyone he bedded wore a lab coat, right?'

I have to smile back at that. 'I think so.'

'Jesus,' she says.

'Jesus Christ, Amen,' adds Gary.

I take a piece of bread from the basket on the coffee table before me. I laugh while feeling strangely responsible. It's stupid but I do. My father ruined her sister's life. That one is a fact, the rest—what on Earth happened to my mother—is conjecture.

'Did she hate me?' I ask.

Monica shakes her head, quite vigorously.

'It could feel like she did.'

She continues the gesture, the denial by proxy. Looks into my eyes.

'Not always but a lot.'

'I think she was too young and inexperienced, didn't think about you on day one. You had a mother she couldn't replace, didn't want to replace. She kind of snuck in and married your father while hoping for no relationship at all with you. Unrealistic, unhelpful. She isn't a nasty person but...Sophie, what is it?'

'It's hard for her, Mon.' Gary talks across her. Not to me, nor excluding me. 'What I saw of Mary was fine but none of us can second guess whatever the hell the police are onto. Her arrest.'

'Mary was clear as day earlier,' says Monica. 'If she was trying to fool us, then I'm a fool.'

'No, Mon, don't say that. You've got lovely childhood memories. We need to learn what Mary has or hasn't done. Don't lose sight of everything else about her. Don't let it all hinge on this. She must have enjoyed your visit...' He turns to me. '...and you going was really something. I understand the history. Monica talks about you so much. You visiting her, Sophie, that's a big deal. We're all going to have to learn in the weeks and months ahead. You and Mon may not see it quite the same. The thing is never to fall out over it.'

I am up from my seat; I take Monica's hand in mine, grasp Gary's with the other. 'Thank you,' I say, directed at the boyfriend I had not expected to like. 'Thank you for understanding. I don't think I am an easy person for others to get. I know that I was unkind to Mary, far more than she deserved, it's just the child I was, the one she locked horns with.' Then I stoop and give Monica a hug which she accepts. 'I think I'm meant to be grown-up now. It can be terribly tricky.

4.

We had a terrific day together yesterday, and today I am alone in the house. Monica has gone up to town to discuss a forthcoming project. Gary is filming. I expect he has sideburns plastered to his cheeks already. I breakfasted with the pair of them—pyjamas and robe; it is permissible when one is going through what I am going through—I find Gary more finely attuned than Grace Topping ever was. A most caring soul. And Monica is the mother I have missed. Only a decade my senior, I have been looking up to her since the interview in nineteen-eighty-six. Since my stepmother acquired the Stephenson surname, even. That other wedding. I think these are the daughter-mother feelings I have kept from Mary. I used to kid myself that Mon and I had a one-sided romance. It is not that. A role model and not a partner.

Yesterday they took me with them to go around Kingsweston Something-or-other. One of these big old country houses which they were casing as a possible wedding venue. I felt completely at ease with the pair. Odd that I should—wedding-bells talk—couldn't have been a greater gooseberry. Unlike prison, apparently it is worth wearing one's celebrity on one's sleeve when looking to spend copious amounts of money. The pair were simply charming. A gentleman—who other staff at the venue called Raleigh, he insisted we call him Charles—gave us the grand tour. He took my presence in his stride, and still asked a few curious questions, trying to fathom my precise role. I wanted to say ménage à trois, because I enjoy watching people's faces if I tease in that manner. It would have been a joke, not a fantasy. I could make no joke at all while my aunt was preparing for what will be her big day. I'll not sully that. In August of next year, the big event will take place, this is forward planning coupled with a certainty that their relationship will last more than six times the length of any I have ever been party to.

I struggle to imagine weddings. Not the raising of champagne flutes and pretty bridesmaids' dresses. They are all right, I've drunk many and even worn one. It is the notion of becoming half a person that takes the wind out of me. When I was younger, I believed that I loved my father, considered myself raised by him. Even thought I might have inherited his roving eye. But I also conceived the notion— game of make believe—that I was really the product of an affair my mother hid from him, my lineage not directly linked to the unreliable Prof Paul. He—I used to review the photograph albums in my Carnforth home, and in my true home back in Epsom before ever we moved up to where I did not belong—embarked upon two marriages with all the pomp and ceremony that my lovely aunt and her doting beau plan to do for theirs; my father had not a gramme of the sincerity which they have in sack-loads. Perhaps Cynthia Hartnell, and later Mary Bredbury, believed Professor Stephenson—or plain old mister which is surely all he was the first time and possibly second too—loved them with an unerring passion. How they could deceive themselves beats me. The man is charming; he understands the relationships which hold together the different components of an atom. People interest him only from his selfish perspective. Shallow as a birdbath. Not a millimetre deeper. Yesterday, my thoughts were of Monica and Gary, the wedding to come. My aunt queried if there might be a way to coax Simon to the event; she wants to be surrounded by family. We never spoke of Mary. She could be guest of honour, or might be languishing, unspoken of, in Holloway or the like. I even made an inner calculation—I have followed one or two murder trials professionally, being a reporter and what have you—Mary may still be awaiting trial. The outcome still to be determined while little sister ties the knot with Gary who isn't really a Victorian-era doctor but, after spending a day and a half in his company, I would let examine me for the sheer thrill of it. Lucky Monica; and odd of me to picture a man's hands on my torso when so beautiful a woman is also in the room. And Mary missing it all through a spot of detention at Her Majesty's pleasure would have felt like icing on the cake three days ago. Now I feel conflicted. Want the best for Monica and think it possible I have misjudged Mary. I'm really not sure either way about her. She seemed like a horrible stepmother at the time, yet I know that I was a ghastly older sister to Simon for all of his early years. Love him to bits nowadays. Childhood misunderstandings; it is terribly sad that Mary's marriage was from the same mold.

* * *

Kingsweston House is set astride lush lawned gardens, a tree-lined approach to the front door. And nicely topiarised trees they are too. Monica was most interested in a converted barn in which one may host an old-fashioned hoe-down. Bells and whistles. When Charles of the evenly tanned pate mentioned a horse-drawn carriage, Monica turned to me and said, 'That really is too much, isn't it?'

'Style, Miss Barry,' said our genial and understated sales representative. I suspect he would hate to be so termed. Showing the palatial trappings for the simple good fortune it might bring to the pairs' collective future, might be his summation of the role. I didn't see the prices but scandal-rag reporters couldn't marry here, even those who can sustain relationships. Of course, if my despicable daddy doesn't see daylight again, nor Mary whose probability either way is quite beyond my calculation, then the boys and I will be very, very rich. Family money, and not hard work, the provider. I could marry in a joint like Kingsweston, and probably find a man who would say yes, sincerely or otherwise if I was flashing that much cash. But I would not enjoy it. The wedding day, maybe, but marriage I believe to be murder. Relationships comprise cold-morning visible breath, tangled fingers, sweat and saliva, and purposefully listening to each other far more than I am any damned use at. Semen too, seeing as there has to be a Gary-type—the male of the species—involved. I've put up with it before now but I'm not a fan. Just pleased for Monica, she looked to be enjoying the anticipation of it: the showbiz nuptials, pictures for a magazine. I hope they are as good with each other as they seem. I have spent two nights in their house now, and either they make love exceptionally quietly or my presence is putting them off. Disappointing to note, actually. I would happily bed either but for the chaos the doing of it would provoke. And in the state of freefall in which I find myself, I need family. Mustn't destroy what little I have.

* * *

This morning, before my hosts left for the kind of busy day that I should be enjoying but for my enforced, and temporary, absence from the Noise, we talked over croissants. Over coffee. 'What will you do while we are out?' asked Monica. She and Gary treat me like I have returned from the front, shell-shocked and not my true self, while building me up to feel taller than my five-feet-five. It is welcome respite from the life I had; very welcome. I think I am my usual self, apart from the bite-size bits of sympathy I feel towards my stepmother.

'Rest, relaxation and phone Darius Pleydwell, get myself an assignment and some normality.' Monica stared at me. I explained my current hiatus from work in the heart-to-heart we shared in the pub in darkest Kent, straight after the visit. Seeing Mary in jail. 'I have no wish to be assigned to this story; I would like it on my mind a fraction less than is currently the case. I don't imagine achieving any more than a fraction. I'm sure you're the same. Worrying about what has gone on nineteen years ago gets all-consuming. Work will be a very welcome distraction. I think that's the only reason most people go.'

Monica laughed at that, squeezed my hand lightly. 'Take as much relaxation as you need.'

'I did a proper job,' said Gary. 'Less than a decade since. I always wanted to be an actor—trained—the parts didn't come. Decorator, painter and decorator, that was my other trade.'

Honestly, I stood up from my breakfast-bar seat, little round and leather cushioned stool that it is, went the three paces to where he sat, leaned in and hugged the man most tightly. 'I love the proletariat,' I said. Not generally true, it just happened that this morning those were my feelings. And Gary would never be a rebellious shouty one. He's a Victorian doctor half the fucking time.

Gary pecked my cheek. 'Thank you. I'm not claiming working-class status though, Sophie. I was sponsored through drama school by a complicated mix of patrons—a Worcestershire church in the mix—never a truly downtrodden worker. I only did the painting job to make ends meet. To keep up my payments on the London flat between acting roles. I enjoyed it more than I probably should have.'

'Hold it right there, Gary Fielding,' I said. 'Two things to clear up. This church congregation you are beholden to: you are their Messiah, I take it? And enjoying painting the houses of others? Explain.'

'I bet it's easier than your job. Stress-free, once you've

learnt not to drip.'

I looked at Monica. 'Funny, funny,' I said. 'Did your fancy man paint this place then?'

She giggled at my term for him. 'A couple of rooms, yes. I've not changed the main rooms since...' She glanced across at the husband-to-be. '...he came on the scene.'

Gosh. That solved a riddle for me, and I wasn't angling this time. My family has money sticking to it like spring burs, this clever girl makes it all on her own, and lives in a more tasteful residence than my father or grandmother ever managed. Grand but a cottage. Deserving it might be the key. 'And the church?' I said with a raised eyebrow. 'Have I to worship you? What's the low down on that one?'

'Not much to it really. My parents were both congregants. I was a member, I guess. Confirmed in it. They used connections to secure the money for The Bridge. Drama school in the Fields. We were not especially well off, you see. Not dirt poor like Monica, just not a lot to spare.'

'London Fields, is that where it was?'

'Yes, up there. I was playing bit parts in musicals in my teens. Shouldn't have needed the painting and decorating sabbaticals. Wouldn't have if I'd Monica's talent.'

'Shut up. You were too much the theatre purist to take a soap back then,' she said.

'Not true...' Gary looked into my eyes while he said this. '...never offered one. Monica was brilliant from the word go; I was a slow learner. Do you know, Sophie, before I truly met her, I fell in love with your stepsister watching her in a Miller play. Fell in love while sitting in the stalls.'

'I think a lot of us have done that, Gary. And she is my aunt, step-aunt, that ballpark. It is working with a paintbrush, not for art but for notes and coins, that I hugged you. Falling in love with Monica must be very, very easy.'

'Ha! What can I say about manual labour? It becomes a very acceptable way of life. The highs and lows of this occupation—tele and theatre—have an edge, mostly because humdrum work has no highs or lows. It just is. A fair whack of satisfaction seeing rooms and houses made over. Very nice. Punters were generally satisfied. Weren't you, love?' He nodded at Monica, and got a little smile back. 'And I think you're right, Sophie. Everyone needs some work to distract from the feelings of kinship and friendship and all the rest of it. To never work might just be too intense. I think unemployed people—and I don't mean this to sound right-wing or unsympathetic—have a burden of time upon them, that might outweigh the absence of money. Might. Having no money must be shit as well.'

'I am detecting something proletarian again, and that is acceptable.'

'Sophie,' said Monica, 'the Noise is a bit of a nasty right-wing rag, although you don't report politics, not as I've ever read. Mary always said your grandmother, Paul's mother, was a bit of a self-appointed duchess. Do I detect irony in your questioning?'

She was outing me as a snob, and this after taking me to see her fairy-tale wedding venue. And Gary's earlier comment, not dirt poor like Monica, was a reminder I shouldn't need. Mary and Monica both look fabulous, could have been born to the manor and all that. Granny Bredbury was the proverbial church mouse, raising them both—dumbbell Stephen too—all on her own in a godforsaken coastal town. I never dwell upon it. Hating Mary and adoring Monica has never left me any room for basic sympathy. 'I don't vote,' was the extent of my reply.

* * *

I think about going back to bed but that isn't really me. I'm a busybody in my own way. Instead, I go into Monica and Gary's bedroom. They have a proper shower through here which she said I may use. The bathroom in this cottage is an old-fashioned affair: big bath, sink and a rather high throne; red and white tiling that looks simultaneously classy and garish. I open the concertina door to the little en-suite. Flecks of shaving foam coalesce around the sink's plughole; I find myself thinking it reassuring—for Monica, not I— somebody taking you just a tiny bit for granted. Not even cleaning up fastidiously, so assured in each other's company are the pair. There is a shampoo bottle in the soap holder inside the cubicle, unisex. I might be stealing from either if I use a tiny blob in a few minutes. My hair is so short, I won't be needing much. I go back into their bedroom and throw my robe on the bed, lower my pyjama bottoms. Before I can unbutton my top, I hear a groan, followed by the tinny ringtone of my phone. That is how quiet this cottage is: I heard the vibration of my phone two doors along the corridor. I skip away, feeling a little odd, half-naked in a strange house; it might even be Darius, who I plan to ring later. Only on the corridor do I realise it has stopped, the ring was a single announcement. A text. A vast number of people have my number but I already sense who it is.

In my room, I fish the device out of my jeans pocket. Yes, I wore jeans to the fancy wedding venue yesterday but mine are not any old denim. Mode Argent: trousers which cost what a painter and decorator earns in a week. This pair did. Daddy paid, of course. I sit on the bed and key in my password. It's him.

> ***Big Sis, important, Craig has run away. He didn't tell me he was going. Very strange. Upset. Worried for him. Has Sarah told you?***

I feel frozen to the bed. My brother Craig is a little immature, that only makes it harder for him to assimilate these terrible events. He is family, and I cannot lose more; my mother alone is too much. And Monica will need to know. I don't think she is in touch with the Redhill gang.

Sarah is Prof Paul's sister; Monica never tried to ingratiate herself with a single Stephenson.

No. No contact. When did he leave?

Yesterday, a bike ride

Police?

Since early morning

What do you think?

Scared to think

He is an honest boy. I might conjecture all sorts of possible scenarios, to soothe myself or scare myself witless. Our Simon just knows it is not good news. And I focussed overly on Simon, when I was there, knowing that he must have found the move from Lancashire to Redhill hard to stomach, I think I neglected poor Craig.

His phone?

Turned off. Or out of charge

Simon, my friend, I am at Monica's, cannot get across easily. I must let her know

Tell Mica, but she doesn't know us. Can't help

Monica knows me, and I think she might like to know my half-brothers better. They are the blood relatives I am not. It has simply never quite worked out. I even think her relationship with Mary to be stranger than was obvious when I shared a Formica-topped table with them at the prison two days ago. Monica seems to feel a lot of guilt, not justified, but amorphous. She has led a comfortable, hard-working life. Has this cottage to boast of, can headline in the West End or on television. A man a couple of years her junior—one who every woman with a pulse would like to sleep with—adores her and only her. Gary is the faithful sort; I think I can tell. And she has been unable to rescue Mary from a morsel of her depressing life. Lancashire; Professor Cocksure; two boys whom she loves, although it cannot have been easy. Craig the forgotten infant, although he is a spotty seventeen these days.

Simon, Monica may not be able to help but she cares. Can I phone Sarah, tell her you have texted me? I am concerned

Do whatever you think best

Chapter Six:

Water Shall Burst Forth in the Wilderness

1.

I don't care for my stepmother and I don't care that it is her twenty-first birthday. However, Mummy is back in the house which I find delightful. She says that she will put me to bed tonight, and that it needn't happen until I have enjoyed the first two hours of the party. Two hours is a lot. There are sixty minutes in each hour, and that means there are a hundred and twenty minutes in two hours. My father says that there will be forty guests at the party, so I could spend three minutes with each. I've worked it out. And I have also decided that I shall not. My stepmother is the guest of honour, and I won't be bothering with her. That leaves me a certain number of extra seconds for everybody else. I could work out how many if I had a pencil but I am in the bath at present and therefore I am without one. Mummy has left me for a few minutes, she will come in to dry me soon. I can do that for myself, and I would do were it only Stepmummy offering to help. Mary the six-tonne fairy. She is actually very thin but I call her that because it is a very funny name. Because I think it would upset her if I actually said it out loud. Which I shall when I'm older, and then she will have to take my intense dislike of her seriously. At present she tries to make little jokes. Tells me that I am nice deep down, when I am not.

Crack Up or Play It Cool

I don't play with silly ducks in the bath or any other children's toys, instead I have a snorkel, and a proper visor for my eyes so that I can see underwater. Daddy once explained that everything looks different at the bottom of the sea because the light comes through a lot of water. By going down there, divers can see shoals of fish or shipwrecks in the green gloam. In the bath my feet look the same with the snorkel and visor as they do if I just look at them while sitting up. It is still more fun to go under, provided I don't accidentally swallow bathwater. That can taste grim and my knees got dirty from playing in the garden. They are clean now but the water is, therefore, very, very mucky.

Mummy comes into the room and laughs because I have the diving apparatus on. I tell her I am practicing, and she still laughs. Not at me. She is happy that I am going to be a shipwreck treasure seeker when I am older. My best friend will be an octopus.

'Am I clean?' I ask.

'Let's have a look at you then.' She sniffs around me in the bath, then says, 'Stand up.' I do as she asks and she nods, puts a great big bath towel around me. I usually have to use a little one because Six-Tonnes says I am small enough not to need the big. Mummy is much nicer to me than her. She likes me to have the same comfort that she would have, or Daddy has. Big Fat Mary too. Mummy dries me very nicely, takes her time. The towel is soft on my skin. 'You smell of lemons and pomegranates,' she says.

I giggle because I'm sure that I don't. I have no idea what a pomegranate is but Mummy must like them if my smell reminds her of them. 'Will you be putting on a party frock, Mummy?'

'No. Mary isn't one for dressing up. A low-key party; I understand that a lot of her friends will be here. Friends and family.'

'I'm going to wear a party frock.'

'And you will be the belle of the ball, Sophie.'

'After the party, Mummy, will you be sleeping in our house?'

'My house is yours too, Sophie.'

'But will you sleep here? Like you used to before Six...before Daddy went silly.'

'No. You all make me very welcome, it's just I've my own home to go to. I expect to get a cab at the end of the evening. Or Uncle Phil might run me home if he's still sober.'

I give my Mummy a funny look because she is using a word which I don't know yet, and that is a bit rude of her.

'Squiffy,' she says. 'He might get squiffy. Drink too much wine or bubbly, sleep it off on the sofa. Or perhaps Auntie Sarah will stay sober but that's never happened before.'

'Are you going to get squiffy, Mummy?'

'Probably.'

'Can I get...'

'No. Nein. Nyet. Sorry, Sophie-lovey, it's a strict rule at your age.' Then she unwraps the towel and blows a big raspberry on my tummy. It is funny, and feels nice, but it is what mummies do with babies and I am seven years old. Quite big, actually. Just not old enough to get squiffy yet.

* * *

Mummy ties a red ribbon around my black hair, pulls it ever so gently so that it stands up a tiny bit from my forehead. I am staring in the mirror. It is vain to think oneself pretty and, for this reason, I know that I am vain. The party frock that I wear will look nicer than any other worn this evening. Mummy says so, and Six Tonnes doesn't even appreciate nice clothes so she, and all her dumb-dumb friends, will probably dress as if they are about to start painting. Old trousers and the sorts of shirts men wear; they won't even tuck them in. They are all so, so stupid. I'm going to be the apple of their eyes. Mummy says that too.

Twenty-first birthdays are important. You can do anything you want afterwards; however, before reaching that age, you need your parents to agree. When my mummy is explaining this to me, I ask her if it means that Granny Bredbury—who is a right sourpuss—had to agree to the wedding. Stepmummy married Daddy when she had only just turned twenty.

Mummy bursts out laughing at my suggestion. 'Who doesn't want to win the football pools?' she says.

I don't understand her strange comment. 'Tell me? Tell me what it means?'

'Your new almost-Granny and her other two children will all be at the party tonight. Ask them about the union, Sophie. Try to speak each of them alone.'

'The union?' I don't understand this. I think a union means a gathering of nasty men who shout on the television news.

'The marriage. Mary and your father.'

I look around from the mirror into my mother's face. It is as lovely as mine, although I do not know why she is laughing. I think she has given me a test. A kind of challenge. I will do exactly what she asks; she is my Mummy and she is very clever. She must think that I will enjoy talking about it with them. And I don't think I am wrong about the union. Words can mean a lot of different things all at the same time. I like them but they are very, very slippery.

* * *

The doorbell has rung about twenty times in as many minutes and there are too many people here for me to spend more than about a minute with each. I've decided to say phooey to them. Not to their funny faces but in my head. I will talk to my weird new stepgranny, to Uncle Stephen and Auntie Monica, as Mummy said I should, and spend the rest of the time with Mummy and Daddy. If the birthday girl must sit alone, I shall not care a fig. And if she cries at her own party, I will laugh until my pee comes out.

'Here she is!' says Mummy from the top of the stairs. She has to say it very loud—to shout it—because there is horrible pop music wailing out of speakers all over the downstairs rooms. Mummy and Daddy only like proper music, which is when violins and pianos do it right. That is the music I like, as well. Tuneful and lovely. All the people in the dining hall—which is empty of furniture except for a few chairs against the wall and the nice display cabinet—look up at Mummy's shout and it is me that they see. My frock is black and white, and that goes well with my black hair. As well as a red ribbon around my forehead, I have a red sash over one shoulder. I look spectacular.

Daddy claps his hands as I make my way down. And he says, 'Miss Sophie Bumblebee,' which is funny and makes me laugh. Six Tonnes has come to his side and reaches out her hands as I arrive at the bottom of the stairs. I ignore her and do a twirl so she cannot grab hold of mine. A fast one that lifts my dress up my legs, and then I giggle as I fall into Daddy's arms.

In the room are all my family, and also some people I don't know. Boys with long hair and girls in silly short skirts. They actually look nice but Mummy never wears anything like that, so I don't think I should approve. Mary the big fat fairy is a student in the place where Daddy is an important teacher. I expect the people I don't know are her friends from the same place. Imperial College.

A girl who looks even younger than Mary, wearing very scruffy clothes indeed, jeans and a T-shirt with a picture of a llama on the front, puts a hand on my head, rubs me lightly. She says, 'Hey.' I yelp because Mummy did my hair so nicely. The girl bobs down onto her haunches and looks into my face. 'It's me, Sophie. Your pal, Monica.'

I smile now, although I hope the ribbon is still in place. Auntie Monica was nice to me at the horrible wedding last summer. She danced with me through two whole songs and made funny jokes about everything, while all the other guests took the business of Daddy marrying his student so seriously that I wanted to be sick.

I put my finger in the middle of her chest. 'Is it an alpaca or a vicuna?' I ask.

'Very clever, Sophie-dope. You must know the names of all the animals in the world.'

'I think I do.'

I don't understand what it is that Monica does now. She told me that she left school in the summer, and she will go to drama college. I don't know what that is. If it is nice, I might do the same when I leave, for the time being, school does me very nicely. I have the best marks in class and I can bend all my parts better than any other girl or boy when we have the mats out. PE lessons, and I know those letters stand for physical exercise. More than know it, I can spell the actual words out in full.

* * *

I try to talk with Granny Bredbury. She is a hopeless case. Treats me like I'm stupid when it's her. She was talking with my father when I joined them, so I told him that Mummy would like to speak with him. It isn't true. Or if it is true, it's only by luck that I have hit upon it. Mummy hadn't asked me to say it; nevertheless, I like it if he talks with Mummy instead of Six Tonnes. He stands up and goes to find her. I sit in the seat he vacated.

'Hiya,' I say.

'Sophie, are you enjoying the party?'

'In April I shall have my own birthday party because I will be eight. But right now, I am seven, and that divides into the number twenty-one. Which is the age of your daughter. My party might be even bigger than this one. More people. But I shall invite people my own age because they play proper games.'

'I hope you have a nice party then. Are you enjoying this grown-up one?'

'Did you know that seven goes into the number twenty-one? Three times, it goes into it.'

'I do know that, Sophie.' Easy for her to say it now that I've told her. 'Your father is a very clever man.'

I nod my head. Daddy might be the brainiest person in Britain; everything he understands is very important. I think it might be to do with space which is where, in the future, I expect we will all go to live. I think this woman—she has mousy hair in a much shorter style than either of her daughters, and her eyes are dull, although they are a similar shade of green to Auntie Monica's nice shiny ones—might have agreed that Mary could marry him exactly because he is so clever. 'Would you have let my stepmummy marry him if he was a thicky, like the men who empty the dustbins on a Thursday morning?'

She looks very shocked; the smirk leaves her face replaced by the look of eating pickle. 'I don't know. Binmen aren't bad men, Sophie.'

'And if Six...if your daughter, Mary, fell in love with a binman would you have approved their match?'

'That's quite a question, little Sophie. I am very pleased that it is your father whom she fell in love with. Shall we leave it at that?'

'You didn't have to approve their union but you did anyway. Why did you do it?'

My new stepgranny—who hasn't even got a binman who loves her—wears a thinking-face like I have asked her a long-multiplication question. Looking around I see that Daddy has not only found Mummy, she and he are walking up the stairs. I think I guessed right that Mummy wanted to talk to him. If they talk privately—they can use my bedroom for that—Daddy might realise he made a mistake marrying Six

Tonnes. This substandard granny—not a proper one, the step ones never are—can take Six Tonnes back to her funny little bungalow by the sea, and then Mummy will come and live with me and Daddy again. It would make my eighth birthday party ten thousand times better than this noisy racket.

* * *

One of the girls who wears a short skirt is dancing with me. She is opposite my stepmother, and might be her friend. Six Tonnes dances, too, but it is more swaying and waving arms than doing any truly clever dancing. She hasn't learned a sequence of moves, simply bobs up and down. Sways. One of the boys, who is Mary's age tries to cut in, to dance with the girl who is dancing with me but she says 'No.' I am pleased that she chooses to stay dancing with me. Girls shouldn't give in to boys. That's what I think.

A man from Daddy's work came and started talking to Granny Bredbury before she answered my question properly. I don't think he asked her to dance but she might have been hoping he would. On account of not even having a binman. 'Run and play, dear,' she said to me.

'But why did you agree to Stepmummy marrying Daddy?'

'Sophie, Sophie. You can see by now, can't you? Mary always gets what Mary wants.'

That was a strange way to say it. She wasn't even twenty-one when she married Daddy. I think Stepgranny could have stopped it if she wanted to. I love Daddy but even I know he is far too old to marry a student. Six Tonnes will be pushing him around in a wheelchair before she is as old as her mother is now. Very stupid choices all round. I think her answer means that Mary never let her decide anything, that Mary was quite a naughty child. That is how I will be for Mary. Always do as the teacher asks at school, and I behave like an angel for my proper mummy when I am at Spenser Avenue. I'll never do what Mary tells me to do. Never ever.

I hug the legs of the girl dancing with me, put my right ear on her blouse about where her tummy button is. 'What are you doing, Sophie?' says my Stepmummy who is beside us. I am hugging this girl whose name I don't even know, closely and tightly. Like I would never do with her.

* * *

'Hello, Stephen.'

'It's Uncle Stephen.'

'Hello, Uncle Stephen,' I amend. And I was only being friendly, calling him as everyone else does. He must be sniffy about it because I'm so young but that doesn't stop me from being his equal. His better, actually, Stephen is not from Epsom. He was raised somewhere far more common: Dorset where the farmers live. 'What do you do?'

'What do I do?'

'Yes, Uncle. What? Daddy is a lecture and Stepmummy is a student. What do you do?'

'I don't think your Daddy is a lecture...'

'Yes, he is.'

'...he's a lecturer. He gives lectures.'

I don't usually make mistakes but it is after my bedtime. I think this clever-clogs might actually have got this one right. 'And what do you do, Uncle Stephen?'

'I am a laboratory assistant. I work in a medical laboratory.'

'Oh, yuk. I think that means you clean out rats' cages. And I don't like rats at all.'

The bighead chuckles about something. 'No rats,' he says, 'but other laboratory assistants probably do that. I work in a hospital. We wouldn't keep rats there. Test tubes and vials and saline solutions in our lab.'

'And in this laboratory, do you try and bring people back from the dead?'

'Not yet. We haven't figured that one out.'

'And you are a lot older and cleverer than Mary, than Stepmummy. Did you have to agree to her marrying my daddy. Because neither of you have a daddy to do that, and I already know her mummy couldn't stop it.'

'Steady on, Sophie. I hope you and she are getting along okay? My sister—your stepmummy—is great. Really clever. Why would we stop her from doing what she wanted to do?'

'Because he already has a wife, he just forgot. He's upstairs with her now, and has been for ever such a long time. You see, they have more to talk about because they are the same age, and your sister is just like the girls and boys he teaches. A student with a lot to learn. It's a bit one way.'

My Uncle Stephen is chuckling as if I have said something funny; I am revising my opinion about the intelligence of laboratory assistants. They might be binmen in white coats for all I know. 'I think your daddy is very happy to have married to Mary. I think most men would be.'

Thick as a piece of balsawood. My daddy is a man, it doesn't mean he likes the same things as other men do. At school all the other children like pop songs but I don't. Me and Mummy and Daddy are a cut above your average Jane or Charlie. Your Marys or your Stephens too.

* * *

Mummy took me up to bed. I told her not to, and she said my two hours were up. 'This isn't your house, anymore,' I said. It shut her up a bit but she still pulled my frock off and put me into these navy-blue pyjamas. Now I have sneaked right back down the stairs and beckoned Auntie Monica to come to me. I need to find out who in her family agreed to the marriage that is ruining my life. I know that she is more honest than the rest of them. She scoops me up into her arms, carries me straight into the study when I tell her that our talk needs to be conducted in private.

'We shouldn't be in here,' I say, 'because it is Daddy's

private room containing all his work on physics. The books might tell us how to get to outer space, and it's supposed to be a secret.'

'I could read all I wanted, Sophie-bug, I don't think I'd understand a jot. Stephen and Mary are the scientists, I prefer playing.'

I laugh because it's quite a funny joke. 'You must understand science. Your brother does and he's not half as clever as you.'

'Not sure if he is or isn't but I spend my time playing. Not learning physics.'

My auntie seems to be very serious about this. 'With toys?'

'Yes and no. Props. Learning to act just like you see on TV, Sophie. Or in the theatre.'

'Television is for common people; I believe I will enjoy the theatre when I am old enough.'

Monica starts laughing so much that I no longer know if her playing is the joke or if it is something I said. She is sitting on Daddy's swivel chair and can't stop spluttering. Then she pulls me onto her lap and tickles me so much that I join in her laughing.

'Tickling's good fun, you see, Sophie. Common people do it but it's none the worse for that.'

I think I get it now. 'You want to be on the television, don't you, Auntie Monica?'

'You can call me plain Monica on account of us being the right age to be sisters, Sophie-bug. I'm not on TV so I'd better not dream too much about it. What's eating you, little one?'

'If Daddy had wanted to marry you, would you have let him?'

She splutters out another volley of giggles. 'Kicked him in the nuts, more like.'

It's a funny answer, and I don't expect Daddy would have liked it wherever these nuts are. I am pleased nonetheless. It confirms my hunch that young girls marrying old men is silly.

'Then why did Mary let him?'

'Hey, honey-bunch, Mary loves your daddy, okay. I was joking, and I don't kick people. Not in regular times. Your daddy is smart and great and everything. Mary is way too young to even be married, if you want my opinion, and I'm younger than her. I just kind of reacted to your question. If a boy at school asks you to marry him say no. You can change your mind when your older but it's a no for now. Right?'

'Should I kick him in the nuts and bolts?'

'Definitely not.' She squeezes me in her arms, and then picks at my pyjamas. 'Stars,' she says. 'You're covered in stars.' It is true, my pyjamas are the deepest navy blue, with silvery white stars emblazoned all over them. The night sky. 'Are you going to be a star one day?'

The question doesn't make any sense. You can't be a star, they are enormous, far away, and on fire. Although she says some rum things, I still like this auntie the best of all the Bredburys. I like the way she hugs me. Doesn't tell me what to do except for not kicking boys. Not marrying, too, but that is very easy. I even think she told her sister not to, and then stupid Six Tonnes didn't listen because she is older than Auntie Monica. Stephen and Granny Bredbury are the dumbos, said yes when a kick in the nuts would have made my life much more straightforward.

2.

Everything is in boxes. A small construction of them in every room. Sold. My father has sold our family home to somebody who works in television: a producer he told me, as if it might lessen the blow. I didn't know the name but he might run the entire BBC. I don't care, and I hate having it leave the family. When my mother returns, she will not know where to find us. He says that she will, that every person we know, including our family solicitor, is always ready for a call. Would put her through to me wherever I might be, whatever time of day. He has said it many times but saying it doesn't make it happen. Some girls in school would say it jinxes it, while I think it is more terrible than that. I am coming to think she doesn't wish to telephone me. Will not send for me. It might be better if she has been kidnapped. For me if not her.

We are not staying around for the removal men. A friend of Daddy's, called Rinus, has a key, and he will stay to lock up the Epsom home I never expected to leave. We are driving to our new house in Lancaster. We shall stay in a hotel tonight, let these funny men unload our furniture into the new house without us. Daddy said he has paid extra so that Stepmummy and I, plus the horrible little sprog she has spawned, can rest in comfort until the house is ready. I have told him I want to help—I can carry my own things into the new house—he said no, it's cash in hand and he gave most of it to them when they agreed to do the job. The removal men shall do it and we shall not. He is a man with more money than sense. Not stupid, just lots of money. More than you would need to fill a bathtub. A swimming pool even. And no amount of money can fill the void I feel in the absence of my mummy.

I always imagined that she would come back—hoped Mary might move out on the same day—and live in our house in Epsom, as she used to when I was very small. Instead, total strangers will live in it, and the Stephenson family shall not. Daddy even says that Mummy's house is going up for sale too. I shouted at him when he said that. It isn't his and he can't sell it. He nodded, said her solicitors told him it should happen. Mummy has taxes or electric bills to pay, and the only way to get at her assets will be to realise them. I queried this, a very funny turn of phrase. I have always known that she has a house, it isn't something I have just realised. He taught me, because I asked him about the word, that realising can mean turning something into money. A pretty silly use of the word, if you ask me. You realise the house by not having it, by having a big pile of cash, or a long number in your savings account, instead of having a house. When you realise what you have, you don't have it any longer.

Stepmummy asks if I mind sitting in the front of the car for the start of the journey. Simon is awake and she says he might need feeding. 'You can't get your boobies out on the motorway,' I tell her. I don't explain myself, I'm simply sure of it. We will be travelling too fast and they will wobble too much for the little simpleton to drink out of. I even think other motorists will snigger, think it all pretty disgusting.

'Oh, I can you know. Baby's needs come first. Every time.'

I have a shameless stepmother; she will try it anywhere. If I ever have a blubbering blob, I'll give it cows' milk. Undressing in public is what tarts do.

Daddy is having a last word with Rinus, and with the driver of the removal lorry. It feels like the end of my childhood, I am going to have to act like a grown-up in Lancaster. A new school, called Hazelbrook, the pictures in the brochure look very nice but it is hours and hours from every friend I've ever made. I shall hate it.

While we are waiting in the car—waiting for Daddy to come and drive us into the unknown—I ask Stepmummy if she feels the same. 'You don't know anyone in Lancaster either.'

'We will meet people soon enough. Make new friends.'

'Just because there are people there doesn't mean we're going to like them.'

'Honestly, Sophie, the children in your new school will be every bit as nice as the ones in your old school. Don't be so suspicious.'

'I'm not suspicious. I just know they won't be. Don't you think we're all losing everything by going so far away?'

Water Shall Burst Forth in the Wilderness

'No, I don't. Daddy is getting a much better job, for a start.'

I know that this is true. He is going to be in charge of Lancaster University. Or the head of something, rockets and science and what have you. 'But he won't know anyone either. Even Rinus is staying here in Surrey.'

'He is, and it won't stop him from coming up to see us from time to time.' All the while that Mary talks, she has a finger poking Simon in his dimples or drilling into the palm of his little hand. He watches, his eyes follow the finger but he always has the same gormless expression on his jowly face.

Eventually my father gets into the driver's seat and we set off. To deepest Lancashire. The journey is quite boring and Mary and Daddy discuss bills, how much everything costs. Solicitors and estate agents, the removal lorry, and someone who is going to 'tame the wild hedges' in our Carnforth home. I don't think I've been paying attention these last few weeks. Daddy has bought a house in Carnforth although the university he is to rule is in Lancaster.

'It's a pretty part of the country,' says Mary. 'I like that. After growing up in Dorset, I've found Surrey rather nondescript.'

My idiotic stepmother talks twaddle first to last. Epsom in Surrey suits me just fine. Lancashire sounds like pooh-shit, and I really miss my proper mummy. I don't say it because they would both shout me down. They say Mummy has been selfish to leave me, and I sometimes think it too. Or there could have been a ransom letter. Things are always getting lost in the post.

* * *

While we are eating café food in a motorway service station, Simpleton falls asleep. I would say, about time, but he is no bother apart from his demonic stare. He doesn't make a noise, doesn't cry. Doesn't do anything a cleverer baby would. He just looks like a cow in a field looks, waiting for its end to come. The café food is horrible and I try to say so, and Daddy shushes me. He says we are not making a special detour for a decent meal when we have so many miles to travel. 'Why don't they serve proper food here?' I ask. 'It's a bit wicked to have old pie and greasy fried eggs turning into rubber on hot plates. Not nice like my Mummy used to make.' Then, very quietly, I add, 'And Stepmummy even does quite well.' I see her lips turn up. It is a concession, and actually true that she makes dinners and even snacks which are much better than this rubbish.

'Stop complaining, Sophie,' says my father. 'It's just food for the masses and we shouldn't be stuck-up about it.'

'No,' I say, 'but we should be scientific in our evaluation, don't you think?' Daddy is just taking his frustrations out on me, and I've had enough of it. I expect he is going to lose all his friends from Imperial College by moving up to the north of England where this awful food is probably their normal fare. Wanting everything to be good is not being stuck-up, it's actually very sensible. All the things Daddy eats every all the time except moving-house day.

'I'm sorry, sweet pea. It's a long drive and we're only halfway. Let's not grumble about the tiny things, it won't make it any easier. Back to our usual food in a day or two. At the hotel tonight, hopefully.'

* * *

Stepmummy and I play a game of draughts in the lounge of the Aldcliffe Hotel. We've spent the night here, and it is rather a nice one. Daddy has driven to our house in Carnforth to oversee the unloading. Sprog is in his little carry cot. Whether he is asleep or awake makes no difference to the turning of the world. A year or two back I thought Mary quite stupid because I always beat her at these games. I used to tell her I was the cleverer, and she never argued. I have since revised my assessment: she used to let me win. Now she gives me the respect I am due. Tries her damnedest. Wins more than I do, I think, but I expect to overtake her as I grow up. Learn everything she knows and more.

Beside her she has the brochure for Hazelbrook School. I am thankful that it is only for girls. I expect northern boys are coarser than the ones in Surrey, and I didn't like any of them. Living up north, Simon will grow up to become horrible. I point this out to Mary, not to be negative but to prepare her.

'It is all about how we bring him up, Sophie. I have to be a good mummy, Daddy is very good with him, and you will be a caring sister, won't you?'

'I'll take him as I find him,' I say. Many months ago, her sister, Monica, said these words in a play in the West End. We were all watching. Mary heavily pregnant at the time. I think they are very funny words, and fair not rude. Ha-ha, then they turn a little rude if you think about the context: I find Simon to be a big lump of gristle: a body but not a presence.

'We will all help him to grow and learn,' she says while hopping her double over four of my draughts pieces.

* * *

Daddy is still at the new house when lunchtime comes around. Mary asks me if I'd be happy with a bar snack. I ask what that is, and she says, 'Let's see.'

She lifts the carry cot in which my half-brother now sleeps—stuck in a stupor that is not dissimilar to his waking hours—and I follow her into the hotel bar. She places sprog on the floor, indicates I should sit opposite. Watch him. Then she goes up to the bar. I see her exchange a word with a lady in a uniform behind the serving counter, then she returns carrying two bound books, and hands one to me. 'The menu, Sophie. Choose anything you like.'

Crack Up or Play It Cool

It actually looks quite nice, and I ask for halloumi fries and the signature cheesecake. I know that signature means it is the best they can do. Stepmummy talks to me about my bedroom. She says that I will have a room in the new house that is as big as hers and Daddy's, and with a single, not a double, bed in it: there will be lots of floor space. She says that I can have the spare dining table as a making table or an art table if I like. It will easily fit in the room, shelves too for storing the materials of any craft I care to pursue.

'Why don't you go and order the food I've asked for,' I say, 'or aren't you hungry?'

'The lady will be over in a minute or two.'

'If the room is that big, can't I get a cello and learn to play it?'

'Yes, but will you practice? They can sound lovely, or terrible if you don't learn to play it properly. And the cello is not an easy instrument.'

I think this is a little dig at me because of the recorder I neglected to practice upon when I was about seven. No comparison in my view, those things are little better than a tin whistle. Not a part of any orchestra I've ever seen.

'I might work on it every day; it might be enjoyable to do so.'

'Ask me when might turns into will. What about an art table? I would have loved that in my room when I was a child.'

'But you couldn't because you were poor.'

'We were poor compared to all the choices you have, Sophie, but I enjoyed happy times in our little bungalow.'

I turn my face away; she should know not to say that. Money doesn't buy happiness, and she has been a blot on my childhood. The wealth has actually been all right. It is my mummy leaving which has made it all quite unbearable.

'Are you all right, Soph?' I continue to look away, and she places a hand upon my own.

Water Shall Burst Forth in the Wilderness

'I'm not all right because when Mummy comes back, she won't want to live in Lancashire and I can't do this journey two times, or four times, a week.' I hate for Mary to see me crying but I cannot help doing it. Crying a bit.

'If she comes back, we'll work something out. You come first, Soph. You always have.'

'I'm called Sophie.'

The lady in the fancy grey skirt and jacket—very like the stewardesses wear on the boat to France—comes to our table carrying a tray with two iced-up glasses and a bottle of mineral water. 'Have you chosen?' she asks. I eye the drink. I like it, Mary ordered right, I just don't want to say it. She is still a crummy stepmother. Remembering that I like a lot of bubbles in my drink isn't very much at all.

* * *

By the time my father comes to collect us it is already five o'clock. It has been a boring day with Mary, made duller still by sleepy sprog. She has talked a bit about herself, which is selfish but quite interesting. She never knew her daddy although she believes he is still alive. Might be living and working in Australia. Her mummy, the tedious Granny Bredbury, told her that he went out there with another woman just a year or two after my Auntie Monica was born. She didn't even live at the seaside then but up in Wiltshire. She says they only moved to Charmouth because of the shame. I said, 'Did you feel ashamed?' and she laughed at my question.

'I hadn't started school at that time, Sophie. I don't think I knew what shame was. But it was awkward growing up in the nineteen-sixties without a father. There were very few divorces back then, very few single-parent households. I think I learned to feel ashamed of it while also learning there was nothing to be ashamed of. My father was not me; I was never responsible for his actions. I never felt ashamed if I was feeling confident but it's hard to keep that feeling up every day of the week.'

I have been thinking about what she said. I feel every emotion a brain can spark up whenever I think about Mummy running away and leaving me. I feel sad that she enjoyed her life here so little she would do such a thing; I feel angry that she didn't even tell me she was going, nor how I can find her when I grow up and no longer have to go to school; I feel like smashing my fists into Mary's face which is also about this. She looks nicer than Mummy—I know I shouldn't even think it but she does—and that is the only reason Daddy chose her over Mummy. He didn't stop loving Mummy; I know that's true because of what they did behind Mary's back. It is more than two years since I first figured it out. When Daddy came to collect me from Mummy's house, he would let himself in the backdoor, then he would tell me that he and Mummy were just going to have a word. They wouldn't talk in the lounge or the dining room, they always went up to Mummy's bedroom. I listened at the door once and they weren't talking but gasping. And afterward, Mummy's hairdo was crumpled. I remember thinking I could tell Mary and she would divorce Daddy, and then Mummy could come back into her proper house. I didn't do it because Mary might not have believed me and I thought Mummy and Daddy would work it all out for themselves. They are both clever people. Then everything started to change, I don't think they even went to bed together in the months before Mummy ran away.

I have thought about this a lot, and I don't even know why men want pretty women. All the business which they do in the bedroom—I'm not stupid, I understand sex and babies quite well—utilises only the ugliest parts of their bodies. The bits which men and women pee out of. It doesn't make any difference what a girl's face looks like, so Mary's pristine features are worth nothing. I think Daddy liked Mummy's inside-knickers more than he ever has Mary's. I have seen what Mummy looks like down there but I'm not interested in it, and certainly never wish to see my stepmother without her clothes on. It would be awful. It makes me feel a bit funny—sort of woozy—even thinking about it.

'Did everything go all right?' asks Stepmummy.

'They broke a vase and the lower drawer of the wardrobe for the spare room.'

'Not the blue porcelain?'

'No, that's still wrapped away. Unbreakably packed. One of the white flower vases, a shame...'

'Quite replaceable. Not to worry.'

'Have these klutzes broken anything of mine?'

'No, Sophie. I don't think so. They've been very good really. All gone now and we...'

'Did you remember what we agreed?' asks Mary.

'Yes, fifty pounds. Quite a tip, and they didn't look displeased.'

'Thank you, Paul,' she says. It sounds like she has made Daddy give them a lot of money, and all for dropping vases and smashing up wardrobes. I saw them—the removal men—when they first came to pack away the house in Epsom. They looked to be just the type of people to spend it all on beer. Beer and betting shops, fish and chips too.

Now my Stepmummy is carrying the sprog in her arms and he is actually making noises, not words or even close. Gurgling. I know that this means he wants feeding and Mary will probably sit on the back seat and get her knockers out. At least I'll be in the front, I can't stand looking at them.

* * *

Daddy drives fast and we arrive before half-past five. The new house has a name: Windermere Court. We pass through big stone gateposts, pillars almost. The whole place is very grand and very ugly. Big grey slate stones, nasty sharp corners, and a roof of dirty black. There is a television ariel sitting next to the chimney, without it the whole place could be in the nineteenth century. I hope it's got flushing toilets. When we go inside, it is funny. Most of the furniture is in the right places but the men haven't unpacked any of our small things. Daddy probably stopped them when they started breaking everything.

'It smells of smoke,' I say.

'Cigarette breaks. They took more cigarette breaks than they did work, you might think.'

Mary looks a bit concerned. She is terribly anti-smoking. Her arguments seem quite sound but I don't like to agree with her. 'I'm taking Simon up to his room,' she says.

Little sprog is sleeping again, having sucked away at her bust which I am sure he is too big to be doing and too stupid to stop. I follow her up the stairs because I want to see my room. Daddy says, 'Let me give you the tour, Sophie,' but I say no. I want to explore it for myself. I imagine it used to be lived in by a fat mill owner who murdered one wife after another. It's that kind of house.

3.

My form teacher, Mrs Lundt, is a two-faced cow. She smiles a lot, and has told me I may speak with her whenever I wish—she wants to help me settle—then in class she keeps correcting me when I am already right. She's not much of a teacher, understands little. The head teacher, and all the other teachers too, look very frumpy. They wear tweed or long skirts that make them look like vicar's wives. Mrs Lundt is the only one in a proper dress. A good-looking young heifer, I suppose. And then she can't even teach properly. Lancashire is the pits.

Stepmummy Stupid took me to the clothing shop in

Lancaster yesterday. They said I was lucky that they had my size in stock. The uniform is a black skirt with purple trimmings and a white blouse with the name, Hazelbrook, on the left-side breast pocket. I think the lady in the shop was a cheeky madam. I am the most normal size there is, if they didn't have mine in stock, it would be a rum affair. Last night, when I was telling Daddy about the shopping trip, I said it might mean all the girls at this school weigh twice as much as me. I have seen, in our few days here, that Carnforth has quite a few fatties per acre.

'That's funny but not true,' he said. 'Don't worry about the other girls. You'll soon make friends.'

That was more of the patronising nonsense he and Stepmummy have bombarded me with since he first learned he had the head-of-university job. Pretending things are normal up north. He won't take responsibility for ruining my life. It is the way of the modern parent, I am sure. The girls here at Hazelbrook are not fat—except for one called Miriam, and there was a fat one back at Long Grove Prep—they are quite simply freaks. They watch an awful lot of television, call each other 'chicken,' which is a revolting name, and although they try to make their vowel sounds properly—unlike the shop assistant in the clothes shop in Carnforth—they really can't do it. One called me stuck-up because of the way I speak. I said, 'We're all at a private school, dear, you can't hurt my feelings by saying I'm a cut above.' That shut her up.

The trouble is that I don't like any of them. I have to spend the next four years with these goofy girls. We have moved from Surrey to Hell, taken up residence in a haunted house, and my father and his floozy act as if they like my cursed half-brother more than they care for me. I have decided to call my autobiography, The Journey Back to Epsom. My purpose is to ensure it lives up to the title. And I must engineer into real life the triumphant ending that already plays itself out in my head. That yearned for reunion.

4.

I hope I did not outstay my welcome at Monica's super cottage in Bucks. I was there under a week and we both worried ourselves sick for a night about poor Craig. Just for one night, then we laughed a little crazily when we learned the full story, when the police returned him to Auntie Sarah's house. The stupid boy only got himself caught trying to break *into* Retford Prison. Such a funny thing to wish for. I have spoken to him on the phone since; he was a bit embarrassed, wouldn't say much. I didn't laugh during the call. Auntie Sarah said it's because my father—who is one of the poor lad's two jailbird parents—has accused his mother, my stepmother, of murder. He wanted to hear it from the horse's mouth. I did too, and the horse didn't say enough for me to feel certain one way or the other. And I had the sense to get in through the visitor's entrance, not by trying to climb barbed wire.

I spent last night in the flat, Bayswater, and now I've made my way back down to Redhill to meet the boy who tried to get himself banged up. Uncle Philip is out again. Auntie Sarah said, 'More work for him,' but I'd lay a bet that he keeps a spare set of clubs at the office. Moseys on out to the golf club every day he gets bored of Auntie Sarah. I'd do the same in his shoes. Might camp on the course. And he could be idling away the time in the nineteenth hole. I'd do that too. Sarah and Philip never had any children of their own. I'm not the type to ask if it was choice or biology: I have refinement. He's old enough that he really doesn't need to pretend to work, which must be all he ever did a decade ago. Family money and his name on the brass plate on the door of the accountancy firm of which he is senior partner. With only the dreadful Sarah, plus two troubled youngsters in the house, buggering off has become more important, I imagine. Sarah takes her family duty more seriously, no choice but to become a late-life pseudo-mother. She's not a natural. Runs it more like an upmarket bed and breakfast than a loving family home. Simon is a challenge, isolating himself as he does. Craig might be the more mixed up about everything. Whatever I think of Mary Stephenson—and for the longest time I considered her malign parenting the cause of Simon's many abnormalities—she has been a warm mother to her second son. Even Simon will say nothing bad about her. He believes himself a free agent who chooses not to speak directly, or even look into the face of, another soul. He has pictures of Mary and her sister, when they were much younger, hanging on his wall. When they were the age which he is now. He might get off on it for all I know, and that would be weird, and kind of hard to begrudge him. A twenty-stone stay-at-home elective mute. Uncle Philip must think his house has become a silent bedlam.

Before I see Craig, Auntie Sarah wants a heart-to-heart. She went to see Daddy yesterday and clearly found it tough.

'He said it's truly terrible what all this is doing to the lad. He shed tears. I've never known Paul shed tears in forty years. At one point he said, "We should never have had him. Should have guessed this would all come out one day." Both parents in prison for what happened long before Craig was born.'

I do not see it quite like Auntie Sarah. In my own darker moments, I think it is only my family that this pair of horrors have wreaked havoc upon—my mother was the one beneath the shed—Craig and Simon should simply pull themselves together. It is an unkind thought, I know it is. And Simon hasn't even fallen apart; he is simply made this way. Monica has shed tears about her sister, while being most understanding about my mother. She blames Prof Paul—

Sarah's brother—for everything under the sun. For everything but me. She doesn't dislike my half-brothers, simply doesn't have so much to work with. Simon, Craig and I enjoy a shared history. Enjoy! I hope there was a little. That her sister burdened herself with children when leaving her unhappy marriage would have been a better course, dominates Monica's thinking. Has flooded her veins too. She likes to hear about her nephews, the business of meeting up seems a strain for her. She has yet to manage it since they moved down here. Since their parent's incarceration.

'Did Daddy mention me.'

'He did...' She pauses for too long before finding what he might have said. '...knows how hard it is for you, finding out what really happened after so long.'

'But what did really happen, Aunt Sarah? Did he say?'

'You know he can't talk properly in there.'

'I can't wait until court, and Mary talked properly about it, whether she was telling truth or lie. What she had to say...' I let my little rant fizzle away. I don't think I want to talk about my stepmother's infidelity with Aunt Sarah. We have never once spoken of my father's many similar dalliances—his hundreds and thousands—it would upset the balance in our tolerance of each other. If she believes him a model husband I would be surprised but only mildly.

'I hope it never gets to court, Sophie. The real killer could come out of the woodwork and our family can go back to the peace we knew.' She sits upright with a quick lurch. 'What is it, Sophie?'

I am stifling a laugh, that is all. 'He has admitted it, you know? Said he buried her under the shed. Buried his first wife under a shed in the garden of an elderly colleague. That is going to court for sentencing, Sarah. The police think the pair of them did the murder, he says only her. It's a bloody mess. The woodwork contains nothing.'

'He might be covering for the elderly colleague.'

I put my hand on my forehead. Jean Fletcher has long passed away; she was in her seventies when my mother died. My father has not implicated her at all. Not as far as I know. He might have used that venue because she was too dotty to know what was going on in her garden. I have a vague recollection of the lady. Daddy used to wax lyrical about her as a ground-breaker, a woman who worked in academia—in science—before World War two and after. She was once remarkable but looked only a thin old bird when I saw her. Teaching days long in the past; an elderly spinster.

'No chance,' is all I say. If my aunt wishes to delude herself, I am powerless to stop it. 'And what did Craig say about the police. Were they all right with him?'

'He picked up a bruise or two in the skirmish when he was caught. Then he was taken and charged in the police station, then it was dropped...or he was cautioned. Something and nothing. The police lady who drove him all the way back here from Retford came in for a coffee. And she was most sympathetic, I'm pleased to say. She wasn't the one who bruised him. Understood how very stressed poor Craig is. She even advised he have counselling but I don't like to. What with Simon how he is, it seems a bit much to be calling in the professionals for the other one as well.'

'Aunt Sarah, if he's not well, he's not well. I'll talk to him shortly but if they both had broken legs you wouldn't dismiss the second as more than the family can handle.'

'Oh, it's all right for you, Sophie. I have them every day. The sooner that family get back to normal, the sooner I can get my own life back.'

I don't laugh at this. Not at all. She must be more than twice my age, cannot think straight about housework, never mind twenty-year-old murder cases, or teenagers clanking off the rails. She will be crying silent but plentiful tears; it is not just me. Not just me and Craig. Not just me, Craig, Monica and Mary if her denials have a shred of truth in them.

Something terrible has befallen our whole family. Uncle Philip is probably weeping away on his golf course, or even behind a closed office door. Thank God Granny Bredbury is dead. If that sounds unkind it is not how I intend it. The poor lady had a heart attack before she reached pensionable age. I doubt if Mary ever told her the state of her marriage. At least she took pride in her youngest being on television, and never lived to see Mary go to jail.

Uncle Stephen hasn't phoned me, nor me him. It is the way of our relationship. I barely think of him as family. Monica mentioned him once or twice but it seemed she did so out of duty. They are not close. He's still to do the prison visit.

* * *

I play it safe and text before entering. Well before.

> *Simon, my friend, I'm going in to see Craig exactly now. Will call on you after that. To talk and you can listen. I will knock first and promise not to look. A girl cannot live on text alone*
>
> *Stay outside. Shout if you have to*
>
> *Don't be a dick*

* * *

When I knock on Craig's door, he calls the single word, 'Come.' He is expecting me. He sits at a small writing table. It might be a textbook before him, he could have been studying. Staged is my guess but I shan't embarrass him.

'Yo, Craigy,' I say, pulling him into a tight little hug.

'Sophie, don't be cross with me.'

'Never.' There were plenty of times I probably was cross with him, at least I got over myself while he was still in primary school. I've been better to this one than to his brother, civil for a longer duration. 'In your own words, Craigy. What was the plan? And more importantly, what should we do for plan B?'

He swivels himself around properly now that I have released him. His chair is a square shape but he is sitting side on, knees facing me. 'I should have broken into Mummy's prison,' he says.

'Craigy, the women in there would eat you alive. Your mum wants to see you, and she wants out, not you in.'

'You saw her. Will she come out? Is Dad lying?'

'Tricky stuff, little bro. Our dad has lied to me for nineteen years, so whether he is telling the truth now is hard for me to sniff out. What do you know about your mum conducting a little extra-marital something or other? Finding love behind our dad's back. Did you ever have wind of it, up there in darkest Lancashire?'

'What, Sophie? What are you on about? What kind of love?'

'The rumpy-pumpy kind. Possibly with warm feelings attached. Dad says Mary killed Cynthia; Mary says he is only saying it to get back at her for conducting an affair. A postgrad at the uni. Sound plausible?' I've embarrassed him, I see the colour of my young stepbrother's cheeks going through the gears. Pink-red-purple. His sainted mother getting barnacled by a man who isn't the pensionable Prof Paul. Less embarrassing than letting the old man she foolishly married give her woody-woodpecker in my biased book. 'The hole in her theory is she admits she never thought Dad found out. She must have conducted it pretty discreetly but word at the university might have got around.'

He isn't crying or anything, sitting with his head in his hands. 'I have one fucked-up family,' he says. I nod concurrence. 'Did she sound convincing?'

'To Monica, yes. I've been on the fence—or on the other side of it—regarding Mary Stephenson for as long as I've known her. A quarter of a century, Craig. We've had this conversation before. You love her but she was pretty ice-cold with me when it mattered. Hey, hey.' I hug the little wretch again. Something in my words as got him teary and I thought my breezy style was keeping all that at bay. 'Craig, I'm sorry. It's about those two, not about you and I.'

'It's about your mum, Sophie. I know that.'

* * *

When Craig and I have talked out the issues of family and I've heard the detail of his rail journey to Retford and assault by security at the prison perimeter, I query his next steps.

'Auntie Sarah says you have a school lined up here, just haven't gone yet.'

'Getting my head together. I should go but I don't want to be a grade-one fuck-up on my very first day.'

'Yeah, I get that. But are you getting any coursework, getting prepped for entry whenever you're properly ready?'

'My head isn't quite there, sis. I'll do it soon. Really, I will.'

I look at him carefully. His face is handsome but the bruising on his cheek is quite dark. A serious blemish. 'That'll clear up,' I say. 'What do you feel inside?'

'I feel bloody angry about this,' he points to the very part of his face I was discreetly scrutinising. 'They hit me because they could. I was doing nothing.'

'Too right. Wrong place to be, Craig. It doesn't justify what they did, there's just no suing those bastards.'

'If I was a reporter, I'd make a splash about shit like that. Publicising wrong-doing is the way to stop it.'

'Spot on, spot on. I don't think the Noise will print anything I write which is family-related, not at the present time. You get yourself to school and then do a journalism degree, like I did. You're the man to right that wrong.' He smiles quite proudly when I say it. I've no idea when he will hit the school gate. A family falling apart like this would knock anyone out of the game for a time. I'll be racking my brains over how I can help him all night tonight, I know I will. 'Are you and Simon getting along?'

'Sure. He's been a smug git about this...' He gestures his face once more. '...but we're fine.'

'And auntie and uncle?'

'Insufferable, aren't they?'

* * *

I'm outside and I'm coming in

Stay where you are

I'm coming in

Then I start to compose a last text to prepare him. ***Five, four, three*** — I feel my phone vibrating — ***two, one.*** I send it. Scarcely pause before I push down the door handle. When I step inside, big and burly Simon expresses something verbal, that just might have been 'fuck off.' He has never spoken in company before, to the very best of my knowledge, so it might be an Earthly miracle for which I am the catalyst. The poor boy is virtually naked, I wasn't to know. He has pulled some bedclothes across himself now. If he was wanking, it was untimely, and if it is my presence in the house which aroused it, that is a most unwanted compliment. I imagine there is an innocent explanation, shan't ask him to justify himself. 'Sorry Si, I'll give you five minutes and come back.'

When I back out of the room, I click my phone and read his last missive.

No!

It makes sense in the circumstances, and he wasn't to know I was mid-text.

Sorry bruv. Can't text all morning. Are you decent yet?

Stay where you are.

No can do

This big beast could probably push his furniture in front of the door single-handed but it is not in his nature to try. Willpower has been his sword, and he slices the air with it every day. Me too, that is his problem at this juncture.

Five

I wait but he doesn't reply.

Four

Same result.

Three, two, one

If he's naked this time, I'll fucking kill him.

As I open the door, Simon is on his feet. He wears black trousers and a patterned shirt. Blue, red, white. A surprisingly tasteful one. He bows his head forward, makes no eye contact and his hair is quite long. Not ponytail long or anything outlandish but falling over the eyes he keeps from me. I think he is showing me that the nudity was a blip. Not really him.

'How is it going, Simon?' His demeanour doesn't change. He will not say eff-off to that, and it maybe that only involuntary formulations pass his lips. An elective mute with Tourette's Syndrome, very niche. 'I'm worried about Craig, you know. He is more muddled than I realised. His journey to prison was a needed if futile pilgrimage. Showing he's not taking it lying down. What do you think?'

He seems to be looking through his hair into his hands and before I realise what is happening, my own phone vibrates.

He is terrified that both our parents are in there for life

'Poor lamb. I have no idea what will happen to them but there is realism in his fears, isn't there?'

True

'Can you reassure him? Kind of make it clear that you are going nowhere.'

What if they decide I'm a nutjob?

'Make sure I am down as your next of kin. I won't let them.'

My God. Are Craig and I going to live with you, Sophie?

'Ha! You misquote me. These are the guys with a big house. Your aunt and uncle. It doesn't make them next of kin.'

We're a moneyed family; buy a house like this one

'Hey, Simon. I love you guys but what about my life? My plans?'

Like?

'I don't know. What if I choose to settle down? Raise my own family one day'.

You don't settle

'I might one day.'

Two women do not a baby make

'Who told you that?'

Right in one

'Seriously, Simon. I never talk about my personal life...you've not seen me in town.'

I am staring at my phone, waiting for the silent one's explanation. Daddy hasn't a clue. None of them have. About once every three years, I have taken a boy to the family home. Let them dream. Usually, it's been a boy who I have let do a little more than dream. I don't mind that stuff. It just comes second. How does this social misfit know what no one else has figured? Not even Monica, I'm sure.

'Tell me how you guessed that one.'

More of his fucking silence.

'Do I smell lesbian?'

> *There is no olfactory clue*

'You have a sixth sense?'

> *I have sense*

'Have you told Craig?'

> *That is for you to do in your own time, sister*

'You'll give Auntie Sarah an aneurism if you blab it to her.'

> *Then I shall save the news until I can stand her no longer*

* * *

Back in Bayswater in the evening, I am still pondering Simon's unlikely insight, along with the conversation I had on the drive with Uncle Philip. I don't dress dyke, I like normal pretty, it is my way. I like it in myself and in the girls which I like to look upon. And I eye the boys a little, maybe not as gung-ho, tongue hanging out as some, but I spot who's hot. Simon doesn't look at me. And my texts are usually about him. Hats off to the boy but—fuck me—it's scary.

Just as I was leaving, heading for the railway station, a car pulled onto the drive. Uncle was sweet, gave me the peck on the cheek which his wife is too uptight to manage, and asked if I had time to talk. There are half-hourly trains into town, it's all the same to me whatever time I arrive at the station. He mostly wanted to hear how the prison visits had gone. I think he is itching to go but can't without Sarah—the blood relative—and she will only see her brother, as if it would be disloyal to go and see the boys' mother now that he's dobbing her in it.

Water Shall Burst Forth in the Wilderness

I told Uncle Phil that Mary thinks Paul is paying back a personal grudge, and without missing a beat he said, 'An affair.' It took me quite by surprise; I'd never come across a hint that she might have had one until I heard what I heard in South Kent.

I sought to clarify that he meant Mary having the affair, not one of Prof Paul's conquests.

'I think he was worried about that,' said Phil.

'What makes you think it?'

'Last time we stayed—the only time in the last five years—he was getting stressed when she was out longer than her time planner suggested she would be. You must have seen it: they kept university schedules, teaching times, up on his study wall...no...on the kitchen wall. "Where is she? What's she getting up to?' he said. At the time I thought he was just the anxious host, didn't know how to entertain without Mary by his side. It's is only since that I've wondered if there was more to it.'

'And Sarah concurs with you? She didn't say.'

'Sarah cannot believe her brother had anything to do with it. She has no interest in Mary's defence.'

That was the conversation, and now I've time to reflect upon it in my flat, it strikes me that this is the way it goes. Mary—it no longer pains me to say—is beautiful. The men in the room believe her, the women less so. That is the way of the world. Monica is her sister, on Mary's side. I like beautiful girls too, just not that particular stepmother. I'm no fan of injustice—she shouldn't be in there if she didn't do it—nor do I feel any nearer to knowing the right answer to that pivotal question. Bare-faced liar, or as innocent as a philanderer's wife can be. That is: she is entitled to a few murderous thoughts but none of them should have been directed at the ex-wife, towards whom a little residual sympathy would be the more congruent emotion.

I hear my phone ringing. The little mobile in my handbag.

I dip in and pick it out, press green, try to make my 'Hello,' warm while being unsure if I should be steeling myself for whatever I'm about to hear.

'Sophie, Grace here. I'm so sorry to have failed to call you back when I should have.'

Not quite how I remember it. 'Grace, Grace, how are you?'

'I'm probably having it easy, and I'm missing you, Sophie. I got scared; you are going through such difficult times, and everything about you and me was new. For me it was. New, unfamiliar. But it is beautiful, I want...' She lets a small silence hang on the line. Fails to tell me what she wants. 'Should I be phoning you, Sophie? I know I've let you down once. If you'd rather I hang up, just say so now.'

It takes me a moment to take in all she has so succinctly said. 'So happy to hear your voice.' Which I am. She has a soothing, comforting voice. 'Oh Grace, I thought I'd lost you. Frightened you, which I never...'

'No, you are special, Sophie. I took longer to see it than you deserve. Will you see me again?'

'Yes. Yes, I will. Anytime.'

5.

My girlfriend and I have entered The Ottoman, a small and sweet pub in a passageway off the Strand. An early evening drink and back to hers, that is the plan. Grace is describing the rehearsal process for a Brecht revival in which she has a role. I am disappointed on her behalf that her part is to be only minor. I don't say it. I still harbour a fear my role in her life remains small, much as I would like it to grow. In my mind she is my leading lady but I am wracked with doubts about whether this is mostly a fantasy. Ninety percent. She is ever so nice with me, truly, just doesn't throw the kitchen sink at it. Or perhaps she does, and it is with a degree of restraint I have never mastered.

Something in the way she holds her hands and moves her head when she speaks reminds me of my Auntie Monica. A pleasing comparison, and they both tread the boards. Earlier today—we have been in each other's company hours—she grilled me a little about Mica Barry. I have sworn her to secrecy and told her the lot. That interview in Girls in the News; the stars siblinghood with a probable murderer. I regretted using the word probable straight after saying it. I was pretty resolute about it the last time I saw and kissed Grace Topping. Told her my stepmother is a murderer. If I turn into a softy now, whatever will she think of me?

The table we sit at is an upturned barrel, well finished, a small marble-effect top. We are in a stylish bar with a rustic feel. Grace has a Belgian beer, it's martini rosso for me. I have noticed two young men eyeing us from where they stand at the bar, and I am trying to fathom if Grace has noticed them also. If she has dropped all that, or retains a stubborn interest in the other sex. The becocked. Being fanciable must be something we all aspire to. I like it. The snag is it may have contributed to the brevity of my many almost-relationships. There is always promise in starting afresh but the habit of it makes one highly superficial. I lean over the small barrel, a hand upon her smooth cheek, and kiss my girlfriend momentarily upon the lips. Lean back. We have done the same at Camden Market earlier today. This is a better millennium and girls may kiss who they please. I know that the two young men will have seen, will be recalculating their next moves. Exactly what runs through men's heads is a mystery to me. Girls kissing girls might make them look away, quite a few actually stare more. What their calcified brains come up with while they are doing either is a hundred-yard sprint away from the confines of my understanding. Simon is my half-brother, and he has divined my sexuality using the hidden powers of the elective mute.

And still I fear my presence in the house got him more aroused than I have dared ask him to explain, or which he—candid fellow that he usually is—has texted a word of explanation for. A weird and wonderful brain, has my brother Si. Possibly a dirty mind to go with it, and mutism combined with the consideration which goes into texting will generally mask that. My own healthy but broad mind can picture those two young men across the pub sharing a little private time with Grace and I. Such shenanigans are strictly not on today's menu. Too much too soon. For I certainly wouldn't want them sticking around. Young men in pubs are playthings. Not fully formed human people.

'He is the quietest director I've ever worked with. Small chap, scarcely a word during performance. Uses barely discernible facial expressions as his main feedback.'

As she is saying this, the two young men arrive at our barrel. 'Crowded here. Okay if we sit with you, ladies.'

The young man who asks this has a snake tattooed on his very visible arm. He wears a T-shirt telling us all that he works out: very tight, barely even short-sleeved. Grace puts her hand on mine, glances into my face as if querying whether rudeness might be the order of the day. In my life, I have been rude and I have been accommodating, perhaps more of the former, but definitely both. I sense that Grace goes the other way. I nod that the two men may join the barrel. It does not mean we are double dating, or even listening in to each other's conversations. They pull up their little stools to sit upon. Share our barrel, Curly Black Hair and Bicep Boy.

* * *

'Can we buy you dinner?' asks my muscular admirer. I think Grace looks gorgeous but it is me on whom his glance repeatedly falls. And I am sure Grace and I both have a few years on these unlikely dates. Not so many as to put them off but what they are after is nooky, not lifelong relationships. Young men in pubs! Like I said.

Grace looks at me with concern. I think she is worried that I might agree to his proposition, although I have no wish to spend any more time with them. They are here and I have quasi-flirted. A hell of a week, and I mean no disrespect to Grace. It is she whom I wish to spend the night with.

'Sorry boys, were on a date,' I say.

On cue, Grace turns her face into mine and kisses me once more upon my lightly coloured lips. She lingers, they may not see it but I feel her tongue search out my own. As soon as she has leant back, she glances around at Will and Graham, as they have revealed their names to be. A so-there expression on her face. William—my cheeky Bicep Boy—leans straight into me and kisses my lips as Grace has just done. She pushes him with both hands and he desists. Holds his hands defensively in the air.

'It looked good,' he says. Winks at me. 'Was good.'

'You're not welcome,' I say. I hope to have an ironic undertone to my voice. I really didn't mind but I think Gracie did and that makes it very awkward. 'And we really are a couple. Exclusive. Fuck off all boys, I'm afraid.'

'Sorry,' says Will. 'I was out of order. You look like fun but I was out of order. I...' He makes a funny nervous motion, rubs both hands up and down the opposite bicep. Doing it might stimulate his ink-drawn snake. '...I'm mostly a lot more reserved than this, aren't I, Gray?'

'He is. And we meant it when we offered to buy you a meal but no means no. We get it.'

Grace looks more composed now. I put my hand upon hers. 'We've not finished our drinks,' I point out. 'Back to the polite chat and then we can go our separate ways. All right, boys?'

They both nod, and we fall into the awkward silence that is due. Graham dips his eyes at Grace and says, 'Actress,' beneath his breath. We have not shared professions but she continued to talk about rehearsals while they were at the table.

'I'll tell you a weird thing,' says Will. I think he has dredged up a story. A high to end on, hopefully. 'I'm in physics, Imperial. Research post...'

I cut him off. 'Do all physicists hit on random girls, steal unbidden kisses.'

He laughs. I hope I said it playfully. I am interested. Having a father like mine gives me pause to think scientists may all be more forward than the typical portrayal of them prepares us for. 'Have you ever seen me do that before?' Will asks of his friend.

'No,' says Graham, head shaking as he talks. 'He's a straight-up guy.'

Grace and I both giggle at that clumsy phrase, do so until both boys join us. Then Bicep Boy, who must usually hide his muscles beneath a lab coat, continues his tale. 'My supervisor studied under that guy in the news. The Chair at Lancaster; have you followed it?' Grace puts a hand on the small of my back. Sweet girl. I indicate that I have indeed heard the news story, a discreet nod of the head. That I have visited the old sod in prison, I keep entirely tight-lipped about. Grace knows, of course. Must feel for me, having to listen to the gossip and innuendo of Joe Public. 'I can't believe it. Top physicist. Him and his wife bumped off his ex, twenty years ago, hid her body under a shed in their garden. Then they moved away, left it there like it was the most natural thing in the world to leave behind. I don't know any other scientists who might do a thing like that, think they could get away with it, but when I think about it more generally, physicists are pretty practical—put a man on the moon and all that—I guess they have the skillset.'

I don't tell him that he has muddled up the detail. The shed under which my mother was buried was not in our garden but that of Jean Fletcher. There is much I don't know and still I'm sure to be bundles more clued in about the case than this mental and physical gym bunny. Miss Jean Fletcher deceased, as of November the something or other, nineteen-eighty-nine. I understand she vacated the property four or five years before that.

'What does your chappie say? The one who knew...the top physicist. Knew his second wife too, perhaps. I understand they are awaiting trial. Not guilty until proven otherwise.'

'Rinus knew the lot of them. He says the first wife should have killed him, by rights. A randy prof going behind her back with every female in the faculty. The second wife was a kid, according to Rinus. An undergraduate worth keeping. "A looker" were his words. Sorry if that sounds crude. Old scientists, eh?'

'And he—this Rinus chappie—thinks they plotted to murder Cynthia?'

'He doesn't. He can't see why they would. But he also says—the papers say the same—that he's confessed. Says his second wife murdered the first and the pair of them buried her where they thought no one would ever find her. Madness, eh?'

That it is madness might be the totality of my opinion, it is even driving me a little that way. 'It sounds utterly bizarre,' I concur. 'I expect we must await a trial to become certain of our facts. Isn't that the way of proper physicists? Don't get too excited about the hypothesis until all the data is in.'

* * *

Back at Grace's, she and I alone, my girlfriend wants only to talk. 'You need to, Sophie. You've had such a tough time.'

I am quite partial to the distraction of physical comfort, arousal even, expect it can wait. 'I think I may have scared you off with it all, first time around. The nightmare which is my family.'

'Scared me? It shouldn't have scared me off. I'm sorry...'

'Don't be, Grace. I wasn't meaning to bring it up. I meant to say, it is not all about me. I love hearing about your life.'

'Your father...'

'I never hated him until he was jailed.'

'...you knew?'

'That he couldn't keep his trousers on. Too many girls like men like those, don't you think?'

Grace gives a little laugh. 'I think I've been one, once or twice. Always regretted it.' For a horrible moment, I think she is about to tell me that she once screwed my father. 'Good thing I never met him, isn't it?'

A royal relief. An enema. She is on her little sofa and I am in the armchair; I stand up and take a step towards her lean in for a kiss and then roll upon her. She laughs, does not resist. 'Let me hold you, Gracie. I just want to hold you. Talk as well if you like.'

She busses a kiss to the top of my head, my elfin hair, ears slightly on show. She is on her back with me upon her. Fully clothed. Not the way most ladies in their thirties sit, although it is pleasurable indeed. I'm surprised more don't try it.

* * *

The curtains are not thick, and the light that has invaded the flat dances upon Grace's nut-brown hair. She sleeps. Sleeps as I have scarcely done. Now I am on the right of the bed, for much of the night she held me. We were both in the centre. I am wearing the negligée of hers which I considered most revealing, she in pyjamas, insisting we must not be naked. She says she is wooing me. 'Not doing a Will,' meaning the very Bicep Boy who overstepped the mark in The Ottoman. We have kissed, she allows me small pleasures, but this is a true romancing and I am minded to let Grace Topping do exactly as she pleases. Really, I have learned that she is the warmest soul. When I spat out a bit of bile about Mary, she was all sympathy; and when I confessed feeling some remorse—calculated that Mary was as confused as her stepdaughter in that God-awful marriage—she said it was remarkable that I can be so objective about it. Perhaps it is, and it's been a hell of a long time coming. I do still hate my stepmother, although it is now only provisional hate. Is she guilty or innocent? All my feelings towards her hang upon this. They are proxy feelings for my true mother: whoever is proven to be her murderer I will hate until my dying day. It might be Mary, just possibly not.

My phone has been vibrating in my bag for about an hour. Ten little hums on the trot and then it stops. Thank God I've set the ringtone to silent, mustn't wake Grace who must be fresh for her rehearsal later today. Ten minutes go by, then here we go again. Nobody rings me between five and six in the morning. If Darius wants to send me to cover the closure of The Maze in County Down, he can fuck off. He has touted the like before but I won't be getting off my sick bed for that dismal gig. If a reporter has cried off the Olympics, I'm interested. And that only if I can take Grace with me. Three weeks in Sydney would be sweet. Although her Brecht-thingy should probably take priority. And I am clueless about sports. For now, I shall let it ring.

Grace sleeps on her back, she has the most delicate nose. Thin, well-tended, I can see that she tweezes. Eyebrows too. She might have them done professionally. Her lips are together, and then a small opening appears with every exhalation, closes straight after and I never quite see how. I cannot kiss the lips for it would wake her up, nor can I help myself from wanting to. I hear the short vibration of a text. Whoever it is, they are most persistent. I graze my lips across hers and slip out from the side of the bed.

Phone in hand, I am astonished to see it is Monica who made all the unanswered calls, whose text reads: ***Call me.***

Call me. Call me. Many texts and in all of them this is the extent of her message.

I see Grace raise a hand, a sleepy head. The faintest kiss I could possibly execute has woken her. She looks serene, not cross. 'Leave it,' she says, indicating my phone. Gesturing that I should return to the warmth of the bed. Her arms.

'It's Monica,' I say. 'She wants me to phone her.'

'Mica Barry. Wow.'

'I better should.' I perch myself on the edge of the bed. I feel Grace—who has pulled herself upright—run her fingers over the bumps of my spine, then spread a hand to touch the rear of my ribcage through the thin nightwear. I press the green telephone button, mouth the word, 'Sorry,' to her. It is an intrusion into our private time. I love Monica but she had better have a good reason for interrupting morning sex, if that is what Grace would have allowed. I feel a little turned on by the authority my girlfriend is exerting in our relationship. Her lips now touching and tasting the lower reaches of my neck.

'Monica, it's me.'

'Sophie. God, Sophie, thanks for calling. Are you alone?'

'No. Yes. No.'

'None of my business. If it is no, I hope he's a good one. No easy way to say this to you, Soph. It's about four hours since I took the call. Your father is dead. They found him hanging...' She hears me erupt in tears. '...I know, I know. I'm so sorry, little Soph.'

Grace has moved out from the covers. She sits beside me and holds me close. Lovingly. I cannot fault my aunt; Monica had to tell me straight, I know that. Everything has turned to shit. 'Suicide?'

'For sure. Never a caged bird, we both knew that. Look, lovely, I got the call from Philip. Sarah can't handle it, gone to pieces. I said I would phone you.'

'Those poor boys,' I say, and I am not wrong, although it is my own loss that is making me feel sick, feel like I am in a dream that cannot be true. I have a need to reawaken into the presence of a living father, if only an imprisoned one. This severance of a life seems to deprive me of more than a disreputable father. Of knowledge, a link to the memory of my mother. To her truth. He was a dreadful husband to Mary, to Cynthia Hartnell before that. It is easy to see. Then he could be quite a caring soul towards me, to his two boys as well, although Simon tested his understanding of how everything should unfold.

'You, Sophie. This is so tough for you. I'm glad if you are with someone, which sounds the case, and if you want to come up here—stay again—you're most welcome. Bring him. It's good. I want to help you through this God-awful time, little cousin of mine.'

She has used this expression before, many times before. Incorrect but affectionate. 'Can I take a rain check on that? It is more than appreciated; I might be there before you know it, and I'll call first. Life is complicated.'

'It's a fucking nightmare, Sophie. I can't work out where it leaves Mary, just can't see much good in it.'

'None at all,' I reply. 'Love you, Monica.' I press the red telephone button. I cannot spend time contemplating Mary's lot right now. My tears have resumed, they stream down my face. Grace holds me, rocks me. She could not be nicer. I don't think it is helping but I let her. Love her intensely for trying.

6.

Monica drives, and I am riding shotgun. It is a meaningless thought but the only one I am letting across my mind right now. A phrase Craig used when, from a young age, I allowed him to sit with me in the front of the small Audi I briefly owned. One of Daddy's many gifts. Gosling, our family solicitor, was on the telephone for half an hour yesterday. Mine is a father who won't stop giving, showers me from beyond the grave although I no longer feel any connection with him whatsoever. I want one thing only: my mother back amongst the living. I am coming to believe it might be he alone who has determined it is what I will never have. The day before his death he set out a sworn affidavit stating it was Mary who did it. Murder. Why top yourself after that other than to avoid the upcoming cross-examination? I think I should toss a coin. One of them did it, one or both. Coins be damned.

Monica drives directly behind the hearse; this will be a crematorium funeral, not following the well-trodden path down which members of my family usually take their leave from Surrey life. Or the life beyond if they have strayed further afield; Lancaster, Carnforth, my father took a few wrong turns, maybe a lifetime of them. The manner of his demise decided the modesty of the ritual we are to participate in. Prison, an improvised noose: no self-respecting Church of England vicar would have him sent from their place of worship to the ever after. Not after that. Dispatching the bounder to hell, for surely that is the only realm which will have him now. Craig is on the back seat of our car, sitting alongside Gary. I am not sure what the latter is doing here but say nothing. He behaves impeccably. He and Monica have their names in the newspapers now for all the wrong reasons, their association with the reprobate who was my father has become known to all. And the connection, for Gary, at least, is most tenuous. Monica is a stoical as I am not.

'How are you doing, Craig?' says my aunt. A quick glance in the rear-view mirror as she asks.

'Simon is texting me.'

'You think he's okay, home alone?' Looking over my shoulder, I see Craig shrug. Monica must have caught it in

Water Shall Burst Forth in the Wilderness

the mirror. 'I wish he was here,' she says.

For myself, I cannot picture it. Easy to bring his face—porous, perspiring, hair covering his eyes—his enormous frame, to mind. Impossible to think of it in the company that is gathering at the crematorium. He won't so much as come downstairs for dinner.

'I wish I was back there with him,' says Craig, and we must all detect the catch in his voice.

'That bad?' says Monica. 'Lean on us, Craig. It's so sad but we'll get you through.'

He turns and looks out of the window. The cars are crawling now. We are turning in the gate. 'Who has he roped into carrying his coffin?' says Craig.

'He was not in a position to rope in a soul,' I say. 'Dead before a funeral direction was laid down. I've persuaded the prison to send along six lifers. They are to carry it to grave's edge, drop him in the hole and jump in after.'

Craig snorts out a laugh and a few bitter tears with it, I think I've pitched it right. He was a bastard, our father, one way or another, whatever we thought when he was living. 'Do they let prisoners out for funerals?'

'Can't let the dead ones out soon enough,' I try to quip.

Monica gives me a funny look. Craig and I have this sort of relationship all day every day, and we may be the only ones who will miss him. Craig already knows the answer to the point of his question. His mother, Mary Stephenson, once Bredbury, will be in attendance accompanied by a guard or two. A fat lesbian or two if my powers of prophecy are worth squat. They will keep her away from the other mourners—attendees, I cannot dredge up anything about my father that is worth mourning over—not allow her to touch a soul. The undertakers are true pros; they have warned us, advised how we must behave towards Mary—mustn't approach her—and managed it with a level of discretion that made it sound in keeping with funeral decorum. The guards don't care a fig about any of that, only about returning her to South Kent Prison without incident. It should not preclude my stepmother from spitting on the coffin. If she neglects to do it, she's guilty.

* * *

'Dearly beloved...'

The quasi-vicar, sent by the Church of England to see off the unwanted sinner who fathered me, looks to be an outcast himself. A shock of white hair and a face that would frighten a mirror. Angry eyes set in rice-paper cheeks. He wanted to talk over the service with me but I couldn't do it, nor could Craig. And obviously Simon wouldn't. I sent a few words his way by first-class post, not sure they are having an impact on this pitiable ceremony. Even after receiving my helpful letter, he phoned Monica's house, having got the number from Uncle Phil. I pretended to be out and she was cool about it. Eulogy my sweet behind: what is there to say about the man who, at the very least, participated in hiding my mother's body and denying her the funeral that he has now opted for over a trial.

Craig and I are front row, Auntie Sarah and Uncle Phil beside us. The coffin stands on a stone bier, and I could knock it over, pull him from the cask, try to shake a few answers from his cold cadaver. Sarah cries small tears that mean she doesn't dare to think about all that has gone on. Her brother's upended life. She is crying to avoid looking smug. She knew what he was, has lived a better if duller life, in every imaginable respect. I think Phil is going to miss their late-night whiskies. The was-he or wasn't-he a killer dilemma passes him by. Accountants tot up money, not bodies. No interest in a thing with so diminishing a return. We are all trying hard not to look around. I feel I should give Monica supportive looks if ever I can meet her eye. She has been more than wonderful to me these last sixteen days. I have been at her house more than at my own; she has met Grace, couldn't have been cooler on learning of my leanings. My dykedom. Accompanied me to the undertaker. And when, while following a funeral planning guide she discovered on the World Wide Web, we came to choosing a hymn that this gathered congregation could meaningfully sing, she blurted out, 'Let's go with Pants Down Peter.' Ha! Pop music that even I had heard, and far more apt than Abide With Me or The Old Rugged Cross, all the nonsense that the internet was recommending. The Browns comedic song was in the charts this time last year, on breakfast radio every morning, it seemed. When she said it, I nearly peed myself with laughing, and Monica did likewise. A truly splendid idea; should one laugh when planning the funeral of a close relative who has committed suicide? It seemed right.

The press are here in droves. Not inside the church, a gauntlet between car park and entrance. The prison guard who as good as sexually assaulted Monica some seven weeks ago is in attendance, minding my stepmother. I dare not look around, they sit together on the rear aisle, Mary handcuffed to the woman. It might fulfil the prison guard's fantasy but it depresses me. Mary looks wretched, not beautiful at all, although it is in there. The world can see. Features fine, figure in tact in her mid-forties. The butch bodyguard is loving every minute. Courtesy of the Sunday Noise, she will know that it is Mica Barry's sister she has—in imitation of a sex game—chained herself to.

'When we recall the life of Paul Sebastian Stephenson it is surely with mixed emotions. Two wives in his life time, although neither may have been truly satisfied with the manner in which he fulfilled his role as husband...' I wrote none of this bullshit. He plausibly murdered one, cheated routinely on both. If he thinks it unsatisfactory, then this is a vicar with low expectations of this life. '...father of three children...' The brainless old cleric gestures Craig and I, then looks very puzzled that no third child sits in the front row. I put him in the picture with my letter, and now I doubt he has digested a word. '...I trust you have fond memories however painful they may sometimes feel to access.' The nearest to a true sentiment, although a monkey with a typewriter might have fluked across it. 'And his greatest contribution to this world has been in the field of physics.' I haven't spoken to the small selection of random girls in the audience—a couple in their forties, and at least one younger than me—I know who they are, my father's pioneering work in the bedding of lady physicists. Mary at the back— improbably shackled to a lesbian—is just another of them. They really should play Pants Down Peter over the public address system. A couple of choruses then we can all go home.

* * *

Last night I slept in Monica's beautiful cottage without Grace in my arms. A few days ago, we were both there, and— rehearsals have been the impediment—she was quite prepared to be there again, accompany me today. I insisted I do this alone. Or rather, do this without her. I do not wish to be bitter or hard-nosed in Grace's company. She brings out the best in me, while my father has, lately, done the opposite. I fear souring how Monica and Gary might regard me but I have also detected a small acerbic streak in my aunt. Her relationship with Mary is not a twisted one, not exactly. It is on the approaches.

It was only yesterday that the Home Office gave approval for Mary's attendance at this horrible commemoration. This development threw Monica slightly off balance. She felt herself to be attending in Mary's stead. Prof Paul is both a joke figure and the devil incarnate to her. The cartoon lech whom she might castigate Mary for being so naïve as to have thrown in her lot with; and the bastard who ruined a loved sister's life. That is not someone for whom my intelligent step-aunt is ever going to grieve. If I had counted the number of times she has said, usually apropos nothing, that her sister should have divorced my father long ago, I would have required a children's abacus to keep tally, my fingers and toes being insufficient in quantity. And I cannot disagree, I wished it many times in my childhood. She has had the discretion to say no such thing around Craig.

Is there a way to prepare oneself—steel oneself—for moments such as these? Monica tried, yesterday evening, to find some music that would keep my mind from today. She has a Brahms CD which she put on, and I enjoyed. A well-chosen distraction, she understands my tastes. Still, she saw that I was picking at a nail, screwing my face up in a way I would not if my stomach were less knotted, the world a little less grim. She queried why. Suggested we take a stroll together—she is generous to a fault—but I suggested other music. Not a particular artist but that she might try to find music that would calm me. Mozart was not it. Worse. Then she giggled and said, 'This is dreamy.' The music she put on was foul. Electric guitars and miserable lyrics, the singer pining for a woman who wore a long skirt. It failed to make sense; I have never heard the like. It shifted my mind off father and funeral, had the effect Monica sought. When I queried what era of popular music she played—which band had made money performing such tripe—she said, 'Laughing Llamas.' I was none the wiser, may have heard the name before but their oeuvre has not registered itself in my consciousness. Thank goodness. 'Mary played nothing else in her mid-teens,' she said. 'I guess you had to be there. It's a vibe. These are musicians who eschew virtuosity.'

I think Monica a splendid actress, she spoke that summary understatement deadpan. They eschew virtuosity. They may even be strangers to their instruments, so laidback, almost tuneless was the muzak. 'As of today,' I said, 'this is my favourite pop group. I too shall cherish mediocrity and all points south. When life is at its shittiest, these Laughing Llamas capture the mood to a tee.'

Monica's laugh can be mellifluent. One wants to drink from it. Even Gary, silent until now, was holding his sides. 'You are too young, Sophie,' said my step-aunt. 'Mary and co, back in Charmouth I'm talking—if you were even born then you were a long way from the smart girl I first met at my sister's wedding—they all got doped up and listened to this. Hippy music and dancing around like clothes on a washing line. That was Charmouth. About ten years late if you think about San Francisco.'

'My stepmother was never a hippy!' I declared.

'Yes and no. Not by the time she was eighteen but for a little while. Sixth form. Our friend Dennis was the true long hair. Threw the wildest house parties every week or two. Mary went.'

'And you? You danced with hippies in your youth?'

'Not really. I was much younger than Mary; times changed. Dennis was a cool guy though. We were both into him, Mary and I.' She glanced at Gary. He may have heard this story before; they seem too solid a couple to be troubled by talk of old flames. If that was what she was doing; I can't figure out where this Dennis chappie fits in. My stepmother's first love was my earlier guess.

'And Mary did all the drugs? I'm shocked.' I might have warmed to her earlier if she had told me of this misspent youth. I always thought she had a holier-than-thou air about her, or perhaps that was simply the counterpoint to Pants Down Peter.

'Not really. Nothing heavy. Everyone smoked weed. You too, right?'

I nodded. I have certainly attended parties where many did, at which I put a joint to my lips and breathed with proximity to it. I have always been scared of losing control.

Scared witless. I know my way around wine and gin, hate the unexpected. That is why I feared the following day so intensely. And now it is here.

* * *

And before that, two evenings earlier, Grace and I were together in town. The South Bank Tavern. This was after a preview. Kate Gifford in a modern play—Shift Worker by someone called Madley—the work completely unknown to me. Kate is one of the girls whom Grace was with the night I met her. The Kilderkin. She is the oldest of the three, all are talented actresses. Friends who have supported each other through successful or fallow times. Before the pub we watched the final dress rehearsal. My girlfriend smuggled me in, saying, 'Actress,' with a nod to the director. I wish. The whole thing went a bit over my head, a very moving and emotional work. I tried not to engage too closely with it, fragile as I was feeling.

I know with absolute certainty that I am the first girlfriend Grace has paraded in front of her many buddies. Spending time in the South Bank Tavern was terrific, I never thought about Daddy for a second.

'Sophie is my special friend,' said Grace by way of introduction. Then she leaned across and kissed me quickly but demonstratively. When I looked back at them, they were smiling that slightly sickly, slightly wonderful expression that has recently come into vogue. Couldn't quite believe what they had just seen, aware that fully-fledged support is the right response. The thespian's way.

Grace was very tactile with me in the bar. A trait I enjoy being on the receiving end of. Her close attention moves me. I sat between her and the girl whose thunder we might have been stealing. Kate Gifford. 'Loved your performance,' I told her. 'Intense and credible, every second.'

I think others put it better but she was most gracious.

Placed a hand upon my own. 'Grace used to have terrible taste in men. I'm so happy you've found each other.'

As the evening progressed, I worried that Grace had told her friends more about me—about what is going on around me—than I would feel comfortable with, so sympathetic did everybody seem. But there were no questions about my dead father or my Stepmother's forthcoming trial. One or two innocent enquiries about my family and I spoke warmly of my half-brothers. Tried telling Kate and her fella about Simon, his social anxiety. They listened attentively, said he sounds a great kid anyway, so I pitched that right. I also realised that Grace never named-dropped Mica Barry in this company, and only the night before we were both up in the famous actresses Buckinghamshire cottage. Nor did any other raise it, although the Sunday Noise and others are trumpeting the connection with this unseemly suicide. I asked her directly in the taxi back to my flat. 'You haven't told anyone of my connection to the Stephensons, have you?'

'I wouldn't unless you asked me to. You've nothing to be ashamed of Sophie but every reason to keep your privacy. I love Kate, she's a stranger to you. I know that.'

I nuzzled against her, whispered to her that she is the best. The best I have ever known, and I truly believe it. I have found love.

In bed that night, I told her what Kate had said. The terrible taste in men. Grace grimaced a little. 'I tried so many I forgot what I was looking for.' Under the sheets that night I tried a few things that might have been it. She moaned in a manner that suggested I was right. Reciprocated. It was so good to be transported away from the beastliness of recent days.

* * *

The hymn Monica and I settled upon says a bit about sinners but still seems out of place. We pulled our punches, wimped out of her better call of Pants Down Peter. I don't believe my father ever contemplated the cross on which his redemption is dependent. Couldn't see why any God with integrity would contemplate his redemption, I expect. Nothing in the hymn really speaks to the departed wretch who the service is nominally about. The fucker in the box is the phrase on a text I received a few moments ago from you-know-who. Son of the guy we will, presently, shunt into a hole in the ground.

I can hold a tune, and Sarah is very good. Craig is unenthusiastic, Philip not even trying.

> ***And when I think that God, His Son not sparing***
> ***Sent Him to die, I scarce can take it in***
> ***That on the cross, my burden gladly bearing***
> ***He bled and died to take away my sin***

I can sing it but the meaning is worse than elusive. It is repulsive. I want nobody's son to die for my sins, such as they are. My sexual orientation, if you believe everything in the antiquated book which excites vicars everywhere. I guess how I treated Mary back in the day needs a little absolution. And how she treated me. All a bit late for God's intercession. I shan't apologise while she is in prison. Will have to if the facts prove her innocent. It would even please Monica, and that strand of such an outcome would make me most happy. Wrong reasons, I suppose. Damn that theology. Trickier than algebra, it really is. I glance around while I am singing. I can see both the Bredbury sisters are belting out the words. I like the tune but Laughing Llamas carried greater meaning. And they were atrocious. Glancing back over my shoulder, I wink at Monica. I don't think she sees. It is highly inappropriate. My mind is not really at a funeral at all, only my transient body. And could Christ's bleeding and dying really take away my father's sin? What would be the point of that? We are all accountable for our actions. Surely, we are? I've not figured out how it works but I'm okay with it, one way or another. It seems right. Lines and detentions came my way back at Hazelbrook School. I never minded. Understood the rationale. I swore at teachers, pulled girls' hair. Then did my penance. Even contemplated the error of my ways now and then. Learned to regret; there is merit in the right punishment. I've gone on to kill no one.

When we sit again, hymn duly sung, I think over my conversation with Grace. The disinvitation.

'Do you mind if I let Monica do all the supporting on Friday?'

She never contradicted. I think she was trying to avoid looking disappointed. 'If you are sure that is for the best.'

I was sure about nothing. Relationships are precarious things. I might kick the coffin over and stamp on the body; Grace really doesn't need to see that. When, as best I could, I explained my self-consciousness, while avoiding mention of the adolescent ribbing Craig would subsequently give me, or the likelihood that Auntie Sarah would pass out in the crematorium at the sight of my lady-love, the secondary reasons, she listened with that intensity I have so quickly come to cherish.

'I hear you,' she said. 'Never knew your father and never will. But Sophie, I am part of your life after, and I will guess that memories of him—painful as shit, I can see that—will always be a part of you.' Then she took my right hand in both of hers. 'The you that I love.'

And that is the nub of it. I expected her to love me only because of the various facades I successfully maintain. Grace is stepping through them, one after another. And she is still here. Her early wobble was just the understandable reluctance to give up stubbly men and their ever-eager penises. They can make quite a stir; I recall one or two seven-out-of-tens myself. But they are relatively easy to get over, and Grace has now come around to thinking as I do. She is of a different order to any other girl I've had as a partner. My burden gladly bearing. Right now, I wish I had let her come.

Singing over, we are all seated except the dissembling vicar. He prays for my father's soul. We have each of us bowed our heads, I doubt if we are all praying for the same thing. Given up, in my case. He reminds us even that the method of my father's passing was anathema to the Lord. 'The taking of one's own life, however painful its continuity may otherwise appear, is not sanctified. It is contrary to Christian teaching...' And if he took my mother's life? Raising that might be too disturbing for this guy. Or he might just say it breaks rule number such and such. Twenty-seven. He never knew Cynthia Hartnell, doesn't think about her daily as I have since nineteen-eighty-one. Before that too, but that was without the confusion that her disappearance grafted to my thoughts. '...yet we must hope that the Lord finds forgiveness even for so consequential an act. Hope for Sophie, for Simon who has not been able to come into this service, and for Craig. The brave children of Paul Stephenson, whose wellbeing we should keep most prominently in our thoughts today.'

Beside me, brother Craig is sobbing like I haven't heard him do in a decade, and these words—the stumbling ineptitude of them, quite frankly—have me crying salt tears again. I am not brave: in my mind, every link I felt towards my father, I have severed. I remember that recent visit to prison and feel only revulsion for the man across the table. It could have been an assignment, a report I was to make for The Noise, so cold are my feelings now. In his lifetime, I feared that his love for me came second to his pursuit of girls. Those with whom he had minimal connection but could enjoy pleasures which, perhaps to his credit, he never ever sought from me. Now I see it far more bleakly. He was poison. To Cynthia and to Mary. The world is a better place without him, and both those lives would have improved immensely had he never existed. That would change the rubric for us three brave souls, too, but the balance of goodness in the world would still be the greater without him. I make an honest calculation. Feeling desolate, I hug Craig tightly and he allows it.

In the pocket of my light jacket my mobile phone vibrates. The c-list vicar continues, explains for any here who do not yet know, that the body will not be cremated. Later today my father is to be interred in the family grave at Cobham. The family—meaning me and the boys again, Sarah too but her input has been useless, first to last—have requested that no graveside burial take place. 'The ground has been consecrated, and we must hope that the Lord our God accepts his child, Paul, despite all his failings.' While he drones on, I tap my phone, bring up the text and show it to Craig.

I said burn him. Are you with me yet?

My arm is still around this teenage boy, his crying never abated, and now there is a splutter of laughter in it too. Simon will never make professor but he is worth a squillion Paul Stephensons.

* * *

The goons who come with the funeral package, carry the coffin back to the hearse. Load it up for its short drive to the family plot, to lie in the self-same churchyard where his mother, father, grandmother and grandfather and a few uncles and aunts lie. We are outside the little crematory chapel now. Gathered together, not yet venturing to the cars. Monica has stayed as close to Mary as she could without risking a frisking. Craig and I go towards her, make eye contact. She blows kisses with her uncuffed hand, shouts, 'Love to Simon,' and immediately looks guiltily at the burly guard who accompanies her. Then she is escorted back to the black van, a man on one side and the guard who has spent the funeral attached to her on the other. The overblown security is another sign of the abnormality of this hateful funeral. I embrace Craig as his mother cannot. Even Monica, who has spoken warmly and thoughtfully to him before the service and again now, has not the relationship with which to comfort Craig, as I do.

Sarah and Philip stayed back at the crematorium door, not fans of Mary, I presume. They join us only now that the prison van's door has closed. Shamefully shackled Mary removed from their view. 'Honestly, they are vultures,' says my aunt with disdain, gesturing the press, photographers, who have gathered at the railings in the lee of our parked cars. I don't argue the point. In times past I have been party to entering a service, seen the boys from the paparazzi snap away, while a newsworthy funeral—the more disreputable the better—was underway. The Noise is usually the worst and I imagine Darius has asked for restraint only on my account. Other papers filling that void.

Philip is shaking Gary by the hand. Perhaps they didn't meet before the service. It passed me by. He is confirming that he may enter the tight family circle. Come to the smallest of wakes. I think this might be the awkwardness to which I did not wish to subject Grace. We shall drive back to their house. Simon awaits us there but will presumably stay in his room. Not a joiner-in. Only myself, Monica and Gary will be there plus the household regulars. Of course, the two boys have lived there only since Mary has been unable to mother them in person. We didn't even ask if she might be allowed to attend, so obvious is the answer which the prison authorities never had to give.

* * *

Uncle Philip is quizzing Gary Fielding about nineteenth-century medical practices. It is not a conversation I ever expected to hear. Gary must have researched his role well, and he answers more than proficiently. Auntie Sarah is listening in, it is the kind of talk she can manage. Craig has gone upstairs to talk to Simon. Those odd exchanges between younger brother and mute elder have been an integral part of his whole life. Monica is whispering to me about Grace. Have I texted her? I think she is worried I may have snubbed her by excluding her from this episode in my life. To me, it has been frightful. I love Grace Topping and she deserves better than being obliged to attend a funeral for an undeserving man she never knew. Selfishly, I should have liked her here as a comfort. And I have been selfish long enough. I am trying to put Grace before myself, a worthy, if difficult-to-fulfil, about-face in my approach to life.

Then we hear heavy footsteps on the stairs, not Craig's. The lounge door opens, Craig enters first but says nothing, his forehead is creased as if in worrisome thought. He is still in his funeral suit of charcoal, Philip's and Gary's are similar. We three ladies wear black dresses. Simon enters the room, a hand covers his face and he wears tracksuit bottoms, a blue T-shirt that rides up showing a few hairs around a white belly button. 'I'm glad he's gone,' he growls. 'Useless. He was useless.' The voice we hear properly for the first time in our lives is deep, unexpected, with no accent or undercurrent. 'Tell me how Mummy was? It's not fair on her. I don't think it is. Sorry, Sophie.'

A part of me hates Mary Stephenson intensely, and another part of me agrees with Simon completely. Nothing in this horrible saga has felt fair, and my stepmother has borne a heavy brunt. Incarceration. I like to agree with Simon, my brother. With what he says. I find myself thinking of Grace, wanting her hand in mine. She may not have understood this. Has not spent years texting this young man, receiving texts from him even when he and I were together in a room. The dumb shall speak: it is staggering. The interring of our father seems to have been the release. Was that frightful man

Water Shall Burst Forth in the Wilderness

the impediment all the time? The bane of this boy's life. I don't see it precisely; it is possible. Today he speaks.

'Hey, Simon,' says Monica, 'come. Sit beside me.' Gary stands to her gesture, allows the gargantuan man-child to take his place. Simon sits beside Monica as he has been asked. Looks only at his carpet slippers but he is thigh to thigh with our celebrated family member. She rubs his back ever so gently. Simon lets a little groan escape him; does not request that she cease. 'It's been a tough old day, big fella. It's so good to hear from you.'

'Tell me how she was.'

'We weren't really able to talk, Simon. She spent the entire time handcuffed to a prison guard.'

'The big butch lesbian?' he says. I feel all the eyes in the room upon me. Craig, of course, but even my aunt and uncle recognise it as language I have used whether they know of my familiarity with the type or not. And I have never gone in for big.

'I guess it was her,' says Monica.

'Mummy would hate that,' he growls. 'What was she wearing?'

'It was plain, Simon. A long grey skirt and black blouse. A shirt really.'

'She dressed like the prison guard?'

'Not really.'

As they talk, I look around. Philip looks intrigued but Auntie Sarah only horrified. I am unsure what disturbs her: the sudden lurch into speech which her large nephew has elected to embark upon on this particular day, or the indecorous clothing he wears to her brother's wake. It might be something more fundamental. This is a horrid day for our family of near isolates. She has buried a brother in shocking circumstances, all self-inflicted by Paul Stephenson, custody and death. Yet it is Simon she looks upon with a thunderous face. Craig and I share a smile. We are pleased to hear him speaking after so many years without.

Simon asks if his mother shed tears.

'She did. Many, many tears, and for many, many reasons, I expect,' replies Monica.

'Relief that the old bastard has gone.' As he says it, I can picture it appearing on the screen of my phone, it is shocking to hear his gravel voice announce it in front of Auntie Sarah. Simon has not grasped the etiquette of funerals. Never had the opportunity, I suppose.

'Steady on, Simon,' says Uncle Philip, and as I turn to him, I see my aunt has gripped her husband's sleeve, her face riven with anguish.

'It's just true,' says the nephew. 'True, true, true.' Can't stop talking now he has started. My aunt collapses upon her husband. A faint or a diversion, I cannot tell which.

'Whoa, whoa,' says Monica, once more rubbing the back of my enormous half-brother. 'Emotions running high and that includes yours, Simon. Let's step away from these thoughts for a moment.'

My aunt is wailing in Philip's arms. It is unpleasant and, to my thinking, a mock-up of her true feelings. I don't say this, I heed my wiser aunt. The uncle mouths a 'Thank-you' to Monica. Gary—not family, just the visiting Victorian doctor—tries to hand around a plate of cucumber sandwiches, and this brings a smile to my lips, a little snort from Simon who seems to be on the same page. I like Gary a lot, he needs a role beyond Victoriana.

'I can't stand these boys any longer,' says Sarah between gulps. Bitter tears. 'Mary's boys. Perhaps they are Paul's and perhaps they are not.'

I hear Simon say the fuck off phrase, again quite incoherently, but exactly as I heard when I inadvertently entered his room while he was nude. Then he says it distinctly. 'Fuck off.' I see his point; she has said a most hateful thing. I may have expended more emotion hating my stepmother than I did loving all the girls whose company I have enjoyed put together. I got it wrong. And never would I have been so crude, so downright dismissive of these two boys, not in my adult life—Craig is crying like we are back in the gloomy funeral chapel—and Auntie Sarah is wrong. If Uncle Philip has shared the knowledge-forward-slash-rumour that Mary had an affair behind her brother's back, it is of no consequence to the lineage of these boys. I am—her greatest detractor, bear in mind—certain Mary was true to Pants Down Peter for longer than made an ounce of sense. And he—Prof Paul, the bonking boffin—might have a dozen children outside of marriage, for all we know. Unlikely, scientists understand contraception, although I have had my own scares and men are the rarest visitors to my bed.

'They cannot stay here any longer. It upsets me just thinking about them. Both of them have to go. Both of them. I'm sorry, Craig. But this one...' She is shrieking out these angry words, pointing a crooked finger at big Simon. '...pretending that he can't speak! Well for goodness' sake!' Then she storms out of the lounge. Philip stays, looks at his hands not at our faces. 'Gone!' we hear her shout from the stairs. Hysterically yelled, I have to say. Auntie Sarah is a shocker; perhaps it's good to see she has finally got the better of her inhibitions. Saying it how she sees it. Nothing pretty about her true self, is there?

'Pack a bag, my sweet brothers,' I tell them, decisiveness coming to me for the first time in an age. 'You can stay at mine.' It's going to be rather complicated. I have a small spare but it is neither big enough for two, and nor can I imagine Simon sharing. Craig sleeping in the lounge looks probable, and that will make it smell of teenage boy. The rankest prospect which may lead me to crack like Auntie Sarah but I doubt it. I love these boys. I think they will listen in to Grace and I and all we get up to at night. That might be awkward too. We're just going to have to see how it goes.

'Are you sure about this,' whispers Monica.

'You'll be better off with me,' I tell Craig, who has got to his feet. He looks shell-shocked. The funeral, the wake. The Somme.

From Simon come forth the words, 'Thank you, Sophie.' He can do polite, mostly elects not to.

* * *

Uncle Philip helps us to load the car. A simple phrase, 'Sorry about all this,' has past his lips at least a dozen times as we toil.

Craig has been pretty useless and I have packed the vast majority of his belongings that are coming with us. Gary's car will not allow us to fetch it all. Simon has had purpose, quickly unplugging and boxing up the hard drive, monitor, cables and keyboard of the small home computer on which he spends much of his time. He carries all his own belongings to the car. Half of Craig's too. As he does so, without making any eye contact with us, his neck swivels giving him a quick scan of the surrounding area. Glances the other way, eyes raised for yet another quick shifty. Philip and Sarah have a large front garden, quite a low hedge, and a neighbour currently tending it. Shears in hand but there is scarcely any snipped foliage by her feet. I see, and so must Simon, a curtain moving upstairs in the house from which we have come. Infrequently but with purpose, letting the evictor glance upon the mayhem she has caused. Watching to see that these unwanted family members truly leave. Simon periodically waves a V-sign at that covered window. Perhaps only when Uncle Philip is not looking; however, I am not sure whether such niceties register with my expressive half-brother. The new leaf.

Then, when Simon is ensconced next to Gary at the front, Craig sitting between Monica and I at the back, Philip leans into my open rear window. I feel his breath on my cheek as he speaks. 'Nice having you boys for a time.' Craig says nothing; Simon barks like a dog, seems he hasn't cracked laughter yet. Gary waits for the man's head to retract before driving us away. I always thought of Surrey as my home county. If I never come back, I shall be happier for being elsewhere.

Chapter Seven:

Once a Family

1.

My father phones, insists that I pop back over the Pennines for the party on Sunday night. And I specifically booked a Monday night flight to Spain to avoid getting caught up in Mary's birthday celebration.

'You simply must come, Sophie. It's your mother's party.'

'Stepmother.' If she had it on the right day, I'd be up in the air. 'Daddy, it's Tiffany's twenty-first that Saturday night, and then I've got to be back here at the airport by five on Monday. Is it really worth it?'

'Of course it's worth it. Your mother's thirty-fifth. An important landmark. And who's Tiffany?'

'She shares my house, Daddy. You've met her. The ginger-haired girl.' There is absolutely no way I am spending Saturday and Sunday in Carnforth. I couldn't stand it. And there is no Tiffany, just a needed excuse to turn up no sooner than needed. I still favour not going. 'Thirty-five isn't exactly forty, Daddy. I'll be there for every birthday she has with a nought on the end.'

'You're coming to this one, Sophie.'

'But I have packing to do for the Spain trip.' This is with three other girls, not the housemates I long ago fell out with.

'I've said you're coming. Will you tell me what time your train will arrive?'

'I'd rather not...'

'You're coming...'

'I shall be thinking of you all while I am packing a few things for sunny Marbella. Poor me, missing...'

'What time is the train? I can collect you. You can walk up, if you prefer. Or I can cancel the contract for the flat. The rental. I will, Sophie, I'll stop paying for everything if you are not prepared to even come back for an important birthday. Finally do something for your mother.'

Ouch! I should say stepmother again but daren't. I am moving to London now Uni is over. I've got a couple of journalistic contacts. A bit of freelancing, I hope, and Daddy has agreed to pay the rent on a nice pied-à-terre— Bloomsbury: bloody fantastic, actually—but he has pots of ruddy money and I have only what he allows trickle my way.

'I'll be there around five. I can walk from the station. It'll do me good.'

What a mood he's got himself in. And thirty-five is not an important birthday. Not in any sane mind. Closing in on forty and then there's only death to look forward to. That is my stepmother's lot. Thirty-five is one to brush under the carpet. I find it very depressing that he talks of curtailing my autonomy before it's really started. York and Uni have been great but London is the big one. Where I belong. Going back to Carnforth is just stupid. A nod to our sponsors as they say on television. Say over the pond, on all the corny TV programmes State-side. A nod to our sponsors. I will spend as much of the tedious party as I am able in the company of Craig—daft but sweet—and Silent Simon whom I am developing an increasing appreciation for the longer I am away from the house he lives in. He sends me letters. Strange and intelligent. I used to hear Mary on the phone, getting into contact with this and that therapist, hoping to bring him into the fold. He's a weird boy, odd-squared, in fact, but redeems it all by being so at ease with his own idiosyncrasies. His jumbo pack of them.

'The train arrives around four-thirty, doesn't it?' says Daddy. 'I'll pick you up at the station. I need you to be here by five.'

'By five? What...'

'A family meal before the guests arrive.'

'Oh Daddy, that is tragic. Making poor Stepmummy cook her own birthday meal. You know you can't do it. Making pancakes for a birthday would be unforgivable. You mustn't cook, Daddy.'

'Stop looking down on us, Sophie. Everything is in hand. I have a chef booked, coming to the house. Uncle Stephen and his wife are coming.'

This is unprecedented. I went on a date last month with a boy—I still give them a go every so often—from Cheshire, fellow student here, the only one on campus who carries a pocket watch. He talked about his parents having a chef come to the family home to prepare the food for a dinner party. I laughed: my first ever go at inverted snobbery. I told him that taxi's take normal people to restaurants, hoicking the chef around to your own house is frippery.

'Who else is coming?' I ask of Daddy.

'Mica is bringing Granny Bredbury,' he says.

'Mica?' I am laughing at him as I say it. Fairly quietly, he can be a sod when aroused. How starstruck is the old fool?

'Monica,' he corrects himself. And that is who the chef is for, not his ruddy missus. Mica Barry, the young Lady Hornchurch in everybody's Sunday night television viewing. Mine too, I like to watch Monica. She has real depth to her acting and a good dusting of sex appeal running through it. Quite delicious.

When the call is over, I ring Trish. She was to be my date on Sunday night. I suggest we can bring it forward to Thursday, apologise profusely for messing her around. 'Sorry, luvvy,' says Trish, 'I'm seeing a guy that night.'

'I'm sorry?' Her admission disturbs me. And worse still, I

consider the word luvvy to be very common parlance. 'Are you going on a date with a guy? Planning to date a male of the species on alternate days to schmoozing with moi?'

'Yes. A lot of us do you know?'

I do know this. I have dated guys myself. It is the simultaneous days, the pre-planned two-timing that is more than bugging me. 'Some do, some don't. You put me in the wrong category, I'm afraid. Our plans are over, Trish. Trish, luvvy. Enjoy the dick, I don't have one of those to entertain you with.' I put the phone down. It is not like me to be so crude but needs must. I will not be made a fool of. My father aside, of course. He is paying for a flat in Bloomsbury into which I will shortly move. Might live out my days there: it is very small, exceptionally well situated. Ten-minutes' walk from Euston. And the visit to Carnforth will only be for a few grim hours in the family home, a sleep in my old bed and then back here before boarding a plane.

* * *

A points failure, engineering fiasco—something of that ilk—has delayed my train. Well past five it arrives in Carnforth. My father is in the same stinking mood as the one which engulfed him throughout our most recent telephone call. Foul.

'Nothing I could do about it,' I say, holding my hands up in protest at his reddened face. 'The trains don't pay so much attention to the timetable on a Sunday. Day of rest and all that.'

'I know,' he says with resignation. 'Stephen and thingy are here already.'

Thingy is another almost-aunt of mine, through marriage to my stepmother's brother. She is a Bredbury by name these day, and at least Thingy had the good sense not to do her growing up in an insufferably small seaside town, so well done her. And I recall Thingy's other name to be Julia. The

Bredbury clan are a tedious bunch except for Monica. If she was a cuckoo in their Charmouth nest, I'd not be surprised. I grant that she bears a facial likeness to her alleged sister; their characters are worlds apart.

'Mary can entertain them,' I observe. I don't see what the fuss is about even if he had hoped to get our little family together before the Charmouthers started showing up. I think he has insisted on my participation only because I like Mary less than he does. Someone to blame if there's a frosty atmosphere. Daddy likes Mary's looks, I expect. A younger wife on his arm at faculty dinners; a bit of purpose. Useless between the covers, she really must be. He has never stopped foraging in the corridors and laboratories of his university. Imperial, Lancaster: the man could transmogrify any seat of learning into his personal knocking shop. I hope he's slowed down. His ticker won't take many more of those athletic undergrads, I shouldn't think.

'Mary is rather excited about it all, and I'd thank you to get into the spirit of it. A birthday party, this is a milestone in her life.'

Two summers ago, early in the university holidays, seven others and I embarked on the great coast-to-coast walk, Whitby to Whitehaven. I always thought it was madness. Chloe was dating a lad who was trying to get into Sandhurst. He had it all mapped out. Eight days to walk a hundred and eighty miles. We all managed the first four but Chloe—my sweet and foolish friend—was the only girl who did the lot. All eight days. Three out of four boys did it; boys truly are the more stupid sex. And my point is: milestones come along every ruddy day of the week. After a certain length of time, they mean nothing. If a birthday still raises Mary's pulse up a few notches after already experiencing thirty-four of the damned things, it has been an unremarkable life.

'It will be nice to see Monica again,' I observe. My comment is both sincere and in the spirit of the occasion, I believe.

'I don't want you monopolising the poor girl,' he snaps back.

What his foul mood is about I cannot guess. I resolve to find my party-girl soul, enjoy this forced gathering one way or another. And Monica is not a poor girl; richer than her sister by not being married to a philandering crosspatch for a start. And a glittering career; Lady Hornchurch today, and she used to be Sarah Best in Shoes and Slippers.

* * *

'Sophie, good to see you. You know Julia, don't you?'

Stephen is introducing his wife with handshakes all round as we have done when last we met. And the time before that. He has not been married for very long. I may have only seen her three or four times. Or two. I excuse myself from family gatherings if it is practical to do so.

'How's the world of journalism,' he asks. 'Dog eat dog?'

I show him something of mine that was printed in the Yorkshire Herald—a cutting I've been keeping in my handbag—not bad for a student. Co-wrote it but I don't mention I have only a fifty percent stake, no names printed on the article. All about York Uni, not a terribly exciting piece. London will be better, and I explain that I am about to start freelancing.

'I've nearly finished my PhD,' he says, interrupting the answer he had requested from me. He has the listening skills of a cardboard box, this not-quite relative. And getting a PhD at almost forty isn't clever. Mary's older brother and she's been doing a bit of teaching at Lancaster Uni for years. Got the stripe on her arm mid-twenties, not that I celebrated it at the time.

'Is Monica expected soon,' I ask. His PhD is about the tsetse fly, and I shan't be listening to him rabbit on about it. You can actually feel them biting your forearm as he talks.

'She should be here by now but she's not. I'm unsure what the hold-up is.'

Mary is upon the stairs. Still looks slim, I have to grant my stepmother that small compliment. There are many worse-looking thirty-five-year-olds. She might have been dressing, preparing for her big occasion, or she could have been up there for a needed evacuation. This gathering of her kinfolk could fill her with trepidation, for all I know of her emotional life. She walks down slowly as if hoping to attract our attention. The birthday beauty. Her hair is fair, and very nicely styled, and the red dress she wears—sleeveless, a shimmering crimson, actually—looks simply gorgeous. I adjudge that it is a poor choice of colour for her fair skin, light hair. Mine is black and my tan much richer than hers. I'll not raise the matter but the dress would look better still were I the one within it. And I'd have bought one a couple of sizes smaller than Mary for a perfect fit. As it is, I am in my green trouser suit, didn't consider it worth making an effort for this crowd. I'm starting to rue my choice; the red dress would suit me to a tee. And Monica will be here soon, by rights I should be in more than an old trouser suit for her. Well, she will have to take me as she finds me and, of course, we are old pals.

'Sophie dear, so nice to have you home.' Mary pecks my cheek as neither Stephen nor his surprisingly fine-boned wife could manage. I return it, hold her waist in my hands and look into her eyes. I feel towards her as I always have, détente is simply the more advantageous state in which to coexist.

As the family enters the lounge, my step-brothers both still upstairs, I presume, I slip into the kitchen. I expect to meet an Italian in whites or a Frenchie kissing his lips as he tastes an onion soup or whatever concoction we are shortly to consume. A fat lady is cutting parsley. A dinner lady by my estimation.

Crack Up or Play It Cool

'Hello, I'm Sophie.'

'Ooh. Where do you fit in, duck,' she says.

I find myself grinning from ear to ear. Perhaps Daddy could have cooked as well as this northern oik, perhaps not. Or we could have sent out to the chip shop.

'Step-daughter of the birthday girl,' I say.

'And I would have guessed you were sisters. You know we're expecting Lady Hornchurch off the tele, don't you?'

'That's Auntie Monica. And you didn't tell me your name?'

'It's Pat. Of Pat Connor Catering.'

'And what will we be eating today, Pat Connor?'

'Fish. Fancy fish. But I can't even put it in the oven until Lady Hornchurch gets here, or hers will dry out. It's not with a sauce, you see. I wouldn't want nothing below my best for her. For Lady Hornchurch.'

'Baked fish. Delightful.' Even I can shove a halibut in the oven. 'What other delights do we have, Pat?'

'I bought a fruit flan from Marks. You're all in for a treat, luvvy. What was your name again?'

I tell her but I remembered her name first go. And she is only Pat Connor. Of Pat Connor Catering. Daddy is a ruddy clown.

* * *

At half-past six a car pulls into the gate, when the door opens and the interior light comes on, we can see Monica in the driving seat. Granny Bredbury, her passenger. My anxious father has become quite stressed because at seven-thirty guests will arrive for a party, and we have only one hour in which to eat the fancy meal to which he has not invited the unwashed masses who are to spew forth from the University of Lancaster. And it will be fancy in the style of Pat Connor, the second most stressed of our temporary household. A Lady to feed in her myopic view. Craig—who is just seven years old—is the most philosophical. 'If we choke, we choke,' he says. Not really wise beyond his years, he reads notes that big brother Simon passes to him. I don't see Simon write them but somewhere in his lap he must do so. Or perhaps he pulls them from a pre-prepared pocketful of gems.

When she enters the house, everyone gathers to receive Monica's kiss. A tedious obligation for her, I imagine. Wood veneer, no red carpet in sight. I see her lightly flick Stephen's ear with her forefinger as she simultaneously pecks his cheek. He is a prize ninny, talking tsetse fly even as she greets him; Monica deserves better relatives. She is ever so nice with me, stoops to kiss although that is the heels she wears; she has no more than an inch on me. We shared clothes a few years back when I stayed in her hotel room.

We all peck Granny Bredbury in the lee of her daughter. She asks me if living in London worries me. Doesn't seem to know that I've still to move down there. I suppose Mary has been moaning to her about the flat. Thinks I'm spoiled, won't concede that comfort is my birthright. Granny Bredbury talks about the crime rate, and I tell her London is the most civilised place in Britain. York is all right but the capital is our only truly cultured city. A vibrancy that would wake up Carnforth.

'I was so worried when Mary went to college there. She was just eighteen, it can swallow up a young girl. I could scarcely go to sleep back in Charmouth, thinking about her in the big noisy city. Luckily, she met your father. He took her in hand. Kept her from straying off the path, if you know what I mean.'

She talks rot. I sort of remember her mother's first year—or second—but would have thought my father was the type of scoundrel a decent mother would be trying to protect his daughter from. Or perhaps they deserve each other, it is getting harder to discern right from wrong as I grow older. Whatever good tutoring he gave her back then, it is surprising that she has stayed in his life. Professor Pinch-bottom. Mary has been in my life for too long, and she never replicated my mother's warmth for a second. I see she attends to Simon and Craig more lovingly; I get it, the blood that runs in her veins also runs in theirs. Children? I want none. I will love who I choose and if it does not last—the way of things thus far in my life—I shall release them for our mutual good. My stepgranny, this dim Devonian or Dorsetine, wherever she really comes from—silly old fossil—has brought my mood right down by reminding me of all that went before. My blighted childhood. I wonder if she was concerned at all for Mary in the city, or if she is talking old soap. Words she has heard others say. Reassured when Mary took a lover old enough to be the father she never had. Really? And how come Granny Bredbury is thick as two short planks and her children so successful. Even Stephen's PhD is not a bad return, requires the application of a bit of grey matter if only on the topic of mosquitos. My stepmother, Mary, is more envious than actually worried about my forthcoming residence in the capital. I am sure of it. My true mother is ten years out of my life. Not a card, not a call. I should hate Cynthia Hartnell for caring about me even less than Mary Stephenson, once Bredbury, has done. Instead, I find that I love her more and more. Expect a happy ending that becomes more improbable as time accelerates.

* * *

Pat Connor is the dunce to trounce all other dunces. The broccoli soup she has made is rather good, creamy in the right way. Rich. She serves Monica first, and my lovely aunt is embarrassed. 'It's her birthday,' she says, gesturing her older sister. And around this dining table, they do look very alike. Mary is the broader now, and her smile lines are no more. It might be thirty-five or it might be marriage. My father must be unbearable on that front. For a long time, I thought it was having a cretinous son, although she bore all the challenges he presented both stoically and optimistically. I think the boy has benefitted from a loving mother, although I say it grudgingly. She told us all that he understood every word we spoke back when there was scant evidence to support her assertion. My father wasn't really on board, I am certain. Simon's father. And Mary was right all along. I was the worst family member with the poor lad. Used nasty names to his unresponsive face, didn't think they registered in his brain. I had no idea it was a working organ. I also called the garden squirrel, Mr Gonad Eater. Stepmummy hated the term, told me off repeatedly. When Simon began writing the squirrel's name on his notes—fully three years later—I figured he remembered the lot. Thankfully he didn't reproduce them: Gormless Twat and Satanic Blob were examples of the names I called him, and felt subsequently grateful he did not write alongside the squirrel's appellation. Not proud of myself about that. Rushing to judgement is a bad thing. Lesson learned. And duly forgotten, my character fully formed long ago. Perhaps I'll be wise when I'm ninety, I simply don't have the time for it now.

Uncle Stephen is sitting beside Simon and he tells him one thing after another about the tsetse fly. Its prolific proliferation and its blood-curdling diet of blood. To control this fly may be to rid Africa of disease. Simon spoons soup into his mouth as the monologue continues. Craig asks his uncle if he has been to Africa and he confesses that he has not. The flies which he examines are dead on arrival in Bristol, and this state makes them all the easier to observe through a microscope.

While serving the next course—the said fish—Pat Connor asks Monica if she was filming today; the young Lady Hornchurch will fill the nation's screens once more this evening. 'Wrapped that one up in the summer,' she tells the cook. 'I'm playing a girl of dubious morals in a nineteen-fifties drama next. Shooting starts in January.' Then she says, as an aside to me, I believe, but all hear her words, 'Gets herself knocked up. Bad news in those censorious times, truly bad news.'

'Oh no,' says Pat, tea towel over her forearm. 'Your acting is a gift but no one could believe that. Loose morals? It really isn't you, Lady Hornchurch.'

* * *

We ate the fruit flan in double-quick time. I passed on it, my sweet tooth answers only to martinis. Simon wolfed mine down along with his own. Food consumed in the allotted time. Family members praised Pat's culinary skills, and I didn't let on about the shop-bought pudding. She curtsied to Monica before she left. Now a number of guests have gathered in the house. Scientists: my father's tribe, Mary's too. They might even pay attention to the tsetse fly monologue.

I ask Simon to show me his schoolwork. This is a complicated affair, I believe, because he does not attend; a teacher coming to the house on a twice-weekly basis. Leaves him with copious amounts of reading matter which he diligently devours. Three years ago, the best professional assessment they could rustle up predicted that Simon would learn nothing of import. They said that a restricted life awaited him—he was literate but chose to hide his knowledge—no test devised could, at that point in time, fathom that his comprehension of the world went any further than how to dress himself. Now he completes mathematics and logic questions which might challenge children three or more years older than he. I am fascinated by his poetry, not a genre I am skilled to judge but his is original and brutal. When I enquire about this, he shakes his head. Eyes are down at all times. He listens with ears not eyes. 'Have you no new poems?' I try again.

'He's stopped,' says Craig. 'Doesn't like it anymore.'

Simon slaps a flat palm on the wall he stands beside. I don't think it is morse code; however, it is all the direct communication I shall be getting. All his written notes have been for little bro so far this evening.

* * *

Jake Watts is about thirty—I'm so-so at guessing—good looking, knowledgeable about rocketry, practical physics as he styles it, and I think he is chatting me up. I rather like the feeling although I will be doing nothing more than talking this evening, no expectation that I shall see him again after tonight. No wish to, that's the bottom line. He has refilled my wine glass, and takes my chosen profession seriously, which is nice. I ask if he is father's student, and he tells me that Mary is mentoring him. Taking him through his dissertation. She works at the same university and probably works harder than my father. He's the big name: every university loves having them on the faculty. Paul Stephenson has a book on the popular science shelves of all the high street booksellers. Or possibly they are only in the charity shops these days; I didn't read it. Space: How to Get from A to B. That's the title and I've cracked it without buying a copy; from the arse of the world to Bloomsbury. That's the A and the B in my life's journey. To Venus and Mars, I shall not venture.

'And what do you do if you're giving physics a break?'

'This and that.' It is an evasive reply. 'You're not really Mary's daughter, are you?'

'Stepdaughter.' I'm always more than happy to correct that one.

'Phew. I thought she's too young for...' She is his mentor; I suppose all male students would fantasise about an older teacher who has kept her figure as well as Mary's managed.

'She could be my mother if she had been raped at thirteen,' I state. 'For the record.'

Crack Up or Play It Cool

'Oh, Sophie. What a thing to say.'

I tell him about a news story from eighty-six with which I am au fait—analysed it to death for a year-two assignment—all about a lowlife who fathered two children with his eldest daughter, passed them off as her siblings. A wife even playing along, declaring them to be hers.

'It's horrible stuff to report on,' he says, 'not really party stories at all.'

'It's the stuff of life, Jake. Stephen over there will tell you everything there is to know about his beloved tsetse fly. Helpful for the curing of a disease or two, I understand, but the human-interest stories which the newspapers carry prime us for the lives we are living. The people we may come across. You know the Manchester tale, don't you? Their little zinger from a few years back.'

'I don't recall it, Sophie. Not another tale of depravity, is it?'

'A cautionary tale. The Evening Clarion reported the discovery of a body in some swampy grounds far out on the edge of the city. It was the cover story, Body in the Bog, something like that in bold print. A chap went straight to the nearest police station after passing a newsstand. Seeing the horrid headline. He confessed to the murder of his wife a decade earlier. He had left her body, buried it somewhere comparable to the setting of the story. The snag, Jake—it might have tickled the policeman in the station, as it did me—the news report went on to detail the archaeological importance of the find. A five-thousand-year-old skeleton had been found in the bog. The chappie making the confession had read only the headline. Sometimes the small print is quite important, that seems to be the message. I like a story with a moral.'

I laugh but Jake does not. He slopes off. Finds Mary to talk to in my stead. Having the what's-wrong-with-your-stepdaughter conversation, I expect. Being chatted up by a physicist is not my party game of choice. The sciences bore me and any chemistry found would remind me of my father's worst trait.

* * *

School tomorrow and so Craig has been in bed since the meal finished, I slope off from the party to say hey. Craig shouldn't miss out on the education only a big sister can give him. I know the blind spots of these northern schools. No sense of refinement can be disseminated from here: I got mine in Epsom; Carnforth is mostly cloth caps, coarse men who keep a ferret down their trouser leg. When I enter his room, I am surprised to find Jake Watts and my stepmother both in his room already. She is the one who lays down the bedtimes. Did so astringently for me until five years ago, not that I necessarily complied. 'Oh, hi Sophie,' she says. 'Have you come to say g'night to Craig.'

I noticed earlier that Jake puts a little Australian into his speech; I assess that he has spent a little time down under, doesn't actually come from the place. That Mary mimics her student's speech is pitiful. She must think all the kids are doing it.

'I will say goodnight, just hoping to catch up with little bro first. He's off to school, and me to sunny Spain, first thing tomorrow morning.'

'Okay, we'll leave you. Don't keep my precious one awake too long.'

When they depart, I tickle little Craig and he laughs with me. 'How's tricks?'

'Why don't you come and live back here?' He is instantly serious.

'Got to be in London. My kind of town. Ten years and you can come. Live there with me.'

'Granny says there are robbers in London.'

'There might be; I've never seen them. They wear black,

and lurk in the shadows out of sight. Climbing the walls, slipping in the windows and robbing for England. Hey-ho, enough money to go around down in London, don't you know?'

'Could I be a robber? It sounds a funny job.'

'Daddy wants you to be a physicist, Mummy too, I expect. And I have loftier ambitions for you than robbing. Prison if you're caught.'

'What's prison?'

'You know perfectly well what prison is, little chicken. The judge sentences you to be locked in a room with nothing but bread and water until you mend your ways.'

'Mend your trousers?'

'Mend your ways; stop robbing. What did Stepmummy and that man want?'

'She was showing him the house. And me. Showing off me. She told him I am the best one in the family.'

'She never said that. What about poor old Simon.'

'Not good enough. That boy's way too strange.'

'You're the one that likes him, kidder. You always were.'

'You like him.'

'I love him. Like I love you, little chips, but you figured out Simon quicker than any of us.'

Craig giggles at me. 'A brother isn't a puzzle. I've always known him.'

It might be a salient point. Perhaps I'd have been on Simon's side from day one but for all the half-brother nonsense. If my Mummy had stayed and had three children instead of just me. It must be very hard to leave three. To move abroad with three children back in the house. Three times as hard.

* * *

Simon is still downstairs. No school for oddball, he can keep Simon-time all the time. There is music in the lounge, carrying through to the dining room, probably up to the bedrooms too. Not dancing music, not sounds that will prevent young Craig from sleeping. To my untrained ear it's that funny Dario Renzo we hear: electric guitar played with a mellow virtuosity. Mood music. That and physics comprise the sum total of things appreciated equally by my father and Mary. I think the music is pretension on steroids, and Simon agrees with me if I am interpreting his disdainful slouch accurately. He leans against the backdoor, far side of the kitchen. Sitting alone, as an elective mute must. He hates music generally; I think he is only downstairs in order to ensure no one steals the porcelain. With all these penniless students in the house, it could happen.

'Can I talk with you, Si?' I ask as I approach.

He taps a flat palm against the door twice. We don't share a sign language, and he has turned his face from me. I will take it as a yes.

'Do you mind all the people in the house?'

The hand slaps the door a single time.

'Should we go up to your room, Simmy-Simmy. A pen and paper would allow me in on the talk. I want to know what you think, not just have to guess.'

He turns his face towards me, the top of his head just grazes my chin as he buries his head in my breast. I think he is too young to be exciting himself with this, and my breasts are scarcely the size of tennis balls. I tousle his hair while worrying that there is ketchup on his lips, staining the top of my trouser suit. The boy poured half a pint of the stuff onto Pat Connor's fancy baked fish; I expect he drinks it neat when no one's watching.

'Come on, let's go up.' We cannot yet; he holds me very tightly, hands drifting down to my bum. He's eleven years old, Simon's idea of a joke, I hope.

When I have gently extricated myself from his odd embrace, I take his hand and we walk up the stairs. He is funny, likes the feeling of flesh on flesh, I conclude, yet cannot look a person in the eye. He knows the family incredibly well; I enjoy looking into the faces of others, allow them to do the same to me. I think it is how we know others and allow them to glean a little of ourselves. Simon is different. I don't wish to declare that he sees with his heart— his thoughts are sometimes acerbic, not sentimental at all— he has found another window to the soul. A small one situated round the back of the head, wormhole to the core of one's being.

'Oh, that poster is new,' I declare on entering his room. It is an unusual choice for a child's bedroom, a black and white photograph of a windswept landscape, a lone wooden house on the near horizon. American mid-west, I presume.

Immediately he scribbles on paper, passes the note to me.

Our house

I'll think about it, don't know if he is trying to be funny or make a more insightful point. 'How are you and Craig getting along, Simon?'

Good caddy

'What do you mean by caddy, Si?'

My funny half-brother has flopped down onto the floor and pulled the T-shirt he wears over his head to cover his face. His torso shows his ribcage at the sides, does so only when he breathes in. There is twice as much fat on him as there is on Craig. Tiny little boy breasts, even a passing resemblance to my own. The pen and paper are on the floor beside him.

'I don't understand caddy?' He wriggles, I am not sure what he is doing under that shirt. 'You don't play golf, Si.'

He pulls his shirt back down, pen and paper instantly in hand.

I do

I have to figure this one out. Sleep on it, perhaps. He certainly doesn't have any golf clubs. Never makes his way onto a course. I slip onto the floor beside him, my right hip against his left. My arm is across his shoulder, and once more his hand reaches far lower, his fingers back onto my bum.

'Are Dad and Mum treating you well enough?'

Scribble, scribble.

You don't like her

'We've talked about this, Si. She isn't my mum. I've already got one, thank you.'

Where?

'Don't ask that. Don't be a mean boy.'

She must be somewhere

I agree with this. Fear that whatever prompted her to leave me has also changed her irradicably. She knows no way back. If it was for a passionate love affair, it was one so exclusive there was no room for me. I would like such a love for myself, while fearing it also. Fear it like the plague. A love that transforms a person. How shocking to be so mesmerised by another as to lose one's previous sense of self.

'If she never comes back, I still remember how she used to love me.'

Memory is all we have. Everything beside it is slipping away.

Sweet Jesus, this boy is eleven years old. 'Have you any poems to show me?'

He rolls away from me, roots in a drawer by his bedside, and comes out with a lined notepad, turns the pages and passes it to me. As he is doing this, I see his side profile. Pasty face, he never goes out; freckles on the bridge of his nose. I cannot see his eyes directly, he never turns my way but from the side, I see the intensity of his stare. I don't believe there is a bad bone in his body, and yet I think he might frighten me if I were without the pre-knowledge which assures. If I did not know how firmly he is on my side.

I don't read the poem straight away; I know his work. It can be obscure. 'What is this one about, Simon? Will I understand it?'

Us, he scribbles.

'You and me?'

The Stephensons

'Not a poem then, a horror story.'

He headbutts me in the shoulder, not hard. I think I might have made him laugh.

<u>**House Awake, House Asleep**</u>

If they all stayed home, they could wait it out
Find the other side through sleep occasional
Come to rest aware of other's thoughts.
Defying gravity, they throw it all away
Step out where other forces pull them deep
A rain mac for a shower and a cigarette for comfort
And a Martian with blue fingers for a friend.
If we had a dog, I'd call her Sophie
Let her rest upon my bed at night
If someone left the door ajar and Sophie ran into the fields
I'd whisper, she can bring her Martian home

'Oh Simon, that is so sweet. At least, I think it is. Are you really missing me that much?' This question does not get so much as a scribble. It is a pattern I am familiar with; in my mind it is the same as his moratorium on eye contact. My question was too direct. 'Craig said you have stopped writing poems altogether now.'

He flicks a tick on the notebook's page.

'Is that yes? Does that mean you have stopped?'

Another tick appears.

'Why, Simon? Your poems are good.'

He holds the pen but writes nothing. That response.

'What do you think of them, Simon? You must like them?'

Funny but shit

'I think they are far better than that. I think they are better than promising. Accomplished, I would say. You have a style. You say what only Simon Stephenson knows how to say.'

True, and still shit

'I heard that your tutor loves them. Wants to send them away to proper poetry magazines.'

She is science

'I thought she teaches you everything?'

Tries. She is science

'And who is the Martian in the poem? The blue-fingered Martian.'

Simon makes the strangest movements. He puts his pen against the paper, then drops both to the floor. Leans in to me once more, a big hug, his head on my breast this time, and after about half a second, he releases me. Pen and paper back in hand he scribbles.

Jake Watts

Ha! The name of the nerd houseguest who flirted with me. I didn't flirt back, put him off with tales of depravity as a needed alternative. He couldn't take it. Simon must have seen us talk but Jake Watts is not my Martian. Practical physics he studies, probably off to Mars the first chance he can get. PhD students' ideas for a good time freak me out. Or bore me like the tsetse fly. And I won't be telling half-brother that I like lady Martians. He'll write it to Craig who'll tell

Mary, who will use it against me in ways I cannot yet imagine. And Daddy isn't broadminded at all. A product of his stinking times, I suppose.

* * *

I am sitting close to the dining table, which has been moved up against the wall to make space for the dancing such as there has been. My fifth white wine of the evening. On that score, it is a quiet night, I'd drink double if it was a university party. This irrepressible Jake Watts is hounding me again, telling me about growing up in Crewe. I think he is boasting, and then he makes it sound worse than Carnforth. Thieving little twopenny sweets from the newsagents and making bonfires on disused land; shitty highlights by any normal reckoning. Across the room, Daddy is speaking with a girl who might be older than me but probably isn't. I cannot hear every word but 'escape velocity' and 'elliptical orbit' are in there. I see him touch her hand, her upper arm. Standard. Julia, Stephen's wife, is also in the room. She has temporary respite from her insufferable husband. She talks nicely with another of father's young students. Unless this is one of Mary's, same as boring Jake. It is possible: both teach, and I haven't seen Daddy pawing her. Julia and the student are having an animated chat and, in this light, with a few glasses of wine inside, I am beginning to think Stephen's wife to be quite desirable. Beats the man who is hitting on me—the man from Crewe—by a few furlongs.

'And you always lived here?' says my unasked-for flirt-mate.

'Epsom. Born and raised in Epsom. A lovely place, Jake. Truly. Crewe sounds frightful by comparison. I was dragged up here when Daddy got a job at your spanking new university. I was never a bitch before I lived up north; I'm sure I shall turn far sweeter when I finally get back down to London. Do you mind? I want a word with these two gals here.'

Done it, dumped him before he develops too traumatising a crush, poor lamb. And I really don't live in Lancashire any longer. Never again. Giving certain people the elbow is the kindest way. A mercy killing. Once up from my chair, I take the two steps to my step-aunt-in-law or whatever tenuous link she and I enjoy.

'Julia, we seldom get to talk.'

'Sophie, this is Evie, a postgrad. You know Sophie?'

This other girl indicates that she does not. I've never seen her before but I've seen a lot like her. 'Who are you?' she says.

'Oh me, I almost live here. It's my father's house.'

'No! You can't be Mary's daughter?'

'I am not. A product of wife number one, that's me.'

'I see. Do you study physics?'

'Certainly not. I'm a fledgling journalist. Degree done, gossip and scandal will be my stock in trade from hereafter. A bit of crime reportage if those better staples dry up. Are you one of my father's students?' I don't do the inverted commas with my fingers; I'm sure I could have. Or even said conquest in place of student.

'Mary is my mentor,' she says.

'Then you'll know that chappie...' I indicate the hapless Watts now standing alone. 'Do you mind if Julia and I have a little catch-up?'

She nods, if she wished to talk to me the feeling was not mutual. My hard-to-stomach stepmother is thirty-five years old today, who does she invite to her party? Twenty-somethings in search of a decent grade, that's who. Shoot me when I'm thirty-four.

'I was trying to remember the last time we spoke,' says Julia. 'I think it was the wedding.'

'Your wedding?' This surprises me but it probably shouldn't. I have avoided going down to godforsaken Dorset, from where Mary hails. Avoided it every single time. Made easier by Daddy's wish to do the same. Uncle Stephen has come up here a few times, mostly before this fine wife of his materialised. Came on the scene, as they say. 'So how does married life suit you.'

'We're late to it, Sophie. We've both been around married couples for yonks. Never found anyone ourselves until we were past it.' She laughs; doesn't look past it to me but she's right about him. About Uncle Stephen. 'I think we only tied the knot to please his mum.' I don't say anything, still calculating. I've known about her for four years and they've been married for two. I wonder if she has the same leanings as I do, if her fella is just a bit of camouflage. 'Oops. That's your granny, isn't it? I don't mean anything by it. She is just a tad churchier than Stephen or I.'

'No worries, she's not my granny. I'm only related to Mary through Dad. Not directly. You married Uncle Stephen because she disapproved of the pair of you living together?'

'More than that. We're committed to each...'

'I can't imagine ever getting married. Young couples are fine but who wants to be part of an old couple?'

'Sophie, what are you? Eighteen. It's ageing you're railing against, not being part of a couple.'

'I'll take it as a compliment—intended or not—but I'm twenty-one. Mistress of my own fate.'

'Of course. I remember now. Sorry we couldn't make it...'

'No, no. It's all right.' She is referring to my birthday bash a few months back. The one here in Carnforth was an embarrassment, I'm glad this good-looking lady missed it. There was a drunken affair in a pub in York where I celebrated about ten days later, she would have been welcome to attend that one. Or not. Certainly not if it meant bringing my insufferable Uncle Stephen. 'You're a scientist too, I recall?'

'A science teacher.'

'Oh, thank God. A normal job, not an ivory-towered boffin. What's the school like? State or private?'

* * *

Towards two in the morning, I have tucked myself up in bed, my old one. It is familiar but this room belongs to a more dependent girl. I've flown the coup and returning feels stifling. It will be my last night in York tomorrow, then Spain for two weeks, after which I'm Bloomsbury-bound. Will have just a couple of nights here in Carnforth before Daddy moves me in. He's booked a hire van, so it's been worth making this trip back to keep him obligated.

The bothersome Jake Watts was after me all evening. 'Do you share your mother's taste in music?' he asked, and 'Did you not wish to be a physicist like your mother?' I cannot recall how many times I had to insert the word step into our conversation. My mother's opinions about music and her aspirations for me have both become lost in the mists of time. When he was taking a break from the charms that I really did not lavish upon him, he seemed to be talking to her, to Mary. No doubt asking her all about me. What games I played as a child, all the nonsense that the infatuated man must feel duty bound to learn. To help him cherish me in mind and heart. I'm trying to forget every word he said about stinking Crewe. I've no interest in hell-holes, nor in him. And Mary may have put in a good word, he was persistent. If she had told him that I'm actually Satan, I could not have cared less, and I think that was her opinion of old. At least half of the time; she generally treated me better than that, it was just the undercurrent. Jake actually looks a tad handsome; on the other side of the ledger, he is male and hails from Crewe. When I had the opportunity, I tried to find out more about Julia. I could say, Stephen's Julia, but truly I think she is her own person. She described what she called 'later marriage.' Embarking on it when she is the age Mary is now. And a bright kid in reception class could tell you that my stepmother married way too soon. Too young by about half a lifetime. And I might have been the very girl to say it back in my reception days: thought it around the same time I started firing off thoughts of my own. Julia confided in me that she is too old to have children, that Stephen knew before formalising the arrangement that their marriage would be childless. When I tried to say something upbeat, along the lines that women have children when they are quite old these days, she shook her head. Whispered, 'It came on me early.' The phrase made it sound frightful but it could even be a relief. I'm not a fan of children, and the monthlies can be worse still. I get the most stonking headaches if the bleeding is heavy. She told me she has been teaching since she was scarcely older than me. One year older. Julia did her teacher training straight after she completed her degree. And her work has all been in the rough old state sector. I asked her if it wasn't tricky—starting out as a teacher so young— did she root for the naughty boys and girls, kids who copied all their homework and locked poor teacher in the store cupboard. Good sport that she is, Julia laughed heartily at that. 'It's never happened to me but it has happened. And at my school.'

I got a bit daring while we talked, touched her hand or arm once or twice, didn't get the reciprocation I was hoping for. I asked her how old she is; a bit personal but I was scaring myself by feeling attracted to a post-menopausal chemistry teacher. 'Forty next year,' she said. Wow. I think older faces might be more interesting than young ones. They contain a lot of life. And I think she's a total hetero, stuck on the other side, so only dull old Stephen gets to stare into her beautiful green eyes while on the job. I wish her well with it while continuing to find no warmth for him. Champion of the tsetse fly.

Of course, Monica found time for me. She was in demand,

and seemed to be getting along better with Mary than I really like to see. They are sisters, I suppose. When we talked, just the two of us, I asked her if she was going on any hot dates. A television star in her prime should do that, one would think.

'I think my relationships go better when I am adopting another character,' she said.

At first, I thought she was confiding her particular sexual preference, a penchant for wild role play. I imagined she might pretend to be a helpless Russian émigré for the improvement it wrought upon her sex life. I didn't ask in quite those terms, and I'd got the wrong end of the beanpole anyway. My own fantasy. She meant that her love life is pretty patchy, while on-screen or stage she is getting romantic lead after romantic lead. I think she has been my number one since I was sixteen—since that interview—and in practical terms I've given up. She likes men the way I like a decent Sauvignon Blanc. I drank enough of them last night to prompt me to ask her how come she is so cool and her siblings so square. 'Don't ever say that about Mary,' she answered. 'You know I never liked the poor start she got off to with you. She shouldn't have tried bringing up a clever sod like you when she was still a kid herself. That's been tough on you both. But she is cool, or was cool. Cooler than me before she hitched her wagon to Prof Paul.' I think I looked shocked. Felt a little close to tears because it seemed as if she was choosing Mary over me. Never thought that before. Then she hugged me and said, 'Sorry kiddo.' That was very sweet of her. 'Sorry kiddo, I've just been thinking about her a lot lately. She could have been a better mum for you, I know that. Tried her best, just never quite who you needed.' I returned the hug. I do love Monica Bredbury more than anyone else in the world. 'And Stephen is about as cool as cat food,' she confirmed.

2.

I told her to stay at home because she was so anxious about the babysitter, she kept repeating that she wanted to be here, to see me pick up the prize. And now she has left before Miss Wainwright has presented it to me. It's both typical and exasperating. I am at Lancaster Grammar now, no longer attending this poxy little hole; I've only come back to receive the applause I am due for all my past endeavours. And my special prize—for the finest essay writing seen at Hazelbrook in a generation, as the invitation letter puts it—is a bit of a Trojan horse. In a school of just one hundred and twenty girls total, including nine tragic sixth formers who study here in toy town while Lancaster awaits down the road, I stood out. My name on the cover of Girls in the News is the one that Miss Wainwright savours. Getting her school's name in the same article as the young starlet, Mica Barry.

Daddy would be here but committee meetings come thick and fast through the month of October at his University. Ones he cannot back out of. I know it is true, true that this is the month when all the planning committees meet and determine the way ahead for the year. It might or might not be true of tonight. He might be stuffing it to some young science student who thinks black curly hair looks fetching on an old geyser. That explanation would really get my goat—I could have a blue fit—so for the benefit of my otherwise ebullient mood, I am believing the two-faced liar. Mary likely doesn't, not after being let down a million times. For me it is a rarer disappointment. Daddy is coming to parents' evening at the Grammar in three weeks. Won't let me down in November, I still feel pretty confident.

To be fair to my wicked stepmother, her name came over the public address system. 'Phone call for Mrs Stephenson. Is Mrs Stephenson able to come to the main office? Urgently, please.' They could call her Dr Stephenson, one or two letters on the doormat do just that, to her credit, she doesn't put on airs. I know I would if I'd had to study the motion of rocks in space for years and years just to earn the accolade. Her dissertation was titled The Lesser Jovian Moons. If that is an interesting subject, I must have slipped into a parallel universe. Dull as ditch water in the one I've made home. And I think she would have stayed to watch me pick up my prize but for this intervention. The Tannoy thing. She's as cold as a milk bottle but dutifully does all she can for me, and for her unreliable husband. For Simon and Craig, too, but I think she actually likes them.

All she said to me was, 'Have to go. The babysitter can't cope. So sorry, Sophie. And you really have done amazingly well. Deserving of the prize. The recognition.'

I replied, 'aw' and 'ah.' Not words, just those sympathetic noises that epitomise misfortune connected with little children. Nobody listening would have guessed we hate each other. Not for a second. And I know for a fact that two-year-old Craig is not the one who has broken the nerve of the babysitter. Simon is a waste of space. Can't talk, eats with his fingers, covers his eyes and ears and rocks back and forth on his chair if he dislikes whatever is going on. And he has an awfully large number of very strong dislikes. I think he will end up in an institution, and until then Mary is going to have a lot of social engagements curtailed. Mrs Reynolds, mother of my friend, Caz, calls Mary a saint. She says one must be superhuman to do all she does for so needy a child. 'And your stepmother still works part-time at the university,' she gushed during that conversation. I see the sentiment, understand why she says it but it's poppycock. Jovian moons are more stimulating than tending to that big lump of gristle. My stepmother chose to have a baby—a vain attempt to tie Daddy down is my analysis of that—we all reap what we sow. I tell myself I won't be having children, like a Hindu mantra. I'm not having children, I'm not having children, I'm not a fruit and nut case. And if I ever do, I shall have a baby with my own looks and brains. Blood a little less acidic, perhaps. Not a morose little barrel like Simon. I'd have sent it back to the maternity ward. Truly, I would. We throw away broken biscuits in our house, why we bother with him beats me. And it is a balanced judgement; I would keep little Craig. I'm a practical thinker, not heartless.

* * *

Miss Wainwright's speech is quite moving. She holds my work up before the poor blighters who must toil away for her this year and many more to come. She implores them to follow my example. Discipline and originality. Through hard work and the application of all I learned under the school's tutelage, I have achieved something noteworthy on the national stage. And my essay writing at Hazelbrook was outstanding, term in and term out. I must admit, I like hearing my praises being sung; Mary might have hated it. I have always found her difficult to read. She is polite to a fault. Not sure why I like Daddy more, really, he has not even bothered to come. Found a better offer.

Miss Wainwright reads out a quote or two from the Girls in the News article, states that my highly skilled interviewing style brought forth revelations from Mica Barry that few inexperienced journalists would have managed. Drawing out unguarded intimacies. On balance, I am glad that no one from my family is in the audience. They would have seen through that one.

3.

When we arrive in Bayswater, Monica and Gary are very concerned about me. I know exactly what they are thinking. They have the big house—big cottage I should probably say—they could put up Simon and Craig more easily than I. But they do not have the easy rapport I enjoy with my brothers. That is the truth, and I reassure both that I am looking forward to spending time. Say it honestly.

Monica whispers to me, 'Do you need to discuss it with Grace?' And I shake my head.

I am not expecting Grace to be here today. I will text or telephone this evening; I cannot be sure how this will play out on that front. 'Family are family,' I tell my aunt.

I think the lady in the flat across the corridor recognises the pair who have assisted us bringing luggage from car to flat. Recognised our Victorian doctor, certainly, and Monica—Mica to Jack and Jill Public—is the bigger box office draw, if this nosy neighbour has any memory at all. She stays on the landing, pretending to clean her doorknocker. Utterly ridiculous: we buzz in all our guests.

The boys come upstairs. Craig looks lost and I feel immense sympathy, poor boy. His father's funeral and his mother's imprisonment might be killing him. Simon must look like an oddball to the doorknocker polisher, I am peachy proud of him. Beyond compare. I haven't spoken with Monica about him, we haven't had time alone since he started talking. Telling a few home truths.

I suggest a cup of tea before they drive on to the cottage. Both agree readily. In the flat, I show the boys the two bedrooms. 'Have the large one,' I say to Simon. 'Are you okay with the other, Craig?' I explain that I shall sleep on the sofa, or I may stay over at a friend's flat some of the time. I feel expectant eyes upon me, rightly or wrongly. 'A girlfriend, Craig. I have a girlfriend.' He nods as if this is not news. The other three know already.

'She means she's a lesbian,' says Deep Voice.

'Oh, wow,' says Craig. 'Cool. And that explains why you're not married yet. Because you look gorgeous.'

Monica and Gary join me in laughter. I actually like the way my sweet brother phrased that.

When the tea has stewed long enough and I am pouring it

into cups, Simon remaining in my bedroom—the bedroom I have bequeathed him—Craig gets inquisitive.

'What's your girlfriend's name, then?'

I tell him.

'Why don't you and Grace live together if she's a proper girlfriend?'

'We have not known each other for very long.'

His face drops. 'She won't like me and Simon being here. Being in the way. I don't want to ruin your life as well, Sophie. I don't...'

'Ruin?' Who said anything about ruin? I want you here, and if I do stay over at Grace's, I want you and Simon to be very grown-up about it. To treat my flat as your home, and treat it well.' He looks reassured. Not the whole hog but part way there. 'And I've been thinking—only in the hour and a half since Auntie Sarah's meltdown—I might go and see Gosling, our solicitor chappie, see if he can release the money. Then we could move out of here to a three- or four-bed.'

Monica gives a low whistle. 'You are something, Sophie. It's a good idea, be careful of making rash decisions straight after so much has gone on.'

'In Carnforth?' asks Craig.

'Oh gosh, Craigy. You've never known anywhere else, I'm afraid it just isn't right for me. Not for my work.'

He nods his head. Monica has stepped in, gives the boy a hug. I'm not sure he wanted it, he starts to cry, thankfully not the distressed variety. It has been a hell of a day.

* * *

Last night, I was on the phone to Grace for the longest time. I am a bit slow on the uptake sometimes but the thought that she is the love of my life has bedded in. Taken root. I have told her a little about these two boys before. She is excited to meet them, pleased and proud of what I have done. I didn't do it for her, feared Craig's warning. Now I think she would have suggested it had I asked, run the dilemma passed her. I went through yesterday's family drama, a blow-by-blow account that was emotional enough for the Sunday papers but I'll not be mailing it in. Then, when I explained that a twenty-stone reformed elective mute has become the occupant of my bedroom and I am to sleep on the sofa, that I must come to hers if we are to share a bed, she objected.

'I can share that with you. The sofa must fold out to a double. I want to meet them.'

I hoped they were not listening in when I explained why not. I am not so flamboyant as to wish my love-making to be a sideshow for teenage boys.

'Sophie,' she laughed, 'I wasn't suggesting we go at it every night; I just want to be with you. Hold you in my arms. That doesn't make a noise and you said they are almost house-trained.'

She had me in fits with that, and it is sweet. I cannot leave them alone yet, not on their second night in a strange place, a father's funeral ringing in their ears. An aunt's rejection too. And I do want Grace to hold me in her arms. Later today she shall visit. She wanted to fulfil that wish every bit as much as I hoped to receive it.

I phone Mr Gosling. His office is in Epsom, I believe his company has another out at Earls Court, perhaps we can meet there. The secretary says it is unlikely he can speak to me, and then, within seconds, he is on the line.

'Miss Stephenson,' he says—many people know me by that name—'I was just reading about the funeral. So sad.'

I am not so foolish as to buy a newspaper today. And I hope to keep the boys from seeing one too, may ask Grace to check what the rum fuckers are saying. Grace or Monica: the resilient ones.

'Things have changed, Mr Gosling. My circumstances in certain respects.' I put him in the picture. Advise that I see no prospect of the boys returning to Redhill. 'I will buy a larger flat. Maybe a townhouse.'

'Miss Stephenson, you and the young master Stephensons will be wanting for nothing but it cannot be arranged speedily. I do not know what Mary Stephenson, or her solicitors, advise on this matter. Your father's inheritance will go to her although the circumstances are most complex.'

I query how things stand. I thought I was to have access to substantial monies. Mr Gosling confirms that I am to have a pleasing revenue, a private income that many would envy. It shall not buy a large flat. Not in a hurry.

'Rental, Miss Stephenson. It is definitely an option, not one to be rushed into. I can make an appointment with a financial adviser if that would be of assistance to you.'

'I shall bear it in mind, Mr Gosling. I think I need a more thorough understanding of the will. Can you go through it with me?'

'There will be a reading. Not yet. In a few weeks' time, I expect. I need to learn who is to represent Mrs Stephenson. And the young master Stephensons.'

'Can they not be present at the reading?'

He asks me the questions now. It is a simple misunderstanding. He thinks legal matters beyond the comprehension of both boys. Gosling, our family solicitor, turns out to be surprisingly clueless. Not sure he knows an iota about the wider family for which he solicits. Too busy representing the one still in jail and the one who couldn't face up to all he has clearly done. They are the black sheep, not Craig, not Simon. Not even bitter old me.

* * *

When Grace buzzes, I realise how splendid a mood I have enjoyed all day. The boys are good company; Simon has had lengthy periods of silence but always answers when spoken to. Some monosyllabic answers, and I can feel like that now and then. Craig is finally relaxing. He and I talked about school. He's missed quite a bit, not sat behind a desk since Lancashire. I do not think these have been his weeks of optimum performance; he's clever enough to recover lost ground, in my estimation. The importance of doing genuinely intelligent activities was my big message. 'You can push the A-levels to one side. Pick them up next year if what you want to do requires them. But don't become a dullard. It's easy to feel that mindless activities are the best, that they'll see us through a pain-free day. I think the opposite. Not just think, I know it for certain. Understanding the world and what goes on across it might be impossible. Trying to do just that is the only worthwhile course for any life. Finding ways to leave it better than we found it, if only by a fraction. Everything else is atrophy.' I think Simon was on his computer in my bedroom when I said all this. At the end of my little pep talk, he began to applaud. Mr Bat Ears.

Craig smiled at his brother's response. 'I'll try my best.'

When Grace enters the room, I step right in and kiss her on the lips. I know that Craig is watching, and I want him to know it is what we do.

Grace seems slightly surprised, steps back and looks me in the face, and then she also places both hands on my hips. 'Introduce me then,' she says. It is etiquette's sequence I have offended. Kissing in front of others pleases her no less than me.

'It's a pleasure to meet you,' says my kid half-brother holding out a hand for her to shake. Grace and I cannot help laughing. I introduced her as Grace Topping, and when Craig says, 'How do you do,' I repeat, 'Grace Topping, Craigy, not the Duchess of Snot Hall.'

Simon has ventured from his room. 'I have heard a little about you,' she tells him.

'My auntie can't stand me but my sister can?'

'And I know your sister has impeccable taste, Simon.'

She reaches out a hand to shake, and as he thrusts his forward, face always turned away, she leans in and pecks him on the cheek. It is a normal gesture. He doesn't reciprocate but speaks a couple more of these novel words. 'Didn't hurt.'

Takes his education seriously does my economy-sized brother.

* * *

I start to cook an evening meal, and then Grace rather takes over. Her skills exceed mine. And then some. She talks very casually, relaxed and at ease, with my brothers. I defrosted minced beef with a lasagne in mind, and now she suggests burgers. Both the boys are fans. I ask how that works and she says she will show me. The way she shapes them quickly between her turning palms makes her look a little like a psycho-killer; however, if I step back from the discolouring of her hands, I think she does a good job. I look again in the freezer for oven chips and find I haven't any in.

'I'll use your potatoes,' she says. She seems to know how to conjure these up without a fryer.

I do only a modicum of food preparation, the sous chef and Grace is the executive. She even thinks to bake apples and make custard. I ask her not to examine the date on the tin from which she disburses the magic powder.

By the time we sit down, Craig and Simon have concluded my partner is the one to nurture them. I say that she can only stay in Bayswater for one night; final rehearsal and then performances for a paying audience are to be her lot in the coming days. 'Not to worry, boys you may go and live with her, and I will have my flat back.'

I detect something on the bass end of laughter from Simon, while Craig, who is of a gentler disposition, looks mortified. Thinks me offended by his praise of Grace's cooking. He tries to declare that his love for me is greater than his love of hamburgers. It sounds daft. My girlfriend splutters over it. 'Very sweetly put,' she lies. 'Your sister told me it was hell for you living with the old auntie long before it went tits up. Said she should spring you from it, only her place wasn't big enough. Now you're making it work, she won't give you up.'

He looks at me with puppy-dog eyes. 'Thanks, sis.'

Equilibrium restored.

'And you will have to put up with whatever nonsense Sophie cooks from tomorrow night, boys,' says my smiling lover.

* * *

Later in the evening, we all watch a crime drama that Grace and Craig both express an interest in. Simon surprises me by staying in the room. Viewing it with us. I detect a shift in his perspective. He more than talks, he accepts those around him without the hysteria that used to be under the surface. Closer to the surface than felt comfortable for anyone. The eye contact has not arrived yet but he must know I am watching him watching the television. He allows it, as he recently would not have done.

I think the programme is good. We all watch closely, only the TV speaks. My mind is a pinball machine. Simultaneously restless and exhausted. This is my family. All my life I have kept the objects of my romantic eye away from every relative I have. I think that was not romance at all, it was a wall around my heart.

The programme finishes at ten and Grace has whispered to me that she hopes to sleep long tonight. May not manage, she gets very anxious this close to curtain up. Values sleep at this time in a play's cycle. I ask the boys if they mind leaving us shortly. I need to make the sofa up into a bed. I think it folds out but I've never figured it. I slept on it without unfolding anything last night. Simon says Grace and I should prepare for bed—he knows my showering routine already—

he and Craig will make the bed up. It is another surprise, most welcome.

It feels devilish, Grace and I locked in a bathroom with the two boys out of ear shot. She comes into the shower with me and allows a brief embrace, and it is only that. Affection. When we have towelled ourselves—thick pyjamas that will not cause the boys any embarrassment—we go back to them. They have done as they said they would. It is a double bed. A narrow double, and that pleases me too. One of them is a wag, has lit a candle to bring about a romantic ambience. I blow it out.

'Fire hazard. Thank you so much, Simon, Craig.'

The latter mutters something that I don't hear properly. 'He said it's brilliant staying here,' Simon's deeper voice tells me. 'He said it and I think it too.'

Later, lying with my arms around Grace whose breathing indicates she is asleep in the bosom of my family, I think over how much I have enjoyed this night. Not for extravagant pleasures but for the simplest ones. The company I have kept.

* * *

Two nights later, the boys and I are together in the theatre watching Mother Courage and Her Children. I would have gone alone but they both spoke with Grace about her work. Took an interest. When I said, 'Do you want to come?' I expected only one yes. Got two. We are in the banquet seats, all that was available. Simon is rivetted. Applauds vigorously as the first act closes. I find myself wanting to talk about this with Mary. Not to gloat that I have achieved something she has not. To let her know her travails have paid off. I wrote this boy off years ago when she did not. I am the one getting the comeuppance with regard to Simon. Mary has been his mainstay. Perhaps he will come with me. Theatre, prison. Is life getting stranger or more normal?

Chapter Eight:

The Reckoning

1.

The first day and a half of this trial—Mary Stephenson's trial for the murder of my mother—have been an utter frustration. I have waited in a witness room, uncalled and unable to follow the proceedings. Now I am to take the stand.

Some months ago, I was determined to do this: reveal to the jury the sheer cruelty of my stepmother's deception. My motivation is memory. I recall the time—almost twenty years ago now—recall the step change in their attitudes. Mary and the father for whom I do not grieve. Initially the disappearance was a mystery. They offered no explanation; they sympathised with my upset. Subtly, over time—and possibly no more than a month of it—Cynthia Hartnell became a deserter, responsible for leaving me high and dry. Neither said it that directly. Not in words. 'Passport,' was sufficient. My father said it more frequently than my stepmother, she would accompany his words with a look. A contortion of the face that seemed to push the responsibility squarely onto the shoulders of the absentee. If I had been especially awkward—there were days when I was nothing but—the face said my mother left without me because I was such bloody hard work. That a look could say it without words was always going to be hard to explain in a courtroom.

It is how I recalled it, and what I intended to say in the days and weeks after my mother's corpse entered the world of true fact. The notion that she had fled, no longer a breathing thought. For somewhere between days and weeks I could only visualise how deliberately my stepmother had disturbed me, aged eleven. Trashed my mental equilibrium to cover her own tracks. Softened me up for Carnforth, not that it is relevant to the jury that must adjudge her deeds.

The testimony I planned would have implicated my father equally. He is unable to stand trial; his complicit guilt difficult to dispute. His confession before the final act of his life was partial in the worst possible way. A childish 'she made me' before his childish and petulant suicide. His guilt extends far beyond the disposal of my mother's body, I am sure of it. He could have turned her in at the time, would have done exactly that if he wasn't equally complicit. Of the murder, not just the burial. My father fingered Mary alone for the murder, I remain uninformed of any detail. How she did it. If the jury learned the content of his accusation while I have been waiting to testify, I hope someone will fill me in when I'm done. I need to know, upsetting as every new piece of information is to hear.

Something more compelling than doubt about my stepmother's role in all this seems to have wormed its way into my belly. I have visited South Kent Prison with and without Monica, with and without Simon and Craig. She has treated me most civilly, and I understand how stressful her life of incarceration must be. And on that first visit, with Monica, I was moved by the notion—while being unable to entirely trust it—that Mary stayed with my father only for me, to alleviate my loss following Cynthia's disappearance. The Crown Prosecution Service, with my father's pre-suicide affidavit as their principal evidence, might be wrongfully accusing her. Or alternatively, she just might be the coldest murderess in history. It is a heady watershed.

In a telephone call some four weeks ago, back in March, I told the prosecuting counsel that I didn't think I could do it. Declare my stepmother guilty. Mr Pope QC didn't laugh, I felt its sting nevertheless.

'We're not asking you to be judge and jury,' he said. 'There will be others sitting in those seats. We shall call you to the stand and require only that you answer honestly, under the oath you must swear. I understand how young you were at the time of your mother's disappearance. Your story is background, it will give the jury insight into the Stephenson family at the time of your mother's disappearance. Proof of guilt shall come from elsewhere in the case we construct. A household that deceived the one who most needed to know the truth is but a part of the jigsaw.'

I realised after I had made it that my call was foolish; I would take the stand, the oath, and what flowed from it would be justice. If the jury sees no merit in my aspersions, it is because I was young and things felt as they did, I may have over-concluded. I don't believe I drew any definitive conclusions at the time. Until last summer I had always expected to see Mummy again. Truly, I was certain I would.

I ended the phone call as quickly as I reasonably could. A raven chorus retching in my gut at Mr Pope's words. The deceived, the one who needed to know. Me. Eleven-year-old me still more so.

These months have been strange ones; some good has come from the tumult. Darius played hardball and terminated my contract. I was willing to work but it could only have been on my terms. I would not neglect the boys, my brothers. He had no use for a part-time, deadline-shy investigative reporter. Grace and I remain a fixture. No, I do her a disservice with that trite phrase. We are in love: I with her, she with me. It is a fiery truth. I see her when I can but we—the boys and I—move between Carnforth and Bayswater with more of the former. Craig back in school up there and the big house suits us. Grace stays with us in Lancashire when work allows; it can be a bit occasional, although I believe she likes the place more than I do.

I watched News South on television last night, my girlfriend holding me meaningfully as, together, we heard the briefest summary of day one. Simon sitting in the room, silent as the reporter spoke. He talks but not over others.

> *The trial has begun of Mary Stephenson, the second wife of the late Professor Paul Stephenson. It is for the murder of the professor's first wife, Cynthia, in September nineteen-eighty-one. The judge advised the jury that only she is on trial today. The guilt or otherwise of her deceased husband is no longer pertinent to their decision, although it is the prosecution's case that the pair will have planned and enacted the murder and subsequent concealment of the body in unison.*

It weighs me down like a stone. Perhaps the whole family have played me like an old piano, bashed out a tune that I conceitedly felt has worth because it has arisen from me, my experience. Is the son, a baby when my mother disappeared, an unwitting accomplice in my deception? His speechifying, return from mutism, melting my frozen heart. Finally warming me to the mother he loves. Bringing me to hope she is let off the hook from which she deserves a royal hanging.

A young court usher, sombre charcoal suit clashing madly with his two-tone gelled hair, leads me into the chamber.

I know the layout, the bewigged judge, twelve members of the jury. In the dock sit Mary and her ugly lesbian guard. It crosses my mind that they deserve each other. Fairly or unfairly, it is my thought. And, at the bottom of it, prison guard is a worthwhile job. Keeping a semblance of order in this rotten society.

As I take the oath—swear by a God about whom I am as

uncertain as all else in this life—I notice Monica in the gallery. She might smile at me; I cannot return it. What I am about to do will not be to my aunt's liking, although it hurts me to displease her.

Then the questioning begins. The first questions asked are easy to answer. My name. My age today: we celebrated my thirty-first birthday, Grace and I did so quietly just one month ago. I confirm that I was the merest eleven years old when my mother disappeared. Deprived of her life, as I was of the person most precious to me in this world. The prosecuting counsel has done his research, understands the iciness of my stepmother. On this stand, at this moment, I hate her just as I did as a child.

Mr Pope puts a question to me about the visit my father and I made to the home of Cynthia Hartnell after she failed to pick me up from my father's house that fateful Friday. The barrister lets me talk through entering the house, finding the kitchen door unlocked, all the rest of it. My mother's absence from her own home. Then he takes me back an hour, more than an hour. Coming home from school that day, when did I see my stepmother? The accused. How did she seem? Can I recall the words she spoke to me in advance of going to the house? Going there after the initial surprise that my mother, Cynthia Hartnell, had failed to arrive at my father's house, didn't pick me up, as expected.

I cannot recall her demeanour at all. I see the importance of it, that it might reveal a great deal. That she may have been harbouring the guiltiest secret of them all. But it is also plausible that she was not. My testimony on this point adds nothing.

I find myself woffling to the court about how normal Mary seemed that day. 'On the surface.' I use this term without having any capacity to bring her words, mood or manner at that earlier point in the momentous day into conscious thought. 'It might have been superficial. I was a child, unskilled in psychological unmasking.' The defence barrister is on her feet. I am implying more than the question has invited me to confirm, her objection runs. My thoughts are elsewhere; I do not care if they shoot me down. For the first time, I realise she will get away with it. The Crown has seen fit to give it a go, prosecute the ice queen. Their peripheral evidence, the insight their interviews with her gave, must make them feel her guilt like a crush to the chest. Feel it as I do. And yet, the principal evidence is the testimony of a dead man. A man who cannot take the stand. A man who took his own life motivated, I am sure, by the bleak future before him. The guilt which ensued from the significant role he played in this sordid affair.

There is no justice, only competing voices trying to steal away the narrative.

* * *

The following day, Grace and I sit behind Monica and a girlfriend of hers, in the viewing gallery. I understand Gary is working, that he has an important agent meeting or some such. He has been supportive of Monica and I throughout, I do not begrudge him his career. Being handsome and acting quite well with it, it is not the kind of good fortune one should pass over.

The prosecution take time to show the jury exactly how the persons responsible disposed of my mother's body. I think this is solid, although my father is the one most certainly implicated. He admitted it in his sworn affidavit, and Mary denies all knowledge of the event. The murder, the precise when, and which of the couple tugged hard on the ligature, seems to me to be more speculative. I have learned from a quiet word with Mr Pope much that I have thus far missed. There was forensic evidence gleaned from the decomposed corpse but nothing on Mary's person. They never looked when it mattered most. Her involvement in my mother's consignment to that miserable grave seems hard to prove from here. I do hope they have something. She looks far less disturbed than me, and that isn't right.

'This part of Professor Stephenson's confession was most thorough, members of the jury. A complete surprise for the investigating officers, they had never heard the like. Mary Stephenson here,' he throws a glance towards the dock, 'and her husband Paul—late husband—were scientists, distinguished physicists. It gave them insight and knowledge that is far beyond the commonplace. In November nineteen-eighty-one, more than two months after the last known sighting of Cynthia Hartnell, the police searched the grounds and premises of Cloud House, Mogador Lane, Burgh Heath. The property which—as I have already confirmed—has since yielded the grisly find, almost nineteen years subsequent to that search. The police had no tip-off at the time but search it they did. Going the extra mile, you might say. We have heard from several acquaintances of Cynthia Hartnell, from her daughter and her cousin, that the notion she had fled abroad was their received wisdom. The missing passport and the mystery man in South Africa. Something in the demeanour of Mary Stephenson, and of her then-husband also, gave police reason enough to doubt this speculation. That they took the time to search properties belonging to several of their acquaintances tells us the depth of their doubt.'

The picture he paints for the jury is far more thorough than any I have before understood. The reluctance of the police at the time to accept the fled-abroad theory is completely new to me.

'Why was the body not found? Well—for the record—I want to tell you most sincerely, most certainly, this was not a case of police negligence. Far from it. The police were being terribly diligent, they simply could not have foreseen the extraordinary lengths which the pair went to in order to conceal their murderous wrongdoing.'

Randall Pope QC is a very intelligent speaker. He embarks upon the explanation, tells the jury how come the garden at Cloud House, property of Jean Fletcher, appeared completely undisturbed although the accused and my deceased father allegedly and ingeniously lifted a shed from its place in the ground and put it back down again. He holds my attention effortlessly although I had thought engineering acts such as these to be beyond my current attention span. The barrister almost brings this unlikely feat into the room, we can see it before our eyes.

'The principle behind the enterprise, jurors, was to ease the shed up so slowly that no great shifting of the earth would occur, that it would rise up and then slide back down again, no sign of its temporary elevation remaining visible. Professor Stephenson even said, and I quote, "About a week and a decent rain would hide all sign that the shed had ever been moved." It was nine weeks after the disappearance of Cynthia Hartnell when police came to examine this site; these physicists calculated everything correctly. The initial smokescreen of lies made the delay inevitable.'

The barrister goes into detail about the mechanics—the physics—of their actions. The minor feat of engineering that fooled us all. He explains that a high proportion of the devices used in the building industry utilise a simple inter-cog system to activate their many functions. Gearing. He begins by talking about tractors: explains how seed drills and hay bailers couple onto the rotating power take-off shaft at the rear of the primary vehicle. A muck spreader even. The jury laughs at that. Muck spreading—a funny activity to raise in a courtroom—and it was my stock in trade back at the Sunday Noise. 'All those tractor-pulled devices use the rotation of a single shaft on the rear, linked to whatever machinery is needed, to carry out the carefully controlled job. The clappers on a hay-bailer, scooping up and packing the cut grass, even tying the ends of string, of the bailer twine, which held together each rectangular bail in years gone by. Since that time, we have developed a penchant for the great big cylindrical bails one sees in farm fields from June to September. The bigger machines used to make them rely upon the same principles. The power take-off shaft must be rotating at a precise setting, geared to thrash together hay and even periodically knot the string around the bail. Five hundred and forty rotations per minute, for example.'

The learned man tells us that he has not simply plucked the figure from the air. It is a lot but this allows a scaling down, the way to make a slow motion exceptionally slow is to have substantial control over it. To be able to adjust it so minimally that it is barely even movement.

'Members of the jury, in the written statement which Professor Stephenson made before his untimely death, he drew a diagram of a contraption of which he had two. He said they left his possession before the Friday that Cynthia Hartnell was understood to be missing. A simple piece...' He takes several copies of A3 paper from the desk in front of him. Hands one to the judge, who takes it knowingly while indicating he may pass several more to the foreman of the jury. In the gallery, we cannot see but we hear the explanation. A motor car parked close by and both sides jacked up at the front, wheels off. It affords two available and connected rotating shafts to which these crafty devices may be attached. No heavy lifting machine required to enter the grounds of Cloud House. A regular car as any visitor to the professor who lived there might drive.

I see the jury look at each other, someone seems to be doubting the feasibility of it all, I cannot guess why.

Randall Pope raises a cautioning hand before the presiding judge even thinks to shush them. 'The second Mrs Stephenson,' he declares, 'drove a Volkswagen Passat at that time. A front-wheel drive Volkswagen Passat.' I think someone was ahead of me—I might never have got there—

the clever man has cleared it up. Allayed a jury member's logical doubt. And made my stepmother's link to the event a little more certain in my mind.

Miss Jean Fletcher—now deceased, and her former property twice sold since her passing—was out of the country, on a cruise ship, for three weeks at the time of my mother's disappearance. I scarcely know my father's connection to her; I doubt he had keys to her house. She was one of the great and the good of Imperial College, so long retired that her picture—displayed to this day in the front foyer—is in black and white. My father used her cruelly: the poor woman died unaware that her garden harboured his guilt. By Mary too, I am hearing, for all the difficulty Mr Pope may find pinning the deed upon her forensically. My father's shameful confession describes the use of a single car, my Stepmother's car, both front wheels removed, two devices beside one end of a shed, lifting it a millimetre at a time over a ten-minute period. According to Mr Pope—courtesy of my father's written testimony—both parties participated in emptying the shed in advance of the deed. Restocked it on completion of the act of burial. For the raising, Mary stayed in the car, bringing the accelerator to the level required before engaging the lifting device. My father held a garden spade, he watched the soil and surrounding plants move, signalled if revving was to cease while he tinkered with any attached soil, the roots of bothersome plants. The dual contraptions lifted up one end of the wooden-based shed, and when it was high enough—eighteen inches the requirement—Mary turned the engine off. It held in place. 'The pair of them,' intones prosecuting counsel, 'removed what was little more than a small packing crate from the backseat of the car. Thin plywood, nailed shut.' Then he steps right up to the jury, holds the rail alongside those in the front row. 'A crate so small, she was bent double to fit inside, torso forward alongside her legs. A broken spine just so that she could fit in the space.' There is a gasp, and I realise I am crying. Grace's arm around my shoulder. It is an unspeakable wickedness. I look through my tears at Mary Stephenson, I see her dab a handkerchief to her own eyes. How could my father and stepmother be so heartless as to crush a cadaver, torment my poor mother's lifeless corpse. I bury my face in Grace's cashmere.

'The pair of them were able to take this small crate from the boot of the car, and slide it under the raised shed, knowing it would squash down invisibly so long as Professor and Mary Stephenson were as diligent during the descent of the shed as they had been thus far.'

This episode appals me. Sick inside my mouth. I swallow. I cannot leave the courtroom. I may assault my stepmother should I pass near her on a needed trip to the ladies' room.

'In his statement to police, the late professor said...' Mr Pope adjusts his glasses, reads from a paper he has carried in his hand throughout his oration. Voice clear and without a discernible tone to lead us in our appraisal. I hear him speak my father's words.

> *This was intended to be only a temporary resting place. Mary and I agreed upon that. Jean Fletcher was still rather active, we thought we would have a chance to move it again once the fuss had died down. She liked her cruises, the house often empty for months at a time. Instead, we moved up to Lancashire and rather forgot about it. If not forgotten, not spoken of between us. And we couldn't bring her with us, of course.*

Oh God. I spew an ugly fountain. My vomit is upon Grace's sweater. I fear I've ruined it, and she really doesn't deserve that.

2.

There is a break in the trial and Mary has still to take the stand. The boys and I are up in Carnforth, Grace with us. She has pulled out of a play that was to begin rehearsing today. She says she will look after me. That I am more important. I am a killer's daughter—that is what I am—and I fear my brothers are the spawn of two killers. It is a desolate piece of knowledge and something we should not hold against each other. Grace says, 'How could you?' She does not feel the absence, the cruel awareness that for nineteen years my better, loving mother lay squashed and deformed beneath a shed in a garden two miles from her rightful home. From the daughter who missed her so.

Before this unfolding of events—'Docudrama,' Monica calls it—replaying through the words of witnesses from a time when Craig was yet to be on this Earth and Simon had little purchase upon it, we felt so tightly knit. Mary is our lightning rod, our marmite.

Simon, the speaker of logical truth or nothing at all, and for the longest time before that its diligent scribe, has taken to offering reassurances. His deep voice has raised up a little, its growl wearing off—he has run it in—it is me he reassures.

'We know how much you miss her, Sophie. If we could bring her back, we would.'

And it is not the thoughts of these two boys that worry me, it is that a lack of meaningful evidence will free Mary. The woman who murdered my mother may then take these boys away from me. The only family I have. I could not stand that. Nor to be in the same room as her. Or even the same county.

Craig is with us today, Sunday. He attends a small residential school in Oxenholme. I do not mind driving him to and fro when we are staying here; he boards only when this house is empty; he has seen none of the trial. Simon is adapting astonishingly well, whether here or in my flat in Bayswater. He was going to come to court on Friday, when we thought his mother would take the stand, a last-minute change of mind. He called it right, it was frustrating, they never got around to questioning her. Adjournment occupied more than three-quarters of the allotted time. There is talk of new witnesses, possibly this Dennis Harris chap of whom Monica once spoke fondly. All speculation. If not him then someone else in America, and his is the only link I know between my stepmother and the entire continent. Monica had no idea who it might be, heard only that someone from America was in touch with Mary's team.

At Grace's suggestion, we drive out to a country pub; we will eat there. I think it is only the change of scenery we seek; we are constantly together in house or flat, never do we fall out. Surprising given the boys' hope for their mother's acquittal and my dread of such a thing. Or am I wavering; Grace said to me that Mary doesn't look like a killer, and I think she made her observation only after seriously thinking it over. Isn't trying to influence but she is one of us now. An insider in the unfolding docudrama.

The pub we choose—The Falconer—is up on the fell. When we issue forth from the car it is into a stiff wind. It could be a gale. Grace, Craig and I step quickly to the entrance door but I see Simon hold back. And he is the only one of us without a coat. I whisper, 'Just a tonic water,' to Grace. She is our driver but I want no part of alcohol today, yesterday, this month long. I face this trial sober or I shall drown. Craig enters with her and I go to see what eats my more stubborn brother.

'Sophie,' he says, 'the wind blows everything that isn't tied down. Look!' He points: at the field boundary in our vision, a black tarpaulin—the sort farmers use to cover hay and straw—is bumbling its way over a hedge. Untethered, wind-blown.

I smile inwardly. The observation is below par for this astute boy. 'What of it?'

'The wind has only blown in one direction. I was in your flat, unaffected, but the wind has pushed you this way and that. It is not like you, Sophie. I want you tied down.'

'Riddle-me-ree,' I say. 'Shall we get some food and you can explain what the hell you're talking about?'

'It will be warm in there, and I feel cold.'

'All the more reason to go inside, dear Simon.'

'Sometimes cold is all right. I felt warmer when I understood you. When you understood me.'

'Ha-ha. Did I ever understand you, enigmatic boy? I'm not such a great journalist, and I was never a Simonologist. You need eleven A-levels and a crackpot sense of humour to so much as get on the course.'

He grins quite noticeably just for a second, I think he looks at my face before turning away. 'I understood you, and I'm not clever.'

'If you're not clever, what does that make me? A blockhead. And what of me, in particular, do you no longer understand? I am not evasive. I've always been a ready talker.'

'Do we ever truly know anything, Sophie? I know you are the one most affected by all this. Both parents gone. I don't really know what grief is but you have it bad, Sophie.'

I put an arm across his back, and in his inexpert way he reciprocates. Over my shoulders. 'I think you more than understand me, Simon. You want to lift me out of it. But I think it should have been me beneath the shed. Not that my father wanted me dead. And nor do I see why he wanted my mother dead. They actually got along you know. Our father's relationship with your mother has always been the funny one. A twenty-something year marriage in place of a one-night stand. Am I upsetting you by saying this?'

'You should say whatever's on your mind.'

'I never rated Daddy's second marriage but it did produce you and Craig. A good haul.' I let my words fall to nothing. I have more maudlin thoughts: that Mary would have liked me beneath the shed. And I haven't a pinch of proof. It's just how I've always felt about it.

'I never knew Cynthia Hartnell,' says Simon. 'And I don't do my living in the feeling realm. The brain does all the thinking, feelings are only the aftershock. I don't think it is that way round for you, Sophie. I think hearing the events of those years ago is like the wildest wind. You've become untethered, and I want you tied down.'

'So, you stayed out here to feel the wind, and to tell me that you cared. Which I already knew but it is nice to hear it. Especially so in your cryptic telling.'

'I think the wind will change, Sophie. Not today perhaps, but soon. The wind will blow from another direction.'

* * *

Inside the country pub, Grace and Craig seem to be engaged in their own heart-to-heart. I feel that she too is family, one who will endure, grow old among all these people close to me. And if fate and the rough justice that is looking all too likely to tear us apart, divide me from my brothers, then Grace and I will go on. Our love is stronger because she knows me so intimately. Knows me as I've never allowed another. I have explained to her how cruel I used to be to Simon. 'You were a kid,' she said, 'a mixed-up kid.' I used to think myself a prodigy, a child genius, but Gracie has the more profound insight.

The food at The Falconer is exceptionally good. We seldom ate out when I lived here years ago, never in this pub, and for me that is part of the attraction. When we have eaten our main courses, and the boys are perusing the dessert menu, a young lady cradling a baby comes across from a nearby table.

'Oh Caz,' I say. 'It's you.' I rise and try to give my old friend a hug, although the child she holds is in the smallest size they make. Must be no more than a few weeks old, and I wish to be careful that we neither crush it. 'He's delightful.'

'Caroline,' my former friend says rather coldly. 'And my baby's a girl.' I am corrected, and a raised flat palm rejects the offered hug.

'What a lovely baby,' I try again. Caroline Reynolds—who befriended me, and I her, through two schools hereabouts—is looking at me through narrowed eyes. 'Craig and Simon,' I say rather hurriedly, 'You might remember them? And my truest friend, Grace. Grace Topping.'

Caroline snorts at my words. I suspect she has changed the Reynolds to something else, don't recall a wedding invitation but I could even have snubbed it. Living in London is such a frantic social swirl. She is staring at me for the longest time without any pleasure evident. The Reynolds were rather well-to-do, I recall. She may have married into Lancashire society, and if he wears a cloth cap it's fine with me also. A snob no more.

'They used to say we were queer up north, it seems like going down south has done it to you.' And she sniggers after saying it. A cruel laugh that she does alone.

I once rather liked this girl. The spiteful words she has spoken remind me that we were both a bit anti-lesbian for a while. Isn't that just the way of teenagers? A phase.

'When are you going back?' adds Caroline. Caz of old.

I look down, a wave of my hand across my face. This is more upsetting than it should be. I know there are idiots like her in this world; I hate her intrusion into my time with family. Grace and my brothers are all I have. I don't need sneering at today.

Craig has put down his menu. 'You're rude as hell. Maybe your daughter will be the same. What will you think then?'

She laughs at him. 'I'd best go before she catches it then.'

I love that he wanted to protect us. Not the most articulate intervention but thank you for trying, Craig. When Caroline Reynolds has truly gone, Grace says, 'Don't worry about it. Small town, small minds.'

Craig has the arguing bug. 'I'm from here. From a small town. I think you're both great.'

She places a hand upon his, I do not believe she meant to criticise the whole of Carnforth. Then she turns to me, without excluding the boys. 'My parents will be as bad as whoever that was. You can bet your house on it. That's why I've not told them yet. But I have to. We're a real couple aren't we, Soph?'

'As real as they come,' I confirm. Then I start to laugh. I worry that it is inappropriate, nothing very funny appears to have taken place these last few minutes. I give Grace a hug that won't scandalise a northern pub. A quick one. 'Caz from my old private school,' I say. 'She thought my preference for a lovely girl over a smelly fella is something to be pitied, something on those lines. She knew Prof Paul, knew Mary. Must have read the paper or turned on the news, she could have tried to shame us for the dreadful deeds that the generation above us were mixed up in, kept secret all the while they lived here. Some or all of them, boys; just saying. She picked on who I love. That stuff can't be wrong, the world a better place for feeling what I do towards you, Gracie.' My laughter has waned completely. Sentimental tears escape my eyes. In the company of Simon and Craig, I can still hold my head up. It isn't even that they don't judge me. It is that they judge correctly. See precisely what matters.

* * *

Late in the evening Grace sleeps beside me. We have talked quite intensely, with deep honesty on both our parts. She remains embarrassed about the parents she has scarcely spoken of before tonight, and hers are only bigots. Not killers.

I see that she too has a past to reconcile with her present. Disappointing her parents may have been a factor holding her back in those early days of our liaison. And I have learned a lot. Once I was most dismissive of people who worried over how to square their sexuality with the expectations of their wider family, although I simply hid it. Not in my normal life but on home visits. I might have been kidding myself about how outlandish I was. May have exaggerated a story or two, as a tabloid journalist is apt. Grace worried that I would be cross: cross that her parents are narrow-minded; cross that she has yet to confront them, say that she loves a girl. What of it all. She needs to work out where to take the relationship with her parents in her own good time. I am simply grateful that I am the priority. I make no demands upon her, whatever little sod I might have been once upon a dalliance.

* * *

I lie awake all night. I have to drive Craig up to Oxenholme in the morning. School. I think he hates the parting, won't say it, of course. Very reluctant to rock the boat, that brother of mine. Simon will come down to London but probably not to court. Grace and I need to hear it. I need to hear and watch every minute, hate it as I do.

In the still of the night, I think about Mary once more. The third time I visited South Kent Prison, Simon accompanied me. Craig was with us too, his presence quite unexceptional. Simon voluntarily entering the prison was startling for her. It must have been. I wanted Monica there but after much deliberation, the prison welfare officer told us no. That number of visitors could not come together, even three was permitted only because Craig is not yet eighteen. Keeping the family apart, the improbable aim of the so-called welfare service.

My stepmother smiled when we entered the visiting room, stepped up to her Formica table. 'Thanks so much for bringing them both. For being here.'

I coughed. It wasn't a signal but it might as well have been.

'They don't hurt you here do they, mother?' What strange first words for one's baby to utter. Mary looked up at him, her larger son was looking away. He repeated, 'Do they?'

Craig tried to beam at his mother, I think the emotion of it was too great. She looked a bit dismal, to be honest. Hair washed but limp. Not done with any product I would let near my own. Her clothes were not ones I recognised; if she owned them in Carnforth, it would have been for the purpose of decorating or gardening. Given the widest berth from any social engagement. A big butch guard stood four paces behind her. We three, her children and stepchild, formed a group only permitted by exception. And Simon talking. Not rabbiting on, he is more measured with speech than he ever used to be with texts.

I said, 'You heard he started after the funeral. After Auntie Sarah...'

Simon placed a hand on my arm. 'Ran out of reasons,' he said.

'I heard, Simon, Craig. I do read my letters. I am so grateful to you, Sophie. Grateful for all that you have done for us.'

Craig had a few tears in his eyes as he stretched a hand out on the table. His mother touched it; finger ends. Nothing for a guard to get uppity about. I was feeling affronted. She can always do this. Helping us, were the words she used. As if I am not quite of their number.

'I love them too,' I said. I thought it a defiant comment; she may not have noticed.

Craig tried to make Mary laugh, to entertain, wisely or otherwise. 'He started talking when we all got back from the funeral.' Mary nodded. 'Talked about it like it wasn't such a big deal.' I saw him gulp quite visibly after he had said it. A bigger deal to him perhaps. 'Do you think Aunt Sarah is the only one who will miss Daddy?' His voice cracked with just the saying of it. I think he loves his brother more than he ever did his father, or that might be my own bespoke calculation. And I was entirely the other way around for the first eight or ten years of Simon's life.

'I think we will all miss him,' Mary sounded quite flat as she spoke. 'The reasons we will miss him may trouble us. Miss him for better and for worse.'

'I won't.' That was the pronouncement of decisive Simon Stephenson.

'He tried with you when you were young,' said Mary. 'Do you remember that? When you proved yourself intelligent, and he understood quicker than the doctors. It confused him but he was keen to make the professionals understand why he thought it. Recognised you were very able and aware.'

I tried to talk over our travails with schooling for Craig, with housing. I told her that we might return to Carnforth, and Mary said, 'You'd do that for them?' She understood how much I hated the place. Understood it from the day we moved there, I expect. I confirmed that my concern was entirely for their wellbeing. If an older sister cannot put herself out for her brothers, she is really not much to write home about. I used an expression of that ilk.

'You have always been most capable, Sophie. I believe I let you down. That has been the friction between us.'

Simon looked up. Quickly up and down. I had already sensed that he anticipated much of the conversation, found it unexceptional. Something in that exchange piqued his interest. 'Thinking she was abandoned by her own mother was the cause of her low self-esteem. It's in all the psychology books.'

I found myself grinning at my brother's interjection. Low self-esteem, my sweet derriere. I was a conceited fucker all childhood long. A residue of it remains. And I know, from texts he sent me, from long ago, not any recent conversation, that Simon has no truck with psychology. Thought every therapist he saw a fool.

'You don't mind us going up to the house then?' I wanted to make sure this would not be a cause of future disagreement. There may be breakages, who knows. 'I planned to take a friend. A girlfriend.'

I did not say it with any challenge in my voice. Matter of fact, that was what I went for. Craig beamed of course. A nice smile, I think he is very fond of Grace. Mary picked it up astutely. 'I am pleased you've found someone, Sophie.'

It is quite bewildering to fathom the ebb and flow of that visit. Mary took Simon in her stride. She was nicer to me than she used to be, although that had also been so when I visited with Monica. Or with Craig alone. An evolution in our relationship. Perhaps preparing each for the verdict; unfortunately, I was no clearer what it would be. It is all very odd to recall. Troubling and very, very odd.

3.

In court today I expected Mary to be on the stand. I want to judge her as Mr Pope says I cannot. And I know beyond doubt that I shall, that my judgement of Mary's guilt or otherwise will be the one I live by regardless of the opinions of the twelve seated away to my right. They feel nothing. I might send her a birthday card to whichever jail she languishes in if I think they unfairly convict, or spit in her face should we meet on Bond Street after they mistakenly acquit her. I know I must wait until the end of the trial before I conclude but our relationship has never been on shakier ground. It is back under the shed.

A witness from the building company who were clearing the land, taking down the shed, following a successful application to build a new home—infill they call it, utilising garden space between existing houses to add another property to the leafy road on which Jean Fletcher once lived—is describing the ghoulish find. His unearthing of my mother. 'We crowbarred up the shed floor. The wooden crate just looked like more flooring, frankly. Only when I jemmied it open and saw the bones did I realise what I'd come across. Before the police whatsit got there, I thought it was a child. On account of the tiny size of the coffin. But I should have thought really. I mean, it wasn't a proper coffin or anything. But I was a bit sickened by it, quite frankly. Didn't want to study the bones. That's all it was. Bones. I knew it was human, some long ones and I saw the skull you see. They have a certain shape, don't they? Can't mistake them for dogs or cows. It was a sad lot to come across. I didn't have the first idea how long it had been down there.'

'Mr Carter...' Irene Goddard is setting the questions today. I think she is a QC, has to be to speak in a courtroom of this importance. She works with Pope and he seems to be taking a breather. He sits up in his seat, pays attention, while he has clearly left the working-class witness to the younger barrister. Graces-age young, I'd hazard, hard to tell with the funny wig on. '...before you started to demolish the shed was there any sign that it had been tampered with, that a small packing crate could have been placed beneath it?'

'It couldn't. The shed was solid before we smashed it down. That's just our job. No, you've got it wrong, miss. Whoever erected the shed put it on top of the little coffin. That wouldn't be hard. You couldn't have slipped it under. There's no way to do that, miss. The little crate was smack in the middle. I know about this; I work with sheds every day of the year.'

'Ladies and gentlemen of the jury,' says this youngish barrister, 'there you see the ingenuity of Mary and Paul Stephenson. They have outwitted this upstanding contractor. You have heard how he came across the remains of Cynthia Hartnell, the skeleton folded within a small wooden crate. You have heard with what foresight they chose this to be her final resting place. Temporary resting place according to Mr Stephenson's affidavit, although neither culprit made any effort whatsoever to make good on their vow to find her a better burial site. A shed standing in Miss Fletcher's grounds since the nineteen-fifties. There was no evidence of disturbance, nothing to make the police suspect a burial had taken place in this garden. For nineteen long years the poor lady lay where she did not belong.'

That is just what I am thinking. And I can see my stepmother listening very closely to Irene Goddard, her summary of the exchange. Hearing how she—Mary—hid the crime. The corpse of my better mother. She looks a little aloof to me. It might be the effect of her raised little dock, her place of importance in this courtroom, and that is an unintended consequence. It is only the importance which the prospect of notoriety carries in its wake. I understood Mr Pope last week, his underling today. Achieving this cruel and perfect deception was not the work of my father, not alone. He could not simultaneously be in the driver's seat and monitor the raising of the shed end, see that soil barely slipped while revving the engine. By nineteen-eighty-one my father and Mary had rowed but I think they were still a couple making a go of it. They later moved to darkest Lancashire together, for God's sake. I am astonished that my father would cover a crime as grave as murder for anyone. I suppose doing it for his then-wife was more likely than doing it for any other. Preserving that marriage for whatever future it had. More probable still, the murder itself was a joint project. The motive confounds me, as does his suicide. If it was only the covering up which he'd been party to, why act so thoroughly guilty? This goes around in my mind day and night. It is all very hard to bear. Tougher than I ever thought when I shouted at Darius, wanted to cover the story for the Noise. Glad I didn't, I might have written it all wrong. May have failed to file any copy at all, so bewildering do I find it.

Mr Carter leaves the stand at the judge's direction. I wonder why Grace's arm grips me so tightly around the shoulder, then I see the forefinger upon her lips. I am wailing again. Making an awful noise that I no longer truly hear. A mother in a shallow grave is horrifically upsetting.

4.

A day later and finally, she is to address the court, answer questions. My stepmother held to account.

Grace has a screen test; she is not with me. It is a terrific break for her but I am horribly nervous about it. She and I will meet this evening, possibly at her flat; Simon can cope alone in Bayswater. He cooks as well as I do, and we all rely rather heavily on Grace. Today's audition is in Camberwell; and if she is cast, the big shoot will be in Greece. Camberwell and Greece, studio and location. I understand she could be away for weeks and weeks. Not immediately, when filming begins. She says she may not get the part; I think it's in the bag. Sounds that way.

Once more the judge directs the jury, reminds them that they should carefully consider everything they hear from the accused today, reiterates also that this will not be the last of it. This is her cross-examination by the prosecution. The defence case is to follow. It is the civic duty of jurors to keep an open mind. I am not expecting Mary to say yes. To tell the court that it was she who tugged the ligature tighter while my mother's face turned blue. She won't say it but I have been picturing it each time I close my eyes these last nine days. My mind involuntarily producing that image. She has some convincing to do if I am ever to believe her innocent.

Mary wears blue. A skirt-suit in light blue. She could be presenting a paper at a symposium. For as many years as I have known her, she has enjoyed the easy access to my father's money that I have. Easier, I guess. She had turned eighteen when they met, he was more circumspect with the spending money of his children than of either wife, I imagine. For all the finery of clothing, and the attractiveness of the body she was born into, she has poor taste. The cut is nice, the colour clashes garishly with her still-fair hair. Possibly-dyed hair. Can they do that in prison? I expect her defence team have found a way; they will have spared no expense. Hair and nails and many carefully chosen words. The sleep-deprived Mary of South Kent Women's Prison, with her unwashed hair and common or garden clothes, looked guiltier than the well-groomed lady before the court. That is all superficial, yet it will have motivated the defence team. I think they are behind this sprucing up. You'd think they would have settled on a better colour. And when I look very closely at her, try to detect signs of guilt or innocence, I must admit the futility of my calculation: I am utterly uncertain.

Monica sits with Gary. We spoke on the steps but I made a point of coming to this end of the viewing gallery, away from where they sit. She respected my decision, understood that she and I have faced opposite directions throughout these testimonies. I hope our friendship can survive this ordeal, while doubting it with a stoicism I have never before found within. They are sisters, I guess she loves Mary as I do my brothers. I am so grateful that I have Grace. Before the judge began his peroration, an usher came to me and asked if my friend—he could have comfortably said girlfriend—would be accompanying me today. There is a small exclusion zone around me. I smiled and said I would cope alone. I have broken down more than once, and I cannot predict when it may happen again. This absence of a loving mother has afflicted me for twenty years; it is a chronic condition and, slowly, I am learning to live with it.

My aunt has dressed as if in parallel with her older sister, her skirt suit green. She matches it with a wide Alice band of a similar material. Carries off the look her sister cannot. Gary is a fine actor, hair now much shorter than when he was filming his Victorian melodrama. The eyes of the press are on the accused, one or two lurid stories have already speculated what inner demons may have propelled her to do the deed which she pleads was done by another. In the lee of infamy, Monica and Gary's hard-won fame is suddenly of little consequence. Their names made the papers and then were just as quickly dropped from the related articles. They act, everything they do is pretend; never throttle another or bury them beneath a shed. Not in real life.

'I swear by almighty God that the evidence I shall give shall be the truth, the whole truth and nothing but the truth.' I look on as she says these words, declares her intention before a God I think she has less belief in than I. Granny Bredbury went in for it, attended church all her life to the best of my knowledge. Mary told me that she followed Stephen's lead, stopped the day she was old enough to stay home alone on a Sunday morning. Monica is the same. I hope I am not over-concluding: seeing the rationalist and scientist that she is, swear before the court on the holy bible suggests to me that she will lie. The court has heard her take the oath while I have heard her dodge a truer one. The affirmation.

The judge asks if she understands the proceedings, tells her that she may look to him for direction if there are questions which she has reason to feel uncertain about answering. 'I will ensure they are procedurally permissible,' he says, 'but it is your solemn duty, as you have sworn to do, that you then answer honestly and without omission of relevant facts. Unless I—and I alone—have disbarred the question. Do you understand?'

She is still standing, still holding the bible she never reads. 'I do,' she says, then—and it looks like a small curtsey to me, could have been a stumble or an attempt to put the book on the stand without focussing upon it, her eyes still on the judge—she repeats, 'I do, your honour.' I think her first go sounded like the culmination of a marriage ceremony. And I can't see my stepmother ever having another go at that.

'Mrs Stephenson,' enunciates Randall Pope, strutting back and forth like a tomcat hovering in the proximity of a cowed mouse, 'this court has heard that, as far as has been ascertained, Cynthia Hartnell went missing sometime after her morning hair appointment on Tuesday the fifteenth of September, nineteen-eighty-one. Can you tell us in your own words about that week? The Tuesday through to the Friday. You can walk us through it as slowly as you please. I'd like the ladies and gentlemen of the jury to understand what you were doing when Cynthia Hartnell was murdered.' Then he turns away from her, looks at the jury box. 'They are to determine whether you participated in her murder and the disposal of the body. A proposition which you deny.'

Mary is on her feet, looking lost. I think it could be guilt, or perhaps we would all feel as she appears if asked to deny a murder charge. It's a difficult pitch: she can do nothing personable to win the jury over, cannot guide their scientific enquiry as she did her students back in Lancaster. Twenty-year-old recollections will make or break her. 'I was away from Epsom; I have stated this to the police many times...' This is bullshit. She was in the house with me on the Friday, the days before that too. How dare she lie so brazenly? '...from the Sunday morning until after lunch on Wednesday.' Hmm, I try my best to recall the veracity of this. 'I visited my mother in Charmouth. I was with her on the Sunday right through to Wednesday morning. I have thought about this repeatedly. I think my husband—Paul—did it while...'

'Enough, Mrs Stephenson. The question was not what your husband did, indeed, on the days you have referred to, you cannot possibly know what he did. You have just said that you were not there. And members of the jury, you may hear this conjecture from time to time throughout this trial. Mrs Stephenson has said in her statement that she can vouch for her husband much of the time that week but not on the evenings of Sunday, Monday or Tuesday. And you will also know that he cannot possibly have acted alone in the disposal of the body. It was a two-person task, you have heard that in detail. No fewer than two people were involved in it, and the late Professor Stephenson confessed to being one of them.' Then he turns back to Mary. 'Put you at the scene too. On the Thursday night. Thursday the seventeenth of September, nineteen-eighty-one. But we shall come to that. About your supposed trip to Charmouth. Is there proof?'

It has come to me now that this took place as she has said. Not thought about it in years. Maybe not even once since everything happened. I was eleven years old, very pleased to have Mary out of the house, and Simon too. He was just a baby at the time; she took him along for the visit to her mother. Never apart from Simon at that time. That all happened. I don't see how it clears her. She says herself she was back on Wednesday.

'You know that my mother has passed away. She can no longer vouch for it. But I stayed with her, took my baby son with me.'

'Yes, conveniently passed away. Any other proof? I understand that you went there from Epsom by rail. Do you still have the ticket?'

Collette Franklin QC is on her feet. Mary's barrister. The questioning displeases her. 'Your honour,' she says, 'Mr Pope is not seriously expecting my client to produce a twenty-year old rail ticket. He is mentally roughing her up. Seeking to disturb her thoughts before asking questions of proper import. And that is not the right way to assist a jury in making this difficult, indeed momentous decision.'

'Thank you. Sit down, please. I hear the point you make,

Miss Franklin, but I do not sustain your objection. The possibility of Mrs Stephenson retaining a rail ticket for this length of time may be remote, that does not invalidate the question. He is inviting your client to prove the truth of her assertion. The absence of proof does not make it false but it is the absence of proof.'

Mary looks perplexed, troubled. Judge and jury are hearing only the wrong she may have done; there is little defence one can discern from her utterances. There are many circumstances in which I might enjoy the scenario but I cannot today. On this narrow point, her trip to Charmouth ending more than forty-eight hours before my mother failed to collect me as planned, Mary is answering truthfully.

'Mrs Stephenson,' asks Mr Pope, 'I understand from your counsel's interjection that no rail ticket remains. Any other proof you might be able to muster.'

'You know, Mr Pope, that I also met Dennis Harris in Charmouth. On Monday evening and briefly on the Tuesday morning, for an hour before lunch.'

'But he has been unable to support your statement.'

'I have been unable to contact him. We understand that Dennis is in America.'

'Members of the jury, the defendant provides no proof of this whatsoever. A named alibi who cannot confirm the meeting which confers their status upon them is not an alibi at all. Mrs Stephenson, are you happy to tell the court the nature of your relationship with this Mr Harris?'

'He's an old friend.'

'An old lover?'

'No.'

'But you were seeing him when on a trip without your husband...'

'Objection, your honour. This is irrelevant. Speculation and irrelevant.'

The judge looks quite gleeful, puts both hands to his wig

as if to straighten it. 'Objection sustained. Jurors please note, Mrs Stephenson is not on trial for any relationship she may or may not have had with...' He looks over the rim of his bifocals, a piece of paper before him. '...Mr Dennis Harris, nor is it the place of this court to examine it. She has stated, after swearing upon the holy bible, that he is not a...' The judge gives a short apologetic cough. '...a former lover. The only point worthy of note is that he is not here. The meeting is in the ambit of Mrs Stephenson's recollection but it has not been verified by another.'

'I remember,' I say from the back of the court. 'My stepmother did go away on the days she said. Came back on Wed...'

'Miss Stephenson, please respect the procedure of this court. You are not upon the stand and may not address the court.'

'I'm sorry but I was never asked. And I remember it...'

'Usher, remove the young lady from the court.'

* * *

At the next recess, Monica seeks me out. 'I know you were trying to help,' she says.

I was and I wasn't. I am a seeker of truth. End of. 'Monica, everyone in there knows who I am. I get handed counselling leaflets every time I pass by reception. It's my mother's murder which this trial is all about. Will you put in a word for me? I need to hear this. Hear everything Stepmummy can or cannot explain.'

'I know you do, little cousin. I'm hardly the one to get you favours though.' I look at her pleadingly. Her famous face opens doors, I'm sure it does. 'Sister of the accused, it's not a sympathetic role, Sophie.'

What a tangled web: she and I are the best of friends, related after a fashion. The judge might actually be on my side, while wishing me far away from his emotionless courtroom; Monica's likely bias is in a direction which displeases the court. They want Mary's blood; they are trying her for that purpose alone. I want it too, just not if she is innocent. I have a heart—if it is twisted, Grace is on the road to straightening it out—The Old Bailey is without compassion. Wigs and gavels, and hungry dungeons, deep in its merciless bowels.

'If you say you'd like me back there; that it is not Mary's wish to prevent me...'

'Soph, I can't speak for Mary but when you chirped up, she had a little grin on her face. And not when they were ejecting you. She was concerned, never forgets that it is your mum they're talking about in there. You validated her story which the prosecution guy was trying to undermine. The jury heard it; she's not a liar.'

I rock in my seat, show I've taken it in. 'A word can't do any harm. I'll control myself; that was my last utterance in there. The judge won't notice me.'

'I'll try,' she agrees. 'And you sit beside me if it's a yes. We're family whatever goes on in here. You know that.'

* * *

The court clerk speaks with Monica; I stay away. When she returns, my aunt tells me that the clerk was in love with Sarah Best when he was a teenager, in love with her Shoes and Slippers alter ego. He confessed to it before she'd so much as said what she wished to speak about. My hunch is correct. Men's brains go awfully mushy when they meet the likes of Mica Barry. Mine too but it is Grace who has won me from here on. Mine eyes are for her alone. Auntie Monica is my friend, my confidante; a fantasy no longer. 'He also said they are taking an early lunch. One-thirty before we go back in there.'

Gary is with her today, and Monica asks if I want to lunch with them.

'I'm not terribly hungry. A sandwich, perhaps.'

In the event, we go into a small café on Newgate Street. It

isn't far from the courthouse; however, I don't see any others who have ventured from there to here. No one with a central role in my stepmother's trial. The fare in this little snackery is pre-prepared, wrapped in cellophane. They will toast a sandwich for you while you wait. The highlife it is not, although it is with celebrities that I dine. No one seems to notice them in this dive. Never had TV stars in here before, so why would they.

When we have found a vacant table, Gary asks me if I need to be here. 'I know it's probably the most important chapter in your life but the outcome will be the same if you wait it out at home. The detail must be excruciating.'

I know this is the very conversation that could send me into the afternoon churning up inside. I feel light-headed, no wish to think about that question at all. The notion of opting out, retiring to safe distance. 'I'm here for the boys as much as for myself.'

'The boys care very much,' says Monica, 'about you and Mary. I think you are the only person in the place who really dwells on the life lost. Nineteen years ago.'

'Twenty. It's coming on for twenty.'

* * *

On the witness stand, Mary has got as far as Thursday. She says that she and Paul were in all evening. She adds that I was there as well, and baby Simon. This is the evening when my father has alleged—the testimony of a dead man—that he and Mary removed the body from Cynthia's house to that of Jean Fletcher. Did their shed trick. All done after dark, the implication being that Simon and I were both sleeping.

'We had no babysitter that evening and honestly, I could never have left the children, particularly tiny Simon, without adult supervision. I couldn't have lived with myself if I had.'

Randall Pope smirks. 'The offence of neglect is not being directly alleged today, Mrs Stephenson, jurors. It is my supposition that committing so small a misdemeanour, leaving your children alone for a couple of hours, would be an insignificant risk in comparison with the task. The purpose behind leaving them unattended: an unlawful burial of a person previously murdered by you. Children alone in the house for a couple of hours looks like small beer in the company of those grave offences, I should say.'

My stepmother stands awkwardly, not looking at judge or jury. No question asked and she appears disinclined to witness their reaction to his supposition. I cannot entirely trust my recall of that night, the one before I learned of my mother's disappearance. I have retraced those steps many times over the last months. I believe my recollection is real, not a filler-in of my brain's unconscious devising. But I do understand how brains work. That they can all get a bit defective when there is too much riding upon the story they try to bring to mind. Can't really trust them under pressure. I think that Mary was at university in the day, home around five-thirty. Daddy already in the house, his study. He may have been there when I came home from school or I may have been home alone for thirty minutes or so. Backdoor key under the mat. This was in nineteen-eighty-one and we had not ratcheted up our collective fear of intruders to the stratospheric levels we see today. It is a detail that eludes me. I will have let myself into the house either way. Father in the study or out lecturing, bonking. Murdering even. Mary may have collected Simon from a childminder before coming in. More likely she had him with her at the university. He was never alone for a second back then—obviously not—these days it is core to his lifestyle. Her work at that time was not teaching but research, seeking the PhD she would not acquire until the family—such as we were—moved up to Carnforth. Until she transferred from Imperial to the University of Lancaster. I did my homework, I always did it before our meal. I was a good schoolgirl and daughter; obnoxious only in the role of stepdaughter. We ate together,

Simon sleeping through it. Stepmummy and Daddy arguing, not intensely, just some disagreement about the weekend ahead. He was probably trying to get out of a commitment, fulfil another of his own. There was a lot of that. It might have gone over my head at the time but I was on to him in the broader scheme of things. Then they called a truce, agreed to share a nice night in. I wonder if there was a bottle of wine involved, it is in my recollection but that doesn't quite tally with the time. Mary was still breastfeeding Simon. Six months old, little more than that. It is the grown-up me that thinks the wine improbable, it was in my mental picture; perhaps young Mary swigged a little wine while breastfeeding. Nineteen-eighty-one and all that. Or Daddy may have downed a bottle on his own, Stepmummy on the squash. I watched television with them. A programme about a hospital if my dreamlike recall has any purchase. At eleven years of age, I would have gone to bed at nine. Or even half-past eight. Both parents were very strict about my regimen. In my room, I listened to them talking downstairs. Many a child might do so who had legitimate fear of parents rowing once more. Disharmony in the household. For me, there was no fear; I loved to hear them fight and shout. Spent my childhood rooting for the break-up that never came. That has required a suicide, and not of the party I would have scripted. That they did stay together so long is another imponderable to me. Nothing in common, and adultery to contend with. I knew that it went on long before I learned the word for it. And went on in a single direction to my childhood knowledge. Mary's revelation in prison was the surprise. And completely irrelevant to the events of the year nineteen-eighty-one. I think so. No bearing on the conduct of Paul or Mary at the time of my mother's murder.

'Mrs Stephenson, for the jury to be clear, your late husband says he—and you but that is not the point I am establishing here—buried Cynthia Hartnell on the evening of

September seventeenth. The Thursday. Am I right that you are—through your honest recollection—giving him an alibi for that night? Confirming that he remained in your home in Epsom, at no time out of your sight long enough to travel to Burgh Heath?'

'Yes. I wasn't watching him like a hawk. At least, I don't recall doing such. But he never left the house. Never took the car. I am sure of it.'

Then, after a couple more exchanges, the sly Queen's Counsel asks, 'And Mrs Stephenson, Mary, can you recall if, on that Thursday night, you and Paul, you and Mr Stephenson, enjoyed sexual relations?'

She looks stunned. Miss Franklin is on her feet but something in the exchange—Mary's changed demeanour—has everyone rivetted. The barrister fails to utter the objection word.

'Did we have sex that night?' Mary echoes back, her head shaking but it is unclear if it is in answer to the question or incredulity at the asking.

'Yes, did you have sex after you had accomplished the ingenious feat with motor car and shed? The crafty contraption. Applied your engineering prowess. Satisfy each other with your bodies, having done so with your clever minds.'

* * *

In the evening, Grace comes to the flat once more; Simon is with us. A gooseberry but one growing more normal with each passing day. He has made burgers, following the template of Grace's skilled rendition several months earlier. It has become a staple for us, even Craig now a superior chef to me. We eat together and both wish to hear my recollection of the day's proceedings. I confirm that Mary has been on the stand; Simon wishes to know how she has coped. Did I think she was being as truthful as the oath demands. It is exactly the same as when I am with Monica: I do not like the gulf I can feel, the contrary links between ourselves and that woman. Mary Stephenson. I fear a wrong word might lose Simon and, conversely, I dislike his eagerness to hear all is well with my mother's murderess. I might be trying to out-Simon my brother with the wordy interplay I deploy. 'Would you feel bound to tell the truth just because of an oath taken? Isn't it just superstition? "Strike me dead if I tell a lie." That sort of nonsense.'

Simon laughs his deep guttural guffaw. 'I tell the truth,' he states, 'because the alternative is to lose the thread entirely. Oaths be damned.'

And it is true. His honesty is boundless. It is exactly what got him thrown out of crabby Aunt Sarah's. I have come to believe that he sent his father to Coventry for the longest time. Possibly for the way he treated Mary; however, that might be an inference too far. Simon has talked but not about the reason behind his years of not talking.

Grace picks up the theme from a different angle. How did I feel listening to Mary? At one point she says, 'Talking about the past must have made you feel like the girl you were back then.'

I turn my face away, do not want sympathy for the self-pity I feel at those words. No sympathy for the girl whom Grace could never have liked. I know my lover is a few years older than me, that it could not have been, but I often wonder to myself if we would even have been friends had we met as teenagers. The answer my ruminations lead me to is always no. I had friends but that was the consequence of living in a grand house, having an unblemished face, top marks in good schools. I think—and Simon has said as much over the years, if not said, then texted—I was an odious little sod back then. Grace grew up in far more modest circumstances than I, worked hard at what she loved—art, literature—but was neither tutored nor encouraged to the extent which I enjoyed. I would have put her down, failed to appreciate a truly beautiful soul. And she would have dismissed me as a snob. An appraisal hitting the nail most squarely on the head.

'It is unbearable to dwell upon,' I say, without showing them my anguished face. 'I keep thinking that my mother's disappearance—her abandonment of me, as I believed it at that time—was the cause of my caustic personality. And I am ashamed to admit that it makes no sense. Cannot be so. I was bitter and twisted towards that woman—your mother, Simon—long before the disappearance, the events that have put Mary in the dock. She was always on the stand in my mind; I have long wanted her judged for so much as entering my life, seeking to replace Cynthia Hartnell.' I am crying like a small child now. I do not enjoy having Grace see me this way. She is right from start to finish: talking and thinking about our childhoods takes us from the present in every respect. Rekindles what we have lost even if we would be better served to leave it back in the unreachable past.

'You were a harsh judge of Mum because kids always are,' says Simon. 'And now you are letting those feelings render you a harsh judge of your young self.'

I blink my eyes at him, look into his face as best I can. Simon is allowing it, a development I never quite expected. His face is jowly, pasty, astonishingly warm.

'Feelings are the harsh judge. When we are children, they are all that we have. No developed logic to understand the context, ameliorate the rawness of those emotions.'

Looking into his green and hungry eyes is like viewing a new country when first stepping off a plane. I cannot imagine the adventure ahead, that I am ready for it is as much as I know. Did I misjudge Mary from day one, all those years ago when I was a small child? Considered her only as the usurper, the woman seeking to replace my true mother. It made me the unkind person who still bobbles closer to the surface than I can easily admit. Outing myself as unreasonable does not absolve her of the crime for which she stands trial. The police must have their reasons; my father may even have had knowledge. Not that trusting a liar is a wise course of action. Did she pull the ligature because of the years of hell I had given her? Was she punishing me for being the rotten child I certainly was? I allowed her no easy pretence to being a Stephenson. Let her know about it every day. That she did not belong; could not mother me. It was my home she had invaded, not her home. That was my take on our dysfunctional family. Said as much quite a few times. Only when we moved to Carnforth—the house we shall return to this Friday evening—did she find her feet as a wife, and by that time her treatment by my father—his evident contempt for their wedding vows—must have twisted her more than she knew how to come back from.

'I think I need to let the jury decide, Simon. I have been the worst judge of Mary. Of the mother who was so good to you, and might have been better with me than I deserved.'

* * *

For the night, Simon is in the small room, and Grace and I once more share my double bed. I insist upon physical love. Need its release. She seems embarrassed when I groan and moan loudly; she takes me away from here. I forget my brother sleeping, hope he is sleeping when he fleetingly crosses my mind. When I am exhausted—she has done to me as I wished her to—I apologise. 'You take me out of being myself,' I tell her.

Grace runs a tender hand across my body. 'Stay in there,' she says. 'I like you just fine.'

5.

Grace and I sit at one side of the viewing gallery, Monica and Gary at the other. Not because we are on opposite sides in these proceedings, simply not wishing to disturb the other's concentration upon the unfolding past. My aunt is content that my girlfriend's supervision will keep the peace. There is some commotion at the beginning of the session, men in pinstripes whispering at the front. Then Randall Pope and Irene Goddard leave the chamber. Neither judge nor Mary have yet entered. I see Monica slip away; I wonder if she knows what is causing the disruption, the delay.

After some twenty minutes the clerk of court, having just returned to the chamber from elsewhere, coughs as if he is to make an announcement. Before he can speak, the door opens and both prosecuting counsels return to their seats. Pope wags a finger at the clerk, as if advising against his planned speech. Monica, too, comes into the court, comes to my end of the gallery although Gary sits at hers. 'Unwell overnight,' she whispers, 'but she's coming anyway. Wants to get the damned trial over with.'

It is a troubling form of words. The trial might damn her sister and, of course, it troubles Monica in its wake. I wonder if Mary is unwell through guilt, her constant denial could weigh in her stomach as if digesting a gravestone. And yet the stress of this hearing has got to me—an innocent in the matter to hand, if little else—in more ways than I imagined it might. It stirs too much inside us all. If she stands unfairly accused, her plight must be worse than mine.

'All rise.'

I understand courts, did modules about how they work on my journalism degree. The defendant arrives before the judge; that is the order of things. Today it has not occurred. Most irregular. The wizened old crow shuffles in. Bewigged. Acknowledges one or two people with a gesture of the head. Once at his bench, before sitting, he addresses the jury. 'Mrs Stephenson is unwell. Nothing serious, we trust, and a doctor will look her over before she enters this chamber. To make progress, the prosecution wish to tie up some loose ends in their case.' Then he glances down. 'That's right, Randall, isn't it?'

'Yes, your honour.'

* * *

I did not partake of breakfast this morning. Not so unusual for me; however, by eleven-thirty my stomach is rumbling. The same large prison guard—the one we have seen on most of the days of this trial—accompanies Mary into the chamber. My stepmother looks hot, sweaty, burning up. This is a rare sight: my accusations of iciness may be harsh but, at the very least, she ordinarily appears composed. Grace mutters something I do not catch, squeezes my hand.

Once more Mary swears her oath. Randall Pope is oblivious to her discomfort, questions her mercilessly about her relationship with Cynthia Hartnell.

'We got along as well as wife and ex-wife could,' she says.

That doesn't resonate with me, although I concede it might be how Mary always perceived it. So young when she first dated and then married Paul Stephenson. To the prosecuting counsel her words must seem like music, he grows a visible inch as he struts up and down in front of the jury.

'And the late Mr Stephenson? How did he get on with Cynthia Hartnell?'

'I did not see animosity between them. Cynthia had resigned herself to separation long before I became involved with Paul.'

'That was your understanding? Do you recall what your late husband said of Cynthia Hartnell?'

'He said very little to me. Very little directly. They got along; I know they did. Shared the care of Sophie. Their daughter, my stepdaughter.' Her eyes flick briefly in my direction; I see that her face is quite washed out. Not in pain, waiting expectantly at its threshold.

'I think they shared more than that, Mrs Stephenson. I

know from the statements made by you and others that you were fully versed about their continued relationship. Divorced since nineteen-seventy-five but still enjoying frequent sexual relations some six years later. How did that affect "getting along as well as a wife and ex-wife could?" A help or a hinderance?'

Mary slides down onto the seat she stood before, buries her face in her hand. 'Can I have a moment, please?' she asks.

'I'd rather you answered the question,' says Pope quietly.

'Mrs Stephenson...' The judge addresses her. '...we are grateful that you attended today despite your sickness overnight. These proceedings are no doubt stressful to you, needed as they are. If you require a moment to compose yourself, I am both obliged and happy to grant it. Mr Pope, please keep your opinion on the matter to yourself.' Then he looks around. 'Members of the jury, please pay close attention to Mrs Stephenson's answers; however, I advise that you do not try to adjudge her demeanour. A doctor was concerned for her health and advised that she might be wise to give no evidence today in the light of it. Mrs Stephenson has chosen to ignore that advice because—and I think we must take this explanation at face value—she wishes to assist the court. Now, Mrs Stephenson, would you like an adjournment?'

'No, thank you. I will continue.'

'Do you wish to remain seated?

'May I?'

From her small bench in the wooden dock, my stepmother talks about the matter she must most have hoped would stay out of the room. Not just because of the motive it might seem to prompt but more so for the sheer embarrassment of the facts. I see the pressmen, one or two women also, scribbling eagerly in the eddy of these revelations.

'I did not expect it. Shocked when I first realised. Not until the second year of my marriage. Already I knew he sought physical comfort elsewhere although...' My stepmother looks down, talks to her knees. '...I did everything I thought I should to satisfy him. Things I'd not imagined doing before.' Then she lifts her eyes, a penetrating stare in the direction of Randall Pope. 'Over time, I became appreciative. If my husband had intercourse with a person known to me it felt infinitely preferable to the others, the young students in the science department whom I also knew might be amenable to his charms. I was aware of it. Of the relationship he continued to conduct with Cynthia. Long aware of it. Cynthia told me once—not of their couplings, she never spoke of that directly—that living with him, Paul Stephenson, was the hard part of the marriage, not being with him for an hour here and there. I think she was apologising. I've always thought that.'

'Thank you, Mrs Stephenson. Are you suggesting we should believe you did not feel angry because of this? The revelation of their fornication. Angry with her; angry with him.'

'Yes, please. Sometimes there was anger in the marriage on my part, there was and it was caused by many, many things. The behaviour of Paul first and foremost. I never felt anger towards Cynthia. A little confusion perhaps. Not anger. Believe that, please, for it is the truth...'

I feel Grace squeezing my hand. Last weekend, when we were in bed together in Carnforth, I asked her, rashly perhaps, did she crave going once more—enjoying physical union—with a man. We were sitting up, this was Sunday morning and we can lie in as long as we like, neither brother of mine rising early. She shook her head gently, denying, but thinking while she was doing so. 'I couldn't stand it if you did,' I blurted. 'I've withstood it before now. Girls who meant little to me. I couldn't stand it if you were untrue.'

She nuzzled into my ear, whispered to me alone, 'You are the love I wasn't looking for but swear I'll never leave. You know that don't you, Sophie? I've forgotten about men. You've bewitched me.' I have thought myself a witch many, many times; only Grace has made it sound appealing.

'...I was angered when I learned of his womanising at university. Drawing in an undergraduate as he once had me, the pair of them behaving as if I was not there. It was not a way I ever treated Cynthia. She was not in his life...' My stepmother has paused, takes a handkerchief from her sleeve, dabs her eyes quickly, though I see no tears. '...I did not know her to be seeing Paul any longer, not when we met. Only for the purpose of co-parenting their young daughter. And nor did I jump into bed with him, unlike the others. It was different.'

I hear in my stepmother's rambling, her reflection upon marriage to my father, exactly what it is which makes Grace so different. A divergence from any other I have let into my life. My father led my stepmother to believe she was his one love, must have played exactly the same hand with my mother several years earlier. He didn't believe it for a single second. A con. Grace didn't really try to win me, and I have been a most insincere lover all my adult life. If I was true, it was because I never thought a relationship would last. Had no need of cheating: my life was a dance in which partners changed each time the chorus came around. Our love, Grace and I, is a delicious accident, not a calculation of anything by either of us.

'You are not on trial for the seduction of a married man, Mrs Stephenson...,' Pope starts to say.

'Objection,' screeches Collette. 'He is implying something both irrelevant and untrue.'

'Unproven, Miss Franklin. Simply unproven.'

Mary has stood. She shrieks, 'Untrue,' at him also. I am starting to think that Randall Pope could be endangering his own case. Mary looks unwell and he behaves as her tormentor, not the objective inquisitor he must wish the jurors to perceive. I even think he is trying to badger an outburst from her as if a confession might come that way. Hasn't a strong enough case unless she cracks under the pressure he exerts.

* * *

When we are on the steps again—the end of a difficult day for Mary and only the prosecution's closing statements to come before the defence make their case—Monica puts her arm around my waist. 'I don't think you enjoyed that any more than I did,' she observes.

I return the physical affection. 'I've never felt sorrier for her.' As I say it, I feel Monica go quite limp in my hold. She seems worn down by the day's events. Mary really wasn't well enough to testify, it was unwise to take the stand. Exchanges were irritable. Strategically so by Pope, all an error on the part of my stepmother. Still, I have resolved to trust the jury. Twelve men and women, the spawn of Joe Public, exactly the pool whose opinions I would tend to ridicule were circumstances within my control. It is better that I defer to anyone right now; I think my bile duct has packed in and my functioning brain with it. So help me jurors.

We four go to a bar, a bottle of wine ordered, Gary a Belgian beer. I shall sip little, it is politeness. This is the opposite of a celebration. We have had our guts wrenched to the left and to the right; it may have been a little less excruciating for Gary and Grace, still their faces look as if they are surveying a wasteland, and the bar in which we sit is rather swanky. A most emotional day.

Throughout my childhood, I believed myself to hate Mary Stephenson. She did for me mostly what a parent would or should. In the early days, I think she expected an easier child. I was wilfully difficult, and I could see that she did not like me. I expect she would have liked me more if I had made an effort; however, she would not have loved me as my mother did. I did not think it could be done, and time has not changed my view of this small detail. Over the years, and with the disappearance of my mother, we came to an accommodation. I would moan and gripe and mostly plough my own furrow, God knows, my father was the most occasional playmate. A blue-moon buddy. If I rocked the boat, I did it gently. And Stepmummy treated me very well but without warmth. Perhaps our wintry rapport was unexceptional, repeated under roofs up and down the land. The reconstituted family. It all felt hateful to me only through the prism of a grief I didn't even know I was going through. Seeing someone with whom I have shared such large swathes of my life suffer as Mary did today is like being the sufferer. Thinking I would like to watch her drown, and the actuality of looking upon it, are the most dissonant of cousins. For Monica, it is all about sympathy. She has had an up-and-down relationship with Mary, yet I know it was truly warm in their formative years. She looked up to back Mary then, got a return.

'Hearing the defence will be a little less horrible, whether they prove the case or fail dismally,' I say.

Grace and Gary murmur assent. Poor Monica has gone inside herself. A wine glass in her hand, no sip taken from it.

'Whatever you two are going through, lean on us,' says Gary.

I know he speaks for Grace; I have felt myself leaning on her for as long as we have truly been a couple. What has drawn Monica down today evades me. Seeing it is unpleasant. A mirror.

6.

Craig questions me. 'What does it all mean? I have no special insight but, for him, weekends are when he hears more than is reported in the papers or on the TV news. I try to answer although I have never known a case like this one. Defence has made a start but Friday was one long adjournment. Nothing is going smoothly.

On Wednesday the court heard the rest of the prosecution's case, and very wordy it was. They have put great weight upon the statements my father made between arrest and suicide although even I think his credibility shot through. It is the dying squeal of an unwanted pig. There was a time when I loved him. Times that will not come back, and I would not embrace the feelings could it mystically occur. There is logic to the prosecution's assertion. My father was very specific that he and Mary buried the body on the Thursday night, the method—devices attached to the car wheels, used and then destroyed—he described in detail. Experts have confirmed the credibility of his claims. Those same experts say he did not act alone, pulling the shed from the ground one millimetre at a time was ingenious. To have lifted up the shed without simultaneously securing the soil moved, keeping the turf line, would have been open to discovery back in nineteen-eighty-one. The police looked: found nothing. This clear picture—Mary offering my father an alibi for his own confession hardly clears her of complicity—although nor does it prove she did it. A spiteful lie before taking his own life? That must be the defence. Prosecuting counsel point out that Professor Stephenson had no obvious motive. Long divorced and still managing a little nooky. That—the screwing of wife number one under the nose of wife number two—made the papers and the evening news bulletins too. Made Craig blush. Poor mite, a couple of years pre-conceived when all of these terrible events happened. He thinks it will give him a reputation at his new school. I tried to tell him raffish is good in a teen but he heard me all wrong. My younger brother is nothing like his father. He will mistreat no-one, fastidious in his wish to accommodate the feelings of others. And the female party to the furtive tryst was my mother. If it explains my character, I

The Reckoning

am, since meeting Grace, reformed. Entirely reformed, devoted to Grace Topping for all time.

They say that this is Mary's motive; they note that the method of killing, a guitar string as garrotte—which my father alluded to but gave no detail—was not a challenge to a young woman as she then was. Mr Pope described—and I bit flesh from within my lower lip while he did so—how the killer used a simple pre-tied knot to execute the deed. He said, in the face of her denials, that if Mary had worn a glove upon her right hand and that was the one with which she tugged the life out of my mother, no indentation on the hand would remain. He noted that no forensic examination of her hand took place at the time. It might have born witness to the dastardly deed for weeks or months: never shall we know. No scrutiny because it was nineteen years before the murder became apparent, never mind the method used to accomplish it. Twenty years is a long-time for a small ridge cut from a guitar string to heal. More than plenty. The when and the where of it, time and place of the murder, the prosecuting barristers have not specified. They think it unlikely to have occurred at my mother's house because the forensic search there was extensive even though my father, in his affidavit, said it was done there. This is a weakness in their case to my thinking. Beyond reasonable doubt? I have doubt and I am not even a reasonable observer of the proceedings. I started off wanting her to swing for it.

'It is very odd, Craig...' Grace is listening while we talk, Simon back on his computer; he has grilled me about it every London evening. '...for my money, they have proved why Mary should have strangled the life out of Dad. The connection with Cynthia is tenuous. Tenuous and weird, the papers are loving it.'

I get a little stare from him. Craig has been reading them in the school library. He has told me several times during this trial that my fellow news reporters are all scum.

Sometimes he makes a point of saying, 'except you.' Other times I am on the dark side, and I cannot tell him otherwise. Not every week but many times down the years, I used to write some real shockers. The raw meat which Sunday Noise readers love to drool over.

'I'm no longer on the payroll,' I remind him. 'An epiphany and a career change. Just celebrity interviews for Girls in the News from now on.'

Grace snorts a little laugh. She knows the story, and the magazine in which I first made print is no longer on the newsstands. And the fawning pseudo-feminism of it never appealed to me.

'They are as bad,' says upset Craig. 'They make out all celebrities are on drugs or cheating on their partners. Dishing the dirt is all that sells.'

I tell him that he is correct—but I said only good about Auntie Monica all those years ago—so, no, I will not be taking up tittle-tattle journalism. Crusading reporting or nothing.

By this time, Simon has returned to the lounge. 'You can't crusade for the snobs,' he says. I have to laugh; his point might be apt. I sometimes wish the bugger could turn off his honesty button, lie like the rest of us.

* * *

The Sunday papers speculate about the hiatus in the trial. Knowledgably or otherwise, tomorrow will tell. When the court case is to resume. The consensus is that Mary's defence team seeks to make late changes to its case in the light of new information. New witnesses perhaps. 'Somebody in America Knows Something,' screams the headline of my former employer. If it is Mary's old friend, Dennis Harris, confirming that she was in Charmouth until the Wednesday morning, it won't get her off, and nor do I think the prosecution has definitively pinned the murder on her. Maybe she did, maybe she didn't: most unsatisfactory.

The Reckoning

My clever brother, Simon, has always known the content of the newspapers without ever appearing to read them. Done so for longer than I have given him credit for, I expect. I remember that he used to walk around this house in the middle of the night from the age of seven onwards. I expect he was a nocturnal reader when all believed him illiterate. All but Mary perhaps, she was the one with faith. I wish it had been me. Back then, he also had the door to his room ajar. Although he did not come into the room to watch the news on television, I believe his fine hearing rendered him cognisant with the content. Nowadays he has his internet. There is news there, straight and slanted, although I only go for print. Today, he sits at the dining table with the whole stack. Every Sunday paper there is. Going through the reporting of his mother's trial word by painstaking word; he is drawing out a comprehensive understanding of what the world makes of his family. Mother and father. I hope he remembers that the world knows zippo.

Grace has secured a part in the film which is set on Crete and for which she auditioned a week ago. She says it might be piffle but the company is putting a lot of money into it. It will be box office. A couple of big stars.

'An archaeological dig angers the gods,' she tells us. 'Thankfully I'm a digger, not a god. Those guys have to spend hours and hours in make-up. I would hate that.'

I have told her already that she looks like a Greek god—my Aphrodite—that they have given her the wrong part. I say the same when she talks about it today, just to let the boys know how serious I am about her. Don't name the god, I'm not going out of my way to embarrass them.

Grace shushes me. 'Craig, I've seen you reading up on archaeology. Explain it to me, I'll need to understand it by August if I'm to be convincing on my big-screen debut.

My brother has a stab. Does as she requests. Ancient history seems to be his passion, a degree in the funny subject beckons. And he can hone in on Crete, recalls details of Minoan artefacts that I never learned in history A-level. While they talk together, Simon beckons me to the table. He looks into my face. His is still very chubby but I swear he is losing weight. That or he is adopting a more normal pose. He gives me continuous eye contact, has given up whatever thinking precipitated his years of abstinence. 'Sophie,' he says quietly, 'this is getting to me. Mum in the dock. Do you mind if I button up again? Radio silence. I'll send the odd text. Like old times.'

'If it helps you then of course, Si. I didn't know...' I let my expression of ignorance dwindle to nothing. I never thought it might be a comfort, never understood him before or since he talked. Acceptance, which was not my strong suit back in the day either, is what he needs. What I must give him, and he has always given me, his once horrible sister. 'Would you like me to tell Craig. And Grace. Monica.'

'I think they'll figure it out,' he says, then runs an index finger over his quickly closed lips. I think that is it. No more speech for the time being. I smile at him and he returns my expression before looking away. Looking back upon his papers. I spot those mannerisms I had thought fading. Not in extremis, just avoiding my eye while simultaneously roving the room. I do like talking with this clever brother of mine; I wonder if his return depends upon the outcome. He must be as eaten up about his mum as I have been about mine.

7.

On Monday morning, the judge begins the trial by imploring the jurors to pay no heed to anything they may have seen in the newspapers on Sunday. He tells them that they must judge matters exclusively on the evidence brought to trial. Upon what is said to them, set before them in this room. 'Unsubstantiated rumour shall play no part in my court,' he says. I do not envy those two rows of six, weighing up the correct judgement, plotting the fate of my stepmother here on in. All their thinking derived only from the strange medley of improbabilities thrown to them thus far. Unsubstantiated rumour may be the closest thing to objectivity that this awful case can yield. My mother was certainly buried, interred very cleverly, in that most unlikely of graves in the garden of a retired physicist. My late father played a part, he wouldn't have known how it was done if he hadn't. Nothing else is clear to me.

Collette Franklin, QC, talks calmly and sensibly to the jury. Reminds them very quickly of the prosecution's narrative while adding, 'There are many salient points you have yet to be told. Facts with which my learned friend, Mr Pope, is well acquainted but chose not to share for fear of the doubt it might instil. And remember, it is for the prosecution to prove their case beyond reasonable doubt. It cannot be determined by the whim of a dead man's testimony.'

After this opening statement, both Collette and Randall Pope go to the judge's chambers, some technical argument held in camera between the two sides. One seldom learns the nature of these disputes. I understand referees are always reminding boxers about the below-the-belt rule, several times a fight, although they surely know it before ever entering a ring. The same rigmarole goes on here in The Old Bailey. Then, back on the stand, my stepmother takes her oath. Does as she must in preparation for questioning. I expect this will be less confrontational than last week's heated exchanges. Collette is on her side.

'Mrs Stephenson, Mary, can you tell the court, in your own words, the nature of your relationship with Professor Stephenson.'

'I was his wife.' When I glance around, I see that even Monica cannot suppress a smile. We all think it a little more complicated than that.

'For the benefit of the court, could you expand upon that, please?'

'It is difficult. I was only eighteen years old when we met. He seemed rather old-fashioned and...I'm not sure how to explain this...I'd rather stopped trusting my own generation.'

'Mary, that is an unusual admission, please can you remind the court how old Paul Stephenson was when you first met?'

'I believe he was thirty-nine...' She seems unnecessarily doubtful, places an apologetic hand upon her forehead. '...I recall that he was thirty-nine years old.'

'Mary, we have heard already, in the course of this trial that your husband was not a faithful man. Are you able to recall when first you learned that he had broken the marriage vows which he had pledged to you?'

'Yes. I have no idea when such an event first occurred, I recall only when it dawned on me. This was some eighteen months after our wedding, we were attending a student Christmas party—undergraduates, and I was no longer one, there only as a tutor's partner—the room was gloomy, a disco going on, and across the floor I could discern body language between my husband and a young student indicative of intimacy.'

'How so, Mrs Stephenson? Can you tell the court precisely what led you to this conclusion? A discothèque is not a bedroom.'

'I worry it might seem slight. A hand resting on her upper arm for a short time, fifteen seconds perhaps. Standing inside her span of comfort, at a distance where a man and a woman will be aware of each other's smell. Scent.' I know exactly what she is talking about here, woman to woman can be equally aromatic. Pungent if the chemistry is poor. 'This occurred during a week when he had stayed out a couple of nights. Not all night but home very late in the evening. Citing work commitments which seemed rather unlikely. My observation completed the jigsaw.'

'And Mrs Stephenson, were you observing a pattern which you had previously enjoyed with your husband? An intimate student-tutor relationship, prior to your marriage.'

'Not really. No. We were close, of course, but before we...' She looks around the courtroom, then quickly down at her shoes. '...enjoyed relations, I had declared the relationship. Spoken about it to the university staff. Moved tutor group.'

'Could you expand upon that, please. Tell the jury exactly why you moved tutor group.'

'When I was a first-year student, Paul was my tutor. We met outside the university on a few occasions. Dates, although the first couple of times fell short of that definition. We agreed that we should both come clean, tell the authorities so that Paul had no role in assigning or marking my work. I had changed tutor group before we enjoyed relations.'

'Thank you, Mary. And for the record, can you confirm exactly what you mean by "enjoyed relations?" That phrase specifically.'

'Sexual relations,' she whispers.

'For the benefit of the jury I wish to add a little to the point the defendant has so casually made. She was not one of the many flings her husband had throughout his career. And it is also to be noted that neither going out on a date nor participating in sexual relations occurred until long after Paul Stephenson had separated from the first Mrs Stephenson, the late Cynthia Hartnell...'

'Objection, your honour. The jury need no interpretation of what Mrs Stephenson has just said. They are to make of it what they will...'

'I am only enabling them to see through the lie which you implied in your earlier...'

'Enough!' says the judge. 'Ladies and gentlemen of the jury, I think you understand by now that I am imploring you to consider if there is factual evidence behind the various contradictory assertions made. Mrs Stephenson says that she and the late Mr Stephenson had an unhurried courtship prior to...prior to...well, you all heard what she said. That is as much as seems to be before this court. Miss Franklin, please move on. Objection overruled.'

'In your earlier testimony, Mary, you confirmed for the court that you had become aware of your husband's infidelities. Can you remind us, please, how that made you feel?'

'Humiliated.'

'Could you speak up,' says the judge.

'I felt completely humiliated.'

'And did it make you feel like walking out, or kicking him out. Filing for a divorce.'

'Miss Franklin, I was brought up by a single parent, my father left us before I had so much as started school. I don't know if I have been foolish in this regard, I was terribly determined not to repeat the pattern. That my children should not be fatherless.'

'But Mary, you were aware of the difficulty in the marriage before you ever conceived. Before you had borne children.'

I find this barrister's style a challenge; my stepmother is having just as hard a time as when Pope was roughing her up. I expect there is method in it, the jury will learn something of her character and resolve, may even sympathise. Nothing pertinent to the murder. Reasons to stay when leaving is the sensible course.

'I was too young when I married, even when I learned more about his nature than I had understood pre-marriage. I thought perhaps that is how older academics behaved. It seemed plausible. I also thought we were an odd couple, the age gap, and a family would secure our mutual concern for each other. I shouldn't have, it was an error of judgement. My husband would never abandon his commitments; I knew that from his generous parenting of Sophie, his daughter with Cynthia.' She namechecks me while the story she tells absorbs her. Never a glance my way. 'The family money was his security, physics his love, and family a big hammock he would rest in, a hammock he paid for but otherwise contributed only his presence.'

'And his other women, the girls, where did they fit in?'

'It was like a parallel life. Never spoken of, not until it became an abyss which we might both have fallen into.'

* * *

It is afternoon when the building of Mary's character—a better mother than I remember, frankly, but I expect these things look different from each participant's viewpoint—takes its most dramatic turn. Earlier, Miss Franklin very specifically asked my stepmother if, while living in Epsom, she too embarked on any extramarital relations. 'I did not,' was the extent of the reply.

Now, having gone quickly over the week my mother disappeared, a little more talk of the trip to Charmouth—establishing that Tuesday was the day my father might have done anything under the sun, my stepmother not in town and an old diary revealing an evening appointment at university, presumably a babysitter with me although time has taken that detail from us—Collette asks a very pointed question. 'Mary, did you have extramarital relations with anyone after you moved to Carnforth?'

'Yes, Miss Franklin. I'm ashamed to say that I did.'

This is an odd choice of wording to accompany the admission. To me at least. It is a shame if cheated on wives—or husbands for that matter—stay home and take it on the chin. Life passing them by as their marriage turns into an embarrassment. Daddy was the shameless one, blagged it to the last as if he were not. Truly selfish, he trampled on the feelings of others. Two wives and a daughter. I believe myself to be at the heart of his hurtful games: he cheated me out of my mother's funeral.

'It was not something that happened until nearly fifteen years of marriage had convinced me that my husband would never change. Could never be the stalwart to me that I had always tried to be for him.'

'Wow,' says Collette Franklin, and she glances at the jury. 'Seems like physicists can be exceedingly slow learners when science isn't the topic.' A ripple of laughter goes through them, and Mary, standing, rolls her eyes. The butt of jokes from her own counsel; the reporter from the Sunday Noise—and all the other trash-end papers—will be lapping it up. 'And this adultery you committed, it was with a single man, or were there a succession of men?'

'A single man.'

'A single fling, for one-night only, or was it conducted over an extended period?'

'A decade. I was within this other relationship alongside my marriage right up until I was taken in to prison. Accused of what I had not done.'

'A decade? That's not a fling it's a marriage in its own right.'

Mary looks uncomfortable with this, and—someone needs to tell her—Collette is a bumbling comedienne. I am more surprised by the news than I should be given my stepmother's prison-visit confession to Monica and I, those many months ago. Simply can't figure it, the when and the how. I suppose it puts me at university when it all started. Simon probably figured it by deduction and never considered it newsworthy. Craig will be oblivious, a regular lad who loves his mother. I cannot begin to guess with whom she might have taken her pleasures. Ten years' worth, thereof.

'And can you tell the court the name of this lover whom you took?'

'I can but it is difficult. He too is married, has children...'

'Mrs Stephenson,' says the judge, 'may I remind you of the

oath you have taken...'

'...his name is Jake Watts.'

Him! That makes no sense, he was at that party years back. Sniffing around me, as I recall. Or not? Maybe he was only talking to me when my father was on the prowl. It could be true. Young chap. A better fit than my father ever was with Mary. The Jake fella having his own wife and kids is a bit fucked up. I squeeze Grace's hand, grateful there are no such complications between us. Not a stretchmark on my lovely girlfriend.

'Now,' says Collette, a sternness in her voice that has not previously been there, 'how did your husband feel about you sleeping with Mr Watts?'

'He didn't know,' says Stepmummy quietly.

'You conducted an affair for donkey's years, and your highly intelligent husband, a professor, no less, never knew. Really?'

'I thought he never found out...never said...'

'Mary, Mary, Jake Watts was a member of the physics department, was he not?'

'A tutor, yes. A post-graduate researcher when we first...' She does not complete the sentence. What she and Jake did alongside his post-graduate research is self-evident.

'So, Mr Watts was a research fellow and subsequently a member of the teaching staff in the department of which your husband was Chair?'

'He was.'

'And yet you believe he never knew. Never learned that you and he were close. Intimate. What did you do? Biannual liaisons when he was out of the country?'

'Not exactly. But we were careful.'

'Not exactly. Could you be exact for us then? Was it a secret crush? Did Jake Watts even know?'

'Miss Franklin,' interjects the judge, 'your questioning is embarrassing your client. Is it strictly necessary? Is it pertinent?'

'Can we find out your honour? The answer will be pertinent, I believe.'

He nods assent and gestures that Mary should answer the question.

She seems to gulp in air. 'We were lovers. We did not meet so frequently, very often we worked together at the department. For four years I was his mentor.' A little ripple of laughter goes through the court, my own lips have upturned.

'Did you go on dates, Mary? Did you and Jake Watts go out in the world together, or was this strictly a laboratory-based love affair?'

'We did manage a few...we were always most careful where we met. It wasn't entirely university bound, largely...'

'Where did you make love, Mary? I presume you made love; it is the point of love affairs, I believe.'

'I have my own small office at the university.'

'An office with a nice comfy bed in it?'

'A bed is not strictly necessary.'

'Enough!' states the judge. 'Miss Franklin, do you want to move the questions on, we are seeking to establish this lady's guilt or innocence, not feed the newspapers with salacious gossip about people unfortunate enough to have been thrust into the public eye. Ladies and gentlemen of the jury, the issue at stake here is very clear to you. This story may prove relevant but we are trying neither Mrs Stephenson nor Mr Jake Watts for adultery; their alleged liaison concerns us only if it has a bearing on the guilt or otherwise of Mary Stephenson viz-a-viz the murder of Cynthia Hartnell.'

This reminder brings my thoughts clattering back down to Earth. I was rather enjoying the exchanges, and found I did not begrudge Mary her entanglement. Grace leans into me and says, 'Jake Watts will have his name in the papers tomorrow.' As I nod, she adds to her whisper. 'A wife and children.'

I put my mouth to her ear. 'I don't think he had one when they started. Not sure but I think he was single a decade ago. I met him once.'

She looks at me with wide eyes.

'Mary,' Collette Franklin continues, 'on a scale of one to ten, how certain are you that Professor Paul Stephenson, your then husband, never learned of your affair? Never suspected from your demeanour, from tell-tale signs, that Jake Watts may have given away. From an analysis of intimate body language, he may have seen between the pair of you, as you recalled noting he and a female student had done, all those years before. Unexplained absences. A colleague in the department informing him out of a feeling of righteousness, misplaced or otherwise.'

'I don't think...we were very careful. Weeks without...'

'Mary, his honour has made it clear we are not seeking a graphic description of what went on. On a scale of one to ten, how likely...'

'I used to think it a nine, even a ten, but now I really don't know at all. You are right, there were many possible ways he could have stumbled across an indication. Or even have been informed. I thought he hadn't because he didn't raise it, I have more recently reflected on the matter. His silence was never conclusive proof. I think we might have become careless; I certainly became more accepting of the state of my marriage after I found true love outside it. Jake and I were never trying to break up our own...I had a disabled child, did not want to disturb my boys' home lives...'

My stepmother is talking more rapidly than she has at any point on this witness stand. I shan't tell Simon she called him by that term, he would hate it. I fear it will make the papers, upset him via that route. Or maybe he will understand. Agree that she might have seen it that way, and see why she should, having being sworn upon an oath, share the contestable insight.

'Lately, lying on a narrow bed in a prison cell, I have come to think you are most likely right. He found out. God knows how.' She looks up into the ornate ceiling of the courtroom. 'Come back and tell us, Paul! Don't take your leave of this world as a liar!'

The judge pats a flat palm down, must dislike the indecorum of her outburst.

'No other explanation makes sense, Collette. I never harmed Cynthia. Never went near her on my own. She cornered me at parties once or twice, and she couldn't have been more civil. I never saw her the week she disappeared.' She looks at the foreman of the jury, very directly. 'I never killed her; never saw her the week she was killed. I couldn't kill a kitten. I cannot think why Paul should either, although I can see why he might try to frame me for it now. I'd like to have seen him cross-examined about it. He's cleverly avoided taking the witness stand, hasn't he?' She suddenly bursts into tears, the sort of inconsolable sobbing I recognise too well. Her grief is of the bitterest vintage. 'He's laughing at me from hell,' she says through tears. 'Laughing at me from hell.'

* * *

We have come out onto the steps of the courthouse; sunshine greets us. My hand in Grace's, Auntie Monica standing to the other side. I think to myself how odd this trial has been. I have made a fool of myself once or twice, so distressing is the subject matter. Today, rightly or wrongly, I enjoyed the exchanges. Seeing Stepmummy squirm always used to do it for me—her humiliation gave me the most indecent pleasure—and yet now the feeling was different. I do not begrudge her Jake Watts, feel a little foolish that I once thought his interest might be in me. I was mistaken, and vainly so. I admire how honest this private lady—Mary Stephenson—is able to be with herself and the world. Cannot understand my parents' marriage: he and Cynthia, nor he and Mary. But does anybody? Is it the perennial condition, suffered alone by every child? From a certain standpoint, all our parents are a bit bonkers, a daft match. Grace and Monica talk across me, I haven't been taking it in, try to do so now their subject has infiltrated my consciousness.

'Rehearsed,' Grace is saying. 'They slip it all in when the judge is too enthralled to intervene.'

'Tone of voice,' Monica concurs. 'Mary was never much of an actor. She's been coached.'

'What! Are you saying that was staged? The whole interrogation a sham. They practiced...'

'Sophie, Sophie,' says Monica, indicating I should lower my voice. Pressmen have the largest ears. 'She was telling the truth, I'm sure she was, but these guys think out how best to unravel it for the jury. Impress on them the importance of the affair with Jake Watts. God knows there have been enough titillating little asides, the big point could have got lost without a little forethought.'

I shrug off Grace's hand, step two paces in front of her. I like to watch her act, and to watch Monica act, precisely because I know it is only fiction. I can enjoy their performance and then let it go. This was quite different. My hand covers my eyes, I hope to hide my upset. I thought I knew, thought I was getting closer, at the very least. I was hating my father more and Mary not at all, and now these emotions will not settle. They are an ocean inside me.

* * *

Silent Simon has accompanied Grace and I to the Old Bailey this morning. We all took a cab. Once more he keeps his face from me, from Grace. He has reverted to never looking directly at anyone. Mostly he hangs his head a few degrees, his eyes many more; occasionally he makes a grand sweep, I think those sensitive eyes grasp it all, however fleetingly they survey. He knows who's who and what is what. He won't be doing it but Simon would make a better reporter than I by a country mile.

'Nice to see you, Si,' says Monica as we wait outside. He raises a hand in acknowledgement, head unmoved.

She came to the flat last night, needed to talk. I think Monica picked up how upset I was by the thought that my stepmother was acting on the stand. Answering only as would convince a jury. 'She was telling the truth though,' said Monica, 'I'm sure of it.' When I pressed her, she conceded that she has no special powers with which to know such a thing. If the jury must go with their gut, who knows whether they despise or feel sympathy for the handsome adulteress who was too spineless to leave the cheating professor. Monica has dwelt on both sides of that one through the course of her adult life. The difference is only the deep-down love that she feels for her sister. And Mary also annoys her like hell; Monica wouldn't have thought twice about leaving a bounder like my father. Never allowed herself to be beholden to anyone; Gary may be a needed confidante but they are equals. Doesn't need him to pay the bills. I think she long ago learned the lessons of her older sister's degrading experience.

Simon sat himself in one of the lounge chairs, spent much of the time with a towel draped over his face, perhaps all of Monica's visit. Listening. Gary was out for drinks with a couple from his old television show, a female patient he failed to resuscitate in the era of Queen Victoria, plus a pretend member of the landed gentry who now dates the girl who is back from the dead. I felt my phone vibrate in the pocket of the sweatpants into which I had changed. Picking it out, I saw that the brother sitting opposite me was joining in the chat.

There are tells which give away all liars

How analytical he is, even of his mother's murder trial. I would like to retain the objectivity he has; however, I even think his is methodological only. How we interpret our findings is personal. The sun went around the Earth for the longest time before someone posited that it might be otherwise. 'Perhaps, Si,' I replied, showing Monica what he had written. 'But I'm no psychologist and I doubt if those buggers are infallible.'

Simon chortled silently beneath his towel. Shoulders moving.

I'm coming with you tomorrow

'It's a date, mate. Do you really think you will be able to tell?'

It's close to decision time. I must support her

I smiled directly at him—at the towel—told him that he is a truly lovely son. I don't think he is close to being objective. A lovely son cannot be. And then I found myself feeling wretched: I should have supported my mother when she disappeared. Instead, I cried and shrieked, advised parents and police of my theory that kidnappers were holding her somewhere. Then, over time, accepted that she left me—no, not accepted, assumed it was as others decreed—that she wanted a life without me in it. I should have seen the tells on my father's face, read his abominable behaviour. Stepmother's too, most likely. I am still unconvinced by her defence. I have been as dreadful a daughter as I have a stepdaughter, that is the truth. Made so by a cruel trick. Paul Stephenson's experiment with my mind, flicking a switch that made me sometimes hate my mother, hate her for walking out, although I only ever felt loved in her presence. If Mary was complicit, I hate her with daggers, if she is innocent, then I should feel as sorry for her as I do for myself. No one should be so wronged. I don't know how I shall find it in myself to do so, yet maybe I must. I can't see the jury convicting and I have determined I should trust them. It is the whole point of our legal system.

It is merciless, Sophie. I can feel nothing for the loss of your mother. Never met, never seen, never known. What you are going through

bothers me twice around the world. Troubles me as much as Mum's possible life term

I stepped across the lounge and squeezed the big guy's shoulder. 'Thank you,' I said, as he flinched. Movement under the towel.

Bury the sentimental

That was his final communication of the evening. Could have been from one of his long-ago poems.

8.

When we go inside—all sitting together for I cannot leave my brother, and Monica and Si must both root for acquittal, versus my fence-sitting—the court is not in order. Members of the jury have yet to take their places. Ushers and the clerk of court are whispering together. This case has been more fractured, chaotic even, than any I covered in my reporting years. Years which were not so many and, I think, may have come to an end. I can write but I no longer wish to adopt the reporter's mindset. It is not my wish to bring anybody's skeleton forth from a closet. Not in print. I hope it happens for those who need resolution; however, the public eye is a jaundiced one. Everything looks uglier under a microscope; newspaper articles seek to draw out the overreaction of their readers. It is how I have lived my life and I cannot say I am without regret.

What's going on?

Well, he might know as well as I, but for the last time, I will try and pull on a professional string. 'I'll see if one of those boys has any inside knowledge,' I tell Simon—Grace too—pointing at the press gallery.

I have to go out and back in again to get up there, I have still kept my press card in my purse. A court usher, standing in front of the small staircase, looks doubtful. He might remember my face from the witness stand. 'I'll vouch for her,' Keano shouts down from the mezzanine level of the marble staircase.

I step up to where he stands and we move into a small alcove, not the courtroom. Tom Keane is an old-school muck-raker, once of the Sunday Noise but now ploughing his furrow at a paper more disreputable still: The News Explained, an outlet which prides itself on contradicting its own title. He must know that it is my family which has been under the microscope these past weeks, ought to have worked out that his reportage will sicken me. Not that I minded when we were both hacking away at the stories of all the Londoners we didn't know. Hiroshima might have been a pretty sight when seen from Enola Gay.

'What's the delay, Tom?'

'Nice to see you and all. How are you keeping? Family well?'

Insensitive for a hobby, this guy. 'Dead or imprisoned, for the most part.'

'That Mica Barry is your sister or something, right?'

I think this oaf doesn't even read the papers. They've all made the connection, The News Explained too, and yet it seems Keano hasn't grasped it.

'I know her; she is my friend. Sorry, Tom, it is a worrying time for us. You look well...' I point at his stomach and then his head. '...interesting combo: a beer gut and the face of a whisky drinker.'

Tom splutters a laughing cough. 'Never pull your punches, sweetheart.'

'Politeness aside, do you know what's going on?'

'Up in the air. Sworn affidavit in America, a new witness. Not submissible at this hour, of course. Defence hopping mad, prosecution completely mental. I have no idea what it says—what two-pence worth the American has got to add—

but we'll publish it if we can get hold of it.'

'Back up, back up. Is this witness for her or against her?'

'Defence. They think it would get her off the hook but prosecution won't allow it. Nor the judge.

'A guy?'

'Might be. I really haven't heard.'

'I'll wager it's this Dennis Harris chappie. Can't see how he can help much, and he's the only man she knows in America. The only one I've ever heard her mention.'

* * *

We leave the courtroom for an early lunch. Nothing has happened; Simon seems to have had a wasted journey. It will reconvene at two o'clock although the clerk of the court did not sound confident when he pronounced it to be the case. I've never known a trial like it. Or another family like the one at its core.

Simon is reluctant to go into the café we usually use. Monica suggests a more upmarket restaurant, it will be quieter. I am feeling sick to my stomach; I explained what Tommy Beer-Gut told me as best I could. I think they—Monica and Simon—are feeling buoyed: a new defence that has the prosecution on the run. I don't know what to think; can barely think at all. I need to learn what happened, not still more of the old bollocks that News Explained propagates for no greater purpose than the advertising revenue it generates. Hyperbole and exaggeration, fiction if they think they can get away with it.

I suggest that Simon might accompany Monica and Gary, that Grace and I may go elsewhere. It is two hours before we go back in. They agree. I'm not sure that they understand my ambivalence to these developments. I want to hear from the jury, and inadmissible evidence helps no one.

Grace and I take the tube. We can spend an hour in my flat and then tube back here. Central Line, I live only a short walk from Notting Hill Gate. The carriage is virtually empty,

Grace tries to joke that I'm taking her back for a lunchtime quickie. There was a time when I'd have laughed. Tried to do the deed, no doubt. Today, I feel a flatness that inhibits me from saying much at all. I think it has been an ordeal for Grace. Supporting a girlfriend with baggage that draws gasps in the Old Bailey. It's not what she signed up for; bless her, she could not have been warmer towards me. I owe her everything.

When we are walking towards my building, Grace puts an arm around me. 'You are struggling, Soph. Every piece of the jigsaw gets closer to completing the picture. It must make it horribly final. Nothing is going to bring her back.'

'And Grace, tell me what you think of my wicked stepmother, the second Mrs Stephenson. Is she cold and sly or a kid who took a wrong turn in her first year at university? Hitched herself to the cad who is my father, and never got back on track.'

'She's both isn't she? Your childhood was what it was, and your second point is true as well.'

'And is she a killer?'

'Let's hear what's in the affidavit.'

'She was with this Dennis Harris on the Monday and Tuesday. He can't have witnessed the murder from Charmouth, I really don't see how he is going to tell us more than we know already.'

* * *

Over a toasted sandwich, we talk about Grace's forthcoming shoot in Greece. When she says, 'And you won't go chatting up actresses in The Kilderkin, will you?' I find myself sobbing once more. Grace is beside herself for her tactlessness. She trusts me, I'm sure she does, but the doubt I imagined in her voice set me off. 'Everything has been too much, I'm so, so sorry,' she says. Hugs me, and it makes me feel better, but there is something keeping my stomach bubbling, my nerves like the thinnest icicles. I cannot face the court, do not want any part of the drama unfolding there. I'm done. Not going back.

Grace says she should stay with me, also queries if I would prefer that she go to the Old Bailey and report back to me this evening. I do not like us being out of step. In the event I say, 'Let's just get into bed. Hold me and I shall hold you. Simon will tell us all later. He's a very objective boy. Totally.'

I wonder if I have disappointed her, under the covers she seems to think it a ruse, and it is not. If she wants small pleasures, I can distribute them. Want nothing in return. I feel like death.

In the bed, two minutes to two, I text my brother. I should have done this earlier.

> ***Skipping the afternoon. Let me know what I need to know. Love Sophie***
>
> ***It's packing out. More of those horrible press people than ever before. TV crews on the steps***
>
> ***Apologise to Mon and Gary for me, please. Love Sophie***
>
> ***No sign of Pope and the judge is coming in. He's left it to his underling***

I show Grace this message. 'The game's up,' I tell her. 'Gone off in a huff; barristers hate losing.'

'Is it good?' asks Grace. I think she means, am I pleased to learn that my stepmother didn't do it.

'Two people, Grace. Two people buried my mother, there is no doubt about that. My father and an accomplice. And which one of what two pulled hardest on the guitar string?'

She hugs me again. 'I get it,' she says. 'Closure, having a sense of what happened that you can rely on, it would make the past more bearable. And it won't be happening today. It's better that we are here. I can hold you, help you adjust. Maybe something will crop up, the affidavit could be made public. Theatre plays and cinema films have sculpted endings, in real life, we never get better than a marker post. There is always something going on.'

* * *

Mistrial. No outcome. The prosecution reserves the right to retry Mum for the same crime. Police drop the charge. Free to leave the court

I am unsurprised by Simon's text, and nor does it satisfy me. Not in the slightest. It might be a just outcome, yet it leaves me concurrently fearing that the judge has released my mother's murderer. I am still waiting for her to come home. Cynthia Hartnell. Mummy.

9.

Grace has left me. I am certain it is only temporary; she is filming overseas for four weeks, may even fly home for the middle weekend. I am alone and Stepmummy has invited me to Carnforth, where she lives again with Craig and Simon. Monica has resumed her actor's life, a small exclusion zone between her and older sister, which I do not understand. I should go, do not want to lose the brothers I have found. The problem is that layer of memory; it would feel too strange to be living under the same roof as the woman who murdered my mother. Or she may have done no such thing. It's up in the air.

Perhaps she is as innocent as she was when she met and fell stupidly for my bastard father. She walked from the court a freewoman but without an acquittal by the jury. Not in the manner I had determined would absolve her in my eyes too. Perhaps my faith in the jury was just another superstition; she did it or she didn't, nothing caught on camera. Guesswork for everybody left in the world but Mary. My father knew and then opted out. Went to hades. The Sunday following the mistrial—when the papers informed us that a woman, not a man was the person in America swearing a statement so devastating as to collapse a murder trial over three thousand miles away—I felt only further bewilderment. Not Dennis Harris then, and a testament to the remarkable power of words. If the words reach my ears, all may become clearer. The papers had none of them.

I believe Mary wants to explain. I never feared her, even when I saw us as magnetic poles, prided myself on doing whatever kept us bouncing apart. I am no physicist but clever enough to know that such a metaphor implied great similarity between us. We repulsed each other precisely because proximity reminded us of ourselves, prevented us from attracting the opposite which we sought. That was my childhood, hopping apart from Mary as if compelled by a force I had no control over. Mary joined my father's household with the belief that she was the youth who gave it vibrancy; I was his child and thought it me. And my father we could neither attract. In those early years, he disliked neither Mary nor I, simply preferred to eat out.

She might bewitch me. Convince me of an innocence which is false. Or she might have been saying the truth all along. Best part of a year in prison because of the late Paul Stephenson's nasty and unsubstantiated lie. How will I know? When she telephoned inviting me to join them, I asked for time to think about it. About a minute later a text came through.

> ***Come to Windermere Court, Sophie. You are one of us. Craig and I miss you.***

It is very, very touching. For the time being solitude suits me better.

10.

I have driven from London without a break, pull into the

services at Charnock Richard. Less than an hour from my destination. I send a text to Grace, let her know what I am doing. I hope the technology works over the enormous distance my words must traverse. She phoned me two nights ago; I said I wasn't going. She said I should carry on thinking, thought me close to Craig and Simon. I don't think I needed her persuasion to swing it; just needed her to tell me to stop being silly. I will use the facilities here then head along. Brothers in Carnforth.

Can I really spend a long weekend ignoring Mary in the disdainful way I used to as a child?

The invitation is an open one, so I haven't announced my arrival. Simon has sent a lot of texts; I have replied, **Maybe**, which might cover everything I have thought in weeks and months. I used to know my own mind, and now I have lost the thread. I might be a nicer, and a correspondingly more uncertain, person as a consequence. Simon seems fairly clairvoyant much of the time, my arrival may not even surprise him. I realise that it will have turned eight o'clock by the time I get there. Plates in the dishwasher.

I go from the ladies' toilet to the food outlets where I order a large burger with fries and onion rings. Eating what Simon eats, that is the extent of the appeal. A large girl wearing a branded baseball cap bearing the initials of the food chain passes my meal across the counter in a brown bag: it is quite the service. I take it to a small round table, sit down on a hard plastic chair. The unwrapping brings forth a bouquet of hot fat. I try an onion ring; eating it is unpleasant but of a form that must be easy to repeat over and over. A minor self-harm like the smoking of a cigarette.

A man approaches my table, if he is older than me it is by little. 'Can I sit with you,' he asks. It is a motorway service station; I have little ground to refuse. He starts to take food from his bag; he has procured something from a different outlet than I, a small box of noodles in his hands, chopsticks so small they look laughable. 'I've been thrown out,' he says.

I look around; all sorts dine here. 'It is very poor form to be thrown out of a service station. And you've sneaked back in, I take it.'

'Thrown out by the wife. My dad is in Ulverston, my hometown. I'll be there tonight. She can just sod it.'

I presume he communicates that he is writing off his marriage. I have a better story but I shall spare him. 'Do you mind if I eat in silence, please? I don't mean to be rude. It's been a long week.'

He nods assent. Picks at his noodles with his little sticks. Picks a few up but they fall back in the box before reaching his mouth. I bite into my massive hamburger and some tomato sauce which I do not recall ordering spreads itself onto my cheek. I think Kicked-Out and I must look like a couple off a council estate: fast food and no manners. He sucks in some noodles, a turmeric stain taking residence on his chin. With a small serviette, I dab my cheek. Touch it with my forefinger. I think I look better than him. Eat with a fraction more refinement. Should bloody well hope so.

'Where do you live, love?'

'Not here.' It is a stupid reply. I don't think anyone lives in a service station. He continues to look at me like the true answer will put his world the right way up. 'Carnforth,' I finally say, although it is scarcely the truth.

'Can I crash at yours?'

I shake my head. Do so with vigour.

'Please?'

'I've had a most tumultuous week. I am sorry that your life has taken a downturn; however, we don't know each other. It's a no. Resolutely a no. And this food is awful.' I stand, leaving my brown food bag and its contents on the table. Head for the door, my car outside.

'Not a downturn, I'm better off without the bitch,' he shouts to my back. I do not turn around. 'Carnforth, you said.

An address?' I can hear the cheeky blighter laughing. When I reach the door, he calls out, 'Put your waste in the bin like the sign says.' I do not turn my head, my right hand is outstretched behind me, my fingers give him the V-sign he has been asking for since opening his mouth. My old self has not left me, it simply requires greater arousal than used to be the case.

* * *

'Sophie, so good to see you.'

No one heard me pull onto the drive; when I was ringing the bell I could hear voices in the house, saw a curtain move but not who made it do so. Now my stepmother—ten days out of jail and looking resplendent in a red and white dress, a small black cardigan over her shoulders—pulls me into a hug which I never indicated I needed. She clasps me very tightly. 'You've been a lifesaver for us,' she says. I like the word us but have yet to nominate her within my chosen circle. The jury should have said one way or the other, I'd have settled for whatever they plumped for. They could have flipped a coin. This hug is never-ending.

Craig is at her side and when the hug ends—which all things must—I receive another, more welcome, embrace. 'Should have come sooner, sis,' he tells me.

'Have you eaten, Sophie.' Mary is attentive.

'Simon?' I enquire.

'Through here,' shouts a deepish voice from the lounge. Big Si is speaking again. Whatever it means, I am pleased to hear it.

Mary indicates that I should go through. Simon sits in the largest lounge chair, looks directly at me. Headphones are about his neck, not covering his ears at the present time. 'What are you doing?' I ask.

'Passing the time until you showed up.' What a sweet answer. 'I'm discovering music, I think it passed me by.'

'Listening to Puccini, I hope.'

'Johnson Ronson, Sophie. He's hilarious.'

'Music which I used to like,' says Stepmummy. 'I think he is hearing something in it that I never spotted.'

'Funny? You think that maudlin old guy did comedy records?' I ask.

'I listen to the old stuff. Stop at Crazy Maisie. That one's about you, Sophie.'

A shiver goes down my spine. Heard it a few times over the years, it is not my kind of song. I was in primary school when it made the pop charts. Hit record about a small child shooting her parents; it was not me, I never acted on those feelings. A cruel game with the younger Mary, and I felt only warmth toward my true mother.

'La Bohème would trump it many times over. More depth.'

'Baby steps, Sophie. I never got anything out of music before.'

This is something I never really knew. I offer to give this boy a hug but he has still to allow these. I think it may come. I sit on the sofa, and Mary sits beside me. Craig in another free chair. They bombard me with questions, both boys a flurry, Mary the more sensitive.

'I couldn't stop thinking how terrible it was for you,' she says when we are referencing the trial.

I don't want to dwell on that chapter. I tell Mary that it has been a nightmare for her—ten months' imprisonment—'Do you get an apology?'

'I get the sword of Damocles.' When I screw up my face, indicate no understanding of the possible outcomes, she continues. 'A statement from this Davey woman was enough to collapse the trial. I wish we could have got hold of the statement; I understand that the prosecution service must disclose it next week. After they have decided what it means, what to do about it. The judge felt compelled to discontinue the trial; he feared a miscarriage of justice if the new information—which was never going to be permissible so late in proceedings—contradicted the verdict. Collette said that if your father had lived, testified against me, it might have been enough to convict me; however, using his statement as the central evidence always left them with a weakened case. Nobody can cross-examine a dead man. I wasn't really getting a fair hearing without the chance for that to happen.'

I feel all the worries I had about coming. 'Poor prosecution, poor defence, as I saw it. Probably too long ago to get any firm evidence nailed down for either side.'

I hear Mary sigh. I have not really joined the spirit of this household, they must celebrate her release, not rue the lost opportunity to call it one way or the other. 'Very hard to prove what went on twenty years ago. Very unfair having a charge thrown at me to defend in such trying circumstances.' She says it in a most matter-of-fact way. Perhaps the emotions of recent weeks have played out in her, hardened her even. And I saw the sense of it when she said on the witness stand that she had nothing against my mother, no reason to harm her. If it was for having sex with my father which motivated her to murder Cynthia Hartnell, she would have long ago become a serial killer.

'Sophie likes concrete answers,' says Simon. 'Would like to see the perpetrators jailed which appears further from happening now than before we started.'

'I don't want just anyone jailed,' I protest. 'The murder is beyond forensics but who buried her? Who was with my father?'

'It could have been the Davey woman,' says Mary. 'We'll all have to wait to learn that.' Then her hand holds my left shoulder, she looks directly at me, her face has aged five years in a single one. 'It wasn't me. You don't know that but I really do. I was a terrible mother to you, Sophie. I think it was a relief to me that you had a better one. From the word go. Could never have deprived you of her. I knew what I couldn't be.'

11.

The Sunday papers have it. Not the Noise; The News Explained is the one. They do not carry the affidavit which has yet to be disclosed to the defence, to Mary. An interview with Alison Davey is their scoop. Craig has returned from the newsagents with copies of all the Sundays, and within seconds it is but a single one which holds the attention of us all. Mary and Simon sit side by side at the table, the centre page spread open. Craig and I look at it from over their shoulders.

'She was at Imperial,' says Mary.

'I recognise her.' The family turn and look at me when I say it. They all know I was only a child, not an especially attentive one. My witness testimony in the trial was completely useless.

The interview is a shabby ramble, not the work of Tom Keane, but of a journalist no brighter than him. Alison was a third-year student at the time of my mother's murder, forty years old today. For the past decade she has worked as an engineer for an aircraft manufacturer in the state of Virginia. That they have persuaded such a woman to pose in a short skirt, her leg raised upon a sofa and a coy smile for the camera, must be a testament to human stupidity. To the wodge of money News Explained will happily slap on the table. She looks like a liar but it means nothing. I have never believed this newspaper and yet a broken clock tells the truth twice a day. It could just be meaningful.

This stupid woman, once a passenger in my father's car—me in the backseat, I recall—fears for her job. Fears arrest and extradition to the United Kingdom although she is now a naturalised American. Fears suffering a similar miscarriage of justice to the one for which Mary Stephenson appeared bound, prompting her to make the statement. I think I stayed in the car while my father rogered her in a dismal flat within a couple of miles of our own house. I say it, let the table know what a fucked-up family this is; that the true fucker-upper is thankfully deceased. It is not the fault of anyone in the room.

'Sophie, that's awful,' says Stepmummy.

'I don't think it happened often but he understood where my mistaken loyalty lay, didn't he?'

She has turned from the table, slid her hand around my waist. 'That stuff gets in kids' heads,' she says. 'Relationships have been a challenge for you. I'm so glad you and Grace have found each other.'

I lean into her, say, 'Thanks, Mum,' then add a little insolence. 'Not your strong suit either, I'm guessing.'

'Right again,' she confirms. I feel a warmth in her touch, perhaps it was always there. We see everything through such narrow prisms most of the time. Miss more than we pick up, I suppose.

When I mention the trailer for the trip, my father's pretext of taking some old junk into the flat to photograph for posterity, Simon points at a picture in the bottom corner of the news story. It shows the contraption that enabled the infinitesimally gradual lifting of the shed.

'The old bastard was telling the truth.'

'Shagged her too, you can bet.'

Mary says almost the same words as me, says them at the same time using the stronger F-word and I cannot blame her. Then Mary turns back to me. 'Wasn't it my car he used that day? He always used mine with the trailer.'

This article, this family, are piecing together my own fragmented memories.

The gist of Alison Davey's tale is that, long ago and when an undergraduate in awe of my father at his London university, she was going to patent her curious lifting device;

her professor—Professor Paul Stephenson—advised that it was the intellectual property of the university. Her research was being guided by his department, and they were therefore the owners. And, the professor said, it had ingenuity more than applicability, enabling every Tom, Dick and Harry to engineer the environment around them would be like unleashing a few million beavers on the country's river system. They tested it anyhow; her lover told them they would bury a replica of the contraption under Jean Fletcher's shed. A note on it with the date. See if the old lady could figure out how it came to be there, the most famous female physicist Imperial had produced. 'Until you,' my father's flattering words of persuasion. Alison saw one of the three devices made go into the hessian bag, she saw him carry it to the boot of the car. She never saw the switch.

On the Tuesday night, when Mary was in Charmouth—she went down there on the train, Simon too small to sit unattended for so long a journey, her car left in Epsom—Alison and Professor Stephenson buried the body. She swears, in that same affidavit, that she had no idea it was a body they placed under the shed. She admits assisting in the removal of the front wheels and attaching two of the devices to the wheel axles. And it was she who revved the car engine so that the device she invented lifted up the structure, enabling my father to conceal the packing crate beneath it. Thought it contained the third lifting device. She never met Cynthia Hartnell, and feels mortified to learn she has been party to the poor lady's illegal burial.

The British police say she is a person of interest.

'A lot of stupid girls did a lot of stupid things for that damned man,' says Mary.

'Don't mince your words, Mum. He was a cunt,' says Simon.'

Behind them, I hold Craig around the waist. I think his eyes are moist, this family's ordeal has affected him no end.

What he feels towards our father evades me. Teenage boys and their feelings make a potent chemistry set.

'I think science students are the worst,' continues Mary. 'Brilliant with facts, data. They can calculate trajectories, build that...' She gestures the photograph. '...dumb as pigshit on every measure of social interaction. Human-to-human understanding. I certainly was. I must give her the benefit of the doubt. Christ, I've needed it myself.'

'It means he did it alone,' I say. 'Murdered Mummy. But why would he do that.' No one in the room deserves it but my tears are back like a storm. Shoulders judder with the tumult. This makes no sense. They seemed to get along better than most after their marriage had broken down and then an execution by gut wire. 'He did it and never told us why.'

My words are only a splutter. Simon seems to understand them.

'He should have confessed but I've told you what he was. And Sophie, Mum, all that about him and Cynthia having sex years after the marriage ended: it's not normal. He had some kind of a hold over her. I don't get it, not my thing, I can see that he really must have had.' Mary is nodding, rapt with attention for her once mute son. 'She stopped. Found a way to put her foot down. Maybe she found true love. The cunt wouldn't have it.'

My tears continue while Simon is telling me what I've needed to know for eleven months.

Mary has stood from the table. Her arms are around me. 'You poor thing,' she says.

I accept it. She is as innocent as her two sons. I hope Cynthia did find love. I hope Mary and Jake can get it together, whatever that means for his wife. I put my face beside hers, still I am peering over her shoulder, but I hug her as best I can. Hug my stepmother with an enthusiasm I have never before raised in her embrace. I have been her most unfavourable judge for twenty-six years. Outrageous of me. 'Sorry, Mum,' I say. It is hardly recompense.

'Mum,' says Simon, 'I don't try the human-to-human stuff. Never did. Science is what humans are good at, the rest is a mess.'

I am trying to hold each of my family, the span of my arms is not great enough but they must sense my touch. There is enormous relief in this for me, more than I knew to be obstructed.

'It might be a good mess,' I say. 'Love and misunderstanding, the best mix in the world if the right people are in it.'

Mary says she must make us all coffee. I follow her into the kitchen and without the clearest reason, or perhaps a million of them, she embraces me again. It is a splendid relationship to have with her. Who knew? In my ear she whispers, 'Sophie, until this terrible trial, I never understood how much you missed your mother.'

It is a loss I cannot recover but this kind woman is kin. My brothers' mother. I have family enough.

Printed in Great Britain
by Amazon